DEVIOUS VOW

A DARK ENEMIES TO LOVERS MAFIA ROMANCE

VENOMOUS GODS
BOOK TWO

JAGGER COLE

Devious Vow

Cover and interior design by Plan 9 Book Design
Photography by Morizio Montani

Created with Vellum

PLAYLIST

Sucker For Pain - Lil Wayne, Wiz Khalifa, Imagine Dragons
Reasons I Drink - Alanis Morissette
Pictures of You - The Cure
The Chain - Fleetwood Mac
Love To Walk Away - The Vaccines
exile - Taylor Swift, Bon Iver
Hands To Myself - Selena Gomez
High Enough - K.Flay
Habits of My Heart - Jaymes Young
Bullet The Blue Sky - U2
Jake's Piano - Long Island - Zach Bryan
Without Your Love - The Paper Kites, Julia Stone
Decode - Paramore
Sometime Around Midnight - The Airborne Toxic Event
Heartbeats - The Knife
Please Don't Be - Hazlett
Civilian - Wye Oak
It'll All Work Out - Tom Petty and the Heartbreakers
Light On - Maggie Rogers
My Love Mine All Mine - Mitski

PLAYLIST

Listen to the playlist on Spotify!

TRIGGER WARNING

This book contains darker themes and graphic depictions of past trauma, addiction, and mentions of SA. While these scenes were written to create a more vivid, in-depth story, they may be triggering to some readers. *Please* know your triggers, and read with that in mind.

1

ALISTAIR

THE FIRST PUNCH always hurts the most.

No matter how ready you are, how much you brace for it, or how far in advance you see the swing coming. When it connects, when Peytor's fist slams broadside into my jaw? It hurts like a motherfucker.

But after that?

I blink away stars, staggering back and allowing the numbness to creep over me as the crowd roars.

After that, you adjust. The numbness becomes your ally. The pain helps you focus. The smug look on your opponent's face motivates you to recalibrate and slow down time, until you can see the path forward to victory, marked out clear as day.

Which I do. Instantly.

Feign left hook. Block his haymaker. Right fist to ribs, knocking out his breath. Dodge the wild counterattack. Left forearm to right ear, temporarily stunning him. Use his confusion to hit his ribs again, cracking the ones already weakened from the first hit. Break nose. Left hook to temple. Right to jaw. Finish with right uppercut.

This is my zone, shaking off that first blow and relishing the look of triumph on an unsuspecting opponent's face. This is where I see the exact roadmap to victory—clear as IKEA instructions in neon letters hanging in the air in front of my face.

I'm the same in court. Let the opposition draw first blood; garner the first nod of approval from the judge, or the first emotional response from the jury. Allow them to sit back, pleased with themselves.

Then comes my counter, followed by the next, and the next, until finally comes the glee of watching the smug look fade from their faces as I shred them under the blind gaze of justice.

But for now, in the dirty, grimy boxing ring in the middle of the old liquor distribution warehouse in Bushwick, I restrain myself. Again, the instructions for how to obliterate Peytor, my opponent this match, are almost literally glowing in the air between us.

However, this match has a *lot* of interest. And with interest come big bets and wads of cash being waved around.

...Also, I may or may not, via a friend, have put down a sizable "wager" with the on-site bookies on Peytor getting me to the ground in the first round.

Of course, I *also* put big money on *me* knocking *Peytor* the fuck out in that same first round.

I'm not taking a dive for the money. That's not why I bet on shit like this.

It's the rush. The thrill of the coin toss. The uncertainty. Or, as Taylor and my brother are all too eager to point out, there's a chance I'm more of a degenerate gambler than I'd care to admit. But to that, your honor, I call bias, hearsay, and leading the witness.

So, that all said, I don't immediately mount my counter-assault. I allow Peytor to edge in on me. Which, admittedly, is a *shit* idea when you're fighting six-foot-four and two-hundred-fifty-pounds-of-borscht-and-vodka-fed Russian Bratva muscle.

But really, none of this is being left up to chance. I'm ready, even as I shake off the first hit.

The second one slams into my jaw again, momentarily blinding me. But the pain is lesser now that the numbness from the first has set in. Still, I stagger back from that second hit. And even though it bruises my ego, I allow my legs to wobble and a knee to drop to the grimy floor. Predictably, the idiots in the crowd who had the poor judgment to bet against me go wild.

I glance to my right, catching Kratos' eye. To most of the assembled crowd, Kratos Drakos is a younger, though by far the largest, brother of Ares Drakos, head of the Drakos Greek mafia family.

He's also my fence for most of the bets I've placed tonight.

The Drakos family is one of my firm's—that would be Crown and Black—biggest and most notorious clients. We handle almost all their legitimate legal needs, especially now that one of our top partners, Elsa Guin, is married to Hades, another of the Drakos brothers. But we're also on retainer for any, let's say, *less* than legitimate legal needs they might have.

About a year ago, Kratos and I figured out we were both low-key in the same underground fight clubs when we spotted each other at an event much like tonight's, and so we started training together here and there.

Over the roar of the crowd and Peytor hurling insults at me as I take the knee, Kratos rolls his eyes and folds his massive arms over his massive chest.

"*Pay attention,*" he mouths. "*He's going to mess you up.*"

Not. Fucking. Likely.

I draw in a breath, slowing my surroundings. I hear the crunch of the grit under Peytor's feet as he advances, and the dull roar of the crowd, and the thud of my pulse.

I feel the first hit seeping into my soul, hardening and focusing me.

My lips curl dangerously.

That first punch is a gift. It's *fuel.* I learned that the hard way at the age of six, when the "first punch" was an SUV t-boning my parents' car at forty-seven miles per hour and pure terror being tattooed on my soul with each bounce and roll of the car until the lights went out.

Until I opened my eyes for the first time as an orphan.

My parents' death taught me that first punch lesson. It was reinforced a few times over the years, like when my adoptive parents died as well.

But *she* was the one who carved that lesson into my fucking chest.

Eloise.

The first punch hurts the most.

It's the best thing she ever did for me. And I've never forgotten it. In fact, I've made it my personal mantra. I let it flow through my veins with each throb of my pulse. Let it govern every thought. Every decision, personal or professional. Every case. Every move. Every fleeting, meaningless, single-serving "relationship" since.

The first punch hurts the most.

After that, it's just numbness.

And numbness is fuel.

Peytor is almost on top of me as I slowly lurch to my feet. The crowd is screaming and waving cash and betting stubs in the crappy neon lights hanging from the ceiling of the warehouse. Dust, grime, and grit chokes the air as Peytor grins, mistaking my focus for being stunned.

Yeah, that'll cost him.

He's winding up for a wild hit when I exhale slowly and put the plans glowing right there in my mind's eye into action.

Peytor flinches and jerks back to avoid the left hook that never actually comes. He swings a wild haymaker which I block easily with my left forearm as I slam my right fist into his ribs. I hear the wheeze of his breath leaving his lungs and dodge his wild counter. My left forearm bashes into his right ear, and I relish the dazed look in his eyes as the disorientating feeling of having his inner ear turned to scrambled egg stuns him.

His confusion is my friend. I hit his ribs again in the exact same spot, hearing the satisfying crack as one—possibly two—of them fractures.

His nose is next. Then his right temple. Then the left side of his jaw, which turns the lights out behind his eyes.

The uppercut is purely for show at this point, but I do it anyway, sending Peytor reeling backward before he hits the ground like a sack of bricks.

The crowd goes apeshit. Men roar and scream obscenities in seven different languages and fists wave handfuls of cash. Two fights break out.

I roll my shoulders and crack my neck as I walk over to the edge of the ring. Kratos is waiting for me, sighing and shaking his head.

"What?" I shrug as I squirt some water from my water bottle into my mouth, slosh it around, and spit it out again on the floor.

"You don't feel bad about this at all, do you."

I give him a look. "What, winning? Not really, no. Am I supposed to?"

My giant friend chuckles a deep, rumbling laugh. "I mean leading him on like that. Fencing bets against yourself through me."

"What? I want to give them a show."

"Oh, fuck off, Alistair," he chuckles. "You wanted to double your winnings by putting that second bet on him getting you to the floor in the first round."

"It's not about the money, Kratos."

As if underlining my point, I take my Rolex Submariner—the one literally owned and worn by Steve McQueen—from his outstretched hand and slip the two-hundred-and-forty-thousand-dollar watch onto my wrist.

It's *not* about the money. It's about the rush of the fight. The adrenaline high of combat. The fucked-up therapy that comes with using violence to confront the demons of the past. And yes, the thrill of the gamble, fuck you very much Taylor and Gabriel.

But also...especially lately...it's about *her*.

Eloise LeBlanc.

Eloise, who I turned my back on ten years ago when she cut out a sizable chunk of my soul. Eloise, who should have stayed the fuck out of my life after that.

Eloise, who should have stayed if not in my past, then at the very fucking least on *her* fucking side of the country in California with her shithead mafioso husband, instead of moving here.

New York is *my* goddamn town. And having her living in it now as well, even if we're buffered by eight million other people, is...problematic.

Hence, throwing myself into underground fights like this at least three times a week recently.

"Look around you, Kratos," I shrug, glancing around. "Pure entertainment. It's all for show. It's theater."

Kratos rolls his eyes again. "This isn't fucking Shakespeare, bud. Or a courtroom."

"All the world's a stage."

Kratos sighs and nods past me to where Peytor's buddies are scraping him off the ground. "He gonna be okay? That was fucking brutal."

"Cracked rib, maybe two, probably a concussion, macular contusion, loose lower molar, broken nose—and a completely obliterated sense of pride." I pat Kratos on the shoulder. "He's going to be fine."

Peytor moans pitifully behind me and spits a large mouthful of blood onto the ground as his friends drag him away.

"I mean...*eventually*," I shrug.

Whatever. This is my therapy. And besides, Peytor Chernov is a piece of shit anyway.

"You ready to go collect my money?"

Kratos snorts. "After I take my cut? Sure. Oh, and one more thing..." His look darkens.

"That doesn't sound good."

"It depends on what phase of the moon you and your brother are on right now. He's here, looking for you."

Shit.

To be clear, Gabriel, my adoptive brother since I was six, is my best friend in the world. He's my other half. The yin to my yang. The grounding force to my chaos.

We also sometimes want to kill each other, and would probably benefit from beating the shit out of each other in this very ring. But I like to think that's just the sign of a strong and healthy brotherhood.

I glance around, my eyes scanning the crowd of unruly criminal underworld types. A few seconds later, I spot Gabriel standing by the door, looking hilariously out of place in his Tom Ford suit and polished dress shoes. His arms are crossed, and his brows furrow deeply as he glares at me.

"Gabriel isn't the biggest fan of your extra-curricular activities?"

"Whoa. Nothing gets past you, does it, Kratos."

"Har har."

Toweling off my face and bare chest, I clamber over the side of the ring and make my way through the crowd. I get a few jeers from the suckers who lost on my fight, and grins and claps on the back from the smart ones who made money off it. Finally, I find myself standing in front of my brother.

He's got the same dark hair and hazel-green eyes as our sister, Tempest, while I've got dirty dark-blond hair with piercing blues. He and I are the same age, same height, and same build, despite us not sharing a single drop of genetics. Same profession, even. Other than that, we're polar opposites.

"If I'd known you were coming, I'd have gotten you VIP seats."

He gives me a look. "Now, would those seats be next the Nazi biker gang, or the Columbian cartel?"

"For you, Gabriel, it can be both."

He glares at me. "What the *fuck* are you doing here, Alistair?"

"I think it's fairly obvious."

He rolls his eyes as he exhales heavily. "Do you seriously think participating in underground fucking cage fights is in the best interests of the firm?"

"I don't think what I do in my personal time has any effect whatsoever on the firm, actually."

"You do understand that Crown and Black is now *the* most elite and sought-after law firm in all of New York City, right? You appreciate that you and I and Taylor worked our *asses* off to get it to that level? And here you're playing Fight Club with a bunch of degenerates?"

"I prefer to think of it as networking and professional outreach. Degenerates have a way of frequently needing legal assistance, Gabriel."

He arches a brow, clearly unamused.

"And I'm sorry, is this really about the firm's reputation, or your political aspirations?"

I know for a fact that my brother has been meeting with a political consulting firm recently, and frequently. He keeps denying it whenever Taylor or I bring it up, but he's about as sneaky as Elmer Fudd under Bugs Bunny's watchful eye.

"There are no political aspirations, Alistair," he sighs.

"Clearly," I murmur as I rake my fingers down my jaw. "Well? Did you just come to break my balls about being here, or was there something else?"

"You weren't answering your phone, and this is important."

"You have my attention. Is it about the Chinellato case?"

"You really think I'd drive all the way out to fucking Brooklyn to go over that with you?"

"Maybe you just missed me—"

"Alistair."

There's an icy coldness in his tone and a warning in his eyes that has me on edge in seconds.

"What the hell's going on, Gabriel."

He clears his throat and looks away. "We have a meeting tomorrow morning with a very eager, very wealthy, very *notorious* prospective new client."

My brow creases. "That's...generally considered a good thing, no? I don't know about you, but I personally quite enjoy money and making more of it."

His eyes lock with mine.

"The prospective client is Massimo Carveli."

The name is all it takes for me to go from neutral to DEFCON 2. For my blood to turn to acid, my teeth to grind to dust, and my every muscle to tighten and coil.

Massimo Carveli is many things, including the head of his family organization after the death a year or so back of his father, Luca. He's rich, powerful, enjoys expensive European sports cars and fine wine, and recently moved here to New York.

He's also a *complete fucking psychopath* with extremely violent tendencies, a knack for cruelty, and a lust for even more power and wealth.

But there's one thing that Massimo Carveli is that more than anything has a way of stabbing me in the heart and making me bleed, which is quite a feat considering I'm sure my heart was ripped from my chest cavity ten years ago.

He's Eloise LeBlanc's *husband*.

There's a ringing in my ears as the world turns red at the edges. My fists clench so tight my knuckles pop. My jaw is grinding so viciously that I taste copper.

"Look, Alistair, we can—"

"Alistair?"

I blink out of my blood-soaked daze when the second voice interrupts my brother. When I turn around, I see Antoine, one of the organizers of the evening, standing there.

"I don't know if you're up for it. But a lot of the guys who lost on that last fight are looking to see you in the ring again." He smirks. "Probably want to win some of their money back."

Gabriel swears behind me.

"Alistair, we have a meeting with the partners at *nine fucking AM* tomorrow—"

"Who's the fight with?"

Antoine grimaces. "Big Joe."

So, yes, the idiots who lost money on me are definitely trying to get it back. Big Joe is a heavily tattooed Samoan dude closing in on seven feet tall, probably weighs twice as much as me, and has a fist like a fucking freight train.

But after what Gabriel's just told me, I'm a fucking nuclear bomb waiting to blow.

…In short, Big Joe is the *perfect* opponent for me right now.

"Listen, Alistair," Antoine makes a face. "You don't have to. Let me see who else—"

"Nah, set it up. Let's get this party going."

I turn away from a stunned Antoine and slip my watch back off, handing it to my brother.

"Hold this, will you?"

Gabriel grimly takes the watch and pockets it.

"Real talk, right now," he growls quietly. "The money is potentially phenomenal. But if you say no—"

"Let's take the meeting."

He eyes me carefully. "C'mon, man. There's facing your demons, and then there's whatever the fuck this is—"

"Massimo Carveli is not my demon," I growl.

"No, he just fucking *married* your demon!" he snaps back at me. "Which is exactly why I'm worried about—"

"I'm a professional, Gabriel," I say in a slow, measured tone, resting my palms on his shoulders. "So here's what I'm going to do. I'm going to walk into that ring and put Big Joe in a big *hole* in the ground. Then I'm going to go home, have a shower, call someone I don't care about to come over and bounce on my dick. *Then* I'm going to kick them out, get some sleep, and in the morning, I'm going get dressed, walk into our offices, and have yet another business meeting with yet another mafioso tough guy who needs us to keep the law at bay for a sizable markup on legal fees. *That's it.*"

With a nod, I take my hands from his shoulders and start to turn away.

"What if she's there?"

I freeze for a moment, my pulse thudding in my ears. Then, slowly, I turn to level my gaze at Gabriel.

"If she's there," he continues, "then what? Because I—*we*—can't have World War Three going down in a conference room on Tuesday morning."

"She won't be."

"But if she is—"

"If she *is*," I snarl, my teeth bared, my temper throbbing, and my blood scorching my veins. "If Eloise is there, she'll be as dead to me as she was ten fucking years ago, okay?!" I snap. "And that's the fucking end of it."

I whirl away from my brother and storm over to the ring with so much viciousness on my face that even Big Joe looks worried as I hurdle the ropes and level my gaze at him.

Except, that was a lie. This isn't the fucking end of it.

It's only the beginning.

The first punch hurts the most.

And ten years later, I'm still fucking numb.

2

ELOISE

ROUGH, masculine grunts fill the room, mingling with wet, sloppy sounds. Massimo's head lolls back in pleasure, his jaw clenched and his fists gripping tightly as he pumps harder, pushing deeper.

"*Yes, puttana,*" my husband groans as he picks up the pace of his manic, irregular throat-fucking. "Such a good little slut."

I roll my eyes, turning away from the scene in front of me to stare out the window at Central Park. I lift the flute of champagne to my lips, sipping deeply as I try to ignore the disgusting sounds of Massimo getting off not ten feet away from me.

Mercifully, *not* involving me.

"Eloise."

I ignore him and continue to stare out the window of the high-rise penthouse. Present gross scenario and the generally craptastic nature of my life notwithstanding, the view from here of the park and the entire East Side of Manhattan is truly stunning. Not to mention a total change after spending most of the last year staring out at the Pacific Ocean.

And yet I know the splendor of this view, just like the one of the stunning ocean in LA, will eventually fade and tarnish.

A "nice view" only sustains you for so long when the rest of your existence is shit and ash.

"*Look* at me!"

Part of my delay is me purposely ignoring Massimo. The other part is that after three glasses of bubbly on an empty stomach, my response time is *slightly* slowed.

That's another tactic, alongside "nice views", to block out my day-to-day life: alcohol.

"*Look. At. Me. You. Bitch!*" he snarls.

I jerk, choking on my champagne as the shoe he's just thrown at me narrowly misses my head. Turning, I glare daggers at Massimo as he leers at me, his hips pumping his frankly revolting dick in and out of the other woman's mouth.

His lips curl into a malicious smile. "*Yesss.* Watch, my worthless wife. Watch how a real woman pleases a real man."

I only refrain from rolling my eyes because I'd like to finish my current glass of bubbles without getting another shoe thrown at me.

A REAL man.

Says the guy still wearing socks, with his pants around his ankles.

How terrifyingly alpha.

The woman kneeling between his knees sputters a little. But she's a pro—literally—and keeps bobbing her head on his dick as his hand tightens in her hair.

There are few upsides to being married to Massimo Carveli. But the biggest one by a landslide is that he doesn't touch me.

Not once.

Not ever.

Massimo's "thing" ever since I was forced to marry him a little over a year ago—his kink, I guess—doesn't involve touching me at all. In fact, I think it specifically involves *not* touching me.

Humiliation. That's his thing. A sort of reverse cuckold kink where he belittles and demeans me by fucking other women in front of me, usually while calling me worthless, stupid, a bad wife, or sexually frigid.

It's not that I'm in any conceivable way jealous of the man I hate screwing other girls in front of me. It's not that I care what names he calls me or give a rat's ass what he thinks about me. But I *hate* being an unwilling participant in his game. I hate being forced to sit here and watch him abuse some poor girl, even if she's being paid handsomely for what she does.

Massimo's no idiot. He doesn't actually think that his little kink makes me jealous, because he knows full well I despise him. But he does know I hate the forced participation. And *that's* where his satisfaction comes from.

I allow him to lock his gaze on mine, and I swallow back the sickly feeling that washes over me again when he groans in pleasure.

Fucking gross.

I only pull my eyes away to drain the last of my glass and reach for the bottle, topping my flute right back up again.

Massimo laughs coldly. "Ahh yes, my lovely wife the drunk," he sneers. "Planning on floating to bed later, dear?"

I don't respond. I've learned not to communicate with him when he tries to goad me into banter during one of these sessions. He *wants* me to talk back. He wants me to vocalize how much I hate this.

So I don't.

It might be a pathetically small act of disobedience. But I consider it a win nonetheless.

Massimo grunts, his ass lifting from his chair as he continues fucking the girl's mouth.

"Try not to get too fucked up, *wife*," he snarls. "We have an early morning tomorrow."

Mild curiosity ripples through me. But not enough that I'll break my silence and ask him what that means, or what the hell we're doing. Mostly because it doesn't matter, and I don't care.

We all do things we don't want to do when we have to. It's one of the reasons I can sympathize with the woman Massimo is using in front of me. I mean, sure, *maybe* this girl is doing exactly what she wants with her life. Maybe she woke up one morning and realized her superpower was not having a gag reflex or being bothered by blowing mafiosos with huge egos and tiny dicks, and decided she could make a living with that.

But I doubt it.

The far more likely scenario is that this girl is merely doing what she has to in order to survive. Like I am. Again, mercifully, the things I have to do to survive don't involve touching Massimo.

But they *do* involve being married to him. They involve being a part of his demented world and giving up whatever dreams I had left for my own life.

I take another heavy swig of champagne, trying to block out the sounds of Massimo's approaching...ugh...climax. Whatever the hell we're doing tomorrow, I'll get through it the same way I get through everything: by retreating inward, smiling bitterly, and numbing everything with a drink or five.

"That's your last fucking glass," Massimo snaps at me, ripping my attention back to him. "I don't want you walking into the Crown and Black offices tomorrow looking like hungover trash."

Something glitches inside of me. My entire body stiffens, and the sip of champagne rolling over my tongue gets caught in my throat.

"*What?*"

Massimo's gaze is all on the girl between his knees as his pace quickens to a manic level. "I'm..." he grunts. "I'm interviewing new potential legal representation tomorrow. Crown and Black." He grunts again before his eyes raise to mine. "You went to school with two of the partners, I think. Gabriel and Alistair Black."

A knife twists inside me. A vicious wave of nostalgia, pain, ache, and anger surges through me, knocking the air from my lungs. My head feels droopy, like it's suddenly too heavy for my neck.

My hand drops to clutch at my heaving stomach as I stare at Massimo.

Gabriel Black can be classified as "someone I went to school with."

But Alistair?

That's something completely different. Something elemental. Something ingrained into my very DNA. Something painful, like a wound being ripped back open just as it's healing, over and over.

Something I'll never be able to forget, or escape.

I don't realize I'm still staring at Massimo until I realize he's groaning and wildly thrusting his hips. His eyes lock with mine, and I see the sadistic glee in them as he starts to come before I rip my gaze angrily away.

My pulse thudding. My skin tingling.

My heart aching.

"Oh, *fuck yeah*. Take it. Take it all, bitch," Massimo snarls. "Swallow it. Yeah, fuck yeah."

Revulsion washes over me, sweeping away the confusion, the ache, and the vivid memories that come whenever Alistair Black enters my thoughts. But after Massimo's grunts and groans die down, those thoughts come rushing back with a vengeance.

They always do, no matter how hard I try to keep them at bay.

It's impossible to keep Alistair out of my head for very long, and it's only gotten worse since Massimo moved us here to New York.

Where Alistair lives. Where he has his career at his firm. Where I'll bet he spends zero seconds thinking about me the way I think about him.

Massimo sighs as Destiny pulls away from his pathetic, half-limp dick. She pulls the front of her dress back up over her tits and wipes off her mouth in a businesslike way as she stands. She glances over to me, and we exchange a look.

This isn't Destiny's—or whatever her real name is—first visit to our place here in New York. She's seen this routine of Massimo's before.

She knows I hate this. She probably hates it, too. But money is money, and we all do things we hate in order to survive. And besides, it's not like I bear her any ill will because she just blew my husband.

If anything, I should thank her.

Massimo exhales as he pulls up his pants before tossing an envelope at Destiny's feet.

"Get out."

She counts the cash inside the envelope, which is smart, because my husband is *exactly* the type of shithead who would short her on purpose just to make her ask for the rest. But this time at least, it's all there. She shoots me one last look before she grabs her clutch and heads across the penthouse and out the door.

"Why Crown and Black?"

The question pops out before I can stop it. Massimo smirks as he crosses the room to the bar cart and pours himself a scotch.

"They're an excellent firm. And because of their reputation for working with...well..." He smiles. "Men like me."

Gangsters. He means gangsters.

"They also work with the Drakos and Kildare families, though."

I don't know why I'm questioning this. Or maybe I do. Maybe I want to steer Massimo away from this, because my husband working with Alistair would have my two different worlds crashing together. And going to that office tomorrow and seeing him is almost literally too much to even think about.

Which is why I bring up the fact that Crown and Black works with the preeminent Greek and Irish mafia families of New York, both of which Massimo *loathes*.

But mentioning those families doesn't elicit the angry reaction I was hoping for. Instead, Massimo just smirks again.

"Well, well. Look at you. Pretending to be a lawyer again, are we?"

Fuck you.

"I *am* a lawyer."

"Lawyers practice law, Eloise," Massimo sneers with a dismissive wave.

I've learned not to take his bait. But Jesus Christ, sometimes it's *really* hard. He knows damn well that this is one of the biggest buttons of mine that he can push: the fact that I *am*, in fact, a lawyer, who passed the bar in Illinois and again after we moved here in New York, but I don't practice.

Because he won't fucking let me.

"Why do you need me to come with you tomorrow?"

He shrugs. "I want them distracted when we talk business. The two brothers, at least. Last I heard, Ms. Crown wasn't a carpet muncher."

God, he's foul.

Massimo lights a cigarette, which is yet another habit of his I hate, especially when he does it inside, in spaces we share.

"I've had what I want you wearing tomorrow laid out in your room. Spoiler: it's green and short."

My brows knit.

"Green's not my color."

"Look at me, Eloise. Do you see any sign of me giving a single, solitary fuck?" He smirks at me. "You'll wear the dress. You'll fucking smile when I tell you to. Understand?"

"Whatever."

I turn away and walk to the window, staring out at Central Park before suddenly Massimo strides over. The air leaves my lungs in a whoosh, and I gasp sharply when he roughly spins me, slams me against the floor-to-ceiling window, and grabs my chin in his hand.

"The next fucking time you decide you'd like to mouth off to me, *wife*, perhaps it won't be Destiny's throat that I come down. Am I clear?"

I swallow thickly, feeling my stomach turn to acid.

"*Am. I. Clear,*" he growls again.

"Yes," I mutter.

Massimo's hand drops from my chin. "Get out. I have business to attend to."

When I'm back in my room, which I *don't* share with Massimo, I lock the door and sink against it. I really should eat something, because I haven't all day, and the champagne is making my head swim. But instead, I walk over to the credenza by the windows and pour myself a large vodka.

Swallowing the room-temperature shot with a grimace, I turn and let my gaze settle on my open closet door and the dress hanging pristinely on a hanger on it. As Massimo mentioned, it's green, which really is *not* my color, and short. Like, stupidly, scandalously, short. It'd be skanky looking even at a club. For a business meeting at a world-class legal firm, it's a fucking joke.

But the dress quickly goes into the "who cares" file in my head—the place I keep all those little things I know should bother me, but that I also know I have no control over. The file's pretty thick these days, being married to the sadistic asshole that I am and all.

The scene I just witnessed with Massimo and Destiny gets pushed aside too, along with my crushed dreams, my alcohol-numbed existence, and the depressing thought that this will be my life until I die.

Because something else has taken root in the forefront of my head, occupying every single one of my thoughts.

More like some*one.*

Ten years ago, Alistair Black broke me.

Broke my heart. Broke my will.

Broke *us*.

Or maybe there was never any "us" to break at all.

I've seen Alistair once since moving to New York, at a gala event Massimo attended.

He didn't see me. Or if he did, he ignored me, and made sure we never crossed paths the entire evening.

But tomorrow, ten years after he was my bully and I was his, I'll be face-to-face again with the man who left me standing in the ashes after the spark between us went up in smoke.

And this time, there'll be no escape, for either of us.

3

ALISTAIR

THE DOORS to the boardroom have barely shut behind Charles' exit before Taylor jabs her middle finger at them.

"No offense, but your grandfather is a real fucking prick."

"Taylor," Gabriel sighs, dropping his head heavily against the back of his chair. "I think I speak for Alistair as well when I say we will never, *ever,* under any circumstances, be offended if you call Charles Black a fucking prick."

"Or worse," I mutter darkly.

Taylor blows air through her lips, puffing out her cheeks as she stands and runs her fingers through her long red hair. "It's the fucking *entitlement*. I mean…my *God*."

"Are you clear now why our parents didn't involve him in our lives?" I grunt, kicking my feet up on the boardroom table. "Not to mention that the bastard retaliated by not sending *us*, his own grandchildren, Christmas or birthday presents. The man redefines petulant narcissism."

Gabriel and I have never had what most people would call a "good" relationship with our paternal grandfather, especially since he snuck his way onto the Crown and Black board when we opened the firm. It only got worse when he finagled his way—probably though blackmail—into a near-majority voting interest on said board.

But the frostiness hit Cold War levels a few months ago, when we ripped his claws out of his daughter, Maeve—aka Gabriel's, Tempest's, and my eighteen year old *aunt*, courtesy of Charles' young gold digger trophy wife—thereby allowing her to move out from under his control and into Gabriel's place.

In hindsight, we should have expected a counter-maneuver, from the way he let that particular fight go so quickly. And now here it is: at our impromptu meeting just now, Charles made it clear that if we lose the extremely high-profile Chinellato case that we're defense on, he's going to go to war with us, using the boardroom as the battlefield.

Crown and Black always has dozens of cases going on at the same time. There are the three name partners: Taylor, Gabriel, and I. Then on top of that, we've got a dozen equity partners, about twice as many associates, and something like thirty junior associates, not to mention a small army of legal aides. And we all stay busy.

But the Roberto Chinellato case is the star of the show right now. First, because the billable hours are ludicrous. And second, because our prick, wannabe-mafioso of a grandfather does sleazy business under the table with Roberto, and has made it abundantly clear how bad it would be for him if Bobby-boy went to prison.

Gabriel's brow knits. "How solid are we with the Chinellato case?"

Taylor waves a dismissive hand. "Bulletproof, and you know I don't say that lightly."

We do, just like we know just about everything about Taylor, and vice versa. The three of us linked up in law school—Gabriel and I following in our dad's footsteps, and Taylor blazing her own trail. My brother and I were fresh off the pain of losing our sister Layla to heroin, and Taylor…

Well, Taylor's got more scars and wounds under her thirty-year-old skin than you'd ever know by looking at her.

Bottom line, the three of us became inseparable. I'm sure a therapist would eagerly point out how Taylor effectively became our "replacement Layla" in some weird psychological way. Maybe she did, but hey—it works.

The question, or at least the veiled suggestion, comes up all the goddamn time: Gabriel and I are both single, successful, wealthy, and genetically blessed. Here we are, working long hours side-by-side with a gorgeous redhead with runway model legs, a genius brain, and a bank account and success to match our own. So…?

So nothing. It isn't, never has been, and never will be anything like that. Taylor's essentially an honorary sibling to Gabriel, our little sister Tempest, and I, especially since she doesn't have any family of her own.

Gabriel turns to me, looking for any cracks in Taylor's statement. I just shake my head. "No, we're solid. Roberto's alibi the night of the shooting is unimpeachable."

"Unimpeachable and *true*, or just unimpeachable?"

I smile significantly at my brother. "What did we say about asking questions whose answers come with potential consequences, class?"

Gabriel grimaces. I mean, I understand. We went through the same law program. We grew up with the same father, aka the patron saint of telling the truth, helping the weak, and upholding justice above all else.

But this is the game. Our success as a firm early on was in no small part due to our willingness to take on clients that other firms...*wouldn't*. We don't exactly advertise it, but a solid chunk of our client base is criminally connected.

It bothers Gabriel more than it bothers me. After all, he went into law to follow our father's path. I got into the business to know *exactly* where the fuzzy lines and gray areas are. To know precisely how to bend things to my needs.

There's a version of my reality where I found the straight and narrow path. A version where she-who-shall-not-be-named didn't rip out whatever goodness had formed on my heart like moisture on a cold window and grind it under her heel.

Am I a bitter, antagonistic, and at times tyrannical prick because Eloise LeBlanc fucked me up? Or did she fuck me up because I'm a bitter, antagonistic, and at times tyrannical prick?

Shrödinger's sense of self. But I digress.

In any case, I've spent the last twelve hours preparing for my meeting with Massimo today by adhering to a strict training schedule of avoiding sleep, betting an obscene amount of money on myself before taking on—and yes, taking *down*—Big Joe's revenge-seeking brother Big Jack in the ring, and then taking myself on a solo date to Club Venom to drown myself in more gambling, some drinks, and watching the deviance of the place unfold around me.

It's essentially what I did the night before the Bar exam, and that worked out pretty great.

And no, I see zero pattern in how I spend my nights before facing difficult realities.

None whatsoever.

"Relax, Gabriel," I sigh, leaning back in my chair. "The alibi's solid. Also, Judge Hawkins has already hinted that she'll be throwing out Roberto's priors as admissible evidence. We're fine. It's in the bag."

"You remember what dad said *fine* stood for, right?"

"Fucked. Insecure. Neurotic—"

"Is any of this really helpful at the moment, boys?" Taylor sighs, adopting the big sister, almost "motherly" tone she takes with us at times, despite being three years younger.

"Yeah, *Gabriel*. Is it?"

My brother rolls his eyes and glances at his Rolex. "We're scheduled for Conference Room A in twenty minutes with Carveli." He frowns as he glances my way. "Are you…"

"Fine? Yes. Thanks for asking."

He nods. "Just making sure, man. Now if you'll excuse me, I need to make a quick call before our meeting—"

"How *are* your friends at Empire Political Consultants?"

He shoots me a look.

"What?" I grin innocently.

"Nothing," Gabriel mutters back, scowling. "Look, I don't know what you think is going on, but—"

"I think you're going to be late for your call with Empire Political Consultants."

He glares at me. "That's—"

"Please give them my very best."

When he strides out, I roll my eyes.

"What do you think, Tay? Any idea what the fuck that guy is up to, hiring—"

"Alistair."

I turn toward my friend. "*Taylor.*"

Her face twists somewhere between sympathy and concern. "You don't have to do this, you know."

"Do what, exactly?"

She sighs. "The meeting with Massimo Carveli. I know..."

"Know what."

"I know you and Eloise Leblanc have..." She looks away. "*A past.*"

Okay, so the three of us don't know *everything* about each other, just close to it. Taylor knows the basic outline of the Eloise story. But she doesn't know all the specifics.

Neither does Gabriel, for that matter.

"We went to college together. That's the big juicy story, Taylor. The end." I get up from my chair, closing the file folder in front of me before heading for the door. Taylor follows me out, and waits with me for the elevator.

"Alistair. C'mon."

"*What?*"

"I mean... You dated her."

"I think you and I might have different definitions of 'date'."

Truth be told, I don't even know if Taylor *knows* the definition of that word. I've literally never once seen her involved in any sort of relationship. She's the walking, talking definition of "too smart for her own good" and "married to her career". It probably doesn't help that she's beautiful enough to chase away the shy guys, and too clueless about those looks to understand why the bold ones *are* talking to her.

"We didn't *date*," I continue as we get into the elevator and ride down one floor to the executive offices. "I fucked her. Once. And that was ten years ago."

"My, what a romantic you are, Alistair," she drawls flatly.

"Said nobody about me, ever."

She shakes her head as we walk from the elevator banks toward my corner office. "So... Does Massimo Carveli, notoriously psychotic son of the late Luca "The Carver" Carveli, know that his wife is yet another name on the lengthy list of Alistair Black's conquests?"

Katerina, my assistant, does a spectacular job of keeping her gaze firmly on her computer screen and pretending she didn't hear what Taylor just said. All the same, I clear my throat to get her attention.

"That was never said out loud, and I send you on a one-week trip to the tropical destination of your choice on the corporate card. Deal?"

"I'm sorry, Mr. Black, *what* was never said?"

Yeah, there's a reason Katerina has lasted in this job when *so many* before her haven't.

"Excellent. How's your sister, by the way?"

"Still married, Mr. Black," she smiles sweetly.

"Let me know if that changes?"

"You'll be the first one I tell."

Taylor rolls her eyes as we step into my office. "You're a walking cautionary HR training video."

"And Katerina appreciates my sense of humor." I drop the file onto my desk and turn to her. "You were saying?"

"I was asking if Massimo knew that you've fucked his wife."

"What do you think?"

"I think if he did, knowing his reputation, you'd be dead right now," she says with an arched brow. "Or, at the least, without your dick still attached to your body."

"You're amazing at these pre-meeting motivational talks, Tay. You should really take this act on the road."

She grins before she shakes her head. "For real, though. What's the story with—"

"We're going to be late."

4

ELOISE

Ten years ago:

"We think you'd be a great addition to The Order, Eloise."

My cheeks flush hotly as Ansel's dark blue eyes hold mine. The senior, who towers over me, grins a charming, dazzlingly white smile. Before I realize it, he's reaching out and putting a hand on my arm.

I shiver when his strong fingers touch the bare skin above my elbow, just below the cuff of my short-sleeved shirt.

"*I* think you'd be a great addition, too."

Christ, he's handsome. As if I needed any confirmation of that opinion, the girls behind me giggle amongst themselves as I simmer under Ansel's gaze.

"You'll come to the informational meeting for prospective new members next week?"

"I—"

"She'll be there," Demi blurts from behind me.

Ansel's eyes stay on mine another second. "Yes?" he nods.

"*Yes*," I reply, nodding right along with him. "Yes, I'll be there."

He winks. "I'm glad to hear it. See you soon, Eloise."

When he's gone, I slowly turn, grinning from ear-to-ear as the other girls explode into fits of giggles.

"Oh my *God*, E," Christina squeals. "He is *so* fucking hot."

"And he *so* wants to bang you," Demi snickers.

I blush deeply, rolling my eyes. "He just wants me in The Order. I mean, it's initiation time, and he wants me on the list of prospectives...."

"He wants you on his *dick*," Giorgiana cackles in her musical Italian-accented voice.

"Okay, *arrêtez*," I mumble, still red-faced and grinning as the four of us start walking across the stunning Knightsblood campus, full of sprawling Georgian and Jacobethan-style towers and buildings, toward our dormitory.

To the casual observer, Knightsblood is just another old-school, old-money private college tucked away on the quaint, wealthy shores of southern Connecticut, just outside New York City. In the 1800s, when it was founded, the idea was to create a "truly English" university in America for the heirs of lords, dukes, and other royally-adjacent families who were coming here from England. Those lords and dukes wanted a school to match Harvard, Yale, and Princeton for prestige, but—as if that were even possible—to make it even *snootier* by only admitting those of aristocratic lineage.

It's still the school motto: "To the blood of king and crown, cross and knighthood."

Hence, Knightsblood.

But things have changed since then. The school is still outrageously selective. But these days it caters to the heirs of a different *kind* of monarchy.

For instance, there's me, the second daughter of Andre LeBlanc, head of one of the more powerful mafia families in Paris. Giorgiana's father is head of a *huge* Cosa Nostra family back in Sicily. And Demi and Christina, who are cousins, come to Knightsblood by way of the Romano family in Chicago.

Even Ansel, who we were just talking to, is from the Munich-based Albrecht family, one of the biggest crime syndicates in Germany and Austria. Mafia. Bratva. Yakuza. Cosa Nostra. Cartel. Almost every student here comes from money and power and has criminal connections.

The school is often referred to as the Harvard of the underworld. But the students here snickeringly refer to as "Mafia Hogwarts", a reference that makes even more sense once you get into the four secret student societies.

There's The Order, which Ansel was just talking to me about joining, and which he's the head of. There's also Para Bellum, The Ouroboros Society, and The Reckless. Each has its own traits, and tends to attract students of similar interests during pledge week, sort of like fraternities or sororities.

"Fuck, if you get in—"

"Ansel literally *just* asked her personally to come to the meeting" Giorgiana drawls with a roll of her eyes. "She's *in*. Sorry."

Demi, my roommate, makes a face. "I *know*. Which means I'm going to get reassigned to some other loser like me who didn't get into one of the clubs."

Roommate pairings at Knightsblood are for your entire time here. But if you get tapped during your freshman year for one of the four ultra-selective clubs, you move out of the dorms and into one of the four mansions on campus that house those clubs once you become a sophomore.

"Oh, come on, Demi," I grin. "You could still get into one of them. Or there's always next year?"

She gives me a dubious look. Fair: the chances of getting picked your sophomore year for a club are *slim*.

"The Order membership, living in their mansion, *and* you get to screw Ansel Albrecht all day?" Christina sighs. "Life is so unfair."

My face heats.

Since arriving here, these are the girls I've really connected with. And, as college freshmen do, we frequently gab about guys—conquests, boyfriends and flings from back home, any hookups at school since we arrived.

Christina and Demi have their fair share of wild stories. Giorgiana has double the two of them combined.

I have *zero* stories, wild or otherwise. And I can blame my older sister, Camille—who's also here at Knightsblood—for that. After her wild antics in high school, dad clamped down *hard* on me.

No parties for me. No boyfriends. No flings or hookups.

Nada. Zilch. *Rien*.

Not that my friends know that. I've spun them a few lurid tales involving "Stephan", my incredibly handsome, loving, sexually gifted, and obviously *imaginary* boyfriend from high school. I think they assume I've had a fling here and there since starting Knightsblood, but that I'm shy about sharing that type of stuff.

If only.

We round the corner of one of the walled rose gardens that dot the campus and almost plow right into a tall, gorgeous guy with dark hair, blue eyes, and tanned Italian skin.

"Hi, Dante," Giorgiana purrs almost immediately, batting her eyes and sticking both her ass and her tits out of alignment as she cocks a hip.

"Giorgiana," Dante growls, almost without looking at her, not slowing as he continues on toward one of the academic buildings.

"*Masterfully* played," Christina giggles.

Giorgiana pouts and waves her off. "What? Can't hurt to try."

Dante Sartorre, a close associate of the Barone Mafia family, is head of The Ouroboros Society. Except he doesn't seem to be looking for any one-on-one invitational conversations, unlike Ansel.

"Nah," Demi shrugs. "I think he's fucking Layla Black."

Giorgiana frowns and shakes her head. "No, I think they're just friends. Besides, Layla is totally screwing that sketchy townie guy Jason."

"Eww, gross." Christina makes a face. "Isn't he a drug dealer?"

Demi shakes her head. "Someone should tell her brothers. Gabriel would totally kick that guy's ass."

Giorgiana snorts. "Yeah, and then her psycho adopted brother would stab him or, like, eat his heart or something."

Layla's two brothers, Gabriel and Alistair Black, are the heads of two other student clubs: Para Bellum and The Reckless, respectively. I don't really know either of them, but Gabriel's got a reputation as a hero type, and Alistair as a little unhinged.

"Anyway, I need to run to stats class," Christina sighs. "Catch you bitches later."

Giorgiana laughs and flips her off. "I have to run, too."

"Same," Demi sighs, giving me a glum look. "Ugh, *please* get Ansel to invite me to the meeting next week? I mean, he clearly wants you. So, like, blow him or something? For me?"

I roll my eyes, feeling my face heat as she giggles. "I'll see what I can do."

The three of them head toward their classes. But I've got a free period, so I turn and make my way to the huge, almost Medieval looking library across campus.

It's nice out, so I take the long way through some of the rose gardens. I'm near the stables when I pause, hearing the unmistakable sound of *fighting*.

Fists hitting flesh. Grunts. An occasional groan of pain. Then I hear cheering that really sounds more like *jeering*, followed by a final fist-on-flesh sound.

Six guys emerge from behind the stables. I quickly hide in the shadows as one of them turns and spits in the direction they just came from.

"That's for my uncle, motherfucker," the guy snarls. "Tell your father, if he goes after him again, I'll cut off your fucking balls."

The six of them walk away laughing and clapping each other on the back. And then, my curiosity gets the better of me.

Slowly, I make my way around the corner of the stables. I freeze, my hand flying to my mouth when I see the man half kneeling on the ground, his back to me, his clothes torn, and his dark blonde hair disheveled.

He gets to his feet, grunting and turning to spit blood into the dirt. And it's then that I realize who he is, though we've never actually met.

"Are you okay?"

He doesn't jump or whirl. Rather, he slowly turns to face me.

A shiver creeps up my spine.

There's something almost insidiously beautiful about Alistair Black. The grim set of his chiseled jaw. The glinting malevolence in his sharp blue eyes. The air of power and dark energy that radiates from him, pulling me in like a moth to its fiery doom.

"I'm fine," he grunts, cracking his neck and rolling his shoulders. He turns to spit blood again.

"What the hell happened to you?"

"I got into a fight."

My eyes widen. "Like, a real fight?"

"No, a fake one," he mutters sarcastically, turning away from me.

"You seriously fought one of those guys who just left?"

"I fought *four* of those guys," Alistair growls, shoving his hair back from his face. "And I got my ass kicked."

"You fought *four* guys?!"

He sighs, turning to let those piercing blue eyes lance into me again.

"It was just a fight, princess. It's no big deal. I get into them sometimes." He lifts a shoulder. "It's kind of…what I do."

I chew on my lip. "Why did you just call me princess?"

Alistair eyes me. "Because that's what you are." He says it almost with disdain, which pisses me off.

I scowl. "I'm not a princess."

"I know who your father is, Eloise. You're a princess. Are we done?"

He makes to leave again.

"Why the hell would you go around picking fights? Especially against four guys?"

Alistair groans and turns to face me head-on.

"I didn't say I pick them," he growls. "I said I *get into them*."

"So, they have a way of finding you?"

His jaw clenches and his hand comes up, the back of it brushing a spot of blood from his nostrils.

"Is there a fucking point to this cross-examination?"

A smirk teases my lips. "You sound like a lawyer."

"Thanks."

"Is that what you want to be?"

He shrugs. "Probably. It's what my father is."

"Your adoptive father."

Fuck. Why the hell did I say that? Probably because I've still got the conversation with my friends rattling around in my head, and I clearly remember Giorgiana referring to Alistair as the "psycho adopted brother."

Thanks, Giorgiana.

"What the *fuck* did you just say?"

"I'm sorry, I—"

He storms toward me, erasing the space between us until he's looming right over me, his broad shoulders blotting out the sun as his eyes cut into my very soul.

"A word of advice, *princess*?" he growls quietly.

I glare up at him. "Don't fucking call me that."

"*Princess*," he sneers, jabbing his finger against my collarbone. I shiver, electric sparks teasing over my skin briefly before I shove the feeling down and glare at him even harder.

"Don't fucking touch me, either," I hiss.

"Or *what*."

I swallow nervously, a heady mix of fear and something else swirling around me the longer he stands here invading my personal space.

I could back up, but I don't.

I could run, but I won't.

"Or I'll get the rest of The Order to come teach you some manners."

He starts to laugh, loudly.

"I know what this is," he sneers. "You're one of Ansel's new fucktoys, and this is like some loyalty test he's put you up to."

I scowl. "Eww, what?"

Alistair leans even closer. "A *fucktoy,* princess. Ansel has a new crop of them every year. What'd he promise you? Piss me off, and you get to lick his balls or something?"

I wrinkle my nose. "You're disgusting, you know that?"

He makes a face and waves his hand in front of his nose. "Ugh, could you back up? Your breath smells like Ansel's cum."

I stare at him in shock, my mouth open.

"What the fuck is your problem?" I snap. "I only came over to see if you were okay—"

"Which we established I was five minutes ago, *princess.*"

"Stop calling me that!!"

"The sooner you walk the fuck away from me," he grunts. "The faster that happens."

"Ugh!" I blurt, turning on my heel and marching away from him. "Fuck you!" I yell over my shoulder, flipping him off for good measure.

"I'd say try not to choke on Ansel's cock," he calls back. "But from what I've heard of that douchebag, that shouldn't be a problem."

"Try not to get your ass kicked for being a shithead, *shithead,*" I toss back.

"Hey—princess?"

I stiffen, my teeth grinding hard as I turn to glare at him.

"*What*?!?!"

He turns to spit out more blood. "If you've got any brains under that crown, you'll stay the fuck away from me."

"Believe me, that will *not* be a problem."

5

ALISTAIR

GABRIEL'S already in Conference Room A when Taylor and I arrive. He eyes me warily as we take seats at the table on either side of him, facing the door.

"Carveli is on the way up."

"Noted," I grunt. My hand closes to a tight fist on the table.

Outwardly, I may appear calm. Beneath the surface, though, I'm a swirling dark pool of poison and fury. And I *hate* admitting to even myself why I feel that way.

I hate knowing that my barely contained rage at being in an enclosed space talking business with Massimo Carveli has nothing to do with his reputation, or what he does for a living.

...It's about who he shares a fucking bed with every night.

Eloise.

It's *always* about Eloise.

"Hey."

I flinch, whipping my gaze from the table to meet Gabriel's concerned eyes.

"You really don't need to be here for—"

"Excuse me, Mr. Black?"

The intercom on the conference table squawks as Megan, the front desk receptionist, interrupts.

"Mr. Carveli and his team are here."

"Wonderful. Please escort them to Conference Room A. Thanks, Megan," Gabriel chirps, all business. He turns to me as we all stand. "Look—"

"I'm fine."

I turn away to face the door, effectively ending that tedious conversation. A few seconds later, there's a discreet knock before Megan opens the door with a small smile and then steps back.

I turn to stone as Massimo steps inside, and don't realize my hands have curled to fighter's fists until Gabriel kicks my ankle under the table. He clears his throat, putting on his best, most unctuous politician's smile as he steps around the table with a hand outstretched.

"Ahh, Mr. Carveli! Welcome to Crown and Black."

My hands unclench, but I'm still stiff as a board as Massimo and some big Italian guy who looks like he'd fit in better at one of my fight clubs than at a legal office step inside.

"Mr. Black," Massimo purrs with his Sicilian accent, shaking my brother's hand firmly. "I'm glad we could arrange this meeting."

"Likewise, likewise," Gabriel smiles. "Allow me to introduce my associates, Taylor Crown..."

Taylor walks around the table to shake Massimo's hand.

"And my brother, Alistair."

There's no fucking way I'm shaking this motherfucker's hand, so I don't even make a move to walk around the table. If Massimo notices the slight, he ignores it as his eyes meet mine. He frowns slightly as he shakes a finger at me.

"Alistair Black..." he muses, his brows knitting. "Have we met?"

"I think I'd have remembered," I say flatly, ignoring the "please behave" look on my brother's face.

Massimo shrugs, an easy smile on his chiseled face. "My mistake, then. I could swear we've met before. Maybe we just have more in common than we think."

"I'd bet on it."

Taylor shoots me a pleading look past Massimo's shoulder that I ignore.

"Please have a seat, Mr. Carveli," Gabriel smiles. "Can I get you and your associate anything to drink?"

"Scotch for me. He's fine," Massimo says as he sinks lazily into a chair.

It's nine in the morning.

Gabriel clears his throat, looking completely nonplussed like the pro he is. He touches a button on the intercom. "Megan, would you please have the bottle of the Dalmore 62 from my office brought in, and four glasses?"

Massimo smirks a snake-like smile as Gabriel, Taylor, and I take seats across from him, facing the door.

"Mr. Carveli," Taylor smiles. "Why don't we begin with what Crown and Black can do for you and your organization—"

"I'm prepared to commit fifty million dollars a year in billable hours to your firm."

Holy. *Fuck*.

The room goes silent as Massimo's words hang in the air. That sort of money would make Massimo the single biggest client we have, by about double.

Gabriel clears his throat. "Well, that's wonderful to hear, Mr. Carveli."

He pauses as the door opens, and Megan bustles in with a tray of crystal glasses and the ludicrously expensive scotch from Gabriel's office. When she leaves again, Gabriel opens the bottle and pours a glass for Massimo.

"Now, why don't you tell us specifically what we can do for—"

"Stop talking."

My brows shoot up at Massimo's interruption. Gabriel frowns.

"Pardon me?"

"Stop. *Talking*," Massimo grunts. He wafts the glass of scotch under his nose as he sits back and grins at us venomously. "Let's be quite clear on something, Mr. Black. You and your partners won't be working *with* me. You'll be working *for* me. Are we clear on that?"

I feel my hands curl to fists under the table again. Gabriel's jaw tightens a little, but he nods politely.

"Of course, Mr. Carveli. Now, as I was—"

"And before you start plying me with expensive scotch and knockout redheads with great tits," Massimo snickers, nodding his chin at Taylor.

Fuckhead.

"You should know," he continues, "that my business comes with a...*condition.*"

Fuck. I hate fucking games, and I already hate this fucking guy. The combination is making me come close to boiling over.

"I'm sure you're a busy man, Massimo," I growl, purposely skipping the "Mr. Carveli" shit because *fuck* this guy. "So why don't we just put the cards on the table, shall we?"

His blue eyes swivel to mine, and he wags a finger at me.

"Oh, I *like* this one. You're my kind of lawyer, Alistair. Completely devoid of bullshit."

He sighs as his gaze takes in all three of us.

"My condition is this: I have someone—a lawyer—and I'd like you to hire them."

What?

"Excuse me?" Gabriel frowns.

Massimo shrugs, sipping his scotch. "If you want my business, you'll hire this lawyer. This is non-negotiable."

"We have a very precise and thorough hiring process, Mr. Carveli," Taylor ventures. "But I'm sure we can get your friend into the queue and have them in for a round of interviews."

Massimo smiles darkly and slowly shakes his head.

"That doesn't work for me. No 'process'. No interviews. You'll hire them, today."

My brows furrow. "You can't expect us to—"

"For fifty million a year I expect you to jump through hoops of fucking *fire* if I ask you to, counselor," he growls, a dark look on his face.

Gabriel clears his throat. "Mr. Carveli, could you give us a minute?"

"You have thirty seconds."

Massimo either doesn't see or ignores the glare I give him as Gabriel yanks me away. He, Taylor and I retreat to the far corner of the conference room, by the window.

"No. Fucking. Way," I grunt.

Gabriel rolls his eyes. "You're joking."

"And you're fucking *high* if you think we should bow to this douchebag and hire his mob lawyer buddy."

"I'd hire his favorite fucking *barista* for that sort of commitment on billable hours, Alistair," Gabriel hisses back.

Taylor nods. "I'm with Gabriel. I mean, whoever it is, we can stick them wherever we want. We'll give them a base starting salary, no bonus, and it can come directly out of Massimo's billable hours."

"Except he's the kind of shithead who'll ask for an inch and then take a fucking mile," I mutter.

"Who fucking cares?!" Gabriel hisses back. "Fifty mil lets us finally open that branch in Chicago we've been talking about."

"It's a no from me."

Gabriel sighs and glances at Taylor. "Vote?"

"Sure," she nods. "It's a yes from me. Sorry, Alistair."

"Yes from me, too," Gabriel murmurs, shrugging as he looks at me. "Sorry, pal. Majority carries."

"Aaaand, time's up!" Massimo chirps from his seat.

"This is a fucking mistake," I mutter under my breath as we all turn and walk back to the table.

"Well?" Massimo asks us.

"We have a deal, Mr. Carveli." Gabriel smiles and extends a hand across the table. Massimo grips it firmly as they shake. "I'll have the contract drawn up this afternoon."

Massimo's teeth flash as he smirks. "Excellent."

"So," Taylor clears her throat. "When can expect to meet your lawyer—"

"She's waiting just outside, actually."

Massimo turns to murmur something to his goon. The man nods before standing and slipping out of the room.

"She's excellent," Massimo grins. "Just passed the New York bar exam, actually."

"Always helpful for a *lawyer*," I say, ignoring Gabriel kicking my shin under the table. "Would we know her from any other firm?"

Massimo smiles as the door begins to open behind him.

"You would know her as my *wife*."

The words already hit me like a slap. But seeing her when she walks through that door is like a punch to the dick.

Fuck.

It's not the first time I've seen Eloise since Knightsblood. *That* brutal moment came a few months ago at a gala event, right after she and fuckstick moved to New York.

But that was from a distance. As far as I know, she didn't see me at all.

This time, we're only ten feet apart, and my eyes are the first thing hers latch onto when she steps through the door.

At the very least, I can relish the fear in her eyes. The confusion. The way they fly wide, her heart-shaped lips pulling into an O.

But that momentary victory shatters once I drink in the rest of her.

Goddammit.

If fate or karma had any sense of fairness, Eloise LaBlanc would have walked back into my life three hundred pounds overweight or suffering from some disgusting skin ailment.

But that isn't the case. Not. In. The. *Slightest.*

Ten years ago, Eloise was a pretty, fresh-faced...if mouthy... nineteen-year-old girl.

Today, she stands in front of me as quite possibly the most stunning *woman* I've ever seen. She's still petite, but stands tall and proud, even as her eyes keep darting nervously to mine. Her long blonde hair is up in a sleek, professional bun, though the office appropriate stops there: her attire makes her look like she's trying to score free drinks at the hottest club in Manhattan, as opposed to anything approaching an office dress code.

And it's fucking *green.*

My eyes draw to slits.

Green, just like the night she taught me the lesson I've never forgotten. The night my walls went up and never came down again.

Slowly, she collects herself, and I see her expression transform back into the one I knew ten years ago.

Haughty.

Proud and vain.

Entitled.

For one second, when she first walked in, I felt a surge of something I didn't quite understand and certainly didn't want welling up inside of me. I felt a tidal wave of confusion, the sight of her so close again hitting me like an old addiction and reactivating neural synapses, memories, and cravings I shut down years ago.

But now, seeing that look on her face, so similar to the look the first time I met the snobby little French mafia princess, that momentary lapse in judgment shatters like frozen glass. And that green dress, rubbing my face in that memory, is just a big fuck-you icing on the cake.

The fury comes back. So does the hatred, and distrust, and disgust.

With a *vengeance.*

Gabriel pales. "Mr. Carveli—"

"You're all a bit older now, so I don't know if you recognize each other. But you and Alistair actually went to school with my Eloise."

My Eloise.

I takes a lot—more than I want to admit—to stop myself from putting my fist through the table in front of me.

Better yet, through Massimo's fucking face.

"Anyway, this is who you'll be hiring," Massimo smiles, a glint in his eyes. "Oh, and before you stick her in the mail room or something, let me be clear about my conditions. She works here for real. No bullshit. No sending her on lunch runs. She starts at Associate level."

My face is too tight to react. Not to mention I'm still burning holes through Eloise's fucking head with my eyes. But I can see Taylor and Gabriel both barely contain their own outbursts as they glance quickly at each other.

"Mr. Carveli," Taylor says gently. "And with all due respect, Mrs. Carveli—"

"It's Ms. LeBlanc."

Jesus. It's the first time I've heard her voice in a decade. And I am *not* prepared for the snarling rage it sparks inside of me.

Eloise's face tinges pink. "I…I never officially changed my name—"

Her mouth snaps shut when Massimo whirls on her, his lips curled. Taylor clears her throat.

"Well, *Ms. LeBlanc,* our associate positions at Crown and Black are extremely coveted, and we only promote from within the existing junior associate pool—"

"If my legal representatives don't grasp what 'non-negotiable' means," Massimo snarls quietly, "maybe I should be taking my business elsewhere."

The conference room goes quiet.

"I believe we understand each other, Mr. Carveli," Taylor murmurs.

Massimo grins widely. "Excellent. She starts tomorrow, along with our annual contract."

Fuck no. *FUCK* no. I want to scream. I want to reach across the table and throttle him, or if nothing else, grab Eloise, drag her from the fucking building, and hurl her into the gutter where she belongs.

I can't have her here. I *won't,* even if she's hidden away with the rest of the associates on their floor.

"Oh, and one more thing." Massimo stands and buttons his suit jacket, signaling that the meeting is over. His eyes drag from Taylor to Gabriel and finally settle on me. He grins evilly and wags a finger at me. "Since I like this one so much, and since I think we probably have *much* in common…" His smile curls dangerously. "She works under you. Exclusively. Consider her your personal associate."

What. The. FUCK.

"That's not—"

Gabriel grabs my bicep just above the elbow and squeezes, hard.

"We look forward to working wi—" He stops himself. "*For* you, Mr. Carveli. And we'll see you tomorrow, Eloise."

Massimo smiles a triumphant, shit-eating grin as he picks up his glass and drains the last of his Dalmore 62.

"I'm glad we're all on the same page. Have the contracts ready by one this afternoon, and my people will come collect them. Ms. Crown?"

He eyes Taylor's tits again before shaking her hand firmly.

Gabriel is next. "Mr. Black."

"And *Alistair.*" He smiles broadly as he reaches across the table. I hesitate, and there's no stopping my eyes from swiveling to lock with Eloise's. I extend my hand and shake Massimo's outstretched one, gritting my teeth.

The fucker turns and heads out, followed closely by his goon. Eloise stays where she is for a second, our eyes still locked, my sadistic side relishing the look of horror on her face.

Ten years ago, she fucked me up. She weaseled her way into a place no one gets into, and set the whole thing on fire.

She scorched me. Charred me. Cauterized any remaining weakness in me.

And now—*now*—here we are again, and this time, the power is all in *my* hands.

And she will *rue* the day she stepped back into my world.

6

ELOISE

My stomach churns as the elevator rises to the offices of Crown and Black, occupying the top three floors of the stately Madison Avenue building.

In a parallel universe, this would be one of the best days of my life, walking into one of the most, if not *the* most, prestigious law firms in New York for my first day of employment after years of one step forward, two steps back.

But this is not that parallel universe.

After law school, I was briefly a junior associate at a firm in Chicago. But then my father back in Paris got sick, and it all went down the drain: starting with the stipulations in his living will that I be married off to *Massimo,* immediately.

After the wedding, Massimo forbade me from working, which made it confusing when he allowed me to take the bar exam in New York after we moved there. And it makes it *extremely* confusing that he's just surprised me with a fucking job at Crown and Black.

Because Massimo doesn't do favors, or presents, or surprises—at least, not the good kind. Which means that this position comes with strings. It comes with an "angle".

But even that's not what has my stomach knotting and nervous butterflies fluttering through me. Nor is it first day jitters, or anything silly like that.

No, it's that in a minute, when I step off this elevator into the Crown and Black offices, *Alistair* will be my *boss*. And the resulting cocktail of nervousness, confusion, and outright fear flooding my system has my head spinning.

It's hard to describe what Alistair Black and I were, ten years ago. Enemies, but not. Rivals, but...also allies, in a sense? Oil and water. Fire and gunpowder. If I'd been a man, we probably would have eventually fought each other.

Instead, we *slept* together.

The worst mistake of my life, but maybe the best night, all in one convoluted, dangerous package.

And then it went to shit.

First came confusion. Then came the night of pain and blood and loss. When I actually needed him, he cut me off entirely.

I remember seeing him briefly right before his graduation ceremony. After a month of no contact and him blocking me everywhere, I finally went up to him, against my better judgment, to demand what the hell was going on.

I never got my answer. Well, I did, it just wasn't the answer I was looking for, or expected.

"From the very bottom of my heart, Eloise. Go the fuck to hell, and don't ever cross my path again."

That, ladies and gentlemen of the jury, is my new boss.

With a ding, the elevator doors open long before I'm ready for them to. I grip my bag tighter as I step out and into the main foyer of the law offices.

"Eloise, yes?"

A pretty brunette—Megan, if I remember correctly from yesterday—smiles as she stands from the reception desk.

"Hi, yeah. It's Megan, right?"

She beams. "That's me! Now, I've been instructed to—"

My phone rings loudly. I cringe, scrambling to yank it out of my bag and put it to silent. "Sorry!" I blurt. "I am *so*—"

I freeze when I see the name on the screen.

"*Merde*," I hiss under my breath, wincing and looking up at Megan again. "I'm sorry, it's a family thing…"

She waves me off easily. "Please, go right ahead."

I smile weakly and scurry over to a corner of the foyer before I answer.

"Where are you?" Camille blurts.

Shit.

People have frequently used the words "volatile" or "emotionally fragile" to describe my older sister. Those are the ones being nice about it. It's not that Camille is "crazy", it's just…

Well, it's hard to describe.

It's part drama queen, part narcissism, and one huge part neediness. She hates being alone, despises not being a part of your conversation—even if she really doesn't have anything to do with it—and she's clingy.

And yes, I realize this sounds *exactly* like the sort of person you try to steer clear of, but she's also my sister, and I understand why she's like that.

Losing our mom when we were nine and twelve years old was rough. It really hit Camille at the worst possible time—a time when a daughter really needs her mom around. Add in the fact that I was very clearly Dad's favorite, and him utterly retreating inward after mom died, and you get a recipe for… well, someone like Camille.

She can be a huge pain in the ass. She's emotionally draining a lot of the time. But family is family.

Years and years ago, I secretly came up with a rating system to gauge, emotionally, where Camille was on any given day. One is normal. Ten is "call her therapist, call her psychiatrist, and call the police while you're at it." It's even easier face-to-face, but at this point, I can even give an accurate reading over the phone.

Right now, based on those three words, Camille's at a six. Not great, not terrible.

"Hey," I say brightly, trying to invoke a positivity I don't really feel. "What's up?"

"What's up??" she blurts. "What's up is *where are you*? I'm just sitting here all alone, Eloise. I look like an idiot!"

My brows knit. I even glance at my phone for a second and thumb over to my calendar to see if I've forgotten about something.

I haven't.

"Camille, where are *you*?"

"At Per Se, for lunch!"

I exhale slowly. Yeah, I know what this is. Again, it's not that my sister is delusional, or forgetful. It's that she'll create a scenario in her mind where *you* fucked up, for which she will then "forgive you". It's manipulative as fuck, but...that's Camille. The problem is, once she's come up with this scenario, she genuinely gets into this headspace where she starts to believe her own bullshit.

This is exactly what's happening right now.

Today, Camille has concocted a scenario in which I'm apparently standing her up for a lunch date at the very expensive, very posh, Michelin-rated Per Se restaurant. Normally, the "fix" for this would be to go over there, come up with some sort of apology, and just have lunch with her, because that's the easiest damn solution. And hey, I hear the food's great.

Except today, I can't do that. Because today I'm here, in hell, working my very first day as Alistair Black's underling at Crown and Black.

"Camille, I'm so sorry."

She sighs heavily. "It's fine, I understand. You get forgetful sometimes. Just get here. I'm doing the chef's tasting menu. The uni risotto is supposed to be *insane*—"

"No, Camille, I can't come. Not today."

There's a moment of silence.

"Why not?" she spits in a clipped, annoyed tone.

I blow air through my lips. "I'm at work, actually. It's my first day."

"Wait, *what*?"

"Yeah." I roll my eyes. "Massimo," I mutter, like that's the only explanation anyone needs. "He… He got me this associate's position at the law firm he's going to be using for business."

Camille squeals. "Oh my *God*! Ellie! That's so amazing!"

For all her crazy, again, she's also my sister.

"I'm so fucking happy for you!"

"Thanks!" I gush back. "It's…overwhelming. But I'm *really* excited to—"

"Wait. Which firm?"

Shit.

My silence speaks volumes.

"It's Crown and Black, isn't it?"

I sigh. "Yeah."

"What the *fuck*, Eloise?! Do you fucking hate me?!"

I grit my teeth. "Cammie, it wasn't my decision. Massimo—"

"You're seriously working for *Alistair*?!" she snaps coldly. "After what that piece of shit did to me?!"

To you, and *to me. To hurt me, by hurting you.*

Which sounds so shitty, but I know it's true. Alistair doesn't do random. Whatever happened with my sister and Alistair —however murky the facts are—was done to hurt me. That's bad enough.

What makes it awful is that now I'm working here, under him.

"Camille, I'm *sorry*. It's not at all my decision. Massimo made it pretty fucking clear that I don't have a choice—"

"Yeah, kind of like how *I* didn't have a choice."

My eyes close. "Camille, let's talk—"

"Enjoy reminiscing with your piece of shit ex-boyfriend, you backstabbing bitch."

She hangs up abruptly, and any wind that might have been in my sails when I walked in here dies instantly.

Goddammit.

I sigh as I silence the phone and slip it into my bag again. Then I turn and plaster a smile on my face as I walk back over to Megan.

"Sorry about that."

"No worries." She smiles, then lowers her voice. "I wasn't trying to eavesdrop, but...sibling?"

I make a face and nod.

"My brother's a handful, too," she grins, clearly trying to put me at ease. "I totally understand."

I smile weakly. "Thanks."

"But we should hustle," she says, her smile a bit more nervous now. "Not, uh...not *everyone* might understand, if you know what I mean."

I do.

She means Alistair won't understand. Or care, for that matter.

I follow Megan down the hall into a huge, open-concept office space full of low cubicles.

"This is the main floor, where the associates, junior associates, and aides all have their workspaces. The conference rooms are here too. Third floor is for the legal libraries, boardroom, and offices of the board members"...she gives me a conspiratorial wink..."when they're even here, that is."

I follow her up a gorgeous, sweeping glass and steel staircase in the middle of the huge open space that leads up to a second floor that rings above the first.

"Here on level two..." she continues as we get to the top of the stairs. "Partners' offices and conference room." She turns and indicates a gorgeous, all-glass corner office filled with stunning art, beautiful mid-century furniture, and flowering plants. "Ms. Crown's executive office. Down *there...*" She points to another glassed-in corner of the building, this one far more masculine; all wood, brass, and dark hues. "Mr. Black...*Gabriel* Black, that is," she adds. "And then, if you'll follow me..."

I swallow the large lump in my throat as I follow Megan to the last corner of the floor. This office is glass, too, but unlike Taylor's and Gabriel's, the blinds are drawn, obscuring the interior.

"Mr. Black's office," she says with a slightly nervous smile as we stop outside the closed door. A young, pretty woman smiles at us from behind her desk just outside. "Mrs. Carveli?"

I smile. "It's actually Ms. LeBlanc."

Her brows knit as she glances back at a stack of papers in her hands. "Oh, well...hmm."

Megan pats my arm. "I need to run back downstairs. Anything you need, just come ask, okay?"

I smile weakly at her. "Thank you."

When she's gone, I turn back to the confused-looking girl—Katerina, if the birthday cards tacked to the wall behind her desk are to be believed.

"Is everything okay?"

"It's just..." She smiles brightly at me. "It's definitely *Ms.* LeBlanc?"

"I never changed my name when I got married. So, yes, technically, still Ms. LeBlanc. Is that a problem?"

"No!" she says, with all the sincerity of a punchline. "Not at all. I mean, it *won't* be...as soon as you go down to HR and redo all your paperwork and on-boarding documents."

My face falls. "Oh."

"Yeah, it's..." She makes a face. "Well, I'm sure it won't take too long. In the meantime..." She glances at the closed door to Alistair's office. When she looks back at me, the look on her face screams *good fucking luck, sister.*

"Well, he's ready for you."

"Sorry I'm a little late. I had a family thing on the phone I had to—"

"Yeah, I wouldn't mention that to him."

"It's my sister—"

Katerina cuts me off by stabbing the intercom button on her desk. "Hi, yes, Mr. Black? *Ms.* LeBlanc is here."

She's got an earpiece in, so I don't hear his reply. But the way her smile falters and the color drains from her face tell me everything I need to know.

Ten years ago, I made the mistake of sleeping with my enemy. My bully. Though, I suppose I was *his*, as well.

But if any tiny part of me was thinking that ten years later, he'd let bygones be bygones and consider it all water under the bridge, the naked look of fear on his assistant's face dashes that idea in a heartbeat.

Katerina's eyes drag up to mine. "Like I said: he's ready for you."

Cold dread drags its nails up my spine as I turn toward the door. I walk to it slowly, my breath coming shallow and fast.

My fingers close around the knob. I twist, push, and then with as deep a breath as I can muster, I step into the room.

Alistair is sitting behind his desk—jacketless, with the sleeves of his Oxford shirt rolled up to mid-forearm—and I freeze when his eyes lock with mine, ice blue, piercing, like he's trying to flay open my very soul with his gaze.

"Close the door."

I quickly turn to shut the door behind me. When I turn back, my gaze momentarily drops to his forearm and to tattoo ink that I don't remember from before.

"Eyes up here, *Ms. LeBlanc*," Alistair growls. My gaze drags up to his, over the chiseled line of his jaw and cleft chin. Over the sinfully perfect lips and regal nose, until I'm once again captured by that lethal look in his eyes.

"Or is it *Mrs. Carveli*," he says with a hint of a sneer. "I seem to be confused on that point."

"It's…" My throat closes, choking me for a second, and I quail at the way his lips curl at me. "It's Ms. LeBlanc."

"Well, Ms. LeBlanc," he growls. "You're late."

"Alistair, I'm so sorry. I—"

"First. Of. All."

He stands abruptly, his voice barking across the space between us.

"You will refer to me as Mr. Black. Or *sir*."

I stare at him open-mouthed.

Sir? He can't be fucking serious.

"Is that clear, Ms. Leblanc?"

I nod. "Yeah, sorry."

"Save the *yeahs* for someone who isn't your fucking boss. It's *yes, sir* and *no, sir*. Got it? And apology accepted."

My brows knit. "Wait, *apology*? I wasn't—"

"I don't care."

I flinch at how abrupt his words are—how viciously he's staring at me. How cold the room feels as his gaze stabs into me.

"Just as I don't give a single fuck why you were late. Just know that it's never happening again."

I nod. "I understand."

"You understand…?" Alistair raises a significant brow.

You're fucking joking.

I swallow my pride and clear my throat. "I understand, *sir*."

"Good."

"So, what should I—"

"Whatever I ask, *whenever* I ask it."

He slowly stalks out from behind his desk and moves toward me. It's like watching a jungle predator prowling through the shadows, and just as triggering to my adrenaline. My pulse quickens as he moves closer and closer, and I keep waiting for him to stop, but he doesn't. He just keeps coming closer.

And closer.

And *closer.*

I gasp, my spine jerking ramrod straight as he stops *right* in front of me, looming over me with his broad shoulders and black gaze. With his masculine scent of something woodsy, citrusy, and spicy engulfing my senses, arresting my pulse.

"I...I'm not sure what you mean..."

Every nerve in my body explodes as he suddenly grabs my jaw, lifting my gaze to his as it slices into me.

"What I mean, *Ms. LeBlanc,*" he snarls, "is that from now on..." His thumb and forefinger tighten on my chin, making me shudder.

"From now on, *I fucking own you.*"

7

ELOISE

I FUCKING OWN YOU.

Holy shit.

The Alistair I knew was dark and brooding, sure. He had demons, and a malicious edge to him. And yeah, he was a dick.

But the man standing before me, towering over me with a malevolent energy almost literally radiating off him, is pure *wrath*. He's not dark; he's Darkness personified. And brooding doesn't even remotely come close to describing the viciousness etched into his face as his ice-blue eyes carve into me.

He was a switchblade when I knew him at school. The tall, stoic, cold man standing in front of me today is a fucking broadsword. A weapon of mass destruction.

Death, on a pale horse.

The moment drags on, and the utter silence of his office feels like a shroud. I can hear the rhythmic ticking of a clock on one of his shelves, seemingly in time with the thudding of my pulse in my ears.

Alistair turns away, strides easily back over to his desk, and sinks into his chair. He leans back, stroking his jaw with one hand as he drums the fingers of the other on the edge of his desk.

"I'd ask whose dick you had to suck in order to get this *highly* coveted position without so much as a single fucking interview." His smile turns brittle. "But I suppose we both know the answer to that."

My jaw clenches. "That's…"

"Not fair? Unkind? *Un-pro-fessional?*" he snaps coldly.

"Inappropriate," I fire back.

"You're a lawyer—sue me. And while you're at it, try and forgive my dislike for hiring completely inexperienced *whores* for positions in *my* firm they neither qualify for, nor deserve."

Terrified as I am, I still bristle at his words. It's "the French in me", as my mother would say, and there's no stopping the heated retort that flies from my mouth unbidden.

"You don't get to speak to me like that," I hiss.

Alistair barks out a loud, menacing laugh.

"No?"

"*No,*" I mutter, feeling my face heat and my insides churn as his gaze zones in on me.

"Or what, Eloise?" Alistair says icily. "Or you'll tell your hubby?" His lips curl dangerously. "You'll go tell Massimo all the mean widdle names I call you? Or maybe you'll just make some shit up. We both know how gifted a storyteller you are."

My face burns, and as much as try and resist, my eyes drop from his, looking down at my hands as they twist in front of me.

"I—"

"You *what*," he snarls. "Is this a fucking apology I'm about to hear? Have you practiced this in front of the mirror, Eloise?"

I don't have to think very hard to know what he's talking about.

"I…" I shake my head, picking at my cuticles.

Be the bigger person. Offer the olive branch.

"I… I had no right to spread that rumor about you."

"No *shit*," Alistair barks coldly. "That rumor almost kept me out of law school."

My teeth rake over my bottom lip. "I… I'm sorry."

"Oh, well, that's nice," he deadpans.

"Listen, Alistair—"

"No."

I frown. "Wait, I just—"

"And I said *no*. A, you don't, under any circumstances, dictate to me what to do. And B, I don't, as a rule, listen to opportunistic backstabbing whores."

My face turns to fire as I glare at him sharply.

"Stop calling me that."

"Which part, specifically, Eloise," he growls, "do you take offense to? The whore part, or specifically the opportunistic and backstabbing descriptors?"

"You—"

"I always like to be precise, which is why I ask."

I bristle as he sneers a cold, malicious smile at me.

"I don't want to be here anymore than you want me to be."

"Well, there's the door," he rasps, jabbing a finger past me. "Problem fucking solved."

"Come on, Alistair!" I bark back. "We're adults, okay!? What happened when we were kids is…regrettable. But given that we both have to be here, how about we act like grownups about it?!"

I was half expecting to be cut off by some biting remark. So when he actually lets me finish without interruption, the ensuing silence hangs awkwardly, my eyes darting over his face like I'm waiting for the comeback.

The seconds tick by until slowly he raises his brows.

"Oh, was that the whole thing? I was waiting for you to launch into the next stanza of your grandiose speech."

I grit my teeth as I look away. "You are *such* a fucking asshole."

"Pot, meet kettle," he snaps. "Or is it pot, meet *whore*—"

"Stop calling me that!!"

"Or *what*?!"

He lurches out of his chair, his face livid as he slams his knuckles onto the edge of his desk.

"Or *what*, Eloise?" Alistair hisses viciously. "Or you'll go cry to your husband?"

"Maybe I will!" I hiss back.

"By all means, go ahead." He smiles. "And then I'll tell him all the ways you took my cock."

The words hit me like a slap in the face. And, mortifyingly, like a zap of electricity through my core.

Goddammit, do NOT let your thoughts go there.

No.

Alistair is a bastard and a supreme asshole. And it was *one night*, ten fucking years ago. But even as I try to talk myself back from that edge, and desperately tell the heat on my face to abate, he starts to move from behind his desk. My skin shivers and prickles to goosebumps as his eyes narrow on me and he moves toward me again.

"Please, Eloise," he growls. "*Please* run and cry to Massimo. He doesn't know, does he?"

I look away.

"Does he."

My eyes close as I drag in a ragged breath of air, the nearness of him closing my throat. "What do you think?" I whisper.

"I think your husband has no idea what a greedy slut his innocent bride is capable of being."

My eyes snap up to his, fury and something else I'm not willing to admit to pulsing through me.

"Is that a threat?"

"*Most definitely,*" he hisses back. "So please, go boo-hoo to Massimo. I'm *dying* to tell him all the things he doesn't know about his wife."

I shiver, my breath coming in staccato bursts as he leans down close to me, and then even closer, until I can feel the heat of his breath against my ear. My eyes flutter closed in spite of myself.

"All the wet holes I fucked..." Alistair murmurs darkly.

My core clenches and heat pools traitorously between my thighs.

"All the ways you were my eager, willing, *greedy* cock slut..."

"*You're a bastard,*" I choke.

I almost gasp at the coldness that sweeps over me as Alistair pulls abruptly away. He steps back and turns sharply on his heel before stalking back over to his desk and sitting behind it again.

"Noted," he spits. "Anything else?"

Goddamn him.

Ten fucking years later, and he *still* does this to me. Because Alistair Black is my drug of choice. My sin. My temptation.

My undoing.

"We're done here. Katerina will find you a cubicle—"

"I'm an associate, Alistair."

"No, you're a *parasite,* Eloise," he snaps back. "Let's be crystal fucking clear about something. You're here strictly because your fucking husband demanded it in exchange for his business. He *bought you* a place here at the firm. And for that, I, the other partners, and the firm itself, owe you *nothing*." He laughs coldly. "What do you want, Eloise? A fucking corner office?"

"How about an ounce of respect!"

"*Fresh out of it*," he fires back. "Find a fucking cubicle and start in on the case files that'll be sent to your desk. I'd move fast, by the way. The stack will be taller than you before lunch, I promise."

Gee, thanks, asshole.

He fixes me with a look. "Something you'd like to share with the group?"

"No, just..." I clear my throat. "Katerina mentioned that I'll need to change my name with HR. You have it down as Carveli."

"Yes. That's your fucking name."

I shake my head. "It's still LeBlanc."

Alistair's brow cocks. "So..."

"So...I'll need to change it—"

"Which you can do on your *own* time, after work."

"Okay, but—"

"There is no but," he barks. "That's *it*. Matter discussed; case closed. Now, is there anything else you'd like to waste my fucking time talking about?"

My mouth purses tightly as I glare at him.

It's not like I *need* this job. The problem is, I *want it.*

Yes, part of me knows that if Massimo finagled to get me this position, it's for a reason, and that reason isn't the kindness of his heart. I also know *leaving* would only incur his wrath.

But the other thing that stops me from telling Alistair to go fuck himself before I quit on the spot is more…personal.

It's that I *want this*.

I *want* to be a lawyer, especially at a prestigious firm like Crown and Black.

So I'll be *damned* if I let Alistair the Asshole scare me away. Yeah, I might not "deserve" to be here. And there might be… okay, definitely are…ulterior reasons for me having this position, even if I don't know yet what they are.

But it's a foot in the door. And that's what matters.

My head shakes. "No, there's nothing else."

He cocks one brow meaningfully. My face heats, and I bristle.

"No, there's nothing else, *sir*."

"Good." He frowns, bringing a hand up to his ear as a concentrated look creeps over his face. Then he fake gasps. "Fuck, do you hear that?"

"Uh, no?"

"It's the sound of your workload already piling up. I'd hop to it. Oh, and try not to turn any tricks on the way to your desk, if you can help it."

My teeth flash before I can stop myself. Alistair grins darkly.

"*Say it,*" he growls. "Say whatever it is you're dying to say. You'll do us both a favor if you give me the ammunition to fire your sorry ass right now."

Fuck you, you shit-eating, cocky, narcissistic prick. Go fuck yourself, and fuck yourself again, and fuck yourself one more time to be sure.

I plaster a sugary smile on my face.

"There's nothing else, *sir*. Shall I get to work now, sir?"

Alistair glares at me, almost like he's pissed that I've denied him the fight he so clearly wants. I start to turn when his words stop me, barking across the divide between us.

"Why are you really here, Eloise."

I swallow and shake my head. "I don't have an answer for that."

"Well, then I suppose I'll just have to find it."

His eyes slide over me, his lips curling dangerously. When his hand comes up to stroke his lethal jaw, the tattoo ink on his forearm ripples. "And I *will* find it, Eloise. By *any* means necessary."

8

ALISTAIR

THE EIGHTH-CENTURY general and strategist Sun Tzu once famously wrote in his book *The Art of War,* "keep your friends close and your enemies closer".

I've read it…twice…which isn't really that big a brag because every high-level lawyer, Wall Street trader, CEO, and Silicon Valley entrepreneur has, too. But while Sun Tzu was a genius when it comes to knowing the opposition, I'm willing to bet serious money that he did *not* have Eloise fucking LeBlanc suddenly working under him.

With him.

Around him. All. The. Fucking. Time.

In my head, I keep it as "Eloise fucking LeBlanc", because I have no idea what else to call her. She's not an "old friend", nor an "old flame". She's not my ex *anything*. If anything, she's my enemy. What else do you call someone you went to war against? Someone who spread lies about you that almost ended everything you'd worked for?

Someone who pried her way inside you, only to fuck you over and pour gasoline on the fire she lit inside your chest?

I'm loath to say I hate *her,* because it feels like giving her a win to use words that strong with her. No, what I really hate is that ten years later, she's still able to get under my skin and piss me the fuck off like this.

Ten years ago, I was weak. I was open to manipulation, especially the sort that came from pretty girls with big blue eyes and sharp, sassy tongues.

I've spent a decade changing all that. Burning out the weakness. Shoring up my defenses with iron and sheer will, almost as if some part of me was waiting for the day she'd try to storm her way back into my life and fuck my shit up all over again.

Good thing I did, too, because...well, here we are.

I stand staring through the glass of my corner office—not the window looking down on midtown Manhattan, with the sort of view my father only dreamed of in his career as an in-the-trenches lawyer.

No, I'm standing at the interior glass wall that looks down onto "the pit" below—the maze of cubicles on the first floor teeming with junior associates and legal aides.

Specifically, I'm looking at our newest hire, who's currently sitting sulking in her—admittedly shitty—new cubicle.

I *may* have had a hand in picking that particular cubicle for her. Closest to the distractions of the bathrooms and the break room, sitting directly under one of the air vents—the one that persists in rattling every single time the air blasts out of it, no matter how often we get it fixed.

Oh, and it's also situated so that the afternoon sun is goddamn *blinding* unless you've come to work with a welder's mask.

Is this a childish, petty move on my part? Hell yes. Do I give a shit?

Hell no.

I'm fully aware that it's not Eloise personally who bullied her way into working at Crown and Black with the promise of fifty million a year in billable hours. But as big a piece of shit as I think Massimo Carveli is, he and I don't have a history that merits petty vengeance.

Eloise and I, however, do.

Currently, as promised, she's *buried* under the mountain—more like mount*ains*, plural—of case files I've had my underlings bring her. They're not important cases, or even ones I have really anything to do with. And that's *not* just because of my history with Eloise.

Well, okay, it's maybe *half* because of my history with her.

It's also because she's wormed her way into a position normally reserved for someone who's put literally *thousands* of hours of their life into this firm. Someone who's given everything to get that coveted associate's position.

Not a goddamn mafia princess who simply switched from one team to the other.

When I first heard that Eloise had married Massimo a little over a year ago, I was angry. But I was also confused. Eloise's father, Andre LeBlanc, is the head of one of the biggest old-school mafia families in Paris. Or he *was*, before his illness—his number two, Luc, is apparently running things now. But the LeBlanc family is a French Mafia institution who, historically, gets along with the Italians about as well as Tom gets along with Jerry. As the Road Runner gets along with the Coyote, or Bugs Bunny with Elmer Fudd—

You get the picture.

So, yes, color me twelve shades of surprised when Andre gets sick and it turns out his living will stipulates an arranged marriage between his youngest daughter and *Massimo*.

Almost as surprised as I was to discover that Eloise actually *is* a lawyer. Not one with any real experience, but at least, on paper, a good one.

I've checked.

She worked for one firm in Chicago—and one I can't even shit on: they'll be our biggest competitor if we do open a branch there—after graduating top of her class in law school, and did well there. But that all ended when she married Captain Fuckstick. Then they moved to California, and then here, and she actually passed the New York bar, which is impressive, much as I hate to admit it.

And now here she is. Right. Under. My. Nose. In my crosshairs.

Under my *control*.

Instantly, I regret thinking of it that way as my dick stirs and throbs in my slacks. My eyes narrow onto the pit, staring right at her.

Imagining vengeance.

Imagining stripping her.

Remembering the night when I had all of her.

Until it shattered.

And again, as I stare at her like I did in the conference room the other day, I'm overcome by the sheer unfairness of what time has done to this woman. If whatever divine power you choose to believe in was fair in any capacity, Eloise would have walked in here post-stroke, with half her face numb and slack.

Instead, she strolled in looking ten times as gorgeous as she did the last time we crossed paths.

Parts of her haven't aged a bit. Her skin is still glowing and flawless. Her heart-shaped mouth still plump and way, *way* too enticing. Her long blonde hair still shimmering and youthful. But at the same time, it's like somehow her goddamn legs got longer. Her ass got rounder and lusher in ways it has no business doing. And the years have only somehow made that sharp look in her big blue eyes even fiercer and wilder. There's even a tinge of violet in them now that gives her a witchy vibe, like she's staring into your soul.

Nineteen looked good on Eloise LeBlanc.

Twenty-nine looks downright lethal. And it infuriates me to think who gets to see all that fierce, stunning lethality up close and personal, every day of his life.

Every night.

"Everything okay?"

I blink. Slowly, scowling, I pull my gaze away from Eloise and to Gabriel, who's just walked into my office. He nods at my right hand, which I realize now is gripping a contract I was reading over in a tight fist.

"Fine," I grunt.

"And before you throw a hissy fit, I *did* knock. But you were in dreamland and didn't answer."

I shoot my brother a look before I let the contract drop to a nearby side table and turn to walk back to my desk.

"What's up?"

"She settling in okay?"

"Who?"

Gabriel gives me a bored look. "Fuck, are we really going to do that?"

"Do *what,* Gabriel."

He sighs. "Are we going to talk about it? And before you ask again, I specifically mean Eloise—aka the girl who fucked you up in college—"

"She didn't *fuck me up,*" I growl. "I fucked *her,* once, if that's what you're referring to."

Okay, it was more like four times, in the span of one "encounter". A mere technicality. Sue me.

"Alistair—"

"Would you like me to declare *prior carnal knowledge* with HR? If so, just let me know which form I'm supposed to use to disclose that my newest associate once swallowed my cum before getting down on her hands and knees and asking me—quite vigorously, I should add—to—"

"Are you done? I don't need to hear this."

"Christ, when did you go get squeamish?"

"It's more like self-preservation." He cocks a meaningful brow at me. "Given that the woman you're so casually recalling fellatio with happens to be married to our biggest client, Massimo Carveli."

Yes, because I need *another* reminder of that.

"In that case, don't you think filing an HR report might do more harm than—"

"Alistair, *stop*." He sighs, pinching the bridge of his nose. "Look, you can stick with the version where you don't give a shit about her, in which case we should all stop talking about whatever *vigorous* way she asked you to do I-don't-want-to-know—"

"Anal, while pulling her hair and choking her," I grin.

"I *said* I didn't want to know," Gabriel snaps, glaring at me. "As I was saying, you can play that card, where *whatever* it is that happened between you stays in the past, and we can all move on like adults. *Or*, you can hate her, and be super vocal about it, and whine and carry on like a three-year-old, and Taylor and I can try and figure out how to juggle your tantrums on top of the ten million other things we've got going on. But you don't get to have it both ways. Either you give a shit, or you don't. Pick a side."

I grunt, shrugging. "Easy decision. I don't give a shit, Gabriel."

"That's your story?"

"That's the *truth*."

"Well, good. Stick with that, because if you flip-flop, I don't exactly see Massimo as having much of a sense of humor about you defiling his wife in college."

"When on Earth would I ever even talk to that muppet?"

Gabriel, Taylor, and I sat down this morning and discussed the obvious, i.e., that I will *not* be interacting with Massimo as a client.

Gabriel smiles wryly and glances at his Rolex. "In six hours."

What.

"Excuse me?"

"Your presence has cordially been requested at Club Venom tonight, in Massimo's private lounge."

Goddammit.

"Lucky me," I groan, sinking into my chair before I glance up at my brother. "What the hell does Captain Fuckstick want to see me for?"

"Let's hope just business. And if he wants to bring up college glory days and sexual shenanigans, you'd better superglue your fucking trap shut."

"Heard loud and clear."

He sighs, nodding. "I'd go with you, but he specifically requested you and you alone."

"Sounds romantic."

Gabriel frowns. "Sounds *dangerous*. I'm going to call Dante and make sure his people are aware of the...possible friction."

"This is hardly my first after-hours sit down with a mafioso client at a place like Venom, Gabriel."

"Yeah? And have you fucked the wives of any of those other mafioso clients before having after hours sit-downs with them—goddammit, you know what, do *not* answer that," he grumbles, glancing at his watch. "Shit, I've got a deposition."

"Have fun."

He frowns as he raises his eyes to mine. "Look, if you want to talk about this...I mean, with Eloise working here now, and with what happened at Knightsblood..."

"Feel like talking about your political aspirations yet?"

His lips purse. I grin.

"Yeah, thought not. I'll be fine, Gabriel. I'm a big boy. I can handle it."

But first, I'm going to have Katerina deliver another metric fuckton of busy-work to Eloise's cubicle.

To describe Club Venom as a sex club isn't really doing it justice, or even painting an accurate picture. It'd be like characterizing Wrigley Field and Fenway Park as simply "baseball fields", or the Highland Green 1968 Mustang GT that McQueen drives in *Bullitt* as "a nice car".

It's a place of deviance and depravity. A palace of sin. Hidden away on a dull, unassuming side street, in a dull, unassuming building, Club Venom is a private kink club that caters to the wealthiest, most connected, elite, and *dangerous* of New York City. Mafia dons, Bratva kingpins, underbosses...Venom is where they all come to play, tasting whatever flavor they choose.

Well, not vanilla.

There are no names. Everyone wears a mask, and bracelets of various colors signify different kinks and roles. In addition to the main space there are bars, cocktail lounges, cigar rooms and private suites, and the "adult activities" can happen either in private, or, frequently, out in the open.

In short, it's not exactly a place for prudes.

Gabriel, Taylor, and I have been members for years, though Taylor and my brother go exclusively for business reasons: either to schmooze prospective clients, or to meet with existing ones—A, to show them a good time, and to prove that their choice of legal counsel can "hang" with the dark underworld cool kids of New York. And B, because the anonymous nature of Venom gives an assurance of privacy when discussing sensitive legal issues to clients who may or may not be under the scrutiny of law enforcement.

I go to Venom for all of that, too, of course. But I also come here for *fun*. I even have two masks kept behind the concierge desk: one for business-Alistair, and one for play-time-Alistair. Wouldn't want those two worlds colliding.

Lately, coming here has become slightly more complicated, now that Gabriel's and my little sister, Tempest, has married Dante Sartorre, who owns and runs Venom. It's not that Dante and Gabriel and I don't get along or anything. I mean, yes, at one time, we were enemies. But a guy has a way of growing on you when he saves your sister's life.

No, it's become complicated because, as much as he assures me it's never going to happen, the last thing on the fucking planet I need to see when I walk into an underground sex club is my goddamn *sister*.

Tonight, though, when I thank Michelle at the concierge desk and slip on my business-mode Alistair gold and matte black mask, I can rest assured that I won't be having any unfortunate family encounters. I talked to Dante an hour ago, and apparently Tempest is out to dinner with his sister,

Bianca and one of our best equity partners at Crown and Black, Fumi.

He also mentioned that he'd have some of his own security people close to Massimo's private room and was tactful enough not ask why I might need extra muscle when meeting with my own client.

I make my way through the interior of the club, letting the low lights and sultry techno music piped through hidden speakers envelop me. I pass through one smaller lounge, glancing briefly toward the blood-red couch against the far wall. On it, a gorgeous dark-skinned girl is kissing a blonde on the mouth as they both moan, both getting fucked silly from behind by two men with Russian Bratva tattoos.

As I step into another smaller room, I'm greeted by the sight of a very petite brunette wailing in ecstasy as three Italian-looking guys take all three of her holes at the same time.

Welcome to Club Venom. And it's only Wednesday.

It's not late yet, though, so the "show" in the main room when I arrive is still minimal. Only a few of the array of couches and large beds in the middle of the floor are occupied, mostly by couples keeping to themselves, though, obviously, fucking in front of a crowd of onlookers.

I'm not here for anything but business tonight. So I bypass the show and make my way to the bar to grab a whiskey. I'm only one sip in when a masked beefy guy approaches and coughs discreetly.

"Mr. Black? Mr. Carveli is this way."

I mean, the whole point here is anonymity, what with the masks and all. But I know from the jagged scar running down the man's neck that this is Rocco, Massimo's close confidant and fellow douchebag.

Wordlessly, I follow Rocco down a black hallway with brass sconces until we get to a dark, blood-red door with the club's emblem of a viper on it, in black. Rocco nods at the two guys standing guard before we step inside.

"Ahh, Alistair." Massimo, in a gold and matte-black mask with devil-horns, grins over the rim of his drink in greeting. He stands as I approach and shakes my hand firmly. "Please, have a seat." He nods at my whiskey. "Need a top-up?"

"I'm good."

Massimo smiles curiously at me, almost studying me. Here's the thing about Massimo Carveli: as much as I'd love to write him off as a trust fund mafia ass-wipe who spends all day getting off on his own hubris via the silver spoon shoved firmly up his ass, I know there's more to him than that.

I read people for a living: judges, prospective jury candidates, the legal counsel across the aisle from me, even my own clients. Everyone—and I do mean *everyone*—has a version of I that they want the world to see. Often, the truth is very different, hidden far away.

And that's my superpower: the ability to pull aside the veils of bullshit to see the real person underneath. But with Massimo it's nearly *impossible* for me to see what's underneath, which means he either really is a machismo-huffing douche canoe, or else he's *very* good at hiding the other part of him.

And much as I hate to admit it, I have a feeling it's the latter.

There are too many random "strokes of luck" that have put Massimo where he is at the head of the Carveli family. His father's untimely, oddly quiet death. The last-minute will that clearly stipulated Massimo as the heir to the Carveli throne and fortune, even though they'd been famously at-odds with each other for years.

And marrying *Eloise,* of all fucking people.

So when Massimo studies me with those piercing dark eyes, I'm sure to keep my walls up.

"Please, have a seat." He turns and snaps his fingers at Rocco, who nods. Immediately, he and the handful of guards turn and file out. Massimo shrugs, smiling ghoulishly at me. "This conversation necessitates privacy."

"Of course, Mr. Carveli," I say. "But honestly, if you'd like to discuss business, I think my brother and Ms. Crown should be here, too. Perhaps even in place of me. As much as I enjoy Venom, Gabriel and Taylor are your legal liaisons at—"

"How do you know my wife, Alistair?"

I've spent a career molding my entire body into an impenetrable fortress when it comes to showing my emotions. That said, it takes *a lot* to keep myself from flinching when I hear that.

"College," I say easily, shrugging. "Though I'm not sure I'd really say we *know* each other. I was a few years ahead of her, and we didn't run in the same circles."

"Ahh, I see," he nods slowly, sipping his drink. "But you obviously know her *sister.*" His lips curl into a devilish grin.

"I don't."

Massimo chuckles. "That's not the way *I* hear it."

"I can assure you, I'm not acquainted with your sister-in-law."

I am, of course, in a way that infuriates me. But that's nothing I need to discuss with this asshole.

"Interesting. The way I hear it, you're *intimately* acquainted with Camille."

"I believe that's what they call hearsay, Mr. Carveli."

"We're not in court, *counselor*," he chuckles, reaching over to slap my knee. "Come on! We're both men of the world! Cut from the same cloth!"

Like fuck we are.

He snorts a laugh. "I mean, it's not like *I've* never wondered how tight that little French cunt is myself, eh?" He chuckles, leaning back on his couch. "So, please, put me out of my misery. Tell me how she was."

A blackness creeps over me as that particular night comes crawling out of the dark hole I shoved it into.

I never slept with Camille LeBlanc. But not for lack of effort on her part.

"Like I said, Alistair, we're the same. You don't have to play coy with me," he grins. "I'm not the me-too movement or the politically correct police. You're like me. You saw something you wanted, and you took it."

Bullshit. That's not what happened. It's more like *she* saw something *she* wanted, and tried to "take it". My memory of that night might be a mess, but I know damn well I never touched Eloise's psycho sister.

"I'm afraid you've been misled, Mr. Carveli," I growl. "Nothing ever happened between me and Camille."

He's quiet a moment, a shadow crossing his face like he's disappointed in me.

"Ahh, well…" He finally shrugs. "My mistake."

Just then, the door to the private lounge opens and a stunning masked blonde woman wearing a sheer, almost see-through gold dress steps sensually into the room. I frown as she walks over to Massimo wordlessly, and my brow furrows even deeper when she curls her legs underneath her and sits at his feet.

What the fuck?

"Alistair, meet Gemma."

I nod briefly as she smiles at me, and then twists to face Massimo.

…who suddenly undoes his belt, tugs his zipper down, and pulls out his fucking dick.

"Christ," I grunt, looking away.

Massimo chuckles. "What's wrong?" He grins, his eyes dropping to his erect, definitely below-average dick. "It's not for *you*, counselor," he snorts with a wide grin. "If that helps."

"It doesn't. What the fuck are you doing?"

"What people come to Club Venom to do." He smirks. "If another man's nakedness makes you that uncomfortable, maybe you need to ask yourself why, counselor."

I roll my eyes. "My disinterest in seeing my clients with their dicks hanging out has nothing to do with my sexuality, Mr. Carveli."

"*Mr. Carveli* seems a bit formal, given the present circumstances." He grins. "How about we stick with Massimo, yes?" He points a finger at himself. "Massimo." He turns the finger toward me. "Alistair. Like friends."

"I'm your legal counsel, and you're my client," I grunt.

"Does that mean we can't be friends?" Massimo reaches out and grabs a handful of Gemma's hair. "Pull up your dress."

Gemma, her ass to me, reaches back and tugs at her shimmery gold dress, confirming that she is *not*, indeed, wearing anything underneath it. Massimo grins.

"Feel free to join in—"

"I'd prefer to keep our relationship professional, Mr. Carveli," I say frostily.

"I see."

He pulls Gemma toward his cock. I frown and look away when she opens her lips to take him into her mouth. I'm hardly a prude. I mean, look where I am. But I do *not* need to see this fuckstick get head four feet away from me. And there is a snowball's chance in hell of me engaging in a fucking three-way with him.

Massimo groans loudly as Gemma's blonde head bobs in his lap.

"You're a betting man, aren't you, Mr. Black?"

I don't answer.

"Not an accusation. Merely an observation." He winks. "We have mutual friends and interests, it would seem." He shrugs, groaning again as he fists the girl's hair tighter. "I know for a fact that you like to gamble. Just like I know that you're good at it. Or maybe just lucky."

"I think that you have to make your own luck."

He smiles widely. "I agree." He grunts deeply, his mouth opening as he pumps Gemma's head up and down. "Which is why I want to make a wager with you."

I frown. "I don't think that's—"

"If you can tell me"…he smiles a dark, shark-like smile…"how *exactly* you know my wife before I come down this whore's throat—*oh fuck yeah,*" he groans. "Then I'll commit another two million a year in billable hours to your firm."

I stare at him. "Excuse me?"

"You can have that in writing, Mr. Black."

I stand. "I think it's time for me to go, Mr. Carveli."

"*Sit. Down,*" he growls menacingly. Then the anger melts and his lips curl into a grin. "Go ahead," he smiles widely. "Ask."

I need to get the fuck out of here, and away from this lunatic's psycho head games.

"Ask *what,*" I hiss.

"Ask what happens if you don't make the cutoff. If you *don't* tell me before I—"

"Mr. Carveli, all due respect, I have *zero* interest in playing this game."

"Who says it's a game."

In one motion, he reaches into his jacket and pulls out a Beretta. I freeze when he points the barrel of the gun at Gemma's bobbing head.

"How do you know my wife, Mr. Black." His jaw clenches. "You don't have long, FYI."

What the actual fuck.

"Mr. Carveli," I hiss, glancing at the door and trying to gauge if I have time to get the fuck out of here, past whatever guards Massimo has outside, and find Dante's men before this psychopath shoots this poor girl. "I *don't* know your wife."

"Tick...*unngh,*" he groans deeply, his mouth opening. "*Tock,* Mr. Black."

"Put down the goddamn gun—"

Every muscle in my body tenses, every nerve jangling like a livewire as Massimo grunts loudly and explodes down Gemma's throat. His hips pump a few times before he slumps back on the couch. Slowly, his eyes drag to mine.

He presses the gun to Gemma's forehead.

"Maybe you're not so lucky after all. At least, she isn't."

"No—!"

He squeezes the trigger.

My heart lurches as a loud "click" snaps through the room as the empty gun dry fires.

Blinking, my pulse racing, I stare at Massimo.

He's insane. He's fucking INSANE.

Massimo tosses the gun aside and then pats Gemma's cheek. He grunts as she pulls away, wipes her mouth with the back of her hand, then straightens her dress as she stands. She glances at me briefly before she smiles at Massimo and casually walks out.

When we're alone, he raises the gun and dry-fires it at me with another click.

"Bang," he snickers.

I just glare at him, my face stoic and cold, and he starts to laugh as he tucks his cock away.

"Jesus Christ, your face!" he chuckles, standing and tossing the empty gun onto the couch. "Lighten up, counselor! I'm just fucking with you!"

"Mr. Carveli," I growl quietly, my pulse still thudding. "Don't *ever* point a gun at me again."

"It wasn't even loaded!" he laughs, shaking his head and smiling to himself as he strolls over to the bar at the side of the room and pours himself another drink. He turns to eye me. "What the fuck did you think I was going to do? *Shoot her?*"

"It's time for me to go."

He sighs, shaking his head again. "C'mon, Alistair. I'm just messing around with you!" He grins. "This is who I am! We're going to be working together..." He lifts a shoulder. "I want Crown and Black to know who they're dealing with. I'm a wild card!" he crows. "A maverick!"

Fucking psychopath, more like.

"Well," I growl, buttoning my jacket. "I'll be sure to tell my partners what a humorous guy you are."

He chuckles. "I've offended you. I apologize for that."

"I'll see you next time you're at the office, Mr. Carveli."

I turn to leave.

"Wait."

I stop and slowly turn back to him.

"You still haven't answered my question."

I meet his eyes without flinching.

"Mr. Carveli, your wife and I attended the same college at roughly the same time. *That* is how I know her."

He says nothing, neither of us blinking. Finally, his mouth curls into a grin.

"I know," he shrugs. "Thanks for coming tonight, Mr. Black. I'm glad we could get to know each other better."

9

ALISTAIR

"Uh, Mr. Black?"

Katerina jumps out of her chair and steps in front of me before I can open the closed door to my office.

Assistants physically stopping you from entering your own office is never a good sign.

Her brow furrows. "I tried to call your cell, but—"

"It was on silent. I was in a meeting with Roberto Chinellato's people."

I yank my phone out of my pants pocket. I groan internally when I see the nine million missed calls and texts from Kat. The first one alone is enough to get my blood boiling.

KATERINA:

RED ALERT. CAROLINE IS HERE.

Son. Of. A. *Bitch*.

"She's in my office?" I sigh, pinching the bridge of my nose.

"I'm *so* sorry, Mr. Black," she blurts quietly, looking flustered. "She...I mean, I *obviously* told her she wasn't allowed—"

"It's fine, Katerina." I exhale slowly. It's not her fault. My step-grandmother is the kind of obnoxious bitch that makes you feel like you're insulting *other* obnoxious bitches when you lump them in together.

They say people deal with grief differently. But I doubt they ever meant to include Charles Black in that statement. He dealt with the loss of our grandmother by immediately going out and dating a string of women a third his age who look like they belong on a reboot of *Jersey Shore*.

I mean, he took one to our grandmother's fucking funeral as a *date*, for Christ's sake.

The one that stuck around is Caroline. Charles was fifty-seven when the then twenty-year-old managed to get him to put a ring on it. And the single smartest thing she did afterward was throw her birth control away and get knocked up immediately.

Remember Maeve, my eighteen-year-old *aunt*? Yeah.

"I can call building security..."

"I think animal control might be more appropriate."

Katerina gives a wry smile.

"Seriously, no need to call anyone," I mutter, rolling my shoulders. "I can handle Caroline."

Maybe.

The gold-digging queen herself, clad in black leggings, sky-high *Pretty Woman* stilettos, a fur-trimmed short jacket, and talon-like gel nails, is sitting *at my fucking desk* when I walk in. I glare at her as I close the door behind me, leaning against it with my arms folded.

"Hello, Alistair."

"I assume you still have the same address, Caroline?"

Her manicured brows furrow deeply. "Excuse me?"

"For when I bill you for a replacement office chair," I grunt. "God knows what I'd catch from it now."

Caroline scowls. "Still an asshole, I see."

"Still gargling my grandfather's wrinkly balls, I see." I wince. "Fuck, I hope he can *afford* to replace that chair, now that I think about it."

I relish the look of fury tinged with genuine worry on Caroline's face.

Yeah, that one hit a bit close.

I imagine Caroline's always been a bitter, mean-spirited cunt. But she's extra bitter these days. Charles, once a kingmaker of the underworld, is slowly losing his empire. He's no longer the man to whom mafia dons and top city officials crawl in order to kiss the ring. It's why he's focusing so hard on Crown and Black at the moment. And Caroline *hates* that her extravagant lifestyle might have an expiration date.

She married a kingpin. Now she's just forced to fuck an old man who's rapidly losing his power.

I sigh. "Why the fuck are you here, and what the fuck do you want, Caroline?"

"I want to see my daughter."

That would be Maeve. As of a month or so ago, though, Maeve is living with Gabriel while she finishes high school, instead of with our prick of a grandfather and this festering hemorrhoid of a trophy wife.

"Take it up with Gabriel."

"As if you had nothing to do with that?"

I laugh. "Oh, no, I had *a lot* to do with removing Maeve from your household." My smile drops as I stride across the room to her. Caroline gulps, scrabbling out of my chair and backing up against the wall as I press my knuckles on the edge of my desk and lean over it toward her. "I know you allowed my grandfather to smack her around," I snarl. "And don't for one single *second* think that Maeve hasn't also mentioned your *own* physical and mental abuse toward her."

Caroline pales. "A pack of *lies*, from a spoiled little brat—"

"I'd advise you to shut the fuck up, immediately."

She glares at me. But to her credit she does shut her fucking mouth.

"Now, if there's nothing else, Caroline, I think it's almost time to change Charles' bed pan. He'll probably want you to blow him, too."

"You're disgusting," she mutters. "Anyway, discussing your kidnapping of my daughter isn't all I'm here about. Where are we with the Chinellato case?"

I roll my eyes. "Really?"

"I can ask."

"Sure, but I'm not going to answer."

"I would consider it a personal favor."

I snort. "In that case, I'm *definitely* not answering."

We have rules in place preventing members of the board from sticking their noses into cases. Firstly, the board members are *not* our clients' attorneys. Some of them, like Charles, aren't even attorneys at all. Discussing cases with them or allowing them privileged information could open us up to a host of lawsuits and mistrials. And secondly, them sticking their noses into things prevents us—Gabriel, Taylor, and I— from running a tight, and that means *profitable,* ship. And the board, much to Charles' chagrin, wants a tight, profitable ship. They voted these bylaws in themselves just a little while ago.

So Charles has sent Caroline here to pester me about the Chinellato case, because he *can't*. Meddling asshole.

"Get the fuck out of my office, Caroline."

She huffs, straightening her shoulders. "I have something else from your grandfather."

"Shingles? Ooh, wait, I know. Antibiotic-resistant syphilis."

"You're *disgusting,* Alistair."

I sigh. "Well? What? I'm on tenterhooks."

Her mouth purses. "He wanted me to remind you not to let this Chinellato case go. If it goes bad, well…the threat remains."

Yeah, I've heard this one before.

"You mean his bullshit about kicking Gabriel and I out of our own firm if we lose the case? Yeah, good luck with that," I sigh. "Charles has clout, but he doesn't have the majority vote—"

"He does now."

I'd laugh in her face, except there's something gleefully vicious in her eyes.

Shit.

"Haven't you heard, Alistair? There's a new board member."

I stare at her, my jaw tightening. "No, there isn't."

"Oh, believe me, there is."

Caroline plucks her Louis Vuitton purse from the corner of my desk, batting her too-long-to-be-remotely-real eyelash extensions at me as she struts over to the door to my office and opens it.

"I should know," she smirks. "Since it's *me*."

"HOW THE ACTUAL *fuck* did this happen!?"

I pace the floor of Gabriel's office like a caged animal, my teeth bared, breathing hard. Across the room, Taylor stands looking over Gabriel's shoulder as he peers at his laptop.

"He can't hold a meeting, much less a vote, without us there."

"We don't technically have to *be* there, but yes, we do have to be invited to non-scheduled meetings," Taylor mutters.

"Yeah, well, I seem to be missing my fucking invite—"

"Goddammit," Gabriel suddenly snaps. He points to his screen. "Okay, Charles *did* technically invite us to the meeting, thereby satisfying the requirement to give us the opportunity to attend. But the invite was sent to the three of us on a separate email, where he included the word "FREE" in all caps in the subject line together with about forty fucking emojis. It—as he hoped, I'm sure—went straight to our spam folders."

"He can't vote his fucking wife onto the board!"

"He can," Gabriel mutters. "And he did. Ratified by a narrow margin this morning."

Mother. Fucker.

"I need to vent," I hiss. "I'm going downstairs."

Gabriel and Taylor glance at each other. They know what that means.

"Try not to break your hand again." Taylor frowns. "Looks terrible in court."

THE CROWN and Black offices proper occupy the top three floors of the midtown building we're in. But we also rent a giant space in the sub-basement to house old records, dead files, and anything else that would collect dust up in the main offices.

It's a stuffy, sweaty, miserable place to spend much time in. But that means no one *ever* comes down here unless they need to get something. Which makes it perfect for me.

In a far corner of the maze of metal shelving, I keep a practice bag, for when I just need to hit something.

Right now, I *really* need to do that.

I go at it the second I get to the far corner. My snarls fill the silence, my grunts echo off the metal shelves. I lose my jacket as the heat of the sub-basement begins to cook me, together with my fury. I pause to roll up my sleeves before I attack the bag again.

Jab, jab. Dodge, weave, jab, elbow, knee. Fuck you, Charles.

Sweat begins to roll down the small of my back. I grunt, pausing again to yank my shirttails out of my pants and unbutton it all the way before I start to go at the bag again.

Something clatters to the floor behind me.

I whirl, my eyes blazing. My fists are still raised as my chest heaves. I peer into the dim light before I march over to one of the huge metal shelves groaning with Bankers boxes and storm around to the other side of it.

Eloise gasps, her spine snapping straight. Her hair clings to sides of her flushed face in the humid heat of the sub-basement. Her blazer is gone, along with her heels and her blouse, leaving her standing in front of me barefoot in just a skirt and a skin-tight tank top that clings to her every curve.

My eyes drop to the hard points of her nipples before dragging back up to her wide eyes.

"What the fuck are you doing down here?" I grunt.

She sets her jaw and scowls. "You *sent me* down here, dickhead. Remember?"

Shit. That does ring a bell. I vaguely remember telling Katerina this morning to send Eloise down here in search of some ancient files I may—but most likely will not—need for one of my cases.

I lift a brow at her. "Again, I feel the need to remind you that I am *your boss*."

"And yet, why do I get the impression you can't fire me?"

I grit my teeth, my lip curling as I step closer to her, relishing the way her skin flushes deeper when I do.

"Because of your dear husband?" I snarl.

"Ding ding ding," she smiles icily at me.

My eyes narrow. "I might not be able to fire you, Eloise…"

She gasps as I back her into the shelves behind her.

"But I can make your life *hell* here. For starters," I glance down, letting my eyes drift over her. "Do you fucking call this office attire?"

She stares at me. "I've been down here for three hours and it's hotter than Hell down here." She arches her brows at me, a glint in her eyes as she sweeps them over me in return. "And you're one to talk! Really?"

"I was exercising," I mutter.

"Rules for thee, not for me?"

"It's called executive privilege." I turn away from her, casting my gaze over the random boxes she's pulled from the shelves looking for the files she was sent here for. There's a half-nibbled apple sitting on one of them. I frown when my gaze lands on the shelf behind it, where I spot a paper coffee cup and a bottle of vodka.

I walk over and pluck up the cup, bringing it to my nose. After sniffing it, I turn to glare at her.

"Are you fucking serious?"

She gasps as I move toward her, caging her against the shelves.

"Were you *drinking*, Eloise?"

Her mouth sets. "That was down here already."

Okay, that's clearly bullshit. But for some reason, I don't push it. She's obviously not *drunk*, and, let's face it, if I were married to Massimo fucking Carveli, I'd probably need some medicine to get through the day, too.

Not to mention, if *I* were my boss.

So I let it go. For now.

Eloise clears her throat. "Why were you…"

"Hitting things?"

She nods.

"Anger issues."

"Okay, aside from the obvious."

I glare at her, trying not to notice the teasing little smirk on her far-too-tempting lips.

"Reasons," I mutter.

"So fights still have a way of finding you, huh?" She half-smiles, her teeth sinking into her lower lip. For a second, something flickers in my chest.

Then I stamp it out. Hard.

"Don't."

Eloise swallows. "What?"

"Don't bring up the past like that. We're not having a moment, Eloise."

"I'm not the one caging you against the wall, *Alistair*," she says quietly.

Her tongue wets her plump lips. Her chest rises and falls with every breath. Her throat bobs as she swallows, and my eyes latch onto a tiny drop of sweat as it trickles down her collarbone and between her breasts.

Need roars in my veins. Desire throbs throughout my body. The way her fucking pheromones still start little fires everywhere in my system turns my head inside out.

I need to get the fuck out of here.

"Get back to work," I mutter quietly, turning to leave.

"*Why do you hate me so much*?!" she yells angrily at my back.

I freeze, my jaw grinding.

"I don't hate you, Eloise." I glance at her over my shoulder, the toxic mix of desire and a damaged past scorching my veins before I turn away again. "I'd have to give a shit about you to do that."

"What the *fuck*, Alistair!?" she shouts at me. "Seriously! Yeah, we were dicks to each other in school, but—"

"But *what*?!" I snarl, whirling back on her. "But then we *fucked*?! Is that what you're clinging to, Eloise?!"

"I just don't understand what made you so fucking mean."

"*You* did," I growl. "And don't for a second try and pretend otherwise."

Without another word, I whirl, grab the bottle of vodka from the shelf and storm away.

I toss the bottle in a trashcan near the door, and I make it almost all the way to the utility elevator before I pause.

Shit. My jacket is still by the practice bag.

Grim-faced, my pulse still racing from my close encounter of the Eloise kind, I storm back to the far corner of the records room again.

"*Merde!*" Eloise is hissing from the other side of the shelves, where I just left her. "*Merde! Merde!!*"

Jesus Christ, *now* what.

Grabbing my jacket, I storm around the shelves.

Oh shit.

I watch as it happens. Eloise is standing on a stack of boxes, struggling to reach one on the top shelf. Just as I walk around the corner the bottom box of the stack starts to crumple, and the whole thing collapses.

Eloise gasps sharply as she twists and falls…

…Straight into my arms as I race over to catch her.

Her body slams into mine, torso-to-torso, face-to-face, her legs wrapped around my hips as my hands grab her ass. The force of the hit sends us tumbling backward, and I grunt as my back hits the shelves behind me and her face almost slams into mine.

Time stops. The sweltering heat of the room pulses around us, as if the very air is pushing us closer together.

I can feel her heart thudding against my chest. Fuck, I can also feel the hard, pebbled points of her nipples through the thin tank top. My hands instinctively tighten on her ass, my fingers sinking into her soft yet firm flesh as my cock thickens between us.

Her lips part, inches from mine. And I swear to fuck, her hips roll against me. Eloise's suit-skirt is bunched up, and I *know* she can feel the throb of my erection against the soft, warm mound of her pussy through her panties.

For a nanosecond, standing there with her literally in my arms and her mouth barely an inch from mine, I almost cross the line. I *almost* slam my mouth to hers, yank her soaked panties aside, and ram every inch of my hard, hungry cock into her greedy little pussy.

But then I remember to breathe. I remember that this is reality, not fantasy.

I remember that this is *Eloise fucking LeBlanc.*

Liar. Backstabber.

The enemy.

Her lip quivers. Her hips roll oh-so-subtly again as her eyes lock with mine. But the moment is over. Shattered. Broken.

My face hardens as I drop my hands and Eloise gasps quietly as she slips to the ground. Her face heats as she scrambles a step back from me, hugging herself as her eyes snap to mine again.

"Maybe this is how you operated at your last job," I growl quietly, "or how you managed to catch Massimo. But don't ever try that shit with me again."

Her eyes widen in fury as her mouth drops open in shock.

"You insufferable, egotistical, *ass*—"

"*Sir,*" I snap, silencing her. My lips curl into a snarl as I move a step toward her. "It's yes, *sir,* or no, *sir,* and nothing fucking more. Is that clear?"

Her lips purse tight and there's hellfire in her eyes as they stab into me like twin blades.

"Is. That. *Clear*. Eloise."

"Yes," she says coldly. Suddenly, the room no longer feels sweltering. It's as if someone's opened a window in winter to let the heat out and the chill in.

"I mean, yes *sir*," she sneers before she turns, grabs her blouse, jacket, and heels from a nearby box, and storms off.

10

ELOISE

Holy fuck.

It's close to midnight when the Uber drops me off outside our penthouse after yet another exhausting day at work. My feet are on fire. My legs hurt. I'm cross-eyed from staring at a screen, not to mention archived legal files in eleven-point font all day and well into the night.

I'm not an idiot. I know how things work, how the new person gets "hazed" or jerked around—how they get all the shitty work no one else wants dumped on them, like an initiation thing.

But that's not what's going on here. These are shots fired across the bow. These are power moves, done expressly to show me "my place" by *Alistair*, making sure I'm fully aware of his opinion when it comes to me working at Crown and Black. As if that was unclear before.

I finally got a chance to go fix all of my paperwork with HR, switching my name from Carveli to LeBlanc. When I got back to my desk, the files had literally doubled. It got to the point today where I couldn't even swivel my chair left or right in my shitty, tiny cubicle because of all the boxes. I swear, if I sneezed, one of those towers was going to crash down on me and bury me alive in busywork.

But I stayed, working until the screen in front of me was blurry and the janitor asked if I was okay. It's only then that I realized I was the very last person on the floor.

Trust me, if you're there past the aides and junior associates, you're working late.

But I'll be damned if I'm going whine to King Asshole about anything. Fuck him. It's not my fault that Massimo made him hire me in exchange for billable hours. And if he thinks he can overwork me into quitting, he's dead wrong.

I mean, I'd rather be at Crown and Black bleeding from the eyeballs and fingertips than at home with Massimo, anyway.

...Especially after today.

My cheeks burn hotly as my memory flashes to the records room in the basement, and I pause outside the building, chewing on my lip as it all comes flooding back. The bitterness of our words. The anger in his eyes.

...The raw heat in his hands and his body when he caught me as I fell. The single second of being *this* close to kissing him that seemed to last an eternity before it scattered like dust in a breeze.

I quickly shake my head as I go into the lobby. Whatever the *hell* that was, it's most certainly never, ever happening again. I won't let it. Because it's screwing with me, badly.

Two of my husband's guards escort me up to Massimo's gaudy penthouse, which looks like it could be used for photoshoots for *Cocaine Life* or *Douchebag Weekly*. The whole place is strip-club chrome, neon blue, and white marble, and looks like it was decorated by a martial arts instructor in the 80s.

I hate it.

One of the guards uses a keycard to open the front door, ushering me in before closing and locking it behind me. I drop my stuff in the entryway and head to the kitchen to get a *very* much-needed drink. I also make a mental note to stash another bottle in my bag for when Alistair inevitably has me working until midnight again tomorrow, since he confiscated the one he spotted today.

Yes, I understand it's not exactly the greatest to be drinking vodka out of a coffee cup in the middle of the afternoon *at work*. But, point of order, your honor. There are more than a few "extenuating circumstances" going on in my life right now.

The sound of Massimo grunting, a woman fake moaning, and flesh slapping flesh does and doesn't surprise me. But I ignore it, making a beeline for the fridge and pouring myself a gigantic glass of Chardonnay. I take a hefty sip, then another, before topping it up and heading into the living room to face the inevitable.

I mean, it's not like Massimo is fucking some other girl in our living room so that I *don't* catch him.

Sure enough, he's railing some poor brunette from behind on our living room floor when I step in. He looks up and grins savagely, his fingers digging into her hips as he starts to fuck her even harder.

I suppose you could call Massimo a classically handsome man. He's got dark eyes and hair and tanned skin thanks to his Sicilian background. He's no Marvel superhero actor, but he still keeps in extremely good shape.

But there's just something I find so disgustingly unattractive about him that watching him fuck like this is literally nauseating to me. On top of that, the girls he aggressively screws like this are almost always hired professionals. It always ends up feeling like I'm watching someone get assaulted.

Massimo grunts, his hips slapping against the girl's ass. She glances up in surprise, seeing me standing there.

"Oh, I didn't know this was a couples thing—"

"It's not. She's just watching," Massimo mutters, not missing a beat.

The girl looks confused. "Okay. Well, it's still extra if she's—"

"Shut. The. *Fuck…*" he snarls, fucking her even harder, until she winces. "*Up*." He looks up at me, accusatory. "You're late."

I shrug, refusing to show my exhaustion or pain from the long hours. "I texted Rocco."

"Is *Rocco* your fucking husband?"

I sigh, looking away and gulping my wine as Massimo plows into the woman on the floor.

"How was your day?"

"Peachy," I mutter.

"Tomorrow," Massimo grunts, "I need you to do something for me at Crown and Black."

I frown, still looking away. "Do what?"

"There's a file. I want it."

I bark out a cold laugh. "There are about a million files at that office."

Trust me. They're all sitting in my cubicle.

"I don't want...*ugh, yeah, bitch,*" he snarls at the escort. "I don't want a million files, you dumb cow," he grunts. "I want one specific file—goddammit, Eloise, *look at me*!"

I flinch at his brutal tone, finally dragging my eyes back to his. Massimo's upper lip curls.

"My father did some business with Crown and Black, and they're currently in possession of a copy of his will."

My brows furrow. "*You* have your father's will."

I've seen it, several times. It's the one giving Massimo complete control over the Carveli empire, as well as the entirety of his father's fortune, even though the two of them had been at odds for years.

"Well, I want *that* copy," he snarls, fucking into the girl as she winces. "And it's somewhere secure in that office."

I wrinkle my nose. "And you want me to take it?"

He glares at me. "Did I stutter, bitch?"

"You're asking me to steal confidential legal documents from a law firm, for whom I *work*."

Massimo sneers at me. "Why the fuck do you think I got you a job there in the first place?" he snaps, thrusting hard. "You think I was doing you a fucking favor?"

Anger surges inside of me. I mean I *knew* there had to be a catch, some sort of motive. But this is bullshit.

"You're asking me to steal a personal legal document."

"And?"

I shake my head, looking away as I swallow another large mouthful of wine. "No."

"The fuck do you mean, *no*?"

"I mean no," I snap testily. "As in, I'm not doing it."

Massimo doesn't reply. But I can hear the mewling cries of the girl he's fucking getting louder and more desperate.

"Massimo," I hiss quietly, still looking away. "Stop it."

He starts to fuck her even harder.

"You're hurting her. Stop—"

"Have you spoken to *Camille* recently?"

Slowly, my gaze drags back to him. Massimo is looking at me with an unhinged, sadistic look in his eyes.

"Alistair Black fucked her once, didn't he?"

My pulse turns to ice in my veins.

"I don't exactly blame him," he grins. "She's a pretty girl."

"Fuck you."

"Such a pretty *mouth*, too." He's not smiling anymore as his gaze lasers in on mine. "I bet she sucks dick really well. Maybe I'll ask Alistair next time—"

"Keep my fucking sister out of this," I snap, my jaw clenched.

Massimo grins. "I'd like nothing more, dear wife. And as long as you do as I ask, I will."

The brunette looks like she's barely holding back tears as he savagely slams into her.

"*Stop it*!" I choke.

"Will you get what I asked for?"

"Yes!"

"You're sure?"

A tear beads in my eye as I look at the way he's brutalizing the poor girl. "*For fuck's sake,* Massimo!" I shriek. "*Yes,* okay?!"

His eyes roll back and he groans deeply. "Oh *fuuuck* yesss..."

I look away as he goes still, enjoying his release.

"Fuckkkk, that was good."

I'm wiping a tear from the corner of my eye, still looking away as I shake my head furiously.

"Eloise."

"What." Fuck, I hate him so much.

"*Eloise.*"

I grit my teeth as I whirl on him. "*What*?!"

In one motion, he reaches for his jacket on the couch behind him, grabs the gun from underneath it, and aims it at the back of the brunette's head.

My eyes widen as my mouth falls open. "NO—!"

The gun goes off with a thunderous bang, spraying blood and gore across the floor between us. Whirling, I drop the glass, letting it shatter on the ground as I bend down and start to vomit and cry at the same time.

I can hear Massimo behind me, walking over to the bar cart. "The next time," he murmurs quietly, "they'll send me the fucking blonde I asked for."

I convulse and puke onto the floor again, tears burning my face and stomach acid on my chin.

"Look at me, Eloise."

I can't.

"LOOK. AT. ME."

Shuddering, I turn to him.

"Do as I say and *get that fucking will,*" he growls quietly, standing there, naked, blood on his chest and a drink in his hand. He waves the gun in the other one. "Or the next time you witness that, it'll be your dear sister with my cum in her cunt and her brains on the floor."

11

ALISTAIR

Ten years ago:

If my life were a movie, this would be the part where I'd ruefully reflect on how my father would never approve of such childish pranks in the name of rivalry.

But this is real life. And my father fucking *loves* pranks.

We're talking the full range here: fake snakes or bugs in the cereal box, olive oil in the soap dispenser, plastic wrap over the toilet bowl. It's one of the things I love about him.

Ironically, it's one of the things about Vaughn Black that can also drag a blade across my heart. Not because of anything he does. But because his childish sense of glee in just about everything in life is a sobering reminder for me that *I am not of his blood.*

I'm not able to find genuine joy in things with a snap of my fingers the way he is. Maybe I never was, or maybe that ability was ripped from me by fire and broken glass.

I was six when my world turned upside down. Oddly, but perhaps mercifully, I don't remember much of life with my birth parents before the car crash. Most of what I do know comes from my father, and even then, it's mostly lacking in detail.

I don't have names—first, or last. My father told me when I was young, though, that they were using fake IDs, as they were in the US illegally. I know they were unmarried, but madly in love. They were clients of a friend of Vaughan's. And he always told me that when they heard about the accident that rainy night that killed them and spared me, he and my mother knew *instantly* that they would take care of me—that I was meant to be a part of their family.

And I am, in every conceivable way. I've spent a lifetime rewiring myself as a Black, rather than...whatever name I had before. Which is why I get fucking enraged whenever someone tries to attack me with the "A" word.

Adopted.

I fucking hate that word.

I hate how it acts as an asterisk after my last name with a disclaimer. As if my name isn't Alistair Black, but rather "Alistair Black...sort of."

It feels dehumanizing. I also consider it an affront and an insult to Vaughn and Marilyn Black—two strangers who saw a shell-shocked, scared little boy in a hospital room who'd just lost everything, and selflessly decided to give him a new life.

That's part of the reason I'm here tonight. Because a few weeks ago, when she barged in on me—after Michael

Machiani and his buddies had jumped me because my father was a prosecuting attorney in a racketeering case against his uncle—Eloise LeBlanc called me the "A" word. And I still need to get that out of my system.

The other reason, though, is *rivalry*.

Historically, there's all manner of pissing contests between the four student clubs at Knightsblood. These days, Para Bellum and The Reckless are on fairly friendly terms—what with Gabriel being the head of the former and me of the latter.

This school year, the biggest contentiousness seems to be between The Reckless and The Order. I think it initially started with the football team's quarterback, a guy who happens to be a member of The Order, being replaced by Paolo Cortillo, a Brazilian cartel heir who's a member of The Reckless. It doesn't help that I think Ansel Albrecht is a raging douchebag and a fucking predator.

Back to Eloise. By now, it's a number of things: the fact that she pissed me the fuck off with that "adoption" slap, the fact that she is now a pledge member of The Order, and don't get me started on the water bottle incident the other day.

I was in the gym, shadowboxing with a practice bag until my arms felt like they were going to fall off. There were a number of The Order members in the gym at the time, including Eloise.

I didn't think anything of it until I was done with my workout and grabbed my water bottle—the kind that football players or boxers use, where you squeeze the bottle to squirt a stream of water into your mouth.

Which is what I did, eagerly gulping it down and letting it trickle down my chin and neck.

Until the whole gym erupted in laughter.

That's when I turned to glance in the mirror and realized my entire mouth, all of my teeth, my chin, neck, and front of my workout shirt were now dyed bright blue.

Honestly, if she'd just kept her mouth shut, there's a chance I'd never have known it was her. But it was the eager way Eloise stepped forward and gleefully crowed "You look like you went down on a Smurf!" in that musical French accent of hers before looking hopefully at Ansel, as if searching for validation, that gave her away.

That's actually what pissed me off the most. I could give a fuck about a blue chin for a day or two. I simply don't care. It was a club-related rivalry prank.

What I *do* care about is the craven, pathetic search for validation I saw in Eloise's eyes when she looked at that fuckhead. What makes it worse is that I don't even get *why* that part pissed me off the most.

Anyway, that's how I guessed it was her who put dye in my water bottle. The half empty package of "anime blue" hair color that I found later that night after breaking into her gym locker confirmed it.

Which brings us to now.

Eloise might be a new pledge of The Order, but she won't move into the club mansion until next year. Until then, I'm sure she considers herself lucky to have been placed in Wellington House, the dorm known for each two-person room having its own ensuite bathroom. Maybe her French

Mafia king of a father paid extra to make sure his princess ended up here, I don't know.

Whatever. She's not going to think of it as lucky after tonight. Not after I'm done with my plan.

You look like you went down on a Smurf.

I pause at the half-open third-floor window of Wellington House. My head slips under and then through, my eyes and ears scanning the quiet bathroom attached to Eloise's room that she shares with Demi Romano.

I've got their schedules and I know neither of them is home. Demi's at soccer practice for another two hours, and Eloise is in a calculus study group at the library for another forty-five minutes.

After that, she'll come back here for her usual cup of decaf tea, shower, and hour of studying in bed before she turns out the light.

It's that second step of her routine that's going to bite her in the ass tonight.

Slipping into the bathroom, I momentarily frown at the light on inside the dorm room itself, past the slightly open bathroom door, but I shrug it off. They must have left a light on. Again, I have their schedules down to a tee.

I move to the shower, opening the glass door and slipping into the stall before reaching up to the showerhead. It unscrews easily, and I grin as I pull the big packet of hair dye —anime blue, because irony is *hilarious*—out of my back pocket. The contents get dumped in before I screw it back in place.

I look like I went down on a Smurf, huh? Well, Eloise, after your shower, you're going to look like you got bukkaked by about thirty of them.

I can shrug off the water bottle thing, because I don't give a shit. But Eloise LeBlanc very much does give a shit. She already walks around campus like a spoiled, bratty little princess. Add in being a new pledge to one of the coveted and exclusive student clubs? And being a clear favorite of Ansel Albrecht?

Yeah, that's got her sitting *tall* on that high horse of hers. And what I'm about to do will humiliate her.

I grin darkly.

It will also almost definitely mean she cancels on Ansel, who, I have it on good authority, has invited Eloise to "study with him" tomorrow night. The predatory little fuck.

I'm about to head back to the window and make my exit when I hear it and *freeze.*

A sound, from inside the dorm room.

Not just any sound.

A fucking *moan.*

I tense, my eyes stabbing through the darkness at the dim light coming from the crack of the slightly open bathroom door. I crane my neck until I can peer through the gap.

Instantly, I go still.

And *hard.*

Eloise is alone, lying on her bed with headphones in, her eyes closed, her head turned to the side, and her hand buried between her legs.

She's naked.

I groan inwardly as she moans again and arches her back. Her pale, bare tits thrust up toward the ceiling, giving me a clear view of the creamy mounds capped with hard, dusky pink nipples. My gaze teases down over her flat stomach and rolling hips, to where her hand is rubbing between her thighs.

Pale, creamy skin. Pink, slick lips. Trimmed blonde hair. Plunging, wet, eager fingers.

I'm cupping my cock through my pants before I can stop myself. My eyes glue to Eloise as she touches herself, and I start to stroke in time with her fingers.

I shove aside the inconvenient truth that there's a strong chance it's fucking *Ansel* she's thinking about.

Ansel isn't here right now. *I* am.

Ignoring the words running through my head like "creep", "stalker", or "predator", I pull my thick cock out of my jeans and wrap my hand around it. Eloise starts to finger herself faster, rubbing her clit with the other hand. I start to stroke myself harder, keeping pace with her.

She moans again, her face crumpling as she thrashes her head back and forth. Her back arches, her taut pink nipples begging for my mouth. The wet, squelching sounds of her fingers in her sweet little cunt fill the room, until both of us are past the point of no return.

"Alistair…"

It's the shock that sends me over the edge. Even though I can clearly see that her eyes are closed and that she's wearing headphones, a part of my brain still dumps adrenaline into my system, thinking I've just been caught. And it only makes the climax that detonates through my entire body a thousand times more intense than anything I've ever felt before.

The rush. The thrill. The danger. The dark, depraved, secret knowledge that I shouldn't have.

She's fantasizing about me.

Eloise gasps and arches her back again, her thighs clamping down on her hands as she comes hard. With a grunt, my eyes still locked on her, I twist my torso just as the cum erupts from my swollen head. I blast rope after thick rope into the shower stall, letting it splatter onto the drain.

Clarity hits me hard. Not shame. Not any sort of post-orgasmic reality check. Just the realization that any second now, I really *will* be caught in Eloise's bathroom with my dick out.

It's time to go.

For a second, I glance at the showerhead and contemplate removing the dye.

Yeah, *no*.

I smile maliciously.

Even if I'm the star of her fantasies, the dye stays.

I am *exactly* the devious fuck most people at this school think I am.

But Eloise?

The wheels in my head turn slowly as I slip out of the window and climb back down the ivy-covered latticework outside.

Eloise, it would seem, is much, *much* more interesting than I would have ever imagined.

12

ELOISE

I BITE DOWN HARD on my lip, ecstasy twisting my face as I choke out a moan. My hands tighten on the chrome handle of the detachable showerhead, my legs buckling as I sag against the tiled walls of the shower.

The rush of warm water pulses against my clit, and suddenly, I'm crashing through my climax. I bite on my lip again, whimpering and moaning and twisting as the orgasm wrenches through me.

Heat tingles over my skin as I slip the showerhead back into its cradle with shaking arms and sink back against the wall of the shower, catching my breath and lazily sliding my hands over my wet, slick skin.

But then, shame and confusion settle in. I reach out and abruptly turn off the water. I wrap one towel around my body and another around my head, trapping my long wet hair before stepping out of the bathroom.

Obviously, Massimo and I have always had separate rooms. I can't imagine a reality where I share a bedroom, much less *a bed* with that bastard, considering our "marriage" is based on a solid foundation of distrust, disrespect, and *disdain* for each other.

I sigh as I step into my walk-in closet. Standing in front of the floor-length mirror, I start to towel off, my thoughts scattered and confused, a mix of pleasure and shame.

Because it was Alistair I was just thinking about in the shower.

What the *fuck* is wrong with me? Why do we want the very thing we can't have? Why do we crave the forbidden? And why *the hell* do we desire the people who hurt us the most?

As usual, my silent questions get silent non-answers. Just more confusion and more questions.

I slip on a cream Chanel skirt, black heels, and a fitted black blouse for work. Just as I step out of the closet, my phone rings from the bedside table. My heart instantly chills when I walk over and see who's calling.

"*Tout bien avec mon père*??" I blurt anxiously into the phone.

"*Bonjour*, Eloise," Marie sighs in a bored tone. God, I *hate* the lack of urgency in her voice.

"My *father*," I hiss to my stepmother. "Is everything—!?"

"*Oui*, he's fine. Be calm."

I frown. "Okay, it's just..."

It's just that Marie fucking hates me and has never, and *will* never, call me just to chat. And since she's technically my father's medical proxy...

Yeah. A random call from her has me closing in on a heart attack.

"He's okay?"

"*Oui*," Marie sighs with some exasperation. "*Tout le même*."

Same as always.

I exhale slowly. I might be angry with my dad these days for what he did, marrying me off to Massimo...okay, there's no "might" about it, I am...but it wasn't always like that.

Growing up in the sort of family I grew up in—i.e., a *mafia* family—the concept of arranged marriages wasn't exactly foreign to me. But Papa always told me I'd never be forced into something like that.

My father Andre runs—or, rather, *ran*; his second-in-command, Luc, is in charge now, given my father's medical state—one of the more powerful mafia families in France. Which I suppose makes it extra ironic that I decided to go into law, of all things.

But Papa was okay with that decision. I went to Knightsblood University here in the US like so many other heirs of mafia families, and when I chose law school over the family business, my father told me it was my life to live.

Then he got sick. Then he got sicker. Next came the medically-induced coma. And with *that* came the living will, outlining provisions in the event of him becoming incapacitated.

Provisions like what his *actual* wishes for me were: marrying the loathsome, violent Massimo Carveli in exchange for my family getting control of a paltry smuggling route into North America.

And the rest, as they say, is history.

"Your father is fine, Eloise," Marie says in a bored tone. "I merely wanted to call and let you know that I'll be on holiday for the next few weeks or maybe months in St. Tropez."

My eyes widen. "I'm sorry, *what*?!"

"*Mon dieu*. Don't try and guilt me. I've been at your father's side for months."

I'm sure the fact that my father, who's thirty years older than Marie, by the way, is worth *millions*, has nothing to do with that.

"And I deserve a break."

"Marie, you're his medical—"

"I've hired a nurse; Rosa. She's very good. She'll be staying here with your father full time."

I squeeze my eyes shut and take a deep breath. "But Marie, you can't just up and leave—"

"*Oui*, I can, actually," she says curtly. "Anyway, that's all I wanted to tell you. Hello to your husband."

She hangs up abruptly.

Goddammit.

I debate calling her back, but I doubt she'd pick up. And also, shit, I have to get to work.

My room is on the first floor of the penthouse, unlike Massimo's sprawling master suite, which sits on the second floor, and the hallway that leads from my room to the main living area takes me past his home office. I'm walking by it with every intention of grabbing my bag and leaving for the day without saying goodbye when I hear something that makes me freeze.

"No, no, listen. Eloise is already in place. Trust me, she'll do what I tell her to."

I stiffen, shrinking against the wall next to the slightly open office door.

He laughs coldly. "No, they don't suspect a thing. Why the fuck would they? She's a nobody lawyer that I shoehorned into an associate's position. They're humoring me by keeping her there."

My teeth grit.

Asshole.

"But she's *in*. When the time is right, she can nuke the whole Chinellato case from there. And when that little snitch gets sent upstate, your people on the inside will finish the job. *Capice?*"

I slam a hand over my mouth, my eyes going wide.

What. The. *Fuck.*

Stepping out of my heels and picking them up, I tiptoe silently past his office door and bolt into the kitchen. I grab a banana, fill a flask with vodka for later, and all but sprint for the front door. Slipping my shoes back on, I reach for the knob—

The scream dies in my throat as a hand slams down on the door, keeping it firmly shut. Whirling, my eyes snap to Massimo's dark, piercing, suspicious ones.

"I didn't realize you were still home, *wife*," he growls.

Massimo has always scared me. I'm not ashamed to admit it, because that's just basic self-preservation. But it's gotten so much worse since the other night, when I watched him kill that poor girl.

I've seen his violence before. I've seen his dark side.

Or at least, I thought I had. Because *that* was something else entirely, and I've hardly been able to sleep in this apartment ever since.

I smile weakly at him. "Yeah, running a little late. I should go—"

"Freshly showered, I see."

I don't reply. Massimo leers and leans forward.

"And such a *long* shower, too. Making sure *every* part was nice and clean, were we? I swear, Eloise," he murmurs, "sometimes I can *smell it* on you after you've touched yourself."

I look away, feeling sick.

"I have to go to work, Massimo."

"Yes, you do," he says quietly, unblinking. "Because you've been there over two weeks, and I still don't have what I asked for."

"I—I've been busy, okay?"

"M-hmm, I'm sure," he growls dryly. His eyes narrow on me. "Where the fuck is my father's will, Eloise?"

"I don't have it."

"*Clearly*," he snarls. "But where *is* it?"

I shake my head. "I *don't*—"

"Stop saying that word and start giving me answers I can use," Massimo hisses.

I take a shaky breath as fear drags its nails over my skin. "Okay, well..." the wheels in my head spin uselessly for a second before they latch onto something. "Who was your father's attorney there?"

"Alistair," Massimo growls. "Alistair was his attorney."

I bite back a shiver. "Then it's in Alistair's office."

The emotions that wash over me the second I say it are... awful. I feel gross, and used, and conniving, and devious, and all the things I hate being.

"Go on," Massimo grunts.

"The name partners...they keep the private records of VIP clients in their offices, locked up."

My husband smiles viciously. "Then unlock it."

"I—"

"No excuses," he growls. "Do whatever it takes, *wife*."

His hand drops from the door. I swallow, shuddering slightly under his piercing, cruel stare before I turn and reach for the doorknob again.

"Oh, and Eloise?"

I freeze.

"Don't forget that you live here, like a fucking queen, thanks to me. Even more, *your sister* lives *her* life, unhurt and unmolested..."

My face goes white as I slowly turn to face him. Massimo's mouth twists cruelly.

"*Also* thanks to me," he murmurs. "I want you to remember that whenever you think you've heard something through an open office door. Do we understand each other?"

"*Yes*," I choke, nodding.

Massimo smiles a shark's smile. "Wonderful. Enjoy your day at work, *dear*."

My palms are clammy as I walk up the staircase from "the pit" to the second floor of Crown and Black. The small of my back feels slick, and I swear I can hear the *Mission: Impossible* theme in my head as I surreptitiously glance behind me. God, I must look suspicious as hell.

Timing is everything. Gabriel is meeting with a client on the first floor. Taylor and Alistair are both out of the building; her for court downtown, and him for an off-site deposition. And I know exactly when Katerina takes her lunch hour.

Sure enough, she's not at her desk outside Alistair's office as I approach with a to-go coffee cup containing the fancy chai latte with two shots of espresso that he occasionally has her get him from the ultra-trendy café down the street.

I've noticed that *occasionally*, one of the associates or junior associates will bring little "gifts" up to the partners—nothing crazy, just small things like a coffee, or a brownie from the bakery across the street. Taylor highly discourages it, because it's obviously people attempting to curry favor and it creates an awkward, unspoken competitive atmosphere. But it does happen here and there.

I've yet to see anyone bring *anything* to King Grump himself, but that's my "cover" if anyone questions why I'm up here:

I'm bringing Alistair a coffee as a small token of appreciation for hiring me.

...Against his will, of course. But who's counting?

I slip behind Katerina's empty desk, deftly open the top drawer, and pull out the pink lanyard keychain with the two keys on it.

Annnd cue the *Mission: Impossible* soundtrack in my head again.

I pause for a second, glancing around and making *sure* no one's watching before I use one of those keys to unlock and then quietly slip into Alistair's office. I close the door behind me, feeling a thrill as I turn to survey the room I'm definitely not supposed to be in.

I have mixed feelings about being in here, and why. Even if Alistair *is* an asshole and a complete prick to me, I know that this is wrong. But then Massimo's threat echoes in my head again. The recurring image of him shooting that girl on our living room floor makes me flinch, along with his promise.

The next time, it'll be your sister...

I steel myself as my gaze lands on the locked filing cabinet. I walk over to it, and slip Katerina's second spare key, which I heard her mention in the break room yesterday morning, into the lock.

Click.

I set the chai latte down on top of the cabinet and start with the bottommost of the three drawers. My heart races as my fingers flip through the files, trying to make sense of Alistair's bizarre filing system. Ugh. It's not alphabetical, that's for sure. Though I doubt someone as detail-oriented and meticulous as he is has such important files locked away in no order at all.

Finding nothing on "Luca Carveli", I close the bottom drawer and move to the one above it. Five minutes later, crouched down uncomfortably, frustration and panic take over as that one *also* results in nothing.

Shit.

Panicking, I slam the drawer closed as I start to rise to try the final drawer.

...Which is exactly when the cup of chai sitting on the top of the cabinet tips over, dumping half of its contents down the bottom of my blouse and *all over* my cream-colored skirt.

"Fuck!"

I grab the cup out of my lap and right it before it can empty onto the floor. I hiss in pain as the hot liquid stings my thighs, scrambling to my feet. My eyes dart around the room for *something,* anything, before they land on the door to Alistair's ensuite private bathroom.

Bingo.

I bolt into it, closing the door before stripping off my skirt. I groan as I assess the damage. My black blouse is fine, but my skirt is a *wreck,* with a huge beige stain rapidly settling into it.

Quickly, I turn on the cold water and start soaking the skirt in Alistair's lavish marble and brass sink. I use toilet paper to blot at the hem of my shirt, and then strip off my trashed, chai-sticky nylons. Mercifully, the red marks on my thighs from the hot liquid aren't too bad.

My heart sinks when I pull the skirt out from under the cold water, though. The stain is mostly gone, but the whole thing is *drenched,* and I have like twenty minutes before Katerina gets back.

It's not like I can walk out of Alistair's office and back down into the pit with a soaking wet skirt without raising at least a couple of brows.

Merde.

I start blotting like crazy with a hand towel. Then I remember that Alistair frequently keeps a gym bag in his office. I pause, my mind concocting all sorts of solutions. What might be in there? A larger, fluffier towel, maybe? A *hairdryer,* if I'm luckier than I have any right to be?

I glance at my watch.

I've got time.

Barefoot and only half-dressed, I grab my soaking skirt and ruined nylons, yank open the door back to the office—

And almost *scream* when I stop just short of plowing directly into Alistair's firm chest.

"*I—I—*"

"Hmm, well, let me know whenever you find the right words," he growls. "*I,* however, have *several.*"

His eyes drop. I can feel my face burn as I scramble to yank the wet skirt in front of me to cover my bare legs and panties.

"Well," he rumbles quietly, shaking his head. "This is a new low."

My eyes dart past him to the file cabinet. Mercifully, the drawers are all closed. But the key with the pink lanyard is still in the lock at the top.

Did he notice it?

"I—" I frown, stammering. "I was just bringing you a coffee, and—"

"Come on, Eloise," he hisses. "I mean, seriously? The 'oops I spilled my coffee' porn-plot routine? What are you, trying to *seduce* me?"

Despite my embarrassment, I can feel anger surging inside of me.

"*No*, You conceited ass! I fucking spilled—"

"Yeah, you're just *so* clumsy, right?"

I glare at him. "Fuck you."

I shove past him, but then remember I'm wearing a fucking thong and feel his eyes burning hotly into my ass. I whirl, red-faced, awkwardly hopping on one foot, trying to wrestle the other one into my still-wet skirt.

That is, until it's suddenly yanked from my hands and tossed across the room.

I gasp as I try and cover myself with my hands.

"What the fuck are you doing!?"

Alistair smirks as he steps to the side, blocking my way as I move to retrieve my skirt.

"Seriously, Alistair!"

"And *seriously*, Eloise," he snarls, the look on his face somewhere between dark and hungry, "what would your *dear husband* think of his wife, standing in my office in her panties?"

My lips curl. "You don't know a *thing* about my marriage."

"I don't *want* to know a fucking thing about your fucking marriage!" he roars, making something throb in my core. Alistair snarls as he surges into me, grabbing the front of my blouse and yanking me close. "Just as I don't want to have a fucking thing to do with *you*!" he rasps, fury swirling like twin flames in his eyes. "Now put your fucking skirt back on, *princess*. You're making a fool of yourself *and* your fucking marriage—"

"It's fake!"

The room falls silent for a second. I take a shaky breath, my skin tingling and the whine of my pulse humming in my ears.

"You think I *wanted* to marry Massimo?" I choke, my eyes blurring. Something inside of me is breaking; walls I've put up are cracking.

The cement I've sealed the gaps with is crumbling.

"I don't *care*, Eloise—"

"He hates me! I mean he honestly hates me, almost as much as I fucking hate him!" I scream in Alistair's face.

"Go play victim somewhere else, princess," he snaps coldly. "Because I simply don't—"

"He doesn't even touch me!"

Alistair's eyes blaze. His nostrils flare.

"I—I mean—he never has," I say, more quietly. "Not once."

His mouth thins to a line as his eyes flicker with something lethal and primal. Then his lips pull into a sneer as he starts to turn away.

"I don't honestly give a shit—"

"Yes. You do."

He goes still. So do I, the second it tumbles from my lips. Alistair turns back to me, eviscerating me with that razor gaze.

"I *said,* I don't—"

"But you do," I repeat quietly. "You do give a shit."

My pulse is roaring in my veins, making every inch of my skin tingle. The nearness of him—the heat of his body, the spicy clean scent of him—throbs against me, like there's a dark magnetic power under the surface pulling me closer.

His eyes narrow. "*Careful.*"

"Of?" I choke.

"*Me.*"

My body quivers as a tremor of heat chases through me.

"*Why?*" I breathe. "Because you're just as dangerous as you were before?"

His lips curl dangerously. "*No,*" he murmurs. "Because I'm much *more* dangerous than I was before."

My breath comes fast and shallow, my chest rising and falling quickly, my breasts almost touching him from how close we are. His hand tightens on my shirt. My pulse hums like an engine in my ears.

"Interesting," I mumble quietly. "How much more dang—"

"This much."

That's when his lips crush punishingly to mine.

When my world turns upside down.

And when the walls inside me suddenly lie in shattered ruins.

13

ALISTAIR

PART of me rebels when it happens—a screaming part of me that seethes with rage and betrayal when I grab Eloise and slam my mouth to hers.

But I swallow that down, along with her moans.

Because even though my initial self-loathing when I kiss her comes from the fact that it feels like I'm giving her what *she* wants, despite everything she's done to me, there's a flip side to it.

I'm not giving her a thing.

I'm *taking* what *I* want.

Whatever our past, whatever our sins, at the end of the day, this woman drives me fucking *insane* in a way no woman ever did before, or ever will. I haven't been a saint in the ten years since Eloise LeBlanc crashed into me. But there's not a single face I can remember. Not a single night I can replay. I'd honestly be hard pressed to recall a name.

With Eloise, I remember. Fucking. *Everything.*

Every gasp. Every kiss. Every touch, every single *second* that she was mine. I couldn't burn it out with booze, drugs, sex, or any other poison I could find. So when my lips taste hers, it's like waking up from a coma.

None of that means I have to feel a goddamn thing for her, of course. This isn't about emotions. It's purely chemical and physical. It's pheromones, nothing more.

Christ, who even fucking knows.

The point is, I don't have to forgive her to fuck her. I don't have to *care* about whatever drama or bullshit she's got going on in her marriage to Massimo.

When she first walked into Crown and Black, I told her "I fucking own you".

Now, I'm going to make good on that promise.

So when I kiss her, it's not just a kiss. It's punishment, laced with poison. It's a venomous chemical addiction that I must sate.

It's revenge, and it tastes fucking *sweet.*

Eloise moans like she might come apart at the seams when I kiss her. My tongue delves into her mouth, aggressively tasting and devouring her. When I grab her hips and shove her back against my desk, she whimpers and shudders like she hasn't even been touched in ten goddamn years—

Wait.

I tense and pull away, relishing the way she desperately tries to chase my lips with hers.

"What the fuck did you mean, *he doesn't touch you,*" I snarl.

Her face heats as her teeth rake over her bottom lip.

"I...I mean he literally doesn't touch me."

"Massimo," I growl, "*your husband*, doesn't fuck you?"

She swallows, shaking her head.

What. The. *Fuck*.

It could be so many things—that Massimo is gay and closeted, or asexual, or who knows what. I don't ask.

Because I don't give a *fuck*.

Her scent in my nostrils and her taste on my lips are like delicious toxins seeping into my nervous system.

She's fucking *mine*.

When that massive explosion went off in Beirut a few years ago, they later said it was the result of highly combustible fertilizer, TNT, and chemicals being kept cramped together in a warehouse for years. Then there was one spark, and half the seaport of a major city was leveled.

That's basically what this is with Eloise and I.

I'm the TNT. She's the chemicals slowly breaking down the last safety measure in place.

And then with one touch, one kiss, my whole goddamn world goes up in flames.

I snarl viciously as I kiss her hard, drowning in her moans as I swallow them down. One of my hands wraps around her throat, the other yanking the buttons of my shirt open. We go crashing backward against the wall behind my desk, a writhing, groaning tangle of limbs and lips.

Somehow, my shirt and jacket end up tossed clear across the room. Her blouse gets yanked half open, and my hands rediscover places on her skin I haven't touched in ten years.

"The fuck do you mean, he doesn't touch you," I growl, groaning as she whimpers into my mouth.

"Exactly what I said," she gasps, her breathing coming in heavy pants, her hands running greedily and eagerly over my chest.

"So that *fuck* has never touched you *here...*"

My hand slides from her neck, down her chest.

"*No*," she whispers, shaking her head.

"Or here..."

I cup one of her full breasts, squeezing enough to elicit a deep, guttural moan from her throat.

"*No...*"

"Here...?"

My fingers pinch her nipple, hard, twisting as she cries out in pleasure. Her nails dig into my abs.

"*Alistair...*"

"*Answer me.*"

"*No!* Never..."

I pinch and twist the other nipple until her legs shake and her mouth falls open. My hand slides lower, teasing over her ribs.

"Here."

"*No...*"

I move lower, my fingers tracing over her stomach and feeling her tremble at my touch.

"*Here.*"

"*Jamais…*" she breathes.

Never.

My fingers slip into the lace of her panties as my pulse howls like a demon in my veins. As my cock turns to pure steel in my slacks. Eloise whimpers softly, trembling as I twist my hand, my palm against her lower stomach before I push deeper.

And deeper.

And *deeper,* until my fingertips find the slick, hot, eagerly throbbing nub of her clit.

"*Oh fuck…*" she chokes.

"*What about here,*" I rasp into her ear, nipping at the lobe as she shudders.

"*No one's touched me there since—*"

"Now they have."

Her breath hitches, her eyes bulging wide and her mouth falling open when I sink two thick fingers deep into her greedy little cunt. She's fucking *soaked.* Her messy pussy eagerly sucks my fingers inside and squeezes them tightly.

"*Alistair*!" she moans, clinging to me as I start to curl and stroke my fingers in and out of her velvet-soft pussy. My thumb presses on her clit, rubbing and rolling in deliciously slow circles as she trembles against me.

I push my fingers deep inside, stroking against her g-spot as I keep rubbing her clit. My teeth rake down the soft skin of her neck, biting and sucking and probably leaving marks and bruises that I honestly don't give a fuck about.

My other hand slides up to cup and squeeze her breasts, rolling and pinching her nipples as I finger her dripping wet pussy until my whole hand is sticky and slick.

Fuck, do I need her. It's an urgency I've never felt before.

...No, that's a lie. It's an urgency I've felt exactly *once* before.

One time. One night. One girl.

And now...here we are again.

I'm two seconds away from bending her over my desk and fucking her until she screams the whole goddamn building down when there's a loud knock at the door.

Mother. *Fucker*.

Eloise spasms like she's just been electrocuted, a terrified gasp on her lips as she struggles to pull away.

That's not happening.

I keep her pinned to me, pinching hard on her nipple as I sink my fingers deep into her greedy, messy pussy.

"*Alistair*!" she hisses.

But I ignore her, and the *second* knock. I'm sure it's Katerina, and she's smart enough to know that if she's knocking and I'm not answering, it either means I'm not here, or to fuck off.

Either way, she'd never just walk in.

So I keep fingering Eloise's hot little cunt, my thumb rolling her throbbing clit as she bites back a moan, her eyes hooded with lust.

Then that fucking knock comes again.

"Alistair! It's me."

Son of a—

Not Katerina. *Taylor.*

"Look, whatever prickly mood you're in, I know you're in there."

The knob starts to turn.

Shit.

I'm shirtless, with my clothes halfway across the room and my hand in Eloise's panties.

It's not an elegant solution, but it's the only one we've got time for.

In one move, I pull my hand out of her thong, yank her to my desk and shove her down into my chair behind it.

"*What the fuck?!*" she hisses, her face white as chalk.

"I'm not here," I growl. "You're working in my office, on my orders. Sell it."

"*What?!*"

Eloise gasps, looking terrified as I lurch under my own desk and yank the chair close to it.

"*Blouse,*" I hiss, just as I hear the door start to open.

Eloise scrambles to button it as I go still under the desk.

The door opens.

"Oh! Eloise?" I hear Taylor say.

"Oh, hi!" Eloise chirps back. "Ms. Crown! I'm... Sorry, were you at the door? I had headphones in."

It's a shit plan. But come on, I had one-point-three seconds to put it together. With Eloise sitting at my desk, Taylor can't tell that she's got nothing on from the waist down except some *very* wet panties. I can only hope she doesn't notice my shirt and jacket on the floor.

"I—" Eloise takes a breath, and I see her legs clench as she comports herself. "Sorry, is this okay? Mr. Black wanted me to finish some stuff up involving some confidential files that he didn't want leaving his office."

Taylor chuckles. "Well, there's a first time for everything, I suppose. Including Alistair letting an associate anywhere *near* his office without him here." She laughs again. "But, absolutely fine with me."

I exhale slowly.

"Is that his shirt?"

Fuck.

"Oh, yes, Mr. Black went down to the sub-basement," Eloise lies. "He said he had to 'work through' some things. He... seemed angry?"

Good girl. All of that tracks if you know anything about me.

Taylor snickers. "Sounds about right. Oh, by the way, you can just call me Taylor. *Ms. Crown* seems so formal."

I can see Eloise visibly relaxing under the desk. The problem is, I can *also* see the slick wet spot on her panties, and the way they cling to every little detail of her pussy. And I'm still rock fucking hard.

This is a bad fucking idea. But *everything* I do when it comes to Eloise is a bad fucking idea.

She jolts when my finger drags up her slit through the sticky lace. But she covers it with a coughing sound, like she's just swallowed down the wrong pipe or something.

"You okay?" Taylor asks.

My finger drags up and down Eloise's slick cunt again. She reaches a hand under the desk to try and grab my fingers, but I snatch her hand with my free one and yank it away.

"Oh, yeah, I'm fine, Ms. Crown." Eloise laughs nervously. "Uh...Taylor."

"You're settling in okay?"

"Yeah!" Eloise says brightly. "Yeah, I'm—"

She chokes back her words when I slip a finger under the edge of her panties and tug the gusset to the side.

"I'm *good,* yeah. I know Massimo forced you all to hire me—"

"Please," Taylor says easily, "it wasn't like that. Well, okay, cards on the table, yes, it was a condition of his deal. But, Eloise, you're a good attorney. I talked to some people at your old firm in Chicago, and they had nothing but good—" Taylor pauses, and I can almost picture the concerned look on her face. "Sorry, are you *sure* you're okay?"

Oh, she's *very* okay. I've just started dragging my tongue up her thigh as I rub her clit with my fingers.

"Oh...yeah," Eloise breathes. "Totally okay."

"Well, again, don't overthink it. Sometimes in life we get a leg up or an *in* somewhere, and that's fine. Take whatever opportunity presents itself to get where you need to—"

She's cut off by Eloise coughing again to cover the gasp as my mouth presses between her thighs. My tongue drags up her pussy, hungrily tasting her sweetness as her thighs clamp against the sides of my head. Her hand grabs my hair, trying to push me away. But again, I snatch her hand in mine and yank it back to the side. It's a firm warning.

So is the little slap I give her inner thigh before I start to devour her cunt again.

"Sorry!" Eloise says. "Something's been stuck in my throat all morning."

Taylor laughs it off. "Don't sweat it. Listen, Eloise, there's not a *lot* of female talent in this office. And, I mean, if you ever wanted to grab a drink or something, I'd love for us to get to know each other better."

Under normal circumstances, I'd have a quip or two about Taylor's abysmally awkward social skills. I mean, she's an absolute stone-cold killer of an attorney. But her interpersonal skills smack of a robot reading a teleprompter.

But these, obviously, are not normal circumstances. These are circumstances where I am *thoroughly* distracted, shoving my tongue as deep into Eloise's pussy as I can.

"I'd love—" Eloise gasps sharply, squirming on the edge of my office chair as her thighs clamp around my head again. "I'd love to, Taylor!"

"Great! Well, I'll get going." Taylor chuckles. "Lest the grump king himself comes stomping back up in a mood."

"Is he ever *not* in a mood?"

Taylor laughs.

I return fire by sucking Eloise's clit *hard*, making her almost jolt right out of the chair.

"We'll touch base soon. Seriously, though; if you see Alistair, would you tell him I need to talk to him?"

"Will..." Eloise shivers, her thighs quivering. "Will do."

The door closes with a click. Instantly, I'm pushing the chair back, shoving Eloise's legs up until her ankles are on the edge of my desk, and diving between her thighs.

This time, we're alone. There's no distraction.

And I'm going to fucking *devour* her.

Eloise moans and squeals into her arm, shuddering and squirming as I tongue her clit and sink two fingers back into her greedy pussy. Her legs shake, her ankles on my desk as I groan into her pussy. Then her whole body starts to jerk, her velvety walls clamping down around my fingers as her back arches and her hips launch off the chair against my mouth.

"Alistair—!"

She chokes, biting down on her hand to muffle her screams as she comes like a neutron bomb.

Unstable explosives and chemicals.

One spark.

And a detonation to level half a city.

Her sweetness floods my tongue, her thighs clamp down against my head, and her moans fill my ears.

14

ELOISE

"He's...prickly." Taylor shrugs. "When he wants to be."

She raises her glass of wine and takes a sip, grinning at the way Fumi snickers next to her. Then Taylor catches my pointed silence and grins.

"Go ahead, say it."

I shake my head. "No, it's...nothing."

She laughs. "Eloise. We're not at the office."

In fact, we're—Taylor, Fumi, and I—at Terroir et Pays, a gorgeous rooftop wine bar in Soho festooned with twinkling lights and vine arbors. I love that Taylor invited me out for after-work drinks along with Fumi Yamaguchi, Taylor's friend and one of the top equity partners at Crown and Black. They're both super cool, not to mention successful and confident. And I have to say, having not really had any girlfriends over the last few years at all, it feels fantastic to be included.

But all and of those thoughts do is make me feel shittier. Here Taylor is, making an effort to be my friend—which she doesn't have to do, I mean she's my boss—and all I can think about is how I'm not just her employee.

I'm a *spy*.

A reluctant one, for sure. But Massimo's threat still hangs over me, like the sword of Damocles. A week has passed since I tried hunting through Alistair's locked VIP files for Luca Carveli's will.

...But instead found myself screaming into my arm with my ankles on his desk as Alistair made me come like a hurricane on his tongue. Things have...*cooled* since then: both my hunt for Luca's will, and whatever sparked between Alistair and me.

With the will, I simply haven't had another chance to sneak into Alistair's office. I only barely managed to grab the key from the filing cabinet while he was putting his shirt back on the last time, and even then I had to wait a full day until Katerina's next lunch break to get it back into her desk drawer.

As for Alistair and me? Well...

Massimo has, of course, been a bastard about the delay in getting what he wants, and upped his threats to me involving my sister. But those threats surrounding Camille hit me in even more ways than Massimo knows.

...Because it's a sobering reminder that I'm not the only LeBlanc sister with a "history" involving Alistair Black.

And *God*, does that make me livid.

It happened a few months after he cut me out of his life. It's as if severing all contact, blocking me everywhere, and walking away from whatever "we" might have been, all on the worst night of my life, wasn't enough of a fuck-you from Alistair.

He also had to screw my sister.

Or, according to Camille, he *took advantage* of her.

However shitty it sounds, however awful it is for me not to believe my own sister...well, consider me in "camp doubt." I love Camille, but this is what she does. She embellishes. She reconstructs stories to make herself the main character. The story you hear from her is *rarely* the truth.

Camille's version of that night is that she was out drinking a bit too much with some friends. She bumped into Alistair and "gave him a piece of her mind" for blowing me off. At which point, he supposedly fed her drinks, coerced her into a car, and drove her to his apartment where he essentially took advantage her when she was barely conscious.

It's a lot to unpack. But, and as much as I hated Alistair at the time, *zero* part of me believed he was that sort of man. Also, it wasn't the first time Camille casually tossed out a rape allegation that had zero truth to it.

Actually, it was the *fifth* time she'd done it, and always for attention. To garner sympathy. Again, I know it sounds *so unbelievably shitty* to doubt my own sister's claim of assault. But I do.

Unfortunately, that's where the lies end.

I wanted so badly to believe that she invented the *entire* story of bumping into Alistair that summer, not just the bogus assault part, but that became impossible once I heard from

Demi, who was randomly *also* at that same bar, that she'd seen my sister and Alistair climbing into a car together.

So, *yeah,* when Massimo threatens my sister, it makes me remember the awful reality that she and Alistair once went home together.

And *that* is why things have cooled since that one time in his office when I was reminded how strong a drug Alistair Black really is, and let my guard down. .

"Or…don't?"

I blink, smiling awkwardly at Taylor. "Sorry, I was a million miles away, what?"

She laughs. "I said, we're not in the office!"

Fumi tucks a strand of her jet-black hair back from her slender neck, raising her glass of Riesling. "No joke, Eloise. These nights out Taylor and I take are basically mandatory decompression with having to work alongside Captain Grumps."

Taylor snickers, shrugging. "I mean, I love the guy like a brother—"

"Well, that makes one of us."

Taylor rolls her eyes at Fumi. "Fair enough. But in any case, Eloise," she says, turning back to me. "It's good to vent. You can say what you like about Alistair. I swear to God, I'm not HR, and I won't repeat a thing."

I smirk, arching a brow.

"Ooo, do the dollar bill thing," Fumi snickers.

Taylor nods, and then looks back at me with a sigh.

"Okay, give me a dollar."

I frown. "What?"

"Do you have a dollar bill on you?"

"I…think?" I pick up my bag and rifle inside for my wallet before pulling out a crumpled bill. I hand it to Taylor and she grins.

"Okay, I am now officially and legally acting in the capacity of your attorney. This is now a protected, confidential conversation."

I laugh. "*That's* how badly you want me to talk smack about Alistair?"

"Yup."

I sigh, grinning as I look down into my wine. "You said before that he could be prickly when he wants to be. My immediate response was 'well the mood sure does strike him a lot'."

Taylor and Fumi both crack up.

"*That* it does," Fumi giggles, standing and draining her wine. "Be right back. I gotta pee."

When she's gone, Taylor shakes her head as she takes another sip of wine. "If it makes you feel any better, Alistair's been like that since I met him in law school."

"Oh, he was like that before, too."

The table goes quiet, awkwardly so. Taylor starts to open her mouth as if to change the subject. Then she pauses, her brow furrowing.

"Okay, screw it, I'm just going to say it so we can stop tiptoeing around the elephant in the room." She glances over her shoulder, as if to make sure Fumi is out of earshot. Then she gives me a soft, sympathetic look. "I know you two...have a history."

My face pales a little, and I swallow the lump that forms in my throat.

"No, hang on," Taylor shakes her head. "I'm not interested in drama, it's none of my business, and I don't know any of the details. I don't *need* to know. But..." Her brows knit.

"Massimo doesn't know," I say quietly. "If that's what you're getting at."

She sighs. "Again, not trying to pry, it's just...well, Massimo is..."

"Sure is," I mutter.

"Eloise, if you don't want to work with Alistair, that is *completely* fine. I get it. I can rearrange things—and I'm *not* saying that just to headhunt you for my team or anything. You could work under Gabriel, if you wanted."

I smile wryly, shaking my head.

"It's fine. Really. But I appreciate the offer." My brows wrinkle. "Has he told you anything? Alistair, I mean. About—"

"Your history with him?" Taylor finishes for me, shaking her head firmly. "Nothing that affects how I view you, either as an attorney or a person. That's the truth." She pauses. "Can I be honest, Eloise?"

"Please."

"I've seen the way he is around you—yes, *prickly*, and I think we can both agree that that's putting it mildly. And sure, some of it might be the history you two have from Knightsblood. But, do you think some of it might also be because of what happened with your sister?"

My stomach drops along with my jaw.

"He…he *told you* about that?"

She shrugs. "We're close."

I am *not* prepared for the sudden twist of…goddammit, is that *jealousy* swirling like venom inside? I'm still trying to shake it away when Taylor reaches across the table and places a hand on mine.

"*Nothing* like that, Eloise. I mean close like the brother I never had," she says quietly. "He and Gabriel both are, actually. So, yeah, he told me about what happened. I mean, look, it's not my place, but I really can't help but wonder if some of the…*friction* you're getting from him is because he's now working closely with the sister of the woman who tried to assault him."

It feels like a punch to the stomach.

Hang on, *what*?

I stare at Taylor, my pulse quickening.

"Sorry, what did you just say?"

Her face pales a little. "Forget it. This has nothing to do with me, and it is *not* my place to—"

"Taylor, no, wait!"

She starts to stand, grabbing her bag and pulling out some cash to drop onto the table.

"Drinks are on me. I sincerely apologize for bringing this up—"

"*Please*." I grab her arm, stopping her. "Please, I need to..." I frown. "Look, I... I know they met at a bar here in the city one night and left together. I know they..." I swallow back the bile as horribly vivid images of Alistair and my sister fucking swirl through my head before focusing on Taylor again. "But why would you say she tried to...you know."

Taylor bites her lip.

"My sister is a train wreck," I hiss quietly. "She's unstable, she's a liar, and she's a raging narcissist. And I say all that to let you know that literally *nothing* you say could change what I already think about her."

Taylor exhales slowly.

"*Please*," I croak. "I just want to know the truth."

She nods, looking away as she draws in a deep breath. "Eloise, Alistair almost lost his life that night. He was *extremely* drunk, and it was later shown that he had Rohypnol in his system."

My mouth falls open. "But that's..."

"The date rape drug, yes."

I blanch, staring at her. "What the hell happened?"

"Camille was driving him back to her place when she got pulled over for blowing through a stop sign."

"Drunk?"

Taylor's mouth thins as she shakes her head side to side. "Stone cold sober. The cop gave her a breathalyzer test on the spot. She wasn't even buzzed." Her jaw tightens. "*Alistair*, on the other hand, almost fell out of the passenger seat, couldn't obey the officer's commands, and tried to run off before he collapsed in the street. They took him to Mt. Sinai, gave him adrenaline to get his heart going again, pumped his stomach, and found the Rohypnol in his system." Her face is stony as she looks away. "He could have died, Eloise."

What. The. Actual. *Fuck.*

"I've never heard a word of this," I breathe. "Why the fuck isn't Camille in *jail?*"

Taylor's mouth twists. "Alistair didn't want to press charges."

I stare at her. "Why the *fuck* not?!"

She looks down into her wine and takes a deep breath before lifting her eyes back to mine.

"*You.*"

AN HOUR LATER, there are two things I know for sure.

The first is that Fumi probably thinks I'm a psycho and Taylor is probably terrified of me now. Because I just all but forced the latter to take us back to the Crown and Black offices and give me a copy of the police report from that night that had been locked in her files.

The second is that I'm going to *kill* my sister.

I was always Papa's favorite in terms of true affection, getting hugs and deep, bonding conversations. Camille, however, wasn't left out, and got *money* and her lavish lifestyle paid for without question. Which is how a grown-ass woman who's never worked a day in her life can live in a stunning three-story townhouse a block away from Central Park West.

Her housekeeper Betina—because *of course* she has a fucking housekeeper—answers my furious knocks on the front door. I blast past her, my face livid and my blood burning like nuclear fire as I storm into the house.

"CAMILLE!" I roar. "*CAMILLE*?!"

"Ellie?"

I look up from the foyer to see my sister up on the third floor, dressed in some ridiculous Parisian silk robe with a cocktail glass in her hand. She frowns.

"What are you—"

"Don't. Move!"

I storm up the winding staircase, and by the time I get to her, her face is pale as she backs away from me.

"Okay, first, your energy is *so* negative right—"

"I want to talk about what the *fuck* happened that night!" I scream at her. "With Alistair!"

She bristles. She quickly brings the glass to her lips and takes a large gulp of her martini.

"I… I don't like to talk about that night. You know that, Ellie."

"Why *not,* Camille?!" I snarl.

Her face turns paler. "You *know* why! Because—"

"Because everything you told me about that night is *bullshit,* maybe?!" I scream. "And you 'don't like to talk about it' because you probably don't even remember what your fucking story is!?"

She looks at me, aghast. "That motherfucker *raped me,* Eloise!!" she yells back. "He got me wasted, and—"

"Really? This says you were fucking sober when you were pulled over."

I yank the police report out of my bag and shove it against her chest, splashing her cocktail over her robe.

"I…I…" Camille stammers, looking white as she takes the paper. "I don't know what sort of lies Alistair told you, but—"

"You blew a zero-point-zero for alcohol, Camille," I hiss. "Alistair, meanwhile, *fell out of the fucking car,* ran from a cop in a daze, and then collapsed in the street with his heart rate in the fucking toilet."

She goes still—so still I almost wonder if she's having some sort of psychotic episode. She stares *through* the report in her hand, a wild, manic look in her eyes. Slowly, she drags her gaze back to me, her mouth twisted in fury.

"Get out."

"You *lied* to me, Camille!!" I scream. "Why the hell would you—"

"Get out!!"

"And *worse,* it was *you* trying to take *him* home?! "I mean, what kind of a sister *does that?!* What the fuck is wrong with—"

"GET!! OUT!!"

The room goes silent as we stare each other down, her bloodcurdling scream still hanging in the air.

"*Gladly,*" I hiss quietly.

I keep my shit together until I'm outside. Then it hits me like a brick in the face. I collapse onto a park bench just around the corner, sucking in air as a million thoughts explode through my head.

There are several reasons why, ten years ago, I had to force myself to stop thinking of Alistair Black the way I used to. Our tortuously enmeshed paths, and the way things went up in smoke when he cut me out is one of them. Later, my fake, unwanted marriage to Massimo become another.

But the biggest one for me was thinking for so many years that he and my sister slept together.

Now that I've just found out that it's all *bullshit,* I have no idea what to do with myself. With my sudden proximity to Alistair again.

...Or with the dangerous notion that I may, in fact, be falling once again for the same boy I fell for before.

Come what may.

15

ALISTAIR

THERE ARE a few things about Eloise LeBlanc that I'm slowly remembering, the more time I spend around her. Sure, some are purely libido-related. Like how fucking sexy it is when she sucks her bottom lip between her teeth when she's thinking about something.

Or the way her luscious ass fills out a pencil skirt *oh* so well. Or the scent of her, which has an immediate Viagra-on-steroids effect on my dick whenever I catch it in the air, which is *very* inconvenient if I'm sitting down with a client just as Eloise walks by the conference room.

Fuck you, pheromones.

But there are other non-sexual things about Eloise that are slowly coming back to me from before as I notice them again. Her tenacity, for example, which might even rival that of my sister, Tempest.

But the *biggest* one—which is fucking with me more that I care to admit—is "the switch".

At least, that's what I called it when we were at Knightsblood together. One day she'd be colder than frostbite to me. The next, one could almost say she was flirting. Then, inevitably, the switch would flip again, and she'd go right back to being that psycho winter witch from Narnia.

To be fair, I probably wasn't much better. But the more time I spend working with her ten years later, the more I notice that switch.

One day, she acts like she wants to cut my dick off. The next, she's allowing—more like *begging*—me to finger her dripping wet pussy before going down on her with her ankles up on my desk and her fingers tangled in my hair.

But then comes "the switch". Not twelve hours after the aforementioned ankles-on-desk incident where she humped my tongue so greedily and eagerly, she was right back to being the Snow Queen of Narnia again.

It's not even the switch, or the back-and-forth, that annoys the fuck out of me. Because I do not give a *fuck* about games.

But *that* is precisely what's fucking me up when it comes to Eloise's mood switches: I suddenly find myself *giving a fuck about them.*

Which, much like the random rock-hard erections the very scent of her keeps eliciting in me, is *very* inconvenient.

Anyway, once again, the switch has flipped. For a week or so after the incident in my office, she was giving me a shoulder colder than Sir Edmund Hillary's or Tenzing Norgay's when they were scaling Everest. But now?

She's all fucking smiles. All batted eyelashes. All blushing cheeks whenever I glare at her. It's fucking with my head.

...Both of them, actually.

And the real problem is, as suspicious as I am of her mood swings to the Dark Side and back again, I'm also fucking addicted to them. Worse, I can't even tell anymore if it's her suddenly being all smiles, or the head-fuck of *the switch itself* that I'm addicted to.

And *that,* ladies and gentlemen of the jury, is my current headspace as I make my way through the Crown and Black offices. I suppose to most of my employees—guessing from the looks on their faces when they pass me—I look like I'm about to go waterboard someone.

The truth is, I'm thinking about Eloise. And not about water-boarding her, either. More like about clamping my lips and teeth around one of her nipples as she bounces up and down on my cock.

Which is how it is that I happen to walk right past Conference Room B before my brain catches up to what my eyes just fucking saw in there. Every muscle tenses. Stone-faced, my mind now clear, I turn and stalk back to the wall of windows looking into the conference room.

Mother. Fucking. Fuck.

Roughly seven seconds later, Gabriel looks up with a start as I barge into his office with murder on my face.

"What the *fuck* is *that*?!" I snarl, jabbing my thumb back vaguely in the direction of the conference room.

My brother arches a brow that screams "now what" as he sighs and collects some papers into a file before tucking it under his arm.

"I can't believe I'm even entertaining this, because I have a meeting in two minutes," Gabriel sighs. "But could you possibly be *slightly* more specific?"

"Happily," I snap. "I would, *specifically,* like to know why the ever-loving fuck Ansel fucking Albrecht is sitting in Conference Room B."

That's the motherfucker I just saw sitting in one of the four-thousand-dollar, custom-upholstered chairs in the conference room.

He doesn't deserve to be sitting in one of those chairs. Honestly, I think he'd be far better suited to the kind of chair that's connected to high voltage wires, and instead of custom upholstery, you get a prison warden and a priest giving you last rites.

Because of all the things about Eloise to be "reminded" of, this is one I'd never need a reminder for.

He's a part of her story I'll never be able to forget. And I fucking *hate* the anger that even seeing him stirs up in me, because of what that says about me giving a shit when it comes to Eloise.

Gabriel nods carefully. "Look, I know he was a douchebag at school—"

"Douchebag would have been an improvement."

Gabriel chuckles, which almost makes my temper boil over before I remind myself that my brother doesn't know anything about that night, and what I saw.

No one does.

No one but *Ansel.*

"Well, douchebag he may have been, and, okay, probably still is, he's also a potential new client ready to commit five mil a year."

"It's a hard pass, Gabriel," I say icily. "Get him the fuck out of here."

My brother's brow furrows. "Excuse me?"

"I said no. We're not taking him on."

"Like hell we're not. *Five million* a year? And, unlike a growing number of our clients, Ansel's business is actually above board."

"I wasn't aware the German fucking Mafia was considered 'above board' these days."

Gabriel rolls his eyes. "There was a split, a few years back. Ansel took his inheritance and disowned the rest of his family. His little brother, Yann, is running the organization now. Ansel himself is totally legit. He runs a securities trading house now."

"I don't give a fuck if he's the Pope and curing goddamn cancer. We're not taking him on as a client. End of fucking discussion—"

"It's not a *discussion* at all," Gabriel fires back, his jaw clenched. "Taylor and I have—come on! Alistair!"

But I'm already out of his office and storming my way toward the elevators, loosening my tie.

I have a practice bag in the sub-basement to annihilate, because if I don't, I'm going to march into the conference room and destroy Ansel's fucking face instead.

It's *not* jealousy.

It's pure fucking *wrath*.

OF THE THREE OF US—GABRIEL, Taylor, and me—it's usually Gabriel who stays at the office the latest, burning the midnight oil. That's not to say Taylor and I aren't *also* essentially married to our jobs, but we can extricate ourselves from this place when we have to. Taylor prefers to adjourn to her office at her apartment for night-time work. And I…especially recently…often find myself needing to take a break to unwind in what most would call self-destructive and violent ways before diving back into work somewhere around eleven or twelve at night. At home.

But tonight, I'm here.

I'm not the only one, either.

Stretching, I push my laptop aside and stand from my desk. At the interior-facing wall of windows in my office, I look down into the pit, where the only light still on is the one in Eloise's cubicle.

She's all but buried in her mountains of busywork, courtesy of yours truly. But as I look down on her now, I'm not as pleased with myself as I was a week ago about handing her all of that.

I dumped the work on her before because of, well, what she once did to me. Then the episode in my office happened, followed by a week of cold shoulders and silent treatment, followed by her unusual and downright suspiciously cheerful about-turn.

I mean the woman brought me another fucking chai latte with two shots of espresso today, unprompted and unannounced, then smiled and told me to have a nice day.

I threw the latte away because I figured it was laced with laxatives or poison, but I'm beginning to think it really was just a kind gesture.

Flip, the switch turns on. *Flip,* it turns off. *Flip,* just kidding! It's back on!

Clap on, clap off.

It's impossible to keep up.

My brow furrows as I stare at the mountain of work crap I've all but buried her in. For what? To satisfy my own sense of revenge? If so, what the fuck does that say about me? I mean, much as I hate to admit it, Gabriel's right: what happened at Knightsblood was ten fucking years ago.

Yes, there are things I saw that I'll never unsee. There was her cruelty. But fuck, I was cruel right back to her.

But I'm not that boy anymore, and she's not that girl.

Maybe it's time to let the past stay where it is.

At least, that's what I tell myself when I buzz her cubicle from my office phone: that I'm simply offering an olive branch. Let's ignore the fact that we're the only two people here, and that my cock is at least sixty-percent hard, and that I'm already fantasizing about bending her across my desk, Massimo Carveli's wife or not.

Fuck. This is a very, very bad idea.

"Hello?" she answers, confused.

"Come up to my office."

Looking down through my window, I smirk when she startles, whipping around to look up at me, like she's only just realized we're the only two here.

I relish the blush on her face when she figures that out.

"For what?" she asks, tucking a strand of blonde behind her ear.

"For because-I-*said*-so," I growl.

I swear to fuck, I can see her roll her goddamn eyes from all the way up here.

"I'm sort of busy right now," she says, *just* tersely enough to make the point that she's aware that she's talking to the guy responsible for said work.

"Working hours are over. You're done."

"I'm salaried, not hourly. What do you care how late I work?"

"Electricity isn't free, Eloise."

She snorts through the phone. "So my single lightbulb, an LED one by the way, is going to bankrupt the firm by being on for another few hours a night?"

"Has it ever occurred to you that the reason you haven't worked in almost two years is less about your dipshit of a husband and more about your inability to just nod and say yes when your boss asks you to do something?"

The phone is silent. Then I hear the click as she puts the phone back on the cradle before standing. I smirk as she smooths down her skirt suit and then makes her way up to the executive level.

I'm at the bar cart at the far side of my office when she steps in.

"You're in a mood."

I shrug, my back to her. "It's not a mood if that's my default setting."

"I'm glad you can admit your flaws, Alistair." She grins as I turn to glare at her.

"Drink?"

She nods. "Whatever you're having. Thanks."

I pour her a whiskey, neat, as she walks over. Turning, I hand it to her and then clink my glass to hers.

"Cheers."

Eloise smiles as she lifts her glass. "Thanks, boss."

"I think I clearly requested *sir,* not *boss.*"

I relish the heat that blooms in her face. "I'll have to remember that," she says through the redness in her cheeks. "*Sir.*"

I'm about to quip back when she suddenly knocks back the drink in one gulp.

"Jesus Christ, I asked if you wanted *a drink,* not shots on Spring Break in Cozumel."

Eloise blushes, then reaches past me to grab the bottle and pour herself another.

"You didn't used to drink like this," I growl quietly.

"I also didn't used to be married to a psychopath," she murmurs, taking a deep sip.

My jaw clenches. Something simmers hotly in my veins. "Would you like to explain to me how the fuck that happened? Marrying *him*, I mean."

She frowns. "Honestly? Not particularly."

"What if I'm not asking."

"Then I'd say our conversation is back on track."

I glare at her. "Eloise—"

"Because my father's living will *demanded* it, okay? When he fell into his coma, his people made sure to…follow through."

"I knew about the will. I'm just confused why you went along with it."

Eloise glares at me. "As much as I hated when you called me *princess* back at school, you weren't wrong," she hisses. "I *am* a mafia princess. And that means family duty. And arranged marriages, even if you fucking hate them."

"So why the fuck do you stay with him?"

She looks away, her face tight. "Can we *please* change the subject? Nine at night after twelve straight hours at work isn't really my peak emotional state to discuss my forced marriage to a psychopath."

Fair enough. I take a sip of whiskey. "I'm sorry about your father."

"Oh, goodie, we can skip over talking about my arranged marriage to a lunatic and talk about my dad being in a coma instead. *Much* better."

I grin. So does she, before she hides it with a gulp of whiskey. Then her brow worries.

"Did I see Ansel Albrecht in the conference room earlier—"

"New fucking topic," I snarl, harshly enough that she jumps. Her eyes widen as she looks at me with a little bit of fear and a little bit of confusion. Then she just shrugs.

"Works for me."

She finishes her drink, and then her brows knit as she looks up at me.

"I wanted to say…I'm sorry about Layla," she says quietly. "When I heard…"

"Thanks." My voice is clipped as I look away.

Layla, Gabriel and I's first younger sister above Tempest in the birth-order, was also at Knightsblood when Eloise was there.

Then she died.

Fuck heroine.

Eloise nods quietly at my silence and reaches for the bottle again. I get there first and cover it with my hand.

"Seriously?"

"Seriously. If you hate your husband so much, try something other than poisoning your liver."

"What, like fooling around with my boss?" she says coldly, throwing me an accusatory look.

"Oh, right, because you were kicking and screaming," I say dryly. "Unless of course your ankles squirming on my desk were 'kicking' and your desperately slutty moans were 'screaming.'"

Eloise's face turns scarlet. "Why do you do that?"

"Do what?"

"Make it seem like…I don't know. A punishment. Like I *owed* you what happened the other day."

"Maybe because you treated it like it was a punishment. You froze me the fuck out eight seconds later," I grunt.

Eloise looks away, her lips pursed. "May I *please* have another drink," she mutters.

"Fuck it. Fine."

I watch as she snatches up the bottle and pours a glass. She takes a small sip, still not meeting my eye.

"It wasn't a punishment. I mean…" She blushes. "It didn't *feel* like a punishment at the time. For the record." Her brows knit tightly. For a moment I think she's going to knock back her whole drink again. But she sets it down instead, her hands twisting before she looks up at me.

"Why didn't you ever tell me about Camille?"

I stiffen. "Let's not go there."

There's a determined look in her eyes as she shakes her head.

"I need to tell you something."

"Eloise—"

"Ten years ago, she told me that you got her drunk, maybe drugged her, and…you know…"

What. The. *Fuck*.

When she trails off, my office goes pin-drop silent but for the angry thud of my pulse. My molars grind painfully, my skin feels raw against my clothes, and my emotions duel with each other.

"You seriously think I'm capable of that?" I hiss coldly.

Eloise swallows, and she shakes her head.

"No,," she says quietly. "But I did hear from someone else that you left the bar with her that night."

My memories of that night are...hazy, at best. But they involve bumping into Eloise's crazy-ass sister at some bar in Tribeca, immediately trying to leave, and then somehow finding myself slumped in the passenger seat of her car.

I dimly remember her hand on my thigh, and me telling her to let me the fuck out of the car. I also remember blurred streetlights and shoving her hand off my leg over and over before blue and red lights filled the night, together with sirens.

Then I remember waking up to see my brother and Taylor hovering over me in a hospital room.

So to say that I feel *rage* at Camille's *very* different account of things is a vast understatement.

"Would you care to hear the *actual* story about that night?"

"No need, I know now," she says quietly. She shakes her head, looking away. "I was so, *so* fucking mad at you," she whispers.

"Because you thought I fucked your sister?"

"*Yes*!" she blurts loudly. Her face falls as she looks away again. "*Yes*," she murmurs again, quieter. "I know we were cruel to each other. But that just seemed...beyond."

She's right. It would have been. Even after every shot we fired at each other. Even after the "pranks" like dying a showerhead blue turned *far* more dangerous. Even after we came at each other with knives drawn.

Even after what I saw that night that almost destroyed me and arguably made me the cold, walled-off fucker I am today.

...Fucking her psycho sister *would* have been crossing a line.

My brows knit. "When did you find out I didn't?"

Eloise looks down at her hands. "Three days ago."

Holy fuck.

She's spent ten goddamn years thinking... Suddenly, a thought hits me.

"You still thought I'd done that—"

"Look, I know my sister," she spits. "I didn't think you did what she *said* you did. But..."

"But you still thought I went home with her that night."

"Yeah."

"And you still thought I'd done that a week and a half ago, when what happened in this office...happened."

She nods. "Pretty pathetic, huh?"

"I was going to say flattering."

She blushes, rolling her eyes as she tries to hide her smile. "You're *such* an asshole."

"And here I thought I was an asshole because I touched someone else's wife."

She goes quiet, her chest rising and falling as her eyes meet mine.

"I'm not—"

"Because I *took* what belongs to another man."

Her lips purse, the bottom one quivering.

"I don't *belong* to *anyone—*"

"Well, that's not true at all, is it?"

In one move, I grab her by the hip and jaw, yanking her against my chest as I crush my lips to hers.

She does belong to someone.

Me.

16

ELOISE

It's the way he touches me that does it. Like I'm *his* to do with what he wants.

If it was literally anyone but Alistair, I'd probably scream or turn violent. With him, it's different somehow.

Always has been, always will be.

I took one of those cheesy "love language" tests once. Mine is touch, and I want to say some of this insane physical chemistry with Alistair, this need I have for him, comes from me being touch-starved.

But it's not just pent-up sexual frustration, or being starved for intimacy.

It's *him.*

His touch, his scent, his dark energy that swirls around me and consumes me. Even when I was furious with him back then, or told myself I hated him, or we were at each other's throats, I could never escape the feeling of being utterly *safe* with him. He's always felt like home to me.

It's why, despite our war back in school, what happened in the elevator the night of the blackout…happened.

It's also why I shut down later, and never let anyone else in.

And it's why ten years later, despite every iota of logic, reason, and survival instinct screaming how bad an idea this is, I'm still aching to let him in again. It's why I can't pull away, why I can't stop this.

I'm not sure either of us can.

Alistair's hands slide over my ribs, running down my body to grip my hips and yank them against him. I moan as he tilts my face up to his, his lips crushing against mine hard enough to bruise as he devours my mouth.

He yanks my blouse out of my skirt as my fingers feverishly race to rip the buttons open on his dress shirt. Our clothes drop to the floor in a blur as I whimper and moan into his lips. I shudder with a manic sort of desperation at the feel of hot, warm skin against my own.

Brain synapses that have lain dormant for ten years fire. The touch-starved part of me comes electrically alive as my nipples graze against his bare chest. As his tongue dances with mine. As his hands hold me possessively against him.

I gasp when he suddenly grabs my ass and lifts me up. He swallows my moans as my legs wrap around his muscled hips, my pulse roaring as he storms across the room carrying me. He sets me down on the edge of his desk, and I groan in anticipation when he reaches past me and uses his arm to clear the whole damn thing in one swipe.

Phone, lamp, books, files…they all go cascading to the ground as Alistair groans into my mouth. He fists a hank of my hair, and I gasp when he tugs it back, pulling my mouth from his.

"Why are you stopp—"

"Because we need to get one thing straight first," he rasps.

"Which is?"

"This doesn't change a fucking thing between us."

My brow furrows. "You mean if—"

"Oh, there's no *if*." I jolt as he shoves my skirt up to my waist and slides his hand between my legs. His finger begin to rub my soaking wet pussy through my panties, making my jaw go slack and my eyes roll back.

"I *am* going to fuck you, Eloise," he growls, rolling my clit under the pad of his finger. "But nothing changes."

"Still enemies?"

"That seems…harsh," he growls, groaning as I reach between us and cup the thick bulge in his pants.

Holy *fuck*. I remember him being big, but…*Jesus*. Do dicks not stop growing after a certain age?

"But true," I gasp, choking out a moan as his finger slips under the edge of my panties to stroke my bare lips.

"I mean it. This doesn't change *us*."

"There is no us," I fire back, yanking his belt open.

"Exactly."

"And there won't be."

"I think I like the new Eloise more than I was expecting."

"Don't go getting all...*oh fuck...*" I whimper as he sinks two fingers into me, stroking against my g-spot as my core melts. "Sentimental...on me."

"*Coming* on you, yes. But you don't need to worry about sentimentality."

I whimper as his mouth crushes to mine with a brutality that somehow makes me even wetter.

"You're still *you*," he growls. "And I'm still *me*."

"I'm aware of...*Alistair*—!" I choke as he shoves me down across his desk.

"*You're* still my fucking employee, *I'm* still your goddamn boss, and I still trust you about as far as I can *throw* you. Is that fucking clear?"

He says all of this with his fingers stroking my g-spot and his muscles rippling in the low light of his office, his eyes piercing into mine.

"Eloise." He growls savagely, fingering me even harder as I start to moan. "Is. That. *Clear*."

"*Yes, sir*."

Something dark flickers triumphantly in his eyes, and his jaw grinds as I whimper out the words.

"*Good girl*."

He all but rips my panties off my legs, grabs my thighs, shoves my knees up and lewdly apart, and drops between my legs. And suddenly, his mouth is on my pussy, his tongue snaking around my clit.

Merde...

My back arches like he's touched me with a live wire. My vision goes black at the edges as his mouth hums against my pussy and his tongue dances over my aching clit. He groans into me, shoving my legs back even further and plunging his tongue into me.

I cry out, writhing and squirming on the desk, my thighs desperately trying to clamp around his ears. But he's too strong, and he keeps them *exactly* where he wants them as he devours my pussy like I'm his first meal after being stranded on a deserted island for a year.

It's not just frenzied licking. The man is *gifted*. Frighteningly so. It's like he's inside my freaking head and knows every single place to touch and taste me, and how fast, and how hard, to have me shuddering and trembling and turning into a puddle on his desk.

My whines and moans fill the office, my hands cupping my breasts and pinching my nipples as my head lolls back. I drop one hand, sliding my fingers into his hair. Instantly, he's grabbing it.

"Greedy girl."

He snatches both of my hands and plants them on the backs of my thighs.

"Hold your legs apart," he growls in a demanding tone. "Keep them *just* like that."

When I start to open my mouth to protest, he spanks my ass, making me yelp and whimper, before his mouth delves back to my slick, swollen pussy. His tongue drags up my lips, swirling around my clit as he sucks it between his lips. His fingers curl into me again, coaxing me higher and higher, until suddenly, I feel everything start to detonate.

"Alistair..."

I'm coming so hard it's almost embarrassing. My body arches off his desk, my legs shaking as my fingers dig into the flesh at the backs of my thighs. My moans fill his office as I come on his tongue, spasming from head to toe as he keeps humming and sucking on my clit until it happens all over again.

Suddenly, he pulls away and stands between my legs. My pulse thuds as his abs clench and his forearms ripple as he reaches for his pants. The button pops, the zipper is next, and they drop.

Holy what the fuck.

Alistair is *huge*. As thick as my wrist, and long, with a swollen, gorgeous head and veins running up the entire length of him. He fists his cock slowly, stroking himself as he steps between my thighs. My eyes drop to the clear bead at the slit in his crown. Then I'm gasping quietly as he pushes my thighs apart and stokes the head over my slick lips.

He pauses for just a second, his eyes sweeping slowly over me as if drinking me in. Something fierce and wild sparks in his eyes as he grabs my hips and centers his swollen cock right at my entrance.

"*What a fucking idiot,*" he murmurs.

I frown. "Who?"

"Massimo," he growls quietly. "For never doing *this*."

Oh, FUCK.

My breath whooshes out of me, and my whole body ignites with heat as Alistair starts to push into me. He doesn't just ram inside, thank God, because his dick is honestly gigantic.

He guides himself in slowly, easing inch after inch into my tight, soaking pussy, and my entire body begins to melt with pleasure.

"*Prends-moi,*" I moan softly, gasping wide-eyed as I stare between my legs. He's so fucking big, and *God* does it look hot as he stretches me open to fit inside. I whimper over and over, gasping and trembling with pleasure as he slowly pushes more and more of his cock into me.

Finally he's all the way in, stretching me to my absolute limit and filling me so deep it feels like he's in my fucking throat.

I choke out a gasping moan, my toes curling as my hands slide down my body to grip my thighs and pull them even wider open.

"There's a good girl."

It's the second time he's called me that. And same as the first time, it unlocks something inside me. Those two little words push me over the line from eager and turned on to wanton and *dick-crazed.*

"*Fuck me…*" I choke.

"Oh, I plan to."

He slides out, and then sinks right back in, making me whine loudly as I arch my back and the sensations ripple through me.

He's right: this doesn't change anything. He's still him, and I'm still me, and there's still the bloody battlefield between us littered with the aftermath of our war.

But I want what I want, and despite who he is and all that's happened between us…

He *still* fucking feels like home.

I don't know what the hell that means, or what it says about me, and I don't care. Right now, all I know is his body and mine melding together, and the pure heat and desire that has ignited inside me.

Alistair groans, his hands sliding up my body to grip me tightly around the waist. His hips roll, the V-line grooves under his abs rippling as he thrusts into me. He starts slowly, but gradually he starts to fuck me harder and deeper, until the wet, slapping sounds of his thick cock plunging into my eager pussy fill the room alongside my moans.

His hands move higher, cupping my breasts and squeezing them. He pinches my nipples mercilessly, bringing a cry of pain mixed with pleasure to my lips that sizzles through my brain. His hips roll faster, his cock ramming into me as he wraps my hair in his fist and roughly pulls me upright into a sitting position on the edge of his desk.

Alistair kisses me fiercely, letting me taste myself on his tongue as my legs wrap around his waist. His gorgeous cock fucks into me over and over, until we momentarily break apart, gasping for air. His forehead drops to mine, our eyes an inch away from each other as we fuck each other raw.

"*Fuck*..." I choke, shaking. "*Me*..."

"*Such* a greedy little thing," he growls. "And so *very* desperate for my dick."

"Arrogant bastard."

"*Princess.*"

"Fuck...*you.*"

"Sorry, I'm far too busy fucking *you.*"

He plunges into me hard, each thrust punctuating his words, and suddenly my body starts to clench. A ball of heat forms in my core and then explodes outward. It hits all my nerves, rippling through my system and igniting every little bit of me until it hits my extremities, shooting out of my fingers and toes as my eyes go wide and the scream is in my throat.

"Alistair—!"

"No need to yell, I'm right here," he grunts. "Now why don't you be a good girl and fucking *come* all over my big, fat, hard cock."

Everything goes white as I detonate. My senses blur, and I'm only barely aware of my whole body wrenching and writhing before his mouth crushes to mine, swallowing my cries. Alistair grunts, thrusting his perfect cock deep inside me as I feel him swell and start to pulse.

It pushes me over the edge again, and instantly, I'm coming a second time as his hot, sticky cum spills into me.

As his arms wrap tight around me, and his hands grip me. Like I'm his.

The scariest thing isn't that I might be.

...It's that I might never *not* have been.

17

ELOISE

Ten years ago:

My heart almost stops when my eyes scan the words on the page in front of me.

We regret to inform you...

No.

My throat closes up. My skin feels too tight.

This can't be fucking happening.

Every year, the Hamilton Foundation seeks out five—*five total*—individuals bound for law school and pairs them with a tenured professor at the school they're applying to. It's a mentorship on crack, and it pretty much guarantees you a spot at that school, not to mention employment afterwards.

Naturally, there are something like ten thousand students vying for those coveted five slots. The first round decimates it down to five hundred. The second cuts that number to fifty, and the third cuts it to fifteen…three candidates per slot.

I made it into the third round, and even had a video call with Dr. Shoshana Mendel, the *brilliant* civil rights attorney I'd be paired with if I made the final cut. She's even at my dream school, Yale University.

Making that final cut depends on an in-person interview. It was going to be even easier for me given that Yale isn't that far from the Knightsblood campus.

I made all the arrangements. I had my interview notecards memorized, and knew all the right things to say.

And then two days before that interview that would decide the course of my life, Alistair fucking Black snuck into my bathroom and put blue dye in my shower.

There wasn't any way in this world or the next I was showing up to that interview looking like a fucking Smurfette. So I cancelled, and sent a long-winded, highly apologetic email alluding to a medical condition that was preventing me from attending, and asked about rescheduling.

That was two weeks ago. The letter in my hand right now is the first I've heard from either Yale or the Hamilton Foundation since.

Dear Ms. LeBlanc: We regret to inform you that we are unable to reschedule the final interview of your application process. The positions in our program are highly desired, and we regret to say that you have been eliminated from our selection process. We wish you all the best in your future endeavors.

That's it. Do not pass Go, do not collect two hundred dollars.

One of the reasons the Hamilton Foundation's selection process is so cutthroat is because you only get *one* chance at it.

There's no "we welcome you to apply again next year". You take your shot, and if you miss, that's it.

Fin.

The paper falls from my hand to the floor. My pulse thuds low and heavy in my chest. I want to cry, but no tears come. I want to scream, but I'm too stunned.

I'm going to fucking kill him.

I know it was Alistair. Days after the shower incident, having taken time off from my Knightsblood classes and about five thousand more showers, scrubbing a layer or six of skin from my body to get rid of the blue, I was finally back in public again.

My skin still had a slight blueish tint, and my blonde hair was still tinged green. But I was back in class. When I locked eyes with Alistair across the main quad, the fucker just *smiled* at me, raising a single, purposefully blue-colored middle finger.

My stomach drops further as the full weight of it hits me.

That *fucker.*

That fucking mother. *FUCKER.*

Anger boils in my blood like acid. This is beyond a prank now. He just destroyed an entire trajectory of my *life.*

I'm still sitting on the edge of my bed shaking with rage when Demi walks in with Giorgiana.

"Hey! We were—" Demi stops when she sees the deathly look on my face. "Oh, fuck, what happened?"

Slowly, I kick the letter under my bed with my heel. I turn to look at her.

"It was Alistair Black."

Demi's aware of the blue shower incident, obviously, being my roommate. And she guessed that it was somehow related to me being tapped for one of the four clubs. But I haven't told her more than that. Not even after I saw the fuckhead flip me off and grin, virtually bragging that it was him.

I don't know *why* I didn't tell her before—maybe because I've always viewed this rivalry, this prank war between me and Alistair, as just a private battle.

But he crossed a fucking line.

He crossed *way* over a line.

Demi frowns. "What?"

"The blue dye in the shower," I hiss quietly. "It was Alistair."

Both of my friends' mouths fall open.

"Alistair *Black* is the one who hit you with the blue dye?" Giorgiana chokes.

I nod.

"But… That means he was *in* here. Like, it means he broke into your fucking room."

Demi pales, looking around as she hugs herself. "That's fucking creepy."

"I have to tell you guys something."

It's like watching yourself driving toward a cliff, knowing you need to hit the brakes, screaming at yourself to stop, but ignoring your own pleas and driving right over that edge all the same.

I know it's a lie. I know it's supremely wrong, and well, *well* beyond the pale. If Alistair dying me blue was crossing a line, this is vaulting a mile past it.

But fuck him. He just ruined the Hamilton Foundation placement for me.

Demi looks concerned as she moves toward me. "How do you know?"

I shake my head, exhaling slowly. "Because I was here when he broke in."

It's the pebble that starts the avalanche. The one little lie that lights the fuse of an atom bomb.

"*What?!*" Demi blurts.

"You're joking!" Giorgiana gasps.

I shake my head again, hugging myself. "No joke. I was here, and I was getting changed. He..." I look away. "He saw me, and he tried to...you know."

Demi looks like she's going to be sick. "Oh my fucking *God*, Eloise!"

"I screamed," I lie, warming to my story. "I think that rattled him, because he told me not to tell anyone and left. I had no idea he'd already put the dye in the shower."

"Forget the fucking dye!" Giorgiana blurts. "He tried to rape you?"

Fuck.

"No," I shake my head decisively. "I don't…it wasn't like that. He was just, like, creeping on me. Watching me change."

"Oh my *God*, that's seriously fucked up," Demi chokes. "Jesus, Eloise, have you reported this?"

Oh, shit.

"No, it's…" I clear my throat. "I just want to forget about it."

Giorgiana stares at me. "E, you *have* to report that. I mean what if he does it again, to another girl? What if it's more than watching her change next time?"

"Guys, please," I try and backpedal, not confident anymore, wishing I could reverse time by two minutes. Jesus, why the fuck did I lie like this?

"Eloise, I know you're scared," Demi says. "But…I mean, I live here, too."

God, what have I done. She looks terrified.

"I want to respect your fears, but…" She bites her lip. "If you *don't* report this, I will. I have to."

In the end, my guilty conscience gets the best of me, and I don't report it.

Demi does, though.

A week later, when two other anonymous reports are made with a similar story, Alistair is put on academic probation as the school opens an investigation.

And suddenly, our prank battle has become an all-out war.

Present:

It's after midnight when I slip into the penthouse I share with Massimo. Guilt dogs my every single tip-toed step down the hall to my room, shutting the door quietly behind me.

It has *nothing* to do with what just happened with Alistair. It's not misguided guilt because I'm technically married to Massimo. In no way do I think of what I just did with Alistair as "cheating".

Cheating involves breaking a commitment and a promise. It involves betrayal.

There are none of those things in my marriage to the monster I share a home with. The man who married me against my will. Who doesn't touch me, and who threatens me all the fucking time. The man who fucks other women in front of me expressly to humiliate me, also against my will.

The man who's killed right in front of me.

No, what just happened with Alistair doesn't fill me with guilt. It makes me feel *alive* for the first time in a freaking decade.

The guilt is over what happened *after* the sex.

A few days ago, Massimo cornered me in the kitchen with more threats. He wanted updates on where his father's will was. But he *also* told me he wanted insider information on a big case Crown and Black is currently involved with, concerning a man named Roberto Chinellato. They're defending him on a murder and racketeering charge.

Again, what just happened with Alistair does *not* make me feel guilty.

...It's the part where Alistair went to the bathroom for a minute afterward and I noticed a file folder filled with documents pertaining to that case spilled across his office floor, having been knocked off the desk.

Documents that I quickly took a bunch of pictures of with my phone before Alistair came back, pulled me onto his lap on the sofa, and proceeded to fuck me again until I was shattering into a million pieces.

I crank the water in my shower extra hot before stepping inside. I wince, letting the heat scald me in penance for what I've just done.

The breaking of professional trust, not of my utterly bullshit, at-gunpoint marriage vows to a psychopath.

After a while, I turn off the water, stepping out of the steamy shower stall and reaching for a towel.

"You're home late."

I bite back a scream, whirling and yanking the towel over myself as I glare at Massimo. He's smiling coldly at me, leaning against the vanity in dress pants and a button up shirt, his arms folded over his chest as he leers at me.

My face burns as I grit my teeth, angered by his intrusion. I yank the towel tighter around myself, and even reach for a second one to drape around my shoulders as a nauseous feeling curls in my stomach.

"What the fuck are you doing in here?" I spit.

"Well, it *is* my house," he drawls. "And you *are* my wife."

"Don't."

He snorts, rolling his eyes. Then his cruel gaze drops to the marks on my neck, and a slow grin curls his too-thin lips.

"My my my, what a good little whore—"

"Shut up."

"Do you have anything for me? Anything to show for your whorish behavior?"

My eyes narrow. "You don't get to talk to me—"

I gasp, stumbling backward into the glass of the shower stall as Massimo surges into me. He grabs me by the throat, choking the air from my lungs as he leers into my face.

"I get to talk to you however the fuck I want, *wife*," he snarls. "And I'll ask you one more time: do you *have* anything for me."

I manage to swallow through his grip, nodding quickly.

"Show me."

When he lets go, fear has me racing over to my phone on the vanity. I bring up the pictures I took and show him.

"Mmm, good," Massimo murmurs, nodding as he scrolls through them. A ding tells me he just sent them to himself. "And the will?"

"I'm trying," I blurt, hugging the towels tighter.

"Try fucking harder," he snaps. "Or maybe I need to motivate you the way I motivate my whores."

Oh God.

Massimo reaches for his belt.

"Don't you fucking *dare* touch me," I hiss.

He starts to chuckle, shrugging casually. Then his hand drops from his belt.

"I could," he sneers. "I *could*. But I won't." He grins. "I enjoy torment much more." He wags a finger at me and starts to turn away. "Find that fucking will, Eloise."

"Why are you doing all this?!" I ask just as he gets to the bathroom door. "I mean getting me this job, making sure I work under Alistair, and—"

"And watching you shower after you *fuck him*?" he sneers with a grin that turns my stomach. Massimo shrugs. "Why does anyone play *any* game, my dear?" He winks before he turns and walks out of the bathroom.

"Because it's *fun*."

18

ALISTAIR

I've always thought that one of the reasons Club Venom is so popular—aside from the obvious—is that it stands on its own *without* the gratuitous T&A and public sex.

For instance, right now it's two in the afternoon, and I'm sitting in the stunning and exquisitely designed main lounge. During regular hours, this room is teeming with members in black and gold masks and various stages of undress, either watching or participating in some orgiastic entanglement.

But right now, hours before the guests arrive, you'd think you were in the private VIP lounge of the most exclusive hotel in New York.

Unmasked, given that the club's not open, I sit at a circular table near the middle of the room with Dante Sartorre and Drazen Krylov. Dante, my relatively new brother-in-law, is the founder, primary partner, and de facto king of Club Venom. And he looks the part, too—today he's in a dark three-piece suit that I'd bet is straight from Saville Row in London, and shoes I'd wager even more are custom made.

His penchant for high fashion makes sense. He comes from a family of tailors.

To his left at the table, Drazen cuts a slightly more fearsome figure. The man is fucking *huge*—almost as big as Kratos—with broad shoulders, a firm chest, arms that strain the sleeves of his suit jacket, and a towering height.

Once a bit of a warlord and gun-for-hire, the Serbian is now king of the newly re-formed Krylov Bratva. He's unfathomably wealthy, insanely powerful, possesses a seat at the Bratva High Council, and is near unhinged in his lethalness.

In other words: rich, dangerous, and more than a little nuts. So *obviously* he's a client of Crown and Black.

He's also a new major investor in Club Venom. And again, being how private this place is, it makes sense to have business meetings here.

Plus, Dante's selection of fine whiskies is *perfection*.

"The man you're going to have issues with is Ed Lee," I say, sitting back in my chair and sipping the Hibiki thirty-five year blended Japanese whisky in my glass, which is approaching orgasmic in how fucking good it is.

"Can he be bought?" Dante mutters, steepling his hands in front of his chiseled face.

"Well—"

"Or, if he doesn't care for carrots," Drazen growls, "would he respond well to the stick?"

I deal with a fair number of men you could classify as psychopaths, or sociopaths…violent nut jobs with a lust for power.

Drazen Krylov, although he dresses like a billionaire playboy these days, is another level altogether. I have zero idea which of his mythical origin stories is true, but none of them seems very happy. That he was a conscript in the Russian army. That he was a child soldier in the Yugoslav Wars. That his nickname was once "the headsman".

...Well, you get the idea.

I'm trying to find the most tactful way to remind Drazen of the legal ramifications of killing a city employee when Dante turns to his co-investor and fixes him with a look.

"*Easy*."

Drazen grins and lifts his shoulders eloquently. "What? I'm merely looking at all our options."

"Killing a New York City alderman is *not* an 'option'," Dante grunts.

"I'm not suggesting a public execution," Drazen sighs deeply. "But accidents happen..."

"Speaking as your attorney..." I growl, tapping my glass with a finger.

And as a sane person. Jesus.

"I'd suggest the carrot. If you want to expand Venom into the building next door that's for sale next door, that will involve blurring the lines on about a dozen different building codes. Ed Lee fancies himself a hero of the people. He'll make a big stink about the construction and the permits. But at the end of the day, he wants his taste same as everyone else. He just doesn't want to have to come out and ask for it. And when he *does* get that taste, he wants to get it in private."

Drazen rolls his eyes. "I'm just *saying*: brakes fail on cars all the time. Elevator cables snap." He shrugs. "Bullets fall through the backs of skulls. All purely acts of God."

I arch a brow at him as Dante shakes his head. Drazen grins at me and pats the table. "I'm joking, counselor. Relax." He swirls his drink. "So, he wants a bribe, he just doesn't want anyone involved to call it a bribe, is that it?"

"Pretty much," I nod. "He's on the board of a bunch of charities in this district. You contribute a sizable amount to two or three of those, and also see that he miraculously finds a new Porsche in his driveway, and I'll bet any expansion issues go away."

I want to give myself a pat on the back. Not for suggesting the obvious to arrive at a solution to a client's problem. But for making it through that entire conversation without my mind wandering to Eloise.

Well, at least not so much that I forget what the fuck we were talking about. Because that's been happening of late.

A lot.

After fucking Eloise in my office the other night, I half expected her to freeze me out again. No matter how fake, forced, hateful, and more importantly *unconsummated* her "marriage" is to Massimo, part of me wondered if she'd view what we did as cheating. Dirty. Something "bad" she needed to atone for and abstain from in future.

I would have lost that bet, badly.

Literally the morning after, Eloise walked into my office with an armful of files I hadn't asked for, shut the door, locked it, and proceeded to climb into my lap. I think the time between "door opening" and "my dick sliding into her dripping wet pussy" was *maybe* twenty-five seconds.

In the three days since then, I've fucked her no less than four times in the sub-basement stacks and once more in my office, fingered her in the legal library upstairs, and devoured her pussy in Conference Room B.

I'm not complaining.

But the downside to this sudden and full-scale addiction to Eloise is that the rest of my life seems to be having a hard time capturing even a fragment of my attention. I don't mean putting on mismatched socks or forgetting to rinse the shampoo out of my hair. I mean fumbling my fucking words *in court*. Forgetting to sign legal documents that are about to be officially filed—a mistake Katerina caught, thank fuck. I think I owe her about a month of paid vacation time for that.

So, yeah, making it through an entire meeting with these two without letting my mind drift to thoughts of pumping Eloise's pretty pussy full of my cum, or watching it drip down her ass, is impressive—

"Alistair? You with us?"

Mother. Fucker.

Okay, *almost* through an entire meeting.

I blink, refocusing on Dante. "Sure am. Just crunching some thoughts in my head. I'll have my assistant make a list of Lee's charities and forward them your way, along with my recommendations."

"Great, thanks," Dante nods. He looks past me, frowning slightly before a grin spreads over his mouth.

I sigh, rolling my eyes when I turn to see my sister Tempest strolling into the main lounge.

"Okay, one, I'm in a meeting, T," I sigh. "And two, I thought I was clear that I never *ever* needed to run into my own fucking sister at Venom."

She grins. "Relax, bro. The gangbang I signed up for doesn't go down until ten tonight. You've got plenty of time to avert—"

She gasps as Dante's hand possessively grabs her hip and yanks her down into his lap.

"As if that would *ever* be allowed to happen, *wife*."

He's smiling, but there's no mistaking the jealous glint in his eye. Yeah, Dante is one possessive bastard when it comes to my sister, which is something she loves to rile him up in him by purposefully targeting.

It works for them. I don't think I would have ever imagined someone would be willing to put up with Tempest's, well, *tempestuousness*. Turns out Dante's the man for the job.

"Whatcha doing here, T?" I ask.

She gives me a funny look. "You mean aside from the fact that my husband runs the joint?" She shrugs. "Not much. Just making sure my kneepads are in the glory-hole booth for later."

I cock a brow as I shake my head at her. "You're going to give Dante a fucking aneurysm with your shit, you know that?"

She grins, giggling as she turns to cup her husband's face and kiss him deeply. "He knows I'm just—"

"Keep it up, *wife*," Dante murmurs quietly, his eyes locked with hers, "and we'll see what happens."

She bites her lip. "Is that a promise?"

"Yeah, hi, *brother* sitting *right the fuck here*," I groan in a nauseated voice. Drazen roars with laughter as Dante shrugs.

"Alistair, when two people love each other very much, and they want to express that love in a physical—"

"Finish that fucking sentence and I'm going to knock you on your ass," I grunt. "Right after I vomit, that is."

"And why are we throwing up, exactly?"

Tempest laughs at the sound of Gabriel's voice behind me. "Well, the gang's all here."

"What is this, siblings' afternoon out?" Dante smirks.

"Yes, because a *sex club* is the perfect venue for that," Gabriel grunts, making a face. He turns serious as his gaze lands on me. "Can I talk to you for a minute?"

"You can talk to me for several minutes."

He raises a brow. "Alone?"

I turn back to Drazen and Dante. "Anything else we need to discuss with the expansion, gentlemen?"

"No, we're good," Dante nods. "Send over that list of Ed Lee's charities, and we'll get out our checkbooks."

"And I'll sharpen my stick collection, just in case," Drazen murmurs with a dangerous grin.

After finishing my drink, I stand and follow Gabriel to the far corner of the main lounge, next to one of the bars. It's not odd that he's come here in person to talk to me. Even when it's not open, Dante has a strict no cellphones policy throughout all of Club Venom once you're past the front doors, for security purposes. That's another reason it's such a great place for business meetings.

"What's going on?"

"I'm going to ask you something, and I'm going to be direct, because I have to be," he murmurs.

"O…kay?"

"What the fuck are you doing with Eloise?"

It's only my respect for my brother that stops me from outright lying to him. Instead, I just hold his gaze. Gabriel groans, looking away.

"For fuck's sake," he hisses darkly. "She's Massimo fucking Carveli's *wife*."

"I'm aware of that," I mutter back.

"*Are* you? Because this is beyond your usual devil-may-care bullshit, Alistair," he snaps. "This is a death wish."

"I know what I'm doing, Gabriel."

Such a lie.

"I'm going to go in your place to Massimo's thing tonight."

"*You* weren't invited," I fire back with a snarky smile.

Ostensibly, I was invited because I'm a name partner at the firm, and the cocktail party at his penthouse is, I gather, a who's-who of business associates of his.

Except neither Taylor nor my brother got an invitation. Just me.

"The invite is to the firm," Gabriel insists. "He just wants one of us there to show off to his mafia buddies."

"Funny," I smile as I slip my hand into my jacket and pull out the little white card with gold foil lettering on it. "Because it's specifically *my* name on the invitation."

Gabriel's jaw sets. "If there is *any* chance Massimo knows what you're up to with Eloise—"

"There isn't."

He gives me a look. "Can I take that as confirmation that you're currently involved with her?"

"That's leading the witness."

"Fuck you. Objection."

"Sustained. The defense rests."

Gabriel's lips curl even as he looks away and rolls his eyes.

I step closer to my brother and pat him on the shoulder. "I'll be *fine*, Gabriel."

Probably.

19

ELOISE

I FEEL SICK.

It's not the dress, which is slightly too tight. And it's not the several—I've lost count—glasses of champagne I've already knocked back.

It's the war going on inside my chest, twisting me up and leaving me gasping for air.

"What you've gathered so far is a good start, Eloise."

Guests have already started arriving for this disaster of a cocktail party Massimo has insisted on throwing. But I'm not playing hostess yet. Instead, I'm sitting down in Massimo's private home office with my husband and a man I've just been introduced to simply as Tony.

Tony is a lawyer, though not "officially" Massimo's attorney. He's more of a *strategist,* as he told me five minutes ago when Massimo dragged me in here.

"But we need more," Tony says casually to me, trying to smile like he's my friend.

Bullshit. He's my friend like Massimo is my soulmate.

But I know what this is now. Whatever Massimo is planning for the Roberto Chinellato case, Tony here is helping him plot it.

And *I'm* helping them execute it, however unwillingly.

I stare mutely at the evidence of my crimes spread across Massimo's desk in front of me. At what I've stolen from the Crown and Black offices. Printouts of photos I've taken are mingled with photocopies of other documents I've managed to steal, all related to the Chinellato case.

"Yeah, this is all great, Eloise," Tony murmurs, shifting his heavy-set bulk in the chair next to me. "But we just…*more*."

Across from us, Massimo glares at me, as if daring me to make him look bad in any way.

"Okay, but what specifically are you looking for?"

Tony clears his throat, glancing uncomfortably at Massimo.

"Thanks for your time tonight, Tony," my husband growls, still glaring at me. "Are you staying for the party?"

"Afraid not, Mr. Carveli," Tony wheezes as he pulls his weight out of the chair and reaches across the desk to shake my husband's hand. He gives Massimo a significant look. "If she can get…what we need…we can move forward."

"It'll happen," Massimo grunts. "Just make sure we're bullet-proof. We only get one shot at this."

I stand as Tony exits the office, then linger behind. Massimo glances at his watch. "Okay, time to get back. I need your ass out there smiling for our guests. I think there's probably enough champagne out there to wipe the scowl off even your face."

I purse my lips, glaring at him.

"What are you planning?"

I'm *so* fucking sick of being involved in this. I know Alistair and I aren't anything more than two people who can make each other feel good physically. I know this isn't what it once almost was. But still, the toxic guilt I feel burning a hole through my consciousness every time I even *look* at Alistair is starting to break me.

Massimo smirks. "Don't worry about it."

"I think I need to worry about it, given that I'm part of it."

His eyes glint. "Just keep your eyes open at Crown and Black, and your fucking mouth shut."

"If I get caught—"

"Don't," he mutters.

"But if I *do*?" I spit. "What happens to your little plan then?" My eyes narrow on him. "What's to stop me telling them who put me up to—"

"I wonder if it's too late to invite your sister to tonight's party."

I go cold instantly as Massimo smiles dangerously at me, his lips curling viciously.

"Maybe I should go over there and *personally* invite her."

"You stay the fuck away from—"

I gasp as he surges around to my side of the desk. His hand grabs me by the throat, hard, choking me as fear explodes through my chest.

"Do as I fucking ask, *when* I ask it, *without* any fucking attitude," he hisses coldly, "and I will." His face darkens. "But cross me, bitch," he snarls, "and I'll duct-tape your eyelids open and make you watch what I do to Camille. Do we understand each other?"

"Yes," I choke out.

I'm still unbelievably furious with my sister over the lie she told me ten years ago about Alistair. And she might be insane, and toxic as fuck...

But she's still my sister.

"Now, go out to our fucking party," he snarls. "Smile at our fucking guests, and try not to fucking black out. Think you can handle that?"

I don't say anything. Eventually, Massimo's grip drops from my neck.

"Let's go."

He ushers me out of the office and down the hall to the waiting guests mingling in the large living area of the gaudy penthouse. Massimo instantly turns on the charm, going into "king greeting his subjects" mode as he grabs a drink from a passing waiter's tray.

I grab a flute of Champagne from another passed tray, slugging back half of it before slinking back into the shadows, out of the spotlight.

Originally I had no idea why Massimo was throwing this party. But the reason becomes more and more obvious the longer I take in the guests mingling around.

Massimo's rise to the top of the Carveli family wasn't exactly a smooth one. I don't know all the details, and I never actually knew Luca Carveli. But I do know that Massimo and his father weren't exactly on good terms when Luca died. The cause of death is still debatable, depending on who you ask.

Obviously, this sparked more than a few questions about Massimo's *involvement* with his father's demise. From what I've heard, any such questions from *inside* the Carveli organization were squashed—violently—once Massimo became king. But that hasn't stopped the murmurings about his legitimacy that come from outside.

The five biggest Italian mafia families in the United States, including the Carveli organization, form "The Commission": a round table forum for those families to have open communication and keep the peace between themselves. A rising tide lifts all ships, and all that.

From what I understand, that's where some of the whispers about Massimo and the legitimacy of his claim to the Carveli throne are coming from—specifically, from the older heads of the families, who did business with Luca.

I glance around the party, mentally ticking off who I see. There's Michael Genovisi, the Don of the Scaliami family. I also spot Carmine and Nico Barone, the two sons of Don Vito Barone. I *don't* see Luciano Amato or Cesare Marchetti. A lightbulb goes on in my head.

The Amato and Marchetti families have, I've heard, been the loudest voicing their suspicions of Massimo's claim to the empire. The Barone and Scaliami families, however, have been a bit more...receptive.

He's shoring up his allies.

It makes even more sense as I watch Massimo the asshole utterly *oiling* his way around the room, especially when he gets to the Barone brothers and Don Genovisi.

Slowly, I slip back down the dim hallway, away from the party. For one, because I have zero interest in being a part of Massimo's *Game of Thrones: The Mafia Edition*. But also, because he's so firmly occupied with glad-handing his guests...

...He's *not* watching me.

Quickly, I slip down the hallway, around the corner, and back into Massimo's office. Closing the door behind me, I move to his desk and pull out the file folder full of all the papers I've stolen from Crown and Black, paging through my guilt.

"Do you have a death wish?"

I jolt, gasping sharply as I whirl, white-faced. Alistair's brow is deeply furrowed as he shuts the door silently behind him and leans against it.

Goddammit, he looks good. I mean Alistair always looks good in a suit. In the tuxedo he's wearing, given that this party is black tie?

Pure. Sin.

I don't realize I'm staring at him like a tiger staring at meat until he clears his throat pointedly. I drag my gaze up to his piercing blue eyes.

Alistair's frown deepens. "What the fuck are you doing, Eloise?"

My face scrunches up. "What? I'm allowed to get away from a party I have no interest in—"

"You know what I'm talking about."

My heart sinks.

Fuck. This is it.

I've pictured this scenario before, almost every time I was in some filing cabinet I wasn't supposed to be in at Crown and Black. Every time I photographed a confidential legal document for Massimo.

What if you get caught?

That's kept me up more nights than I care to admit. And now, here I am, living the nightmare, caught red-handed with—

"Look, I can appreciate what you're trying to do," he mutters, his voice slightly softer now.

Wait, what?

"I-I'm sorry?"

He sighs, giving me a look. "Eloise, I know that Massimo is tight with Roberto Chinellato."

I blink. "I…he's…"

Alistair shrugs. "He's asked Taylor, Gabriel, and me about a hundred times *each* how the case is going, and if there's anything he can do to assist with it. I mean, I doubt they're friends, but I assume they have business together."

"He…yeah," I mumble. "They do."

"I also know there was all sorts of bad blood between Massimo and Federico Lombardi."

Federico Lombardi is the guy who was murdered, allegedly by Roberto Chinellato. It's why the alibi that puts Roberto nowhere *near* Federico when he was killed is so important. The racketeering charges rest on the murder charge. If there's no murder charge, the whole case falls apart.

"Alistair—"

"I understand," he growls. "Massimo almost certainly has dirt on Federico, and you want something that puts even more distance between him and Roberto to help with the case." He studies me. "But this is *not* how you do it."

I stare at him. He thinks I'm *helping* him right now?

I wince as something twists painfully in my chest.

"There's a process, Eloise, you know that. When you don't follow it, whatever evidence you introduce becomes inadmissible. Worst case, it results in a mistrial," he continues. "So whatever you've just found there"…he nods past me to the stack of purloined evidence I'm hiding behind my back… "just put it the fuck back. Trust me."

"Alistair…"

I want to tell him. I need to tell him. I *have* to tell him.

…I don't.

Because I'm a coward.

Instead, swallowing the lump in my throat, I turn, shove everything back into the file folder, and slip it back into the drawer where I found it. Then I turn, sitting against my hands as I lean against the edge of Massimo's desk, facing Alistair.

"I'm shocked," I deadpan. "Since when are you the good guy?"

He smiles darkly. "What would ever suggest to you that I'm the good guy."

"What you literally just came in here to stop me from doing."

Slowly, he steps toward me.

"Except that's not why I came in here."

"It isn't?"

My face burns at the squeak in my voice. Alistair keeps moving closer, his eyes never leaving mine as he starts shrugging off his jacket.

Heat pools in my core and my thighs clench as my nipples harden against the shimmery silk of the black and silver cocktail dress.

"W-what…" I stutter, my skin prickling as Alistair drapes his jacket over the back of the couch and takes another step toward me. "What are you—"

"I'm not the good guy, Eloise," he murmurs quietly as he stops right in front of me. The spicy-clean scent of him washes over me. The heat of his body teases against mine. And the way he rolls his sleeves up to mid-forearm…

I mean, Jesus Christ.

"The good guy doesn't get another man's wife alone at a party with every intention of fucking her until she comes all over his cock."

20

ELOISE

My mouth falls open as heat explodes in my cheeks.

"Alistair—"

I whimper as he looms over me, his lips brushing mine as his mouth slips to my cheek. I can feel his breath in my ear as his hand slides sensually over my hip, pulling me against his rock-hard body and the obscenely fat bulge in his pants.

"Massimo is setting up a high stakes poker game out there," he growls quietly. "He wants me at the table, and he'll be looking for you soon."

I shudder. "Then I should go—"

My breath catches sharply as Alistair's hand slips behind me and grabs my ass possessively. Heat throbs in my core as my body trembles.

"There's a scene in *Casino Royale,* when Bond tells Vesper to come to the poker game at a certain time, because he wants the table to be distracted by her beauty."

I swallow. "Is that what you want me to do?"

"No, *princess*," he growls. "I want you to walk in at a certain time *with my cum filling your panties and drying on your fucking skin*, so that when I look at you while I'm sitting across the table from Massimo, I'll remember that I've already beaten him."

It's outrageously hot. But at the same time, it gives me pause.

"Is that what this is?" I whisper. "I'm just a prize you get for *beating* Massimo—"

"You're not *just* anything, Eloise," Alistair hisses as his teeth rake down my neck. He nips at my earlobe, making me moan sharply. "You're the whole fucking deal."

He bites down on my ear again, making me yelp as heat and lust gather in my core. He cups my breast and drags his mouth up my jaw to my lips. He kisses me deeply, making me whimper as he pinches my nipple through my dress.

And I come *alive*.

My hands are suddenly all over him, desperately yanking at his shirt and kissing him eagerly as I melt against him. His shirt opens, and my pulse thuds in my ears as I slide my fingers over his bare skin, my fingertips tracing his muscles and his tattoos.

He suddenly spins me, pinning me to the edge of the desk and yanking my dress up over my hips. He grabs my ass possessively as he reaches up to pull the top of my dress down, letting my breasts spill out. He swats my ass hard with his palm, making me yelp in pleasure and need as I squirm back against him.

"You still think I'm the good guy, Eloise?" he growls as he yanks his pants open. I whimper as I feel him pull his big, thick cock free, letting it slap heavily against my ass.

"Is that what has your greedy little pussy so fucking wet for me?"

I moan as he cups me through my soaked panties, his finger rubbing up and down my seam as my legs start to shake.

"Because you think I'm *the good guy?*"

"*No,*" I choke.

"You're not under some mistaken impression that you're a good *girl*, are you?"

"*Alistair,*" I moan, my back arching as I desperately push back, needing more of his touch. *Fuck,* it's like a craving I can't ever sate. Like an itch that I keep scratching, but it keeps coming back, and he's the only one who can reach it anyway.

"Because I'm not a good guy, Eloise. And you are definitely *not* a good girl."

I yelp again as he spanks my ass with hard, deliberate swats. A moan rips from my throat as he sends electric sparks through one cheek, then the other, then back to the first until my ass is on fire.

My back arches again as he grabs my soaked panties and yanks them down to mid-thigh.

"Because a good girl, Eloise," he murmurs, bending over me. He grabs my hair in a fist, pulling it to the side so that his lips can brush my ear. "*Doesn't bend over her husband's desk like a greedy little slut, begging another man to give her the fucking she needs.*"

Holy shit.

"Is that what you need, princess?" he rasps into my ear. I shudder when his hand slips up my inner thigh and cups my bare pussy. "To get *fucked* like you need?"

He strokes a finger through my lips, collecting my wetness before dancing closer to my clit. He rubs it in slow, deliberate circles, and my jaw falls open when he sinks two fingers deep into my pussy.

"Please—"

"Show me how bad you want it, *princess.*"

His hands slip from between my legs. I turn instantly, sinking to my knees in front of him. I look up at his clenched jaw and piercing blue eyes, my panties down and my dress still hiked up around my waist.

I wrap my small hand around Alistair's massive, throbbing cock. My pulse skips and my core clenches tightly as I slowly stroke the hot velvety skin over the rock-hard iron underneath.

I wet my lips with my tongue and then raise up and forward to kiss the swollen crown of his cock. Alistair groans. I moan myself when he grabs a fistful of my hair.

"Open your mouth, baby girl."

Fuck.

I do as he says, opening my mouth as wide as I can as he guides himself over my pouty lips. I drink in the way he hisses in pleasure as they close around him, and the thrill of tonguing his head as he tenses up is like the purest crack cocaine.

Alistair grunts as his grip on my hair tightens. His jaw grinds as he rocks his hips, shallowly fucking my mouth as my pussy starts to leak down my thighs.

"Good girls don't get on their knees and let their bosses fuck their bratty mouths."

I slurp wetly and loudly on him before I pull away with a lick.

"What makes you think I'm a good girl?"

"I don't."

"You want me to be your bad girl, *sir*?" I purr, looking at him with big, innocent eyes and pouty lips as I lean up to plant a kiss on the swollen head.

Alistair suddenly snaps, yanking me up off my knees and slamming me against the desk.

"You already fucking *are*."

He spins me around and cups my pussy again. His fingers roll my clit as he sinks his thumb into me and drops to his knees. I yelp and moan when he spanks my ass once again, making the tender skin explode with heat before soothing it with his mouth.

His lips and tongue drag all over my ass, moving lower, until suddenly my eyes go wide when his tongue lands on my puckered little hole.

"Oh *God*..."

"It's not God's tongue in your ass that's going to make you come for me, princess," he growls. "It's fucking *mine*."

No preamble. He doesn't "tease" my ass. He plants the tip against my hole and starts to snake it right in.

And my world. Fucking. *Melts.*

It's so fucking sinful and dirty—so fucking *wrong*. But then, all of this is. All of "us"—whatever "we" are—is.

Maybe that's actually what I'm addicted to. Maybe it's the filthy, "wrong" thrill that makes me not just forget the past, but also not care about it. What draws me to this man like a moth to a flame.

It's what has me burning for him, arching my back, and whining for more as he tongues my ass, fingers my pussy, and rolls my clit.

Alistair groans into me, the rumbling sound of his need for me sending me higher and higher as his mouth and his hands move all over me. His tongue swirls, and I choke back a silent scream as I feel my core begin to clench.

"Alistair…"

His palm comes down on my ass with hard spank just as he pinches my clit. I twist my head, biting down hard on my forearm to muffle my screams as the final trigger pulls. I choke, writhing and twisting under his tongue and his fingers as I start to come.

Alistair stands behind me, spreads my thighs with his knee, and centers his huge, swollen dick against my eager slit.

"Fuck me," I pant, whimpering as I cling to the desk, waiting for him to slide in.

Alistair just chuckles darkly.

"Uh-uh," he growls quietly. "Bad girls don't get fucked."

He leans over me, wrapping my hair around his hand as his lips brush my ear.

"Bad girls *do the fucking*."

Holy shit.

"You want this cock, princess?" he growls again. "Then show me how well you can fuck it."

Every inch of my skin tingles. Every nerve ending throbs. I can feel his thick head spreading my lips, hovering *right there* at my opening.

I start to push back, moaning as I impale myself on his fat cock. Christ, he's so fucking big, and I can feel myself stretching open for him as I push back onto inch after thick inch.

Alistair stays perfectly still, gripping my hair with one hand and guiding my hips with the other.

"*There* we go," he groans. "Such a pretty, filthy, eager little slut, taking every inch of my fat cock."

I start to moan louder, whimpering with need as I keep pushing back. Goddamn, there's *still* more of him—there's no end to his cock, even when it feels like he's filling me to my absolute limit.

For a second, I pause, my breath catching, my pulse thudding, my toes curling as my legs quiver.

"Oh, I know you can take more than that, princess," Alistair growls darkly.

My teeth grit and a tremor of heat ripples down my spine.

Yes, I can. I'm desperate to.

I push back, shrieking in pleasure as I sink the last inch and a half down onto his huge dick and feel his balls against my clit.

"*That's* a good girl," he groans, gripping my hair and my hip tightly.

I pull forward, feeling my pussy cling to his thickness wetly as I drag back off almost every inch of him. When I can feel his head about to pop out of me, I push back with a cry of pleasure until I can feel my ass against his abs again.

"*Fuck yes, more,*" he rasps, his cock swelling even thicker in me as I start to ride him. He tugs my hair sharply, sending tiny explosions through my nerve endings that only spur me on. I thrust back harder, choking as I sink down on every fucking inch of him. Then again, and again.

And again.

Alistair grunts, spanking my ass as I squeal in pleasure and bounce on his cock. My whines and moans grow louder and louder, until suddenly he reaches up and clamps his free hand over my mouth as his other one pulls my hair.

That's when the brakes fall off. That's when I lose all control, all sense of sanity, and all grip on reality as I start to thrust back onto his cock like I'm a woman possessed.

Over and over, I can feel myself taking every thick inch of him on the back thrust, and then grip every slick, swollen, veined inch of him on the reverse. My ass smacks against his rock-hard abs and chiseled hip V, his heavy balls slapping my clit with every thrust.

"*Faster,* princess. I want to see how much you *need* that fucking cock," he hisses.

My eyes roll back. My mouth goes slack under his clamped hand as I throw my ass back against him over and over, fucking and fucking and fucking his huge, perfect cock until my world begins to shatter at the edges.

With a choked cry, my nipples dragging across the wood of the desk beneath me and my hips bruising against the edge of it, I slam back onto every inch of him as I *explode*.

I scream into his hand as my pussy clamps down tight around him. My body spasms and jerks, writhing and twisting on his cock as my toes curl in my high heels.

Alistair groans, rocking his hips tight against me. His cock swells thick inside of me and starts to pulse, pumping his hot cum deep inside me as I come around him.

With a grunt, he pulls out, and I whimper as I feel the last hot ropes of his release splatter on my ass, my stretched pussy, and my thighs.

I'm shaking as he pulls me up, slowly turns me, and lifts my chin. His eyes burn into mine as his mouth closes the distance, kissing me and sucking the very air from my lungs as I cling to him.

"We have a small problem."

I tense, my heart skipping. "Was I too loud?"

He smirks. "No. I can't go out there and sit at that poker table smelling like your sweet pussy."

A tremor teases up my spine.

"Oh?" I blush deeper, biting my lip as our eyes lock. "Should I…do something about that?" I purr.

"I think a *really* good girl would clean her cum off of my cock, just to be safe."

Fuck, the way this man carves his way into the darkest, dirtiest, sluttiest parts of me and just…*lives there*, rent-free.

I drop to my knees again. I open my mouth, dragging my tongue up the underside of his still-hard dick. Alistair groans, his muscles flexing and his hand slipping into my hair as I tongue his cock—up one side, then down the other, eagerly tasting myself on him.

I tease my tongue over the slit in the tip, tasting the drop of cum that beads out of it. My lips part, and before I know it, I'm taking his cock into the back of my throat.

"*Fuck*," he groans, his hand tightening in my hair. I moan around him, lost in my own need for *more* as I hum and suck on his swollen dick. My cheeks hollow and my lips tighten around him as I bob up and down, stroking what I can't fit in my mouth.

Alistair's abs clench. His eyes spark with lust as they lock with mine, watching me inhaling his cock and tonguing the underside.

He chokes out a groan, his muscles clench, and I feel his swollen dick pulse in my mouth. I whimper, swallowing eagerly as his warm cum floods my tongue. I can feel it leaking out the corners of my lips, a single drop trickling down my chin to drip onto my breast.

With a gasp, I pull off him, lost in a haze of desire as I squeeze my breasts and pinch my nipples.

I suddenly blush as reality catches up to me and I realize how unbelievably slutty I must look. But Alistair just holds my gaze unblinkingly as he shakes his head, smiling, and pulls me to my feet.

"You're fucking perfection, princess," he murmurs softly, tilting my chin up as his lips descend. "*Such a good girl.*"

God, does that make something warm flood through every single part of me. When he kisses me, completely heedless and uncaring of the fact that he just came in my mouth, I moan as I sink against him.

Suddenly, I stiffen. "We need to get back out there."

His brow furrows. "Shit. Yes."

We both start to fix our clothes. I make to walk over to the bar cart in the corner, where there's a stack of cocktail napkins. But Alistair guesses my intention, and stops me with a tug on my wrist.

"Uh-uh," he growls, reaching down and pulling my panties up for me, tugging them tight against the sticky wet cum coating my thighs and between them. "Remember," he murmurs into my ear, "when you walk into that poker game, I want to look at you and know my cum is still marking your skin." His eyes flicker. "I want to look at you and know how fucking *mine* you are."

How fucking MINE you are.

Ten minutes later, after Alistair has already rejoined the party, I descend from the second level, having taken a back staircase up to avoid suspicion. The glowy, fluttery feeling in my stomach persists as I start down the stairs into the main living area.

There's a big poker table set up in the middle of the floor, with a crowd circling the players—including both Massimo and Alistair—sitting at it.

"Ahh, *there* she is!"

Massimo turns to grin at me as I walk down the stairs. Every eye in the room is on me as well, and I am suddenly *hyper* aware of the fact that I've got Alistair's cum soaking into my panties and still on my tongue.

It's both exhilarating and terrifying.

"The game, gentlemen, is Texas Hold 'Em," Massimo says.

I come to a stop at the bottom of the staircase, my pulse quick as it thumps in my ears. Massimo turns and nods at the dealer, who starts to shuffle the cards.

"And *now* we can start playing."

"Finally!" Carmine Barone, who's also sitting at the poker table, crows.

"Patience, my friend," Massimo grins. He clears his throat and takes a sip of his drink, drumming his fingers on the felt table next to his cards. "This will be one hand, winner take all. *But,*" he adds sharply when some of the players start to look confused, "this particular hand will be worth it, I can assure you."

"Oh yeah?" Carmine chuckles as Alistair's brow furrows, his eyes darting to mine. "Why's that?"

"Because I'm going to sweeten the pot," Massimo murmurs in strange, slightly edged voice that scares me.

Don Genovisi, also at the table, chuckles. "I have it on good authority that you just picked up a vintage Aston Martin, Massimo." He smirks. "You sweetening the pot with the keys and title to that?"

There's a round of chuckles and laughter from the other players and surrounding crowd.

Massimo just smiles chillingly.

"Oh, I can do better than a car, Michael."

I stiffen, a cold premonition washing over me as his eyes swivel to lock onto me.

"The winner of this hand gets *my wife*."

21

ALISTAIR

The whole party instantly falls silent. Then come the nervous titters and half-smiles, as if everyone is trying to figure out if Massimo is joking or not.

I know by the cruel way he's smiling at Eloise that he's not.

At. All.

My eyes snap to her. She also understands, probably better than anyone here, just how serious Massimo is. And I don't get the sense that allowing some other man to "win" his wife is any sort of kink of his.

This isn't about him at all. It's about hurting Eloise. Because he's a bastard.

My hands close to two white-knuckled fists on the green felt table in front of me. Across from me, Don Genovisi glances curiously at our host.

"What's this about, Massimo?"

Massimo grins savagely as he spreads his arms. "I know some of you have doubted my abilities to lead as my father did. Let this convince you that I am *twice* the leader he was. Let this show that I am perfectly happy to do *anything at all* for those who call themselves my friends and allies."

He turns to level a withering gaze at Eloise, who's gone white and is utterly silent.

"*Anything*," Massimo growls. "And let me assure you, I'm quite serious: the man who wins this hand gets a night with my dear wife. And *nothing* is off the table."

I can see protests already forming on the lips of some of the players at the table. These might be hardened men who live lives of crime. But everyone has limits, and this is *clearly* beyond the pale for most of them.

"Isn't that right, *dear*?" Massimo smiles as he stands, knocks back the rest of his drink, and walks around the table to Eloise. Ice-cold lethality burns in my veins as he yanks her to him and dips his mouth to her ear.

Instantly, her eyes bulge. Whatever color was left in her face drains away as she trembles.

I'm going to fucking kill him.

I'm beginning to stand before I even realize it. Suddenly, there's a hand on my arm. I glance to my left, to where Carmine Barone is sitting next to me. He doesn't say anything, but he gives me a knowing look as he shakes his head almost imperceptibly.

He turns to his right, as if looking for something in his jacket pocket draped over the back of his chair. He uses the motion to lean into me slightly and whisper.

"Half the men in this room are his soldiers. Unless you have a death wish, let whatever this is go. Trust. Me."

I don't respond verbally, but my jaw clenches tightly as I sit back down and turn to glare death at Massimo.

"I'll ask you again—isn't that right, *wife*," he says loud enough for the whole room to hear.

Eloise smiles a weak, sickly smile.

"*Yes*," she mumbles awkwardly. "That's right."

Massimo chuckles, turning to grin wickedly at his guests.

"You heard it from the horse's mouth. One night, anything goes. Now, shall we play?"

He cracks his knuckles and strolls back to his seat.

Motherfucker. Whatever he's just threatened her with, it's working. Because instead of screaming, or running away, or telling Massimo to go fuck himself and that there's no way she's participating in this sick game, Eloise is just standing there.

Slowly, my pulse thudding hotly, I swivel my eyes around the poker table. There's me and then Carmine Barone, who seems to understand that there's more than meets the eye between Eloise and me, but is for some reason not saying anything about it. Going around the table, there's a man I think I know as Sammy "The Hatchet" DiFresno, Frankie Paciano, who runs one of the tribute families to the Barone empire, then the dealer, then Don Michael Genovisi, then a grim older guy all in black who I don't recognize, Massimo himself, and lastly a guy who I believe is an underboss in the less powerful Abato family.

"Come on!" Massimo grins as he raps the poker table in front of him. "Let's play!"

I clear my throat, turning to him. "Massimo, what is this?"

"This, *counselor*," he shrugs, "is how I have fun. You don't have a problem with that, do you?"

In fact, I have a *giant* fucking problem with that. But I'm also not suicidal, and falling on my sword right now wouldn't help Eloise anyway.

There's one way out of this: play, and *win*.

"This is how the big boys have fun, counselor," Massimo chuckles.

Across from me, Don Genovisi suddenly turns to level a hard gaze at Eloise.

"*Mrs.* Carveli does not seem to be enthused with this game, Massimo," he growls.

"I think I know my wife better than any other man here, *Michael*," Massimo tosses back.

Don Genovisi shrugs and stands from the table. "Maybe so, but this isn't a game for me."

Massimo snorts. "What, because you're married?"

"Because I'm not an *animal*," he fires back coldly. He straightens his jacket. "Thank you for the party tonight, Massimo. I think it's time I left."

He nods to his number two, Vincent Cave, standing behind him. The two of them and the small contingent of Scaliami men peel away and make their way to the door. Michael begins to take a step toward Eloise with a concerned look on his face.

"Leave, or *sit,* Michael," Massimo barks. "Do *not* presume to talk to my wife."

Michael shoots Eloise one more long, worried look. Then he turns to leave with the rest of his men.

Massimo sighs. "Well, that cuts the pussy out. Are the rest of *the men* ready to play for keeps?"

Every other guy at the table smiles wolfishly and nods.

"How about you, *Mr. Black,*" Massimo grins, turning to level a piercing gaze at me. "I doubt this is how they play in law school. Think you can keep up?"

I have to play, and I have to win.

There's no other option here.

"I think you might not wish to be so quick to assume the fortitude of men you're playing poker with, for these kinds of stakes, before you know how they play, Mr. Carveli."

That gets a round of hoots and chuckles from the crowd. Massimo smiles mirthlessly at me with malice in his eyes.

"So be it, Alistair," he growls quietly.

The dealer begins to distribute the cards. I feel another tap on my arm as Carmine Barone leans close while pulling a pack of cigarettes from his jacket pocket.

"Your reputation at the poker table precedes you, counselor," he mutters under his breath. "You do you. I can run interference."

I turn to arch a quizzical brow at him, but he's already pointedly looking away.

Interesting. He's not the ally I would have expected, but I'm not going to say no to any help right now.

The dealer reminds us that this is Texas Hold 'Em as he reveals the flop. My eyes are squarely on Eloise.

Hers are squarely on mine.

We both know the stakes right now.

Slowly, the game unfolds. Given that this is a single hand game, Massimo and the dealer have announced there are no limits on raises. And so slowly, the pot goes up. And up. And up.

I'm playing my pocket pair of sevens as best I can. The flop doesn't help me, nor does the turn. But when the dealer flips the river, my pulse skips.

Suddenly, I've got triple sevens.

I'm distracted, obviously, by Eloise. I keep looking at her, even if I know how dangerous a move that is right now. But I can't help myself. She looks horrified with every raised bet, and ill every time one of the other men at the table turns to eye her up, or makes a laughing comment about taking what belongs to Massimo.

It takes everything I have not to explode.

Slowly, players begin to drop out. The guy to my right—the underboss from the Abato family—folds first. Next, it's not lost on me how Carmine purposely drives Sammy "The Hatchet" DiFresno past his comfort zone, constantly egging him on until Sammy too taps out. He shoots Carmine a dark, vicious glare before he abruptly stands from the table and storms over to the bar.

The guy all in black is next to fold. Frankie Paciano keeps a strong face going, and he goes *way* past my usual comfort zone. But this time, there *is* no comfort zone.

This is win or lose everything.

Eventually he folds, too. Then, it's just Massimo, Carmine, and me. And Massimo is looking a little more nervous than when the hand started.

The dealer announces a quick break, and we all get up to grab drinks or hit the bathroom. I resist the urge to walk over to Eloise and instead make my way to where Massimo is slugging back a whiskey at the bar.

"Mr. Carveli," I mutter quietly, "I think perhaps this has gone on long enough, don't you?"

He turns to sneer at me. "I thought you had more balls than that, Mr. Black."

I smile as politely as I can. "Massimo, this is your wife we're talking about. I think the game is over."

"It's over when I fucking *say* it's over," he snarls. He turns and claps his hands. "Back to the table! We're finishing this."

When we sit again, the raises continue for two more rounds. Five minutes later, we hit a breaking point. Massimo gulps down his drink, slams his glass angrily on the table, and then clears his throat.

"We're done."

Thank God.

"Show 'em."

What the *fuck*. He's not ending the game? He's saying he actually wants us to show our cards to find out who *wins*?

"Massimo—"

"Show your fucking cards!" he bellows.

I glance at my triple sevens. It's not the world's strongest poker hand. But it's not terrible.

Unless he has better.

Next to me, Carmine sighs. "Fuck."

He flips his cards, showing *nothing*.

"Nice bluff," I mutter pointedly at him.

He arches a brow. "You're welcome." He leans in and lowers his voice as he grabs his jacket. *"I might ask you to return the favor one day."*

Massimo flips his cards triumphantly, showing a pair of aces.

"Pocket rockets. And *that*, counselor," he grins, "is how you—"

I drop my cards on the table. The room goes silent for a second before it explodes with shocked hoots and catcalls.

Triple sevens beat a pair of aces.

I just won.

Men clap me on the back. Some say vile, disgusting shit involving Eloise that makes me want to punch their fucking teeth down their throats. But I just stand calmly. My eyes find Eloise's in the crowd, and I dip my chin as she silently mouths "thank you" to me with relief on her face.

"So, you win, huh?"

I turn to see Massimo stand from his chair and slowly approach, looking at me coldly.

"Massimo—"

"You want to fuck my wife?"

The catcalls stop abruptly. The whole damn room turns chilly as Massimo comes to a stop in front of me.

"Is that it, counselor?" he growls quietly. "You want to fuck her?"

I smile one of my professional, disarming smiles at him. "Take it easy, friend. We're just playing cards—"

"Take it easy?!"

He barks the words, sending a ripple of nervous looks through the onlookers. Massimo starts to laugh.

"*Take it easy,* he says!" he chuckles. "While he plays to *fuck my wife*!!?"

You could hear a fucking pin drop with how deathly silent the room goes. Massimo gets right in my face, uncomfortably close, as his eyes stab into mine with a manic, psychotic glint to them.

Suddenly, he starts to *laugh.*

He grins, guffawing loudly and boisterously as he steps back and whirls, laughing at the guests until the laughter starts to spread nervously.

"I'm joking, counselor!" he barks, still laughing as he turns to me and claps me on the shoulder. "I'm just fucking with you, Alistair!"

Holy *Christ.*

The man is a lunatic.

But the entire room is laughing now. The tension is fading.

"You're such a fucking asshole."

Massimo turns just in time for Eloise to slap his face, whirl, and storm out of the penthouse. The laughter starts to die down again, but Massimo grins and shrugs, getting the good times rolling again.

"Drinks for everyone!" he crows. Everyone's heading to the bar as he turns to smile icily at me. "This is how I joke, counselor."

I incline my head. "Hilarious, Mr. Carveli," I deadpan.

He grins a manic, twisted smile as he steps closer to me, his eyes piercing into mine. "A *joke,* yes?"

"Of course."

"Because you're not *actually* trying to fuck my wife, right?" he says in a monotone, his smile utterly gone.

"No."

Trying? No.

I already am.

22

ELOISE

Ten years ago:

I KNEW this was a bad idea.

The second I see him, I disappear back into the crowd. Music thuds from the big speakers near where the DJ is set up in the kitchen as I push my way through the partygoers, away from the front door.

Where *he* just walked in.

I haven't seen Alistair since the charges were dropped. I've been working extremely hard to make *sure* I don't. I mean, blue dye in his water bottle got him mad enough to break into my dorm room and dye my freaking shower.

I can't *imagine* what the fallout might be from a false sexual assault allegation that was investigated by both the police and the school administration.

And I *know* he knows that's because of me.

Demi might have made the actual report. But I'm the source of the lies, and there's zero chance Alistair doesn't know that. Especially after the investigation into the other accusations revealed that they were bullshit.

There *were* no other girls accusing him of trying to assault them in their dorm rooms. I suspected that from the get-go, but had confirmation a week or so into the investigation, when I went to The Order's on-campus mansion and a snickering Ansel gleefully explained that *he'd* filed the other two reports anonymously as a way to "prank" Alistair.

Pranks are funny, though. There was *nothing* funny about the fallout from my lies.

The police came to campus and literally took him down to the station in town. He was suspended from all his classes. The law schools he was considering for after Knightsblood started calling, saying they'd be passing on his applications "in light of the allegations against him".

Luckily, in the past two weeks, the investigation has exonerated him. I think it helped that I went directly to the Dean of Students and pleaded my case, telling him that in fact I'd *invited* Alistair to my dorm room. And that later, after we'd had a fight, I'd embellished my story.

The only reason *I'm* not on probation now, or straight up kicked out of Knightsblood, is that Dean Garnier is an old friend of my father's.

Papa isn't very happy with me, of course. Neither is the school. And I imagine Alistair is *furious*.

My little stunt almost ruined his life.

So instead, I slip through the party until I find the sliding door out to the balcony, where the alcohol is being kept. On paper, the consumption of alcohol is forbidden on the Knightsblood campus. The mansions that house the four clubs get a complete pass on that, of course. As long as things don't get completely out of hand, the school usually turns a blind eye to other parties as well.

Tonight's festivities are taking place in "The Penthouse", a suite housing five senior students at the top of Worthington Tower, a dorm which at twenty stories is the tallest building on campus by far. Because of the views and the way it rises above the rest of the campus, "The Penthouse" has gotten a reputation over the years as being a party spot.

The wind has been howling all day, and tonight it's picked up even more. I shiver as I step outside, joining a few other partygoers in the weirdly freezing April temperatures. I don't really drink, but when the guy standing at the keg grins and automatically hands me a beer, I take it anyway. Shivering in the chill, I hug my bare arms around myself, wishing I hadn't just waltzed out here in only a sleeveless top and the cute, but short, skirt I wore to the party.

"Here—let me warm you up."

Ansel grins as he steps out onto the balcony and shrugs off his sweatshirt.

"Thanks, but I'm fine—"

"Please. I insist."

He moves closer, draping his—admittedly *super* toasty—hoodie around my shoulders.

"Thanks," I mumble, smiling mechanically.

It's funny the way things change, and how fast. A few months ago, when Ansel walked right up to little old me flashing that charming smile and telling me he wanted me in The Order, I was smitten. I mean, of course I was. He was gorgeous, popular, powerful, and *so cool,* three exclamation points.

But things change. Feelings fade. People show you who they really are.

The first incident was when a girl in Junior year, herself a card-carrying member of The Order, invited me over to the mansion to hang out. I walked in looking as cute as I could, hoping to see Prince Charming again.

Hoping he'd tell me again how much he wanted me "in his club".

I *did* see him that visit. Unfortunately, he was shirtless and standing in the doorway to his room at the time, making out with a girl wearing the dress she'd clearly gone out in the night before.

That killed the luster just a little bit. A few weeks later, I was unimpressed to spot Ansel at an Order mansion party in a lawn chair on the far side of the pool with a *different* girl's head bobbing in his lap.

But what really decided things for me was when he took me aside recently and told me between snickers how he'd heard about my "prank" to frame Alistair for assault. And how he—Ansel, that is—had submitted two more fake reports from "anonymous girls", alleging the same crimes.

That really, *really* rubbed me the wrong way. And I've been avoiding Ansel ever since.

"No problem," he grins, nodding at the jacket as he pulls it tighter around me. "It's part of being in The Order, Eloise. We're family. We take care of each other."

"Yeah, no, totally," I smile awkwardly.

He grins, stepping closer to me. "You know, I'd love to take care of you, Eloise..."

Oh, I bet you would.

"Well, this sweatshirt is perfect," I say brightly, purposefully playing dumb. "Thanks so much—"

"Listen, Eloise," he smirks, pulling even closer. "Let's get outta here. It's a pretty slow night back at the mansion. We can head back there, grab some drinks..." he winks in what I'm sure to most girls is a charming manner. But not to me anymore. I've seen behind the curtain. "See where the night takes us?"

Yeah, right. The night takes us to his bedroom. I'd have to be an idiot not to see that clear as day. A few months ago, I'd have tripped over myself for the chance to hook up with Ansel Albrecht and would have given him my virginity.

But now?

Now that sounds about as appealing as walking back into the party and striking up a conversation with Alistair.

"You know what, Ansel?" I smile pleasantly. "Thanks for the offer, but I'm probably just going to head back to my dorm soon. I've got a long day tomorrow—"

"C'mon, Eloise," he purrs, flashing that "charming" smile at me. "I'll give you a full tour of the mansion. Even the floors that are off-limits to non-pledged members."

Lucky me.

"Thanks, Ansel..." I shrug his jacket off and hand it back to him. "Maybe another time."

I'm starting to walk past him when his hand shoots out to grab my wrist.

"You *do* understand who I am regarding The Order, right? I mean, you understand that *I* have the final say in who gets confirmed and who doesn't?"

Oh, I understand. I also understand that he thinks I'm going to fuck him just to be a part of his little club.

Not happening.

"I do understand that, Ansel," I smile sweetly, pulling my arm away. "And I look forward to being a part of The Order *without* resorting to whoring myself out to the guy in charge."

He falters when I say the quiet part out loud.

"Have a good night," I mutter, sliding open the door and stepping back into the party.

I wasn't really planning on going home yet. But suddenly, that's exactly what I want to do. The wind outside is getting viciously cold, and now I'm kinda bummed out. Plus, I've managed to go this long without having to face Alistair and his wrath, and it might be time to go before I push my luck there.

I spot Demi, who I came here with, on one of the couches talking closely to a gorgeous Korean guy. I grin at the blush on her face: Demi's been crushing on Bang Jin-hu since freshman orientation. His family is one of the most notorious Kkangpae crime families in Seoul, and he's also apparently a really nice guy. So when I catch Demi's eye and arch a brow, she just nods.

That's our unspoken code for me asking if she's okay with me leaving, and her saying yes.

I grab my too-light jacket and step out of The Penthouse. It's a lot quieter out in the hallway, away from the music. I push the button for the elevator, listening to the wind howling outside, wishing I'd brought a better coat.

The doors ding open, and as I step in, I hear the party music get louder for a second and then quieter again, followed by the sound of the door to the suite closing. The elevators doors begin to shut, and they're about three inches from fully closed when a hand reaches through the opening.

"Hold that door?"

"Sure," I reply, shoving a hand out to push the doors apart.

A tall figure wrapped in a black leather jacket with the collar flipped up slips through the halfway open doors. He slides in just as the doors shut again, shoving a hand through his wild brownish-blonde hair.

"Thanks for—"

He turns to me just as the doors shut.

Fuck.

Me.

The smile evaporates from Alistair's face as his eyes land on me. He whips around, but the elevator has already rumbled to life and we're starting to descend.

"*You,*" he snarls.

I swallow. "I—I'm sorry—"

"For almost ruining my life?!" he spits. "Wow, that means a lot. Go fuck yourself, princess."

He turns his back to me, shaking his head angrily. He brings a bottle of whisky up to his mouth, taking a big pull.

I frown.

"Look, for what it's worth, I wasn't the one who reported—"

"A lie?" he snarls, half glancing at me over his shoulder. "No, your fucking roommate did. Gee, I wonder where she got that lie *from?*"

I wince. "It was fucked up, I admit that."

"Fantastic. Still no fucks given over here."

I glare at his back. "Okay, what I said was hugely exaggerated. But you *did* break into my dorm room! You could have walked in on me changing, or—"

I shriek as the elevator suddenly comes to an abrupt stop, the lights flickering. The motor whines and makes horrible grinding sounds before going utterly silent. The lights flicker off and on one more time, then turn off completely.

The elevator goes pitch dark.

Holy fuck.

I don't realize I'm hyperventilating until I jolt when his arm brushes mine.

"Don't touch me!" I yell, lurching backward. Immediately, I conk the back of my head into the elevator wall.

"You need to stop breathing so fast," Alister growls. "I'm serious. You're going to hyperventilate and pass out."

"I—we're…we're…!"

"It's only temporary," he sighs. "The wind probably knocked out the power when a branch fell onto a wire. I'm sure there are backup generators, just give it a fucking second."

He sounds so calm. So unbothered by the fact that we're trapped maybe seventeen stories up in a tiny elevator car.

"But what if no one can get to us!" I blurt. "What if there *is* no backup—"

"Will you *relax*? If you keep that up, you're going to use up all of our oxygen before they can get to us."

My heart drops before I suddenly frown.

"That's not possible."

He chuckles quietly in the darkness. "No, it's not."

"Asshole."

"Do me a favor and keep that princess trap of yours shut."

His face is suddenly illuminated by the glow of his cell phone. His eyes find mine, holding my gaze before he turns away.

"Perfect. Here we go." He opens the little metal door on the wall and pulls the emergency phone out of its cradle. "We'll just call down and let them know..."

He trails off, his brow furrowing as he taps a button on the phone box. He scowls as he drops the receiver back onto the cradle.

"Dead line," he mutters.

I yank my cell phone out of my bag. When my eyes land on the screen, I groan.

"No service," I mutter. "Perfect."

"Same," Alistair sighs.

My pulse begins to roar faster.

We're trapped.

We're fucking *trapped* in—

"*Breathe*, princess," he murmurs.

"Will you stop calling me—"

"Quit trying to provoke a fight and just *breathe*, Eloise."

It might be the first time that Alistair has actually called me Eloise, and not "princess".

It works. My lungs fill up as I breathe in, and then exhale slowly.

I feel better instantly.

"Here. This'll help, too."

He passes me the bottle. I wrinkle my nose. "I don't really drink…"

"Unless it's beer, and involves getting cozy on a balcony with Ansel Albrecht?"

My gaze whips around to see him smirking at me.

I sneer a mean smile. "Aww, are you jea-wous, Awistair?"

"Of you? No. I think Ansel is a douchebag with narcissistic tendencies and a micro-penis."

I snort a laugh, looking away to try to hide it, but failing.

"Seriously, he's all yours," he grins.

I roll my eyes. "I mean jealous of *him*."

"Why, because he had the incomparable pleasure of Her Majesty the Princess *deigning* to speak to him? Can't say that I am."

I glare at him as he grins at me.

"You're an asshole," I mutter.

"You said that. Find new material."

I purse my lips as I lock eyes with him. *God,* he's infuriating.

And yet also…

I shake my head and pull my eyes away.

No. I refuse. I *refuse* to let myself think that word again when it comes to this arrogant dick.

Home.

I don't know how else to describe it. And I have absolutely no idea why my brain is short-circuiting like this, and has been for months. But whatever the reason…or lack thereof… there's something about Alistair, no matter how much he pisses me off, that feels like home.

He feels safe, even though I hate him. Even though I'm scared of him. Even though I know how dangerous he is.

"How long do you think we'll be stuck?"

Alistair shrugs, shoving his fingers through his hair again. I find myself watching the way his perfect mouth and lips move when he's thinking. He shrugs his leather jacket off in the warmth of the elevator, and my gaze lands on his bicep, stretching the short sleeve of his t-shirt.

"Depends," he grunts. "The storm is picking up. I doubt Knightsblood has an elevator tech on staff, which means someone needs to come out. And with the driving conditions like they are…" He makes a face.

"*Merde*," I mumble.

"They also don't even know anyone's trapped in here."

My face falls as I glance at him again. "Are you trying to scare me?"

"I'm facing reality. There's no working phone, we don't have cell service, and nobody saw us get in here."

Alistair shrugs, folds up his jacket, and slides down the wall to the floor. He tucks his jacket behind his head and looks up at me.

"Better get comfortable, princess."

I shiver, hugging myself even though it's swelteringly warm in the elevator for some reason. I start to pace back and forth.

"Will you please sit the fuck down? You're freaking me out."

I glare at him.

"*Sit*," he grunts, pointing at the floor.

"I'm not a puppy, you fucker."

When he shrugs and looks away to take another sip from his bottle, I lean against the wall.

"Tell me something no one knows about you."

I glance at him with an incredulous brow. "What?"

"One thing that nobody knows about you."

I snort. "Why the fuck would I tell you that?"

"I dunno. Why do people go BASE jumping, or run with bulls?"

A smile teases the corners of my lips. Slowly, I slide to the floor, quickly draping my jacket over my legs when I realize how short my skirt is.

"Rain check on divulging my secrets to you?"

"I'll mark my calendar."

The tension and the panic are melting away a little.

Wow, how the hell did he do that?

"Want a drink?"

I shrug. "Fine."

"Apparently *manners* weren't part of your princess classes," he growls, passing me the whiskey.

I sigh. "*Thanks.*"

"You're welcome. Thanks for lying about me fucking sexually assaulting you and almost getting me kicked out of school and blacklisted from a fuckton of law schools." He gives me a sarcastic thumbs up. "Really. Thanks for that."

My heart twists as I look down at my hands. "I said I was sorry," I mumble.

"Are you, though?"

I nod. "Yeah. Truly. That was shitty."

We're both silent for a minute, him taking a drink, then passing the bottle to me. My phone's battery dies and I groan, not that I had service anyway. I swallow a gulp of whiskey and pass the bottle back to him. Alistair coughs lightly.

"In fairness, I did, you know."

I frown as I look up at him. "Did what?"

"Earlier, you said that when I broke into your dorm room I *could* have walked in on you changing. I did. But you…ahh… weren't changing."

My face scrunches. "I don't know what—"

Then it clicks, and my face explodes with heat.

"YOU—!"

He waggles his brows.

"*Seriously*?!"

Alistair grins. "Solid A, A minus performance."

Oh. My. Fucking. God. I want to crawl into myself or melt into a puddle and drip through the cracks in the floor.

Alistair saw me naked. Worse, he saw me *masturbating*.

Just kill me now.

Suddenly I scowl as I yank my gaze back to him.

"I'm sorry, wait, did you say A *minus*?!"

He grins. Asshole.

"I'm just saying, I could have been more drawn in, as an audience member."

I groan as I sink down into a ball, burying my face in my jacket. "You are *such* a dick…"

"Like, I didn't really get what your motivation was."

"Please stop talking."

"And your technique could use some work."

I lift my face again and glare death at him through the fiery blush spreading across my face. "*Excuse me?!*"

He just shrugs and leans back against the wall.

Then his phone dies as well.

Shit. Now we're in absolute darkness.

I gulp, hugging myself again as my pulse quickens.

"You all right?"

"Yeah, I'm fine."

We're both silent another minute.

"My *technique*," I mutter. "Does *not* need *work*."

"If you say so."

"I do."

"Well, that's settled then."

I grin. When did this conversation turn into something that feels like flirting?

"You know what, scrap the minus. Solid A performance."

I roll my eyes, my face still throbbing. "Gee, thanks, professor."

"I'll admit, I might have been swayed by your pandering to the judges."

I sigh heavily. "There weren't…" I shake my head. "What does that even mean?"

"Come on, it was my favorite part…"

My nose wrinkles. "*What* was your favorite—"

"When you said my name."

And the floor drops out from under me.

I forgot that part.

But it all comes flooding back now. I remember touching myself that night, and imagining Alistair as the one putting his hands on me.

Pinning me to my bed, maybe tying me up.

Calling me a bad girl.

Fucking me.

I *said his name out loud.*

...And he heard me.

My pulse starts to thud like a bass drum. My breath comes faster and faster, shaky and trembling as my skin turns to gooseflesh.

"Princess."

I gasp, realizing in the pitch black that he's right in front of me.

"You need to breathe."

"I'm fine," I blurt.

"*Breathe.*"

"I am breathing!"

"No, you're shouting."

"Because *you're* bossing me around!"

"I'm trying to calm you—"

"You're still doing it!"

"*Eloise,* calm—"

"Oh my *God*! Has anyone ever, in your entire life, told you how much of an *ass*—"

I gasp as his hand cups my cheek.

"*Will you just shut the fuck up?*" he murmurs, inches from my lips.

And then there are no more inches, because suddenly, Alistair Black is kissing me like I have *never* been kissed before.

After that, there's no holding back.

None.

In the ensuing explosion of clothes falling away together with inhibitions, and mouths and fingers frantically exploring in the dark, and him swallowing my moans when he first sinks into me, I don't have the time or the wherewithal to tell him I've never done this before.

That this—all of it—is my first time.

In the morning, I wake up groggy and sore, but warm. I realized I'm curled up naked in his arms on the floor of the elevator, our jackets and clothes heaped under and over us like blankets.

The door to the elevator is standing open, and we're back on the ground floor, the dim, gray, early morning light filtering into the empty, silent lobby of Worthington Tower.

I turn to look at his sleeping face. I study the way his eyes flicker under his lashes. The way his dark brownish-blonde hair flops over his face. The hard edge of his jaw and the perfection of his lips.

I dress quickly, and when I'm done, I kneel down next to him. I lean close to his sleeping face, feeling more alive and more full of...*something*...than I've ever felt before. My lips brush his cheek with a light kiss before drifting to his ear.

"Part of you is mine forever."

I have *no* idea why I say it. Honestly, it sounds psycho as hell when I repeat in my head. But it's out there now. I said it.

No takebacks.

I kiss his lips softly. Then I stand, I turn, and I walk back to the real world.

Present:

"WHAT THE *FUCK* WAS THAT?!"

Outside the front doors of our building, I whirl to see Massimo storming toward me, Rocco in tow. His face is livid.

"Excuse me?" I snap back.

"That," he snarls, jabbing a finger vaguely in the direction of the penthouse. "You want to fuck him!? Is that it?!"

I stare at him with a mixture of fear, apprehension, and loathing.

"Are you serious?" I snap. "It was *your fucking game*! *Your* idea! You're the one that offered me up like a cut of meat!"

He smiles darkly. "You *wanted* it to be him."

"You're drunk, Massimo," I sigh.

"And you're a whore."

My lips thin and my nostrils flare as I glare death at him.

"What even was the point of that?"

"To see if you would truly do whatever it takes to get me what I want."

Revulsion curdles inside of me. "You're disgusting."

I go to push past him back into the lobby. Suddenly he grabs my arm, hard, and yanks me back, almost pulling me off my heels.

"Where the fuck is that will, Eloise."

"I told you!" I snap. "I'm working on—"

I tense, barely catching my balance as he shoves me away from him. He turns to Rocco and nods his chin.

"Wait—!"

Rocco's backhanded slap hits me so hard my vision goes black. I see stars, choking on my breath as my eyesight blurs before slowly clearing.

All my fight disappears as I drop to my knees. I'm just numb and scared as Massimo yanks me up and against him, his lips curling as he snarls right into my face.

"Work harder."

Tears sting my eyes. I can taste bitter copper as I bite down hard on my tongue. I turn to glare at Rocco, but it's like trying to look angrily at a wall. My eyes slide back to Massimo, narrowing on him hatefully.

Massimo smiles sadistically. “Something you’d like to say, wife?”

I shake my head mutely.

“Good. Keep it that way.”

He lets me go and storms away back toward the lobby, with Rocco on his heels.

“Get me what I fucking want, Eloise.”

23

ALISTAIR

Ten years ago:

I WAKE up naked and alone.

And smelling like Eloise.

I've never been a morning person, and waking up on the floor of an elevator, slightly hungover, is hardly the day I'm going to start. All the same, I grin as I sit up and reach for my clothes.

I'm not surprised that she dipped out first from a one-night stand.

I smile as I pull my pants back on. I'm actually surprised that Princess Eloise turned out to be the type to have a one-night stand, *period*.

I've got my shirt halfway on when I pause, my face souring as the words "one-night stand" flicker in my head.

Who says this has to be just one night?

Then I'm shaking my head at myself as I finish getting dressed.

What, do I want to *date* Eloise LeBlanc?

Please. It's an absurd idea for about a million reasons. I might have moved past the fact that she almost fucked up my whole future, since she ultimately *failed* at that. But still. Not to mention that she's pledging The Order, and I'm the president of The Reckless.

She's French mafia, I'm heading to law school. She *belongs* at a place like Knightsblood, because of her family, whereas I'm only here because my grandfather pulled strings with his sketchy criminal connections.

Eloise is a prude, I'm...not.

Wait, is she?

I grin to myself, remembering the night we just had.

My dick chimes in, thickening and swelling in my jeans. Yeah... That was no prude I just spent the night with. Not after *four*—thank you very much—times. Not when she kept begging for more. Not when she moaned for me to come inside of her, or when she swallowed my cum the next time.

...I grin darkly.

Not when she asked me to do *filthy* things to her.

I suck my teeth as I step out of the lobby of Worthington Tower and into the cold, gray morning air.

Fuck me, there's a chance I just had the best night of my life, and by far the most fun I've ever had with a girl.

It wasn't just the sex.

It was the talking between rounds. It was her bringing my game up again: "tell me something no one else knows about you."

I didn't barely sleep last night *only* because I was too busy fucking Eloise LeBlanc's goddamn brains out in every conceivable position, and every—and I do mean *every*—hole.

It was because we were talking, sharing things. Shit, I told that girl stuff I haven't ever told anyone. You'd think that would scare the fuck out of me, but it doesn't.

It feels pretty damn good.

Outside, I inhale the dewy morning mist. I think back to my final memory of last night, before I fell asleep. Eloise was already out, wrapped naked in my arms with her back to my chest.

That's when I leaned down. And I have no fucking clue why I said it, or where it came from. It just fell out.

You'll always be mine.

MY EGO MAKES me wait a week. Seeking her out or calling her before that seems kinda desperate and pathetic. But finally I find myself standing outside her dorm room and knocking on the door.

Shit. It's Demi who answers.

"What do *you* want?" she says with a glare.

"Hello to you too, Demiana."

Her face sours. Looking past her, I realize she's not alone in the room as Bang Jin-ho, who's a member of Para Bellum that my brother runs, nods at me.

"What's up, Jin-ho."

"Alistair," he murmurs, buttoning his shirt back up.

"Well?" Demi, who is clearly not in the Alistair Black Fan Club, growls at me.

"I'm looking for Eloise."

Her mouth thins. "Oh really."

"Yes."

"She's not here."

"Where might she be?"

"Home," she shrugs. "She had a family thing back in Paris."

My brow knits. "Got it. Do you have her cell—"

"Dude, you broke into our fucking room. I'm not giving you her number."

I glance past her to Jin-ho. He just spreads his arms and shrugs.

"Okay, well, would you tell her I stopped by when she gets—"

"Nope."

Demi slams the door in my face.

I exhale slowly as I scowl, turn, and walk away.

See, *this* is why I don't do serious dating.

It's two weeks later when a small shape darts in front of me as I'm leaving the gym.

"Hey."

Instantly, I'm grinning like an idiot.

"Hey yourself," I murmur to Eloise.

Her cheeks burn pink and her big blue eyes sparkle as she looks up at me.

"I, um, heard you were looking for me?"

I snort. "Two weeks ago, yeah."

She makes a face. "Sorry. I was back home dealing with some stuff…" She looks away, her shoulders slumping. "My sister. She… She's a handful sometimes."

"Say no more."

"Demi…" she frowns. "*Neglected* to tell me you'd stopped by."

"Fancy that," I say dryly.

She grins, biting her lip. "Jin-ho let it slip earlier today."

My man.

"So…" She shrugs awkwardly. "What… I mean, did you need something?"

Yes, you, oddly enough.

I don't do repeats. Just as I don't "do" thinking of someone over and over, day in and day out. It's freaking me out.

It's also arguably making me less of a prick than usual.

"What are you doing next weekend?"

Her brows knit. "Uh…nothing? I don't think so, at least?"

"You going to the Spring Formal?"

What the fuck are you doing, Alistair?

It just spills out of me. *I* wasn't even planning on going to the dumb formal dance the school throws two weeks before graduation.

Eloise looks at me curiously, her lip retreating between her teeth.

"I…wasn't planning on it?"

"What if you *did* plan on it." I frown. "Going, I mean. With, uh, me."

Fucking *hell* I suck at this.

She's grinning, though. And blushing. Her eyes are locked with mine.

"I could do that."

"You'd want to go to the dance with me?"

"Are you asking me?"

"Yeah."

She giggles. "Then… Yeah, okay."

"I'll pick you up at your dorm an hour before it starts."

She nods, blushing. "That's perfect. Demi is going home that weekend, so…"

"So I can skip the body armor."

She grins. "Exactly." She winces as she looks at her phone. "Shit, I need to run to class."

"See you then."

She beams. "Can't wait."

THAT'S the last happy moment I have for a while. Because when the Saturday rolls around, and I knock on Eloise's dorm room door, whatever high I was on, whatever happiness I'd managed to steal from the universe, turns to ash in my mouth.

When *he* answers the door.

Ansel.

I look past his shirtless shoulders to see what is instantly burned into my brain forever going on in the room behind him with two of his Order buddies.

She's wearing a green dress.

She's moaning even louder than when she was with me.

"You want a turn, bro?" Ansel casually offers. "She's pretty good."

She's not the girl I thought she was. She's not at *all* what I thought she was.

So I walk away, and slam up my walls, and never once look back.

And those walls never, ever come back down again.

Present:

THANK FUCKING GOD.

Eloise is sitting against one of the planters outside my building's lobby when I get out of the taxi from Massimo's place. When she disappeared, and when Massimo came back upstairs alone, I waited as long as I thought I could before making my own exit.

I've been trying to reach her for the last hour.

"You weren't answering your phone," I growl as I walk toward her.

"It died," she shrugs. She looks up at me with immense sadness in her eyes. "Sorry, I didn't… I don't know why I came here."

I shake my head. "It's fine."

"I tried the office first. But it was locked."

"Yeah, we do that sometimes when it's closed."

A smile lifts the corners of her lips as she rolls her eyes. Then she winces and turns to the side.

That's when the light outside my building's front door hits the side of her face.

"What the *fuck*!" I snarl, bolting over to her and gently lifting her chin. There's no missing the ugly red welt and bruise purpling across the side of her face.

"It's nothing, Alistair," she mumbles, avoiding my eyes and trying to turn her face into the shadows again.

"Like *fuck* it's nothing," I hiss. "Was this him!?"

She looks down. Her throat bobs heavily.

"No."

"Are you *seriously* protecting—"

"I mean it wasn't *literally* him."

Her shoulders slump as she looks down. "Like I said, he doesn't touch me." She exhales. "He gets his attack dog, Rocco, to do it. Massimo himself hasn't ever actually struck me himself. I don't know why. When he wants to, he has Rocco do it."

"This is *insane,* Eloise!" I hiss. "Why in God's name would you stay with that piece of shit?!"

Her eyes snap to mine. "Does it seriously look like I'm *with* Massimo?!"

"It looks like you're fucking married to him, yes!" I rage. "Why the *fuck* wouldn't you just leave—"

"Because he'd kill my sister!"

I blink as my mouth snaps shut.

Eloise looks away, sighing.

"I know what she is, okay? I know she's a lot to handle, and meddling, and toxic, but—"

"Can't pick your family," I murmur.

"*No shit,*" she says bitterly. "And she's still my sister. If my dad wasn't in his coma? Yeah, I could talk to him, and he'd get me out of it. But until he recovers, while his greedy captains are in charge..." She barks out a laugh. "They make too much from the deals Massimo throws their way to give a shit. To them, this is just business. I'm the daughter of a mafia king, Alistair," she chokes. "This is what I'm supposed to do."

I exhale slowly, looking away before I turn back to her.

"Let's get you inside."

Upstairs in my loft, I take her through my room to the ensuite master bath to get cleaned up. I bring her some old sweats and a t-shirt of mine, and before I know what I'm doing, I'm pulling her into my arms and hugging her close before I leave so she can shower.

I don't once think what a bad idea it is for her to be here. I don't let myself dwell on what happens if Massimo finds out she's here with me.

Because fuck him.

Let him come for her. I'll *break him* if he does.

I'll break *anyone* who comes for her.

I'm in the kitchen half an hour later when Eloise emerges from my room positively drowning in the clothes I gave her. It makes me grin.

I like her in my clothes.

Fuck, I like her *here.*

She pads into the kitchen and leans against the counter, wrapping her arms around herself.

"How's the face?"

She shrugs. "It'll be fine."

"Here."

I hand her a bag of frozen peas from the freezer. She smiles wryly as she takes it and holds it to the red swelling on the side of her face.

"From what you said, it didn't sound like that was the first time he's had you hit."

She looks away.

"No," she finally murmurs quietly, her voice edged. "It wasn't."

"*Fucker*," I hiss.

"Amen," Eloise murmurs. She looks up at me. "Got anything to drink?"

"Plenty."

"Can I have one?"

"No."

Eloise purses her lips. "Why not?"

"Because you drink too fucking much, princess," I growl.

Her brows shoot up indignantly. "*Wow*, really?"

"From where I'm standing? Yeah."

Her mouth purses. "Well, you're not the—"

"*The boss of you*?" I smirk. "Want to try that again, counselor?"

Eloise groans. "*Please* can I have a drink? It's been a shit night."

"I realize that. Still no, though."

We're both silent a minute, her chewing on her lip as she stares at the floor, me trying to figure out which part of tonight we should even talk about. Then she slowly raises her eyes to mine.

"What happened to you, Alistair?"

I smirk. "What, because I won't indulge your alcoholism?"

She flinches. "Okay, *ouch*."

"The truth hurts."

She scowls at me. "I wasn't *talking* about a drink, actually," she says sullenly. "I mean what the hell happened to you at Knightsblood?"

My jaw grinds.

"Let's not go there."

Eloise barks a cold laugh. "Fuck you. We *are* there."

"*Don't*," I warn.

"Don't *what*?! Alistair! You..." She shoves her fingers through her wet hair. "We had that night in the elevator which was..." Her face burns as she looks away. "*Great*. And then you come to my room looking for me, and then you ask me out to a dance like we were in a fucking John Hughes movie! And then you just *ghosted* me!!" she screams. "You blocked my calls! You blocked me *everywhere*—"

"I *wonder* why the fuck that is!!" I roar back.

"YOU TELL ME!"

She gasps as I erase the space between us, looming over her and grabbing the front of her hoodie.

"You want to know why I did that, Eloise?" I snarl.

"I am *ALL* fucking ears!"

"Because I don't open up to people!" I snap. "Never did. Still don't. Except for you. You managed to fuck up that streak and got inside my fucking head!" My lips pull into a snarl, my eyes narrowing on her paling face. "You want to know why I put my walls back up and fucked off, Eloise?! Because when I went to get you, after you had *asked me* to be there—"

She cuts me off. "Alistair, I wasn't—"

"Please. I fucking *saw you.*"

Ice forms around my heart as my jaw clenches.

"Your little fuck buddy Ansel answered the door, you know."

Her brow furrows. "What the hell are you—"

"His pathetic little dick out, grinning at me. And there you were, Eloise," I rasp venomously. "All dolled up—"

"Alistair! I wasn't—"

"*All dolled up* in your formal dress, bent over and getting double-teamed by two of his fucking friends like a cheap—"

"I wasn't in my fucking dorm room that night, you asshole!!"

The force with which she screams it at me and the pain in her words are like two knives to my chest. I blink, momentarily stunned before I collect myself again and narrow my gaze on her.

"Oh? Then where the fuck *were* you, El—"

"I was in the fucking hospital!" she screams. "Having the worst day of my life!"

What.

"I was in the *hospital,*" she chokes out again, tears starting to stream down her cheeks. "Getting blood transfusions after I almost died from a miscarriage."

24

ELOISE

Ten years ago:

This can't be happening.

I wince as another cramp explodes low in my abdomen, making me choke out a cry of pain. I grip the rails of the hospital bed tightly, my knuckles white. It's the physical pain, yes, that's ripping me in two. But there's a deeper, different type of pain that shreds my every emotion as tears bead at the corners of my eyes.

They told me it's called an anembryonic pregnancy, or *blighted ovum*. It's rare, but not unheard of, and it's normally not that complicated, medically speaking. When it happens, it's before you even realize you're pregnant.

No. Shit.

I wince as another cramp tears through me.

Those movies or TV shows where some inexperienced girl gets pregnant her first time having sex?

Yeah, that's me. I'm that girl you roll your eyes at. It's me.

I was pregnant.

Emphasis on *was*.

And that's a really weird feeling that I'm not quite sure how to process yet. Part of that is I've been too busy *staying alive* since it happened. I was in my dorm, getting ready for the dance, when the pain first hit. At first, I thought it was my period. But the blood just kept coming.

And coming.

And *coming*.

I dimly remember wadding a ton of paper towels into my underwear and staggering across campus, trying to call Camille on my phone as I stumbled into the medical center. They took one look at me, bundled me into an ambulance, and drove me here to Greenwich Hospital.

An anembryonic pregnancy usually isn't that serious. But it is if you start to hemorrhage. The doctors told me it was a bad one, too, and that I was extremely lucky to have gotten here before I bled out.

No part of me feels lucky right now, though.

I'm glancing at my phone to see if Alistair has texted me back yet when the door to my room opens. I look up and smile as Camille walks in and comes to the side of my bed. For all of her crazy, and all her usual "me-me-me" routine, she's been amazing since she first got here. She didn't even bother to change out of the gorgeous emerald-green gown she had on for the dance when the hospital reached her and told her what was going on.

"Ice chips?"

She hands me a cup, and I smile weakly as I take it. "*Merci bien.*"

"*Rien.*"

I slip a silver of ice between my lips, grimacing as another cramp takes hold.

"Have you…"

She frowns. "Heard from him?" She shakes her head. "No. I've left a few messages, though. He hasn't texted you back yet?"

I shake my head and unlock my phone. Then I peer more closely at the screen.

"That's weird."

"What?"

My brow furrows. "It says my texts haven't even gone through to him. But I have service?"

When I look at my sister, her face falls.

"What?"

"Mine…oh, Eloise…"

"What is it?"

"My texts to him went through just fine."

"I don't understand. What are you saying?"

She takes my hand, her mouth twisting. "Honey, I think he blocked you."

I wince, and this time, it's not a cramp.

"Why would he…" I shake my head. "No. That's not like him."

She looks away.

"What," I growl quietly.

"Nothing."

"Camille, just say it."

"Fine, I will. Because I love you," she sighs. "This *is* like Alistair Black, Eloise. You've painted a version of him in your head that isn't real. This is textbook Alistair. He's an asshole."

"Maybe he's just confused why I stood him up?"

"You didn't stand—"

"Well, yeah, but he might think—"

"He read my texts, Ellie," she says quietly. "I explained exactly what happened."

I swallow the lump in my throat.

"No, that's… That doesn't make sense."

"Check your social media."

My pulse thuds as I open Facebook on my phone.

Holy shit.

Blocked. It's the same on Instagram and Twitter.

My hand trembles as I call Alistair's number and bring my phone to my ear. It goes right to voicemail.

Oh my God.

"I..." I look wildly at my sister. "I don't understand—"

"Eloise."

She smiles sadly at me as she takes my phone away and then holds my hand in hers.

"You don't need me to say the obvious, do you?"

"I..."

"He got what he wanted, Ellie," she says quietly.

"N-no," I say, shaking my head, thinking back to that night. It wasn't just my body I shared with him, it was so much more. And *he* shared things about himself—his vague memories of his biological parents. The accident that sent him to the Black family. He said he told me things he'd never told anyone before.

There is *no way* all of that was just to get laid.

Right?

Oh God...

"You didn't want Alistair, Ellie. Not really. You wanted what you thought he could give you. But I promise you, if you'd stayed with him?" She shakes her head. "*Trust* me. I've known guys like him. He would have slowly dimmed your light. He would have cut you off from your friends, and from me. From your own sister!" She squeezes my hand. "You want my advice?"

I nod in a daze.

"Forget that asshole. Forget all about him. You're better off without him in your life." She smiles and squeezes my hand. "We both are."

I manage to hold it together until she leaves to get a cup of coffee. Then it all comes crashing down in a smoking pile of tears, blood, and pain.

Present:

When it comes out, it's like when a dam gives way and the floodgates rip off their hinges.

He tells me the full, awful story about what he saw when he came to my room that night. And when those pieces drop into place, and I realize *who* he saw that night, it's like getting shot in the heart.

Camille.

You're better off without him in your life, Eloise. We both are.

Alistair holds me as I scream into his chest, sobbing with pain and rage at everything that might have been, everything that was taken away from me.

From *us*.

When the fury is gone, and all that remains in me is sadness, he holds me in his arms on the floor as I cry into his chest and tell him about the miscarriage, and the hemorrhaging. His hands tighten on me and his own breath chokes with emotion when that part comes out.

"You tried to tell me..."

His voice is so broken when it rasps from his throat.

As if I could forget.

It was two weeks after the miscarriage. Two weeks of no contact with Alistair. Then finally, right before graduation, I saw him across campus, and I couldn't stop myself.

I still don't know why. It sure wasn't about getting answers from him. Maybe I just needed him to know what I'd gone through.

I made it all the way over to him, and even managed to get out "I have to tell you something" before he stopped me with the words that will forever be etched on my soul.

"From the very bottom of my heart, Eloise. Go the fuck to hell, and don't ever cross my path again."

Then he was gone. And that was the last time we ever spoke.

"Jesus Christ," he chokes out, holding me tighter.

"Alistair, you didn't know. You still thought I'd—"

"I could have listened," he hisses. "I could have *stopped,* and shut my ego down and just. Fucking. *Listened to you."*

Tears run hot down my cheeks.

"I thought you hated m—"

"Eloise."

He pulls back slightly, cupping my chin and lifting my face to his.

"That was the damn problem, princess," he growls quietly. "You could have fucked every man on the planet, stabbed me in the heart, and stood over me laughing while I bled out, Eloise," he murmurs, holding my face in his hands. "And my problem would have always been the same damn thing."

I'm crying as I bite my lip. "Which is what?"

"That as hard as I try, I love you too fucking much to hate you at all."

The breath leaves my body.

My world goes still.

"I've loved you for ten fucking years, Eloise. And the only way I could survive that was to convince myself that the love was hate."

I don't think. I don't hesitate. I don't let the chains of the past weigh me down or stop me.

"I love you."

The words fly from my mouth right before I slam my lips to his. He growls into my kiss, making me moan, his tongue pushing past my lips to dance with mine.

The kiss is feverish and wild, a lifeline we're both clinging to as the storm breaks over us. I whimper, kissing him harder and deeper as my hands shove desperately at his jacket. Suddenly I'm gasping when Alistair stands, still holding me in his arms, lifting me into his chest. I cling to him, kissing him wildly and feverishly as he carries me into his bedroom.

My back hits the bed. Alistair all but rips his clothes off, revealing his *insane,* muscled, tattooed body to my hungry gaze. Instantly, he's all over me. His mouth devours my neck and my collarbone as he pushes the baggy t-shirt he's loaned me up and over my head. My arms are still tangled up in it when he drops his mouth to my breasts, taking my breath away as he sucks, bites, and licks at my nipples until my back is arching off the bed and my body is on fire for him.

He moves down my body slowly, taking his time.

Drawing it out.

Making me *ache* for him as his tongue and lips tease over every single inch of me. My nipples pebble under his touch, my stomach caving and my breath catching as he licks and sucks his way down.

He peels the oversized sweatpants down, his tongue following in their wake, tracing a lazy wet trail down the groove of my hip. His mouth teases right past my pussy, making me groan in frustration as his hot breath tingles over my slick lips.

"*Alistair…*" I whine, lifting my hips desperately toward his mouth.

"*Greedy* girls get made to wait," he growls against my inner thigh. "But *good* girls get what they want." His eyes drag up my body to lock with mine, his mouth hovering an *inch* from my aching, throbbing clit.

"Are you going to be a good girl for me?"

Sweet merciful God.

I'll be whatever the hell he wants me to be right now for just one second of that tongue touching me where I so desperately need it.

"*Yes…*" I whimper, my teeth raking over my bottom lip. "*Yes, sir…*"

The electric fire that ignites in his eyes is just this side of terrifying. But suddenly, he's yanking the sweatpants off me, pushing my legs up, and dropping his mouth between my thighs.

"Oh my fucking God..."

I choke out a whine of pleasure as his tongue slowly drags up between my lips. The tip rolls sensually over my clit, making me cry out before he teases lower again. He does it again and again, dragging his tongue slowly up and down, just barely teasing my throbbing clit on the upstroke.

He dips his head, pushing his tongue deep into me as I cry out. My hands slide into his hair as I shamelessly push my hips against him. His tongue fucks into me, forcing the breath from my lungs and the pleasure from my mouth as I cry out for more.

Alistair's mouth drags up, his lips sucking around my clit as his tongue swirls over it. My moans fill the bedroom as the world around me blurs at the edges.

"Alistair," I moan, my hips lifting into his mouth harder and harder. "Oh God, oh *God...*"

"Are you going to be a good girl and come for me?" he growls into my clit as I teeter on the brink of sanity.

"Yes!"

"Try again," he murmurs, backing off a little and letting the tip of his tongue trace lazy circles around my clit as I hover *milliseconds* from my release.

"Please let me come, sir!"

"Good girl."

His lips seal around my clit, sucking as his tongue bats relentlessly across it. His fingers sink into me, curling against my g-spot, and it's impossible to hold out another second.

Everything blurs and streaks as I scream my release, writhing and shuddering under his perfect mouth as I come *hard* against his tongue. He keeps going, swirling and teasing his tongue around my clit until I'm seeing stars and gasping for air.

Then he's sliding up between my thighs, spreading them to either side of his grooved, muscled hips, and centering his huge cock against my slick, eager opening. His mouth crushes to mine, and I moan when I taste myself on his lips.

"You were always mine."

He sinks every thick, gorgeous inch of his fat cock deep inside of me in one stroke. My head drops back, my eyes wide as I scream a silent cry of ecstasy. Alistair's mouth descends to my neck, biting and sucking the soft skin. His hips roll, sliding his thick cock almost all the way out of me before thrusting back in and filling me again.

My legs wrap around his waist, my ankles locking as my nails drag down his back. His lips slam to mine again, sucking my tongue into his mouth as he fucks into me over and over.

"Harder," I choke.

He growls a deep, throaty groan that drives me wild, and his cock pulses as he starts to ram into me.

"Harder," I moan.

"You want me to fuck you like the bad girl you are, princess?" he rasps.

I whimper, nodding desperately. Suddenly, he's pulling out of me, and I gasp as he flips me onto my stomach. He yanks my hips high in the air, making me yelp as he spanks my ass *hard.*

Without warning, he's spanking me again, pressing the swollen head of his cock against my slick pussy, and plunging in until he's balls-deep.

"Oh *fuck*!"

My eyes bulge, my mouth going slack against the bed as he fucks me like a machine. His palm slaps hard against my ass, making me squeal in pleasure. He grabs my hair in his fist, tugging hard as he spanks me again and fucks the living *hell* out of me.

When I come, it's a ten megaton explosion. I scream my release into the sheets, twisting and writhing. Alistair keeps fucking me, utterly *dominating* me. He yanks my head up by the hair, pulling me up until my back is pressed hotly against his chest. His hips pump into me, his teeth nipping at my neck. I feel his hand snake between us, and when his thumb presses against my asshole, I let out a guttural moan.

"*There's* a good little dirty girl," he snarls into my ear as his thumb slips past my tight ring. I moan, shuddering and shaking, my core clenching and spasming wildly as his cock and his thumb fill me to my limit.

"*Alistair…*"

"Let me feel it, princess," he growls thickly, his hips rocking hard against me, his abs slapping my ass as he fucks me. "Let me feel that messy little cunt come all over my thick cock. Let me feel you *drench* my fucking balls like my good girl."

Oh God.

His hand slides up my body, pinching and twisting my nipples before his fingers wrap around my throat.

"*Come for me,* Eloise," he rasps in my ear. "Right now. Right. Fucking. *Now*. Come for me like a good girl."

Trigger: pulled.

My entire body spasms and wrenches as tip over into the abyss. I scream as he rams into me, holding himself still as I come *so fucking hard* on his cock. He swells inside me as he twists my head around, crushes his lips to mine, and groans into my mouth. Then he starts to explode with me.

I moan as his hot cum spills deep inside, his dick spasming and pulsing as my pussy explodes around him.

Then I collapse onto the bed, with him still holding me in his arms, still deep inside me.

A little later, I'm lying with my head on his chest, lazily tracing my fingertip over his tattoos. I glance up, grinning and blushing when his piercing blue eyes lock with mine, his hand gently pushing a lock of hair back from my face.

"Tell me something no one knows about you."

I grin.

"We're back to that?"

"Seems appropriate."

I giggle, my face glowing hot, remembering playing this on that night in the elevator, in between fucking each other's brains out.

One thing above all else springs to mind. Something he should know. Something I've never told him, or anyone.

For a second, I almost squash it back down. It doesn't need to be said. He doesn't need to know. It will only further complicate an already complicated—

"Stop overanalyzing and just spit it out," he growls with a knowing grin.

Fuck it.

"Fine." I take a deep, shaky breath.

"Eloise, whatever it is, you know you can tell—"

"You're the only one I've ever done that with."

The bedroom goes silent as he peers at me. "Done *what* with," he murmurs quietly.

I swallow nervously. "What…" I look away.

"Eloise…"

"What we just, you know, did." I take another shaky breath and drag my gaze back to his. "You're the only person I've ever slept with."

He blinks. "I—" he frowns. "Come on, Eloise—"

"I'm serious."

He stares at me as my heart pounds.

"Our night in the elevator," he murmurs quietly.

"Was my first time." My lips twist as I blush. "Well, *times*."

Alistair's brows furrow. "But since then…"

I shake my head.

"That was ten years—"

"There hasn't been anyone since," I whisper. "I was…" I look away. "Scared, because of what happened in the hospital. And just…"

"Hurt," he finishes. "Fuck…because *I* hurt you."

I wipe a tear away, cupping his face in my hands as I press my forehead to his. "We hurt each other."

"Yeah… Let's not do that anymore."

I choke a laugh through my tears as I kiss him softly.

"Maybe you could just love me?"

"That I can do."

25

ALISTAIR

The "L" word.

I smile to myself as I lean back in my chair. I drum my fingers on the desk in front of me, shaking my head in grinning disbelief.

I've never said that to a woman before. It's also more than slightly out of character for me to act on impulse and just blurt things out as they hit my mind. I've spent my career honing my ability to craft my words, think them over, and deliver them in the perfect wrapping.

...Or bullet casing, depending.

But with Eloise, there's no "crafting" of my words.

With her, I'm brutally honest, to a dangerous, unprecedented degree. Which should scare me, or at the very least concern me.

It doesn't.

Probably because everything I said to her last night is completely true. I *did* spend the last ten years telling myself I hated Eloise. Convincing myself of that was the only way to get past the brutal truth—that when I walked into that dorm room that day and thought it was her, and assumed it was a supremely fucked up, cruel way for her to mess with me, it broke me more than I wanted to admit.

If Eloise had been just some random college hookup, I'd have gotten over it without blinking. I'd have shaken my head, gone to the dance anyway, and picked up the first girl who even smiled at me to fuck all the Eloise out of my system.

But she was never random. Or casual, or meaningless.

She was the everything.

A knock on my door has me frowning as I shake myself from my thoughts.

"Earth to Alistair?"

I roll my eyes at my brother. "Yes?"

He smirks and steps into my office. "For the record, that was my third knock."

"Court acknowledges the prosecution's evidence but ignores it as unsubstantiated and irrelevant."

My brother grins as he perches on the corner of my desk.

"How'd things go last night at Massimo's?"

"You don't really want me to answer that question."

He arches a stern brow. "How worried should I be?"

"It's nothing." I wave him off as casually as I can. "Massimo got drunk and…well, was his usual charming self. That's all."

Also, I took his wife home and told her I loved her before fucking her all night.

"I see," he grunts. "Can I assume that's why Eloise isn't in the office today?"

"You can."

The truth is, Eloise is taking a personal day to sit tight at my place. She texted Massimo last night that she was mad and needed to stay at a hotel to cool off. His only response was "fine".

Because he's a big charmer like that.

Gabriel sighs. "I really don't need to warn you again about getting involved with Massimo Carveli's *wife*, right?"

"Of course not."

"You're *not* involved with her, correct?"

"Gabriel. You know how much I hate lying to family."

He pinches the bridge of his nose tiredly and looks away.

"I'm just going to pretend you said 'Yes, of course, Gabriel. I would never do anything that reckless and fucking stupid'."

"Wow, you've got my tone down pat."

He sighs. "Well, *speaking* of family, Charles just walked in demanding a meeting upstairs with the three of us."

"I think I'd rather step off the roof, if it's okay with you."

"Taylor's already up there."

Fuck.

"Leaving her alone with him would be pretty unforgivable."

"Yes it would," he mutters. "Don't worry, though, she's not alone with him."

When I frown, his lips twist.

"Our lovely step-grandmother Caroline is in there too."

Shoot me now.

"I DON'T LIKE the way this is dragging out."

God, he's such a pompous blowhard. The fact that Charles is A, not a lawyer, and B, a fucking idiot, seems to be woefully lost on him.

"How exactly is building a solid defense dragging anything out, Charles?" Gabriel says dryly.

"It looks weak, that's why," Caroline chips in.

"Oh, good. The gold-digging sea hag with the IQ of a walnut has some thoughts on the situation."

Both Caroline and Charles whirl to stare at me in shock and fury when I say it. Behind them, Gabriel shakes his head at me and Taylor bites back a grin as she rolls her eyes.

Oops.

"What the *fuck* did you just call me?!" Caroline shrieks. She makes to come at me fighting—which would, in all seriousness, be fucking *hilarious*. Our grandfather grabs her and yanks her back before she can, though.

Pity.

"Now you listen to me, you little bastard," he growls.

My jaw grinds.

My grandfather has called Gabriel and I terrible things since we were eleven, and I'm used to it by now. He's a piece of shit and a terrible grandfather: that's what pieces of shit and terrible grandfathers do. But I *do* take umbrage with "bastard", given the details of my origin, and he knows it.

"You can't speak to her like that," he snaps.

"I literally just did."

Charles glares daggers at me. "Where are we with the Chinellato case? Really."

Taylor clears her throat. "All due respect, Mr. Bla—"

"He's not due a *shred* of respect, actually," I interrupt. "But do go on."

Taylor shoots me a look before turning back to Charles. "You know we can't discuss the case with you, Mr. Black. It's part of the bylaws of the board."

Charles smiles patronizingly at her. "I'm aware of the fucking bylaws, Ms. Crown," he snaps. "But I'm past giving a shit. This is about the reputation of the firm—"

"Yes, *our* firm," Gabriel snarls. "It may surprise you, Charles, but we're more than slightly invested in it."

"Then *get. The ball. Rolling*!" Charles yells, startling even Caroline. He levels a cold smile at us. "You're aware, I assume, that with my dear wife here also on the board, I now control a majority vote."

Obviously, we are. But interestingly, he hasn't used that majority to "get rid of us" like he's threatened to do in the past.

I take it back. That's not interesting.

It's more than slightly *worrying*.

"I've held back, because for all of our bickering," Charles continues, "we're still family. But do you have Roberto's alibi sealed up tight?"

I roll my eyes. "Jesus Christ, Charles. Will you fuck off and let us do our jobs? *Yes*, we have your fucking buddy's alibi down."

It's airtight, too.

During the timeframe when Roberto is accused of shooting Federico Lombardi in Brooklyn, he was in fact clear across Manhattan in New Jersey, rutting away between the thighs of one Mrs. Valerie Siff. And as it happens, Mrs. Siff is more than happy to stand up and court and tell that to a judge and jury.

Now, why is *Mrs*. Siff, who is still very much married to *Mr*. Siff, who happens to be the deputy Mayor of the ultra-rich and snooty Montclaire, New Jersey, so eager to admit to her infidelity involving some shithead gangster like Roberto?

Simple. Because Valerie only fucked Roberto, whom she apparently met at some dive bar, because she'd figured out her husband was banging one of his interns.

Needless to say, the extremely messy divorce is already underway, and this is Valerie's little "fuck you" to her soon-to-be ex.

"Valerie Siff is coached and ready for the stand. We're scheduled for three weeks from now."

"Do it this week."

I frown at Charles. "Excuse me?"

"Reach out to Judge Hawkins and request this week instead."

Taylor rubs her temples. "Mr. Black, that's…really not how any of this works."

He sneers at her. "Trust me, sweetheart."

I wince. Taylor fucking *hates* being called that, especially by scummy old assholes like Charles.

"I have it on good authority that one of her cases this week has been rescheduled and there's an opening Thursday in her courtroom. Make it ours."

He turns to wrap an arm around Caroline's surgically edited waist before leveling a hard look at us.

"Make it happen, or I'll make good on my threat of using the board to remove you. Sweetheart over here can stay, but you two ungrateful pricks will be looking for new jobs. Am I clear?"

No one responds. Charles smiles.

"I'll take that as a yes."

After he and Caroline leave, Taylor, Gabriel and I exhale slowly.

"Is it just me, or is he getting worse?" Taylor mutters.

"Maybe it's something terminal," I shrug.

"We can hope," Gabriel mutters. "*Fuck*," he swears.

I shake my head. "Relax. He's not going to kick us out of the firm. He'd have done that already if he wanted to. No, he wants us here, but he wants us living under his threats."

Gabriel frowns. "You mean he wants to control us?"

"Exactly."

"How is that better?"

"Working on that," I mutter.

"What do we think about this new court date thing?" Gabriel sighs after a pause.

"As much as I hate to say it," I shake my head again, "I think we need to consider it. Not because that asshole's demanding it. But who the fuck knows what's going to happen next week when Valerie and her husband head to divorce court? If she backs out or decides to take him back..."

Taylor nods. "Yeah, I wondered about that, too."

"*Shit.*" Gabriel scowls as he glances at his Rolex. "Fine, I'll reach out to Judge Hawkins' office."

"Keep us posted," I mutter as he walks out.

When he's gone, I suck on my teeth and then glance at Taylor.

"*Sooo...*"

She smirks. "What do you need? I recognize the Alister Black 'I need a favor' look when I see it."

I make a face. "It's a big one. You still heading to Chicago tomorrow?"

Taylor's scheduled a meeting with some prospective new clients, and a few existing ones who live in the Windy City. She's also going to scope out some office space, just to get a feel for things if we decide to go ahead with expanding out there.

Taylor nods. "Yes," she grins. "You want me to bring back a deep dish or Cubs tickets?"

"More like I need you to take Eloise with you."

Taylor's brow arches. *"I see."*

"It's not what you—"

"Alistair."

"Yes?"

"For the sake of both our friendship and professional relationship, please don't ever talk to me like I'm a fucking idiot ever again."

My mouth twists. "Sure. Sorry about that."

She nods. "Apology accepted. C'mon. It's *exactly* what I think with you and Eloise, isn't it."

"Objection. Leading the witness."

"Fuck off. Sustained. *And* guilty as fuck, while we're at it." She sighs. "I'm assuming Gabriel has already told you how terrible an idea this is?"

"Correct."

"Then I'll save my breath." She eyes me dubiously. "Fine, but only because I like you, and might like her even more. She can come."

I smile. "Yeah, well… That's the thing."

"What?"

"I need you to 'bring her'," I air-quote. "But not *actually* bring her."

Taylor, who's the opposite of an idiot, eyes me coolly.

"Okay," she finally says, nodding. "But do you know what you're doing?"

"Mostly?"

"Let's fucking hope so, Alistair."

26

ELOISE

I SPEND most of the morning lying in Alistair's bed, just *breathing*.

Not in a weird way. In an "I haven't been able to breathe without the crushing weight of anxiety or anger in far too long" kind of way.

That's what life under Massimo's thumb has felt like: a crushing weight pressing down on me. Even before him, there were all those years where I was incredibly lost and angry. Now, for the first time in forever, it feels like my head is actually above the water.

Whatever last bricks of the walls between Alistair and I came crashing down last night. And *God*, does that feel good.

I grin, blushing.

Fucking him three times last night did, too. *Very* good. But so did telling him I love him, and hearing him say it back, and knowing deep in my soul how true it is.

I've spent ten years telling myself I hated him for the same reason he apparently did concerning me: because admitting to myself that I was hurt because of what I felt for him was too hard. It was much easier to think of him as a callous, manipulative *asshole* who slept with me and then ignored me forever.

But now the truth is out there.

As if on cue, my phone rings for the millionth time. I glance down and grit my teeth as I silence it.

The truth *is* out there, including exactly how backstabbing and cruel my own sister is. I know Camille has issues with abandonment, and needs to feel important, like everyone's catering to her. But there's a line, and what she did falls about a solar system's length past that line.

So fuck her.

One day, maybe, we'll talk about what she did—both to Alistair and to me. But not today.

Tomorrow's not looking great, either.

I might pencil her in for about a decade from now. *Maybe.*

A few minutes of blissful silence later, my phone lights up with another call from Camille. Then again. And then *again,* all in a row. I'm about to turn the fucking thing off, when I jump at the sound of a fist pounding on the front door of Alistair's loft.

I pad quietly to the door of Alistair's bedroom and crack it open. The landing outside looks down through the open loft below, affording me a clear view of the front door.

Massimo?

The knock comes again, loudly.

I texted him last night, telling him I was "sorry we'd fought", but that I was upset and felt we "needed space", so I was staying in a hotel. All I got in response was "fine", then another text this morning telling me he was going to be working late.

The knock comes again, making my nerves jangle.

It'd be *insane* if it was Massimo. And near impossible. Why would he even think to look for me at—

"Eloise!! I know you're in there! We need to talk!"

What. The. *Fuck*.

My blood turns to fire at the sound of my sister's voice from outside.

"Eloise!! Please! Please, just let me explain!!"

I don't march down because I have any interest in talking to her. I march down so she shuts the hell up and stops screaming my name for every neighbor within a four-block radius to hear.

Camille gasps when I yank the door open in her face.

"*What,*" I snap coldly.

She immediately puts on one of her "faces", her mouth drooping and her eyes watering. It'd be touching, even somewhat heartbreaking, if I hadn't seen it a thousand times before. If I didn't know it was *bullshit*.

Honestly, somewhere in an alternate universe, Camille is an award-winning actress.

"*Hi,*" she chokes.

"If you go into your theatrics, I'm shutting this door right now."

The "trauma" face instantly vanishes. Her lips purse.

"Can I come in?"

I almost say no. I almost *do* slam the door in her face.

"You have five minutes."

I step aside, letting her in.

"This is a really nice—"

"How did you even get into the building?"

She turns, lifting a shoulder. "Flirted with the doorman. I told him I was here for Alistair." She grins. "He didn't even warn me that the gentleman of the house already *had* company…"

My face stays stony. Her smile drops.

"That was a joke."

"I'm not in the mood, Camille."

She nods, chewing on her lip. "Look, I just…"

"Why?" I glare at her. "I mean *what the fuck*, Camille?!"

"I was worried about you!"

"So you fucked three guys in my dorm room so Alistair would think you were me?"

She winces. "I know…it sounds crazy—"

"Because *it is*!" I yell, making her flinch. "Camille, I don't think you even realize what a horrible a thing you did. I mean, lying to me about sleeping with him is shitty enough, but—"

"I already apologized—"

"SHUT. UP."

Her mouth snaps shut, her eyes darting over my livid face.

"But what you pulled…" I squeeze my eyes shut, shaking my head. "I was sitting there in that hospital bed on the worst day of my life, and you looked me in the eye and *lied* to me!"

"I didn't—"

"You *did*!" I roar. "You fucking knew why Alistair was blocking me and ignoring my calls. You were *part* of it!"

"Ellie, I know you don't want to hear this—"

"Correct!"

"You weren't ready for a relationship—"

"That's for me to decide!"

She stammers. "He… He was bad for you!"

"No, he wasn't!"

"He—"

"Camille, I can't do this right—"

"He would have taken you away from me!!"

It's like a record scratch, and the music dies instantly. The loft goes silent as I stare open-mouthed at my sister.

"Is *that* what this was about?" I choke.

"Ellie…"

"You fucking *need me* as an emotional punching bag?!"

I know from the way her face pales I just hit the nail on the head.

"I—you're my sister, and if you were with him—"

"I wouldn't be *available* whenever you felt like acting psycho?!" I hiss. "Whenever you needed someone to confirm you as the main character of the world?!"

"Ellie, that's rude—"

"FUCK. YOU."

The words thunder from my chest with a force that genuinely terrifies me and sends Camille skittering back a few steps. Her eyes are wild as they dart over my face.

"*Okay,*" she says brusquely. "I can see you're upset."

I bark a bitter laugh.

"Stay the fuck out of my life, Camille. I need you gone, now."

Her eyes go wide. "You—!" she sputters indignantly. "You don't mean that."

"I *really* do."

I march past her and yank open the door to the loft.

"But first," I spit, whirling on her. "I want to hear you say it."

"What do you want me to—"

"I want you to admit that you went to my dorm room. How you knew Alistair was coming there because *I told you* he was. And how you fucked Ansel Albrecht and his buddies, and made it look like me."

Her face rearranges back into that pathetic "woe is me" look she had when she walked in here.

"*Eloise*," she fake-sobs. "We're sisters!"

"We sure are," I snap. "And *that* is what *you* do for your sister. Do you know what I do for mine? I marry a psychopath who has me hit, and who abuses and kills women *in front of me*, so that YOU can stay the fuck alive!!"

For the first time since she walked in, Camille keeps quiet.

"I don't owe you *anything* more than that, Camille," I say quietly, pointing to the open door.

Wordlessly, unable to meet my eye, she walks out, then turns.

"Eloise—"

"Goodbye, Camille."

I slam the door. Then I go back upstairs. For another five minutes I hear her knocking. Then, she's gone.

Who wants a drink?

ALISTAIR HAS, of course, hidden or possibly thrown away every drop of alcohol in the house. And I'm too nervous about being seen to leave and get some. Delivery is out, because Massimo has access to my accounts and I'm too paranoid about him spotting me having alcohol delivered to Alistair's home.

So I spend the afternoon watching mindless television, using Alistair's Peloton bike, taking a long bath, and then reading a book—*Hotel New Hampshire*, by John Irving, which is one of my favorites.

I'm about to text Alistair to ask what we should do for dinner, when my phone buzzes with a number I instantly recognize.

My dad's house in Paris.

"*Bonjour*?" I murmur cautiously.

"Ms. LeBlanc?"

I frown. "Yes? Who is this?"

"*Bonjour,* Ms. LeBlanc, my name is Rosa; I'm your father's caretaker."

We've emailed a few times since Marie dipped out to St. Tropez and hired Rosa. But we've never actually spoken on the phone.

Instantly I tense. "How's my father?"

"Oh! *Tout bien*!" She says cheerily. I like her already. "Everything is good, Ms. LeBlanc. He's just fine."

I exhale slowly. "That's great."

"Of course. I apologize if I frightened you. It's just that I've been cleaning out your father's home office at the request of Mrs. LeBlanc—"

That would be Marie.

"—and I came across some things I thought you might want."

My brow furrows. "Oh?"

"*Oui*. Just some papers and a letter—" She laughs musically. "I promise I didn't read them. They were all clipped together with a post-it note with your name on it."

"Weird."

"Would you like me to put them in the mail for you? I can send them express."

I smile, curious. "You know what? That'd be great. Thank you!"

"Ce n'est pas un problème!"

I give her Alistair's address, obviously. Then we end up chatting for a few more minutes about my dad and random stuff before we say goodbye.

I'm grinning when I hang up. My father might be in a coma, but at least now I have a voice to go with the stranger watching over him, and Rosa seems fantastic.

I'm lounging on the couch in panties and one of Alistair's shirts when there's a knock on the door.

Instantly, my mood sours again.

Goddammit, Camille.

I glance at my phone, and of course, there's a bunch of texts that I missed while I was chatting with Rosa.

CAMILLE:

Eloise, we're sisters!

CAMILLE:

Please!

CAMILLE:

Let's talk.

CAMILLE:

i need you

CAMILLE:

I think I'm dying, can you come over?

CAMILLE:

Or I'll come to you, unless I die on the way.

The knock comes again, and I roll my eyes as I reluctantly get off the couch and stomp over to yank it open.

"You're not fucking *dy*—"

My heart lurches.

Rocco smiles cruelly at me. His gaze takes in my attire and bare legs, making my skin crawl before they drag back to my face.

"Mrs. Carveli…"

I jolt out of my frozen state and try to slam the door closed, but he's way faster, and stronger. Rocco shoves the door open as I stumble backward into Alistair's loft. He smiles darkly as he steps inside and shuts the door behind him.

"Rocco, listen to me—"

"This isn't a good look, Mrs. Carveli," he growls. "At another man's house? Dressed like this?"

"Rocco—"

"Mrs. Carveli, I see more than people think I do. It's one of the reasons I'm so valuable to your husband. It's my job to look out for him."

I swallow, my eyes dropping to the gun in the holster at his waist sticking out from under his jacket.

"So when I get the impression that his wife is fuckin' around with her boss—"

"Rocco, hang on! I'm only here because—"

"I think you need to come with me, Mrs. Carveli."

"I don't think so."

He smiles grimly. "It wasn't a request. Let's go."

I shake my head.

"*Now*, Mrs. Car—"

I bolt and *run*, sprinting for the spiral staircase up to the landing. If I can get to Alistair's room, I can lock the door and call—

I don't even make it to the stairs.

Rocco grabs my waist, hauling me backward as I flail my arms and legs.

"Don't touch me!!" I scream, trying to hit him, but failing miserably. "Don't you fucking *touch*—"

Rocco hurls me to the ground and I groan when I hit it hard. As I scramble to my feet, a roar behind me has me whirling back toward him.

Holy shit.

The roar wasn't Rocco.

It was *Alistair*.

He slams into Rocco, sending him backward over a chair before lunging at him. His fists slam Rocco's face over and over before the thug manages to kick him away. He lurches at Alistair, whipping out a vicious looking blade that has me screaming and scanning the loft for a weapon of some kind.

My eyes land on the poker in its little stand next to the fireplace.

That'll work.

I rush over to grab it. When I turn back, I go still.

Alistair is straddling Rocco, the knife knocked to the side, punching him again and again and again. Blood splatters from his fists, and the dull wet thuds of meat being pulverized fill the room.

Abruptly, mid-swing, he stops.

We're both silent. Alistair stares down at the totally still body. His bloodied fists drop, and he turns to stare at me.

"*Alistair*...Are you okay?"

He shakes his head grimly, standing and wiping his hands on his shirt. Then he glances down at the carnage on his clothes.

"*Fuck.*"

27

ALISTAIR

"Thanks for coming."

Kratos nods, planting a heavy hand on my shoulder. "All good." His dark brows furrow deeply. "You okay?"

I nod. "I'm fine."

He glances past me, gesturing with his chin up to my open bedroom door, where Eloise is.

"*She* okay?"

"She will be."

We both turn and glance at the rug he brought over, which is now wrapped around a tarp, which in turn is wrapped around Rocco's body.

Kratos glances to me. "That your first…time?"

He means first kill. The answer is yes. I've hit men. I've seriously fucked people up, and sent them to the hospital, but that's the first life I've taken.

I feel nothing.

Not a poetic "gnawing cold of nothing", I mean I literally don't feel anything remotely approaching guilt, or shame, or any kind of "bad" for killing that piece of shit.

All I know is I'd do it again in a heartbeat to anyone who laid a hand on Eloise.

"You got anything to drink around here?"

I nod. "Yeah."

Kratos follows me into the kitchen, where I yank a bottle of whiskey out from behind the cereal boxes on a shelf above the fridge. Yes, I hid it from Eloise. Sue me.

"Ice? Neat?"

He shakes his head. "Not for me, man. For you."

"I'm good."

He just takes the bottle from me, grabs a glass, and pours me a hefty shot.

"Drink it. Trust me. You're fine right *now*, but there's going to be an edge coming, and this'll dull it. Drink."

Fuck it.

I knock back the whiskey in one heavy slug and set the glass back down as I swallow.

"Better?"

"Yeah, actually." I flash him a grateful smile. "Thanks."

He nods and leans his large frame back against my fridge with his arms folded over his chest.

"So, what happens now?"

"How active is your building? I mean, are residents going in and out all night?"

I shake my head. "Nope."

"Good. I'm going to chill here with the asshole"...he nods at the rolled-up rug..."for a while. If that's okay."

"I get the feeling one of us is the expert here, and it's not me."

Kratos chuckles quietly. "I'll wait until midnight or so, drag his sorry ass out to my car where I parked out back. After that..." He clears his throat. "Let's be real, Alistair. Probably best if you don't know."

"Not your first rodeo?"

He grins and shakes his head. "Nope. Look, you're clear of this. It's never coming back on you, or her. One of my guys swiped the tapes from the building security office before I even got here. And this fucker's car has been..." he shrugs. "Well, again, you don't need to know the details. His credit card is going to show up making some purchases in New Jersey, then in Kentucky, then southern Florida, and that's that."

I exhale, nodding. "I owe you."

"Yeah, probably," he chuckles. "How about for starters you don't mention this to my brothers, yeah?"

I grin, shaking his outstretched hand. "Deal."

Ares, Kratos' oldest brother and the head of the Drakos family, does a *lot* of their business—both criminal and legitimate—through Crown and Black. And of course, Hades, the next oldest Drakos brother, is married to Elsa Guin, one of our top attorneys and an equity partner.

Kratos is helping me today because...well, because he's a friend. But also, the Drakos family has *zero* love for the Carvelis. Not when Luca, and then fucking *Massimo*, tried to force a marriage to Calliope, who is Ares', Hades', Deimos', and Kratos' little sister.

"You two should get out of here," Kratos rumbles. "I'll stick around, clean up anything that needs cleaning up..."

Blood. He means blood.

"And then I'll take out the trash. Sounds good?"

"Sounds like I seriously owe you."

He grins as we shake hands again. "Don't worry about it, man. I'm always up for anything that kicks dirt in that fuck Massimo's face."

ELOISE IS quiet as she stands in the entryway to the hotel suite, drinking it in. She's been silent the whole way here, and my mind is going to the worst possible scenarios.

She shouldn't have seen what she did. But there was no way around it. When I barged in and saw that piece of shit putting his hands on her—especially when I realized it was Rocco, the fucker who slapped her around for Massimo—there was only one conclusion.

But still, she just witnessed me kill a man with my bare hands. She saw me bloodied and savage, the worst, monstrous version of myself.

She hasn't said a word since.

Fuck.

I frown as I close the door to the suite overlooking Central Park West.

"It's just for a few days," I say. "Again, it's going to look like you're on a business trip to Chicago with Taylor. He won't know you're in New York."

I don't know what the solution here is. But I *do not* want her with that psycho. It's not like we'll be able to keep this up forever, but I can buy us some days…a week, tops…before Massimo gets suspicious.

Unless he already is.

Eloise crosses the floor to the windows. She puts her hand on the glass, staring wordlessly out across Central Park.

I walk up behind her, keeping my distance, trying not to startle her.

"Eloise…" I shake my head. "I'm sorry you saw—"

"Thank you."

She turns, her eyes locking with mine.

"Alistair…"

"I know it's a lot to take in, and if you want to talk—even to someone else—about what you saw—"

"I saw you save my life."

She moves toward me quickly, and I catch her in my arms as she hugs me fiercely. Her mouth presses to mine, kissing me slow and deep as she clings tightly to me.

When she pulls away, suddenly, she's the Eloise I know again.

"I don't need to 'talk to' anyone. And I don't see you any differently," she says quietly, as if she's seen the unspoken question in my eyes. Her lips curl up. "And this place is *amazing*."

"Amazing enough to be home for a few days?"

She grins. "Uh, *yeah*."

"Good."

Her hands grip mine tightly, even though I had zero of intention of moving away.

"Alistair?"

"Yeah?"

Her lip worries in her teeth.

"While I'm here..." Her eyes lift to mine. "Will you stay with me?"

"That wasn't ever a question."

28

ALISTAIR

"Have you lost your goddamn *mind*?!"

Two days after I move Eloise into the hotel, I look up from my desk when Gabriel storms into my office. From the look on his face, it's obvious the secret's already out.

"How'd you get Taylor to spill?"

He glares at me, shaking his head. "She didn't. She didn't *have* to, Alistair," he grunts. "I'm a good fucking lawyer. I can smell bullshit when it stinks."

"You're welcome to use the shower in my private bath—"

"It's *reckless*," he growls quietly, stomping over and dropping into one of the chairs across the desk from me.

"I know what I'm doing," I mutter back.

"Do you?"

"She couldn't stay with him, Gabriel," I hiss. "The man's a psychopath."

"I'm not denying that," my brother sighs tiredly. "But exactly what the *fuck* do you think the outcome is of you shacking up with Massimo's *wife*?"

"She's at a hotel, Gabriel, not in my bed."

"Yeah? And which bed have *you* been in the last few nights?"

Touché.

"There's been zero indication from fuckstick that he suspects anything. Their marriage is a sham. He doesn't have any interest in her, doesn't even touch her. He married her in exchange for the smuggling operation he got from her father. That's. It. You can relax."

"Can I?" Gabriel mutters. "What happens after Eloise returns from her *business trip*," he air-quotes. "Is she going to be our perpetually on-the-road lawyer?"

I shrug. "That's not a bad idea."

"It's a terrible idea!" he spits. "Reality is going to catch up to you, Alistair."

"Gabriel, I'm an orphan with a murky background who went on to graduate law school and found one of the most prestigious firms in New York before the age of thirty-four." I smile wryly. "I stopped believing in reality a long time ago."

He smirks. "Okay, fair. I'm just…"

"Worried about me?" I grin. "I know. Thanks."

"I mean, somebody has to be." Gabriel exhales and glances at his watch. "Okay, I have to run and go over my notes."

I nod grimly. As much as I hate to admit it, Charles was correct. Judge Hawkins' schedule *did* have an unexpected opening this week, and she agreed to move our court time up. So tomorrow is the day we'll be dropping our iron-clad alibi and blowing this case out of the water before it even sets sail.

"You've got this, brother."

Gabriel stands, buttoning his jacket. "I know."

I snicker. "Asshole."

There's a knock on my office door, and we glance up as Katerina walks in.

"Mr. Black?" She nods at me. "I just had a call from Mr. Carveli's assistant."

My eyes snap to my brother, whose jaw is clenched.

"What the hell did they want?" I mutter, dragging my gaze back to Kat. When I do, my gaze slips down to her hand at her side, holding a set of keys on a pink lanyard.

It's her spare set that includes the key to my office and one to my locked file cabinet of VIP case files, and I've seen it on her person or desk about a million times. But for some reason, seeing it here in my office is making something ping in the back of my head, like a memory I can't quite access, hidden behind a fog.

I frown at the lanyard, trying to cut through the haze in my mind.

"Uh...Mr. Black?"

I blink as I refocus on her. "Yeah."

"I was saying, Mr. Carveli would like to have dinner with you. Tomorrow night at eight, at Keens Steakhouse."

"Do we know what this is about?" Gabriel asks.

Katerina shakes her head. "His assistant said Mr. Carveli just wanted to catch up." She raises an eyebrow at me. "Is that a no, or shall I call back and confirm?"

"Can I talk to you in private for a minute?" Gabriel grunts at me.

"In a second." I glance back to Katerina. "Go ahead and confirm. Thanks, Katerina."

When she's gone, Gabriel fixes me with a despairing look.

"What? I'll be fine."

"You're shacked up with the man's *wife,* Alistair," he growls. "Exactly how is this going to be fine?"

"He doesn't know," I shoot back.

"And if he does?"

"Don't you have to go study?"

"I do, but I'd like to clarify that my brother isn't going to do something stupid and get himself killed at dinner."

"It's Keens Steakhouse, not a warehouse out in Bushwick," I say flatly. "Massimo's psycho, but I don't think he's quite psycho enough to stab me over a porterhouse and a glass of fucking Chianti."

"You willing to bet your life on that?"

"I'm willing to bet a meal at Keens on that."

He sighs. "Just…be careful."

"You know me."

"Precisely what worries me," he sighs. Then he frowns. "You *sure* you're good?"

"I'm great."

EXCEPT, I'm not.

Not really.

It's not that I feel *bad* at all for killing Rocco. But it is... weighing on me. Sending people that I've beaten pretty badly to hospital is one thing. Taking a life with my bare hands is apparently not something I'm mentally prepared for, even though I know in my blood I'd do it again, if the scenario were to repeat itself.

Normally, my siblings are good sounding boards when something's bothering me. Or Taylor. But there's no way in hell I'm burdening them with this shit. With Tempest, it's that I don't want to see the look in her eye when she realizes I'm a killer. Gabriel could take something like that. I think Taylor could, too. But I'm not putting the burden of criminal liability that comes with knowing about my crime on any of them.

So for now, it's just inside me.

Gnawing at me.

Putting me on edge.

That's the state I'm in when Katerina gently reminds me that my one o'clock has arrived. I don't even glance at my schedule to see who it is. I just float down there in a daze.

Which is why it hits me so abruptly when I open the door to Conference Room B and find Ansel fucking Albrecht sitting at the table, smiling at me.

"Alistair!" he says cheerily, standing and sticking out a hand. "Thanks for sitting down with me!"

I ignore his outstretched hand and take a seat across from him.

"What is this?" I growl quietly. "Taylor and her team are your liaisons with the firm."

Ansel clears his throat, withdrawing his unshaken hand. He stays standing, though, and I really, *really* don't like the way he's looking down on me with this smug expression.

"I thought you and I should meet to…" He shrugs. "You know, clear the air."

"My air is perfectly clear," I growl.

Ansel smiles patronizingly. "Alistair, please. I know you're not my biggest fan."

"I don't follow my clients like sports teams. I'm neither a fan or not a fan of anyone I work with."

But I do think you're a piece of shit.

His smug grin just grows wider as he stands there.

"Alistair, I know you objected to me working with Crown and Black."

I mean, *I did,* but I sincerely doubt Gabriel would have mentioned that. He's just guessing, knowing that I don't like him.

"I'm afraid you've been misinformed, Ansel," I say coldly. "Now, what did you want to discuss?"

He shakes his head. "Nothing, really. I just wanted us to… clear the air."

"Consider it cleared," I grunt, standing and turning to the door.

"You've done quite well for yourself, Alistair."

I stop, turning to eye him coolly.

"I mean, I'm stunned by what you've accomplished with this firm. It's truly impressive. For an orphan, I mean."

A whining sound hums in my ears. My jaw tightens.

Ansel grins. "Normally it would take someone with real *pedigree* to open a firm with this sort of power and prestige. So, I applaud you, Alistair."

Keep it up, motherfucker.

"As much as I'd love to pretend we're still in college and have time to trade insults, Ansel," I mutter, "I'm afraid I have work to do."

He nods. "Of course. I was walking through your offices the other day, and I was amazed at how *busy* everyone seemed!" He grins that smug, condescending smile at me again. "It's truly wonderful what someone like you has accomplished here."

Someone like you.

My eye twitches.

"And the *wildest* thing," he continues, "is who I saw the other day, when I was walking through your offices!"

"Oh?" I grunt.

He chuckles. "I had to do a triple-take, but fuck me if it wasn't Eloise LeBlanc. Working here, at *your* firm!"

"Indeed," I growl.

Ansel beams at me. "Wow…I guess that was one way to get her, huh?"

The whining in my ears grows louder. My hands close to fists as Ansel's grin lasers in on me.

"Don't tell me you didn't pine after her like a puppy dog back at Knightsblood," he chuckles. "Fucking hell, your face that night, when you thought it was her that me and the boys were gang-banging?" He starts to laugh louder. "*Damn*, I wish I'd had a camera."

"I think this meeting is over," I mutter , rage throbbing in my veins.

His brow arches. "Here's the *really* interesting question though, Alistair. See, I'm sure you hired Eloise because she gets you all hard and squirmy. But…" He grins. "When I saw her the other day, she was talking to you. And the smile on her face?" His eyes laser in on me. "Usually, I'd say that's how a woman looks at the man she's fucking. But…Eloise is married, isn't she?"

I meet his gaze unblinkingly. "She is."

"And not to you, right?"

"Ansel, does *any* of this shit have a point?"

He laughs to himself and starts to stroll around the conference room table. "I like this new, all-business Alistair. You were such a prick at school when you were running The Reckless."

"Funny, you're still one."

He grins. "Well, since you're going to be working for me now, I'll let you in on a little secret, Alistair," he sneers. "Sadly, I never did get to fuck your little crush. But even though it wasn't her that you saw that night..." He sighs heavily.

My vision starts to darken at the corners. My brain starts analyzing the way he's standing, noticing he's unguarded, as if I'm in one of the underground rings about to unleash hell.

He *needs* to stop talking and walk the fuck away.

"Here's the thing, Alistair..."

He's smiling at me, clearly taking my stoic silence and clenched fists as me shutting down when he *should* be taking it as the direct threat it is.

"While I was fucking her slut sister," he grins, leering close. "I was imagining that pussy was *Eloise's*."

Something ticks over inside me, like a bomb about to explode.

"The same creamy French vanilla *cunt*, know what I mean?" he giggles. "And while I was fucking that slut from behind, you know what I was doing?"

I'm a hair's breadth away from snapping as he leans close, grinning right in my face.

"I snuck a pair of Eloise's panties out of the laundry earlier, and I fucking held that lace to my nose and inhaled like it was my last breath on Earth while I fucked her sis—"

I fucking *snap*. It's him, and the way he's talking about Eloise, and the emotions still charging through my system from what happened with Rocco.

Ansel goes down on the first hit. But I don't let him off that easily. I haul him back up, and I hit him again, and again, and again. I hit him so hard he flies out of my grip and smashes his face into the side of the conference table, shattering his nose. He's screaming and blubbering when I grab him by the collar and yank him up to his knees as I hit him again.

He's still screaming when four associates rush in and haul me off him.

29

ELOISE

All things considered, living in a luxurious hotel suite overlooking Central Park is pretty darned good. It's like being on permanent vacation, spending my time lounging, taking long bubble baths, eating decadent room service, and obviously, having *phenomenal,* toe-curling sex with Alistair.

In the back of my mind, I know there's danger lurking out there. And I know this can't last forever. I mean, I can only be on a "business trip with Taylor in Chicago" for so long before it gets suspicious.

That said, Massimo hasn't once reached out to me, which is…slightly alarming. It's not as if my terror of a husband has ever been the type to text or call "just to see how I'm doing" or anything like that. It's more like "where the fuck are you", "be sure to look good tonight", and various other vague or not-so-vague threats.

But the fact that he hasn't reached out at *all* is slightly unnerving.

Especially since Rocco is dead. Or, at least as far as Massimo knows, is missing and possibly in south Florida. But again, there's been radio silence. Not even a text mentioning the fact that his guard dog is MIA, like he hasn't noticed—or if he has, it hasn't affected him at all.

To be honest, it hasn't affected *me* the way I thought it might.

After I saw what I did that day, I worried I'd have night-mares, or horrible replays on a loop in my head watching Alistair literally kill someone right in front of me with his bare hands. I worried it would change how I saw him, or erase that safe, homey feeling I have around him.

I needn't have worried. Because if anything, after witnessing that, I only feel *safer* around him. Even *more* protected, like he's a fortress built around me. I haven't once looked at Alis-tair since that day and seen "murderer".

I've just seen a dark knight in black armor.

My dark knight.

But it's on the third day of my hotel staycation when the cracks in the walls I've built around myself and my dark knight begin to appear.

The first one is stupid, and it's my own fault for prying, and I know it's dumb and something I should just brush off. But when it happens, all I can feel is a green, jealous twisting sensation inside my chest.

It starts when Alistair is over late one night, having a video chat with Taylor, who's still in Chicago. He's sitting in a chair by the glass doors out to the balcony, his headphones in as he chats away with her. When he roars with laughter, I look up from the book I'm reading. At first, I just grin, looking at him—at the way the corners of his eyes crinkle, and the smile lines in his perfect jaw. The way his eyes glint with both a promise of danger and a genuine happiness.

But then my eyes shift to the reflection of the laptop screen in the glass behind him. My lip retreats between my teeth as I see Alistair laughing away, with Taylor's face on the screen laughing as well.

Taylor's gorgeous, stunning, successful, powerful face. *Alistair's* gorgeous, stunning, successful, powerful face.

Merde...

It's like there's a little piece of Camille inside me—a tiny snippet of her batshit crazy that somehow lingered in the womb and managed to infiltrate my own DNA. I know—I mean, I *know*—from just watching them together and from the abundance of gossip at Crown and Black surrounding the three name partners that there is *nothing* romantic between Alistair and Taylor. Nor has there, allegedly, ever been. I've even heard him and Gabriel casually refer to Taylor as "their sister".

But ultimately, she's *not* Alistair's sister. She's a wildly beautiful, confident, successful woman seemingly without a shred of baggage who works in very close proximity to Alistair. Whom he's known, closely and intimately, since law school.

Right after he forgot about me.

I know. It's ridiculous. But again, it's like there's a little piece of Camille in me. Because when I see the two of them cracking up and making each other laugh so easily over video as they chat about things clearly unrelated to work, the jealous monster inside of me rises up and *snarls*.

The monster's still lingering inside me the next day. It's early evening, and I'm sitting in nothing but a pair of panties in the kitchen area after a marathon fuck-fest with Alistair.

I glance over at him and grin to myself. He's not exactly all smiles, but he's also not the dark thundercloud that walked through the door a few hours ago.

Apparently, there was a...*physical* altercation with Ansel at the Crown and Black offices today. Alistair won't tell me what it was about. But, I mean, I can guess.

The long-term problem isn't just that he hit a client, or that he broke said client's nose, or even *who* the client is. It's that he's now been reported to the New York State Bar Association, which long story short might result in him temporarily losing his license to practice law. It would be bad for him and *horrible* for the firm.

So I've spent the last two hours fucking him silly to take his mind off that.

"You're so wrong it's embarrassing," he grins at me across the kitchen. We're taking a small break for much-needed hydration and snacks. Which is how we have ended up here in our underwear playfully arguing about Star Wars, of all things.

It's also not lost on me when Alistair glances meaningfully at the can of lemon seltzer water in my hand, rather than a drink.

I haven't had one in days. A real drink, that is. And I have to say, it feels good.

I know probably everyone with a problem says this at some point, but I've truly never felt like I really had *"a problem"* with alcohol. Or at least, I never had a problem with alcohol that "just snuck up on me". Or "got the better of me".

I *know* I had a problem, because I did it on purpose. I did it to escape and to dull out the life I was forced to live. And it's almost as if the more I'm unchained, by Alistair, from that life I don't want to live, the less need I feel to dull out the world around me.

Or maybe, as nauseatingly cutesy as it is, I've just found a new addiction that is *far* more fun than drinking.

Alistair.

"It's 'Luke, I am your father'," Alistair grins, rolling his eyes. "This is indisputable."

I snicker, shaking my head. "Objection."

"Overruled. It's like the most famous line in the original trilogy."

"It's the most famously *misremembered* line in the original trilogy. The actual wording is 'No, *I* am your father'."

Alistair throws an infuriatingly confident yet way too sexy look at me. "You're wrong."

"Let's find out."

"Do it. When you're wrong, you can get on your knees with your mouth wide open, right here, right now."

Heat simmers in my core. "*Oh?*" I grin. "And if I'm right?"

"Then you can lie back on that couch over there and spread your pretty thighs for me to crawl between and lick your clit until you see God."

Holy hell.

"Deal," I blurt, my face burning. I glance around. "Crap, my phone's charging in the bedroom."

He nods to his, sitting on the kitchen island right by me. "Use mine."

I'm googling the answer...which, by the way, I *know* I'm right about...when the text pops up.

JANELLE (BOOM BOOM ROOM WAITRESS):

hey. super random but i'm off tonight and bored. WYD? u wanna chill?

JANELLE (BOOM BOOM ROOM WAITRESS):

i could wear that dress you liked and come over

JANELLE (BOOM BOOM ROOM WAITRESS):

and nothing but the dress

I don't realize I'm glaring *death* at his phone until Alistair says my name for maybe the fourth time.

"Well?" he snickers from across the kitchen. "Am I right?"

It's none of my business. I don't have any right to say a single thing about—

"Who the fuck is Janelle?"

Alistair's brows furrow as I fire a lethal glare at him.

"What?"

"*Boom Boom Room* Janelle?" I snap. "You know, to narrow it down for you?"

His face remains neutral.

"All coming back to you now, is it?" I mutter. "She just texted, if you're interested."

"I'm not."

"She's offering to wear that dress you like so much," I spit. "Oh, and *noooothing eeeelse*," I drawl out in a dumb blonde voice. "Shall I tell her what time to swing by—"

"Eloise."

I shrug, looking away. "Whatever. It's not like we're—"

"For the record, I haven't spoken to that woman in eight months."

"Good for you."

He rolls his eyes. "Scroll up if you don't believe me. Look when the last text exchange was. If I recall, I wasn't too nice."

My lips purse petulantly. I want to say that I don't care. But I so obviously *do*, and he so obviously *knows* it. I scroll up. Sure enough, the last exchange is from well over eight months ago, where bitch-cow Janelle is asking Alistair if he wants to "come over and fuck her however he wants."

Rage shoots through me until I see his reply.

ME:

Janelle, for the last time, please stop fucking contacting me. It was once, almost a year ago, and I'm not interested in pursuing anything. I could be nice and say my work takes up too much of my time. But it is simply that you and I are not compatible. Have some fucking respect for yourself and stop messaging me.

God, he's being a dick but *still* being somewhat of a gentleman about it. That's almost more infuriating, because why is he so freaking perfect.

So—he's right. This isn't some ongoing current hookup. And yet, that knowledge does almost nothing to quell the jealousy churning inside of me.

"How many other Janelles would I find in your phone if I looked?"

Alistair's face darkens a touch as his eyes slide up to mine.

"I don't know, Eloise. How many *current husbands, whom you are fucking MARRIED TO,* would I find in yours?"

There's a cold edge to his voice. I shiver, but I glare back.

"Just the fake one I'm not actually in any sort of real relationship with in any capacity!"

"You're married to the motherfucker," he snaps. "That's real."

"Excuse me?!" I hiss back.

"It's a *legally binding contract,*" he shouts, his face getting angrier, "between you and that fuck-face. So please, Eloise, come after me with your jealous bullshit concerning a woman I barely even remember from over a year ago."

I bark a cold laugh. "Oh, are there just so many of them that you lose track!?"

Alistair looks away, pinching the bridge of his nose. "I've had a *shit* day, Eloise."

"I didn't ask you to fight Ansel Albrecht for me!"

He glares at me. "Look, concerning my dating life, I'm thirty-four years old, Eloise. I'm allowed to have had other adult relationships. And you and I were a long time ago—"

"Oh, there was no *you and I.* I was just one of the random Janelles you fuck once and then drop."

His face turns livid. "I think we've covered—*at length*—what happened in the past." His lips curl. "And it wasn't just once, was it?"

"I don't know, you tell me!" I hurl back. "If you can even *remember* with all of the girls you've plowed since—"

"Since you *got married*?!" he roars back. His brow deepens. "Speaking of which, why the *fuck* have you not filed for a divorce already? Unless the thrill for you in all of this is fucking me while you're still happily married to that—"

"Oh, yes, *so happily*!" I yell. "You caught me, Alistair! This is my kink: sleeping with you while I'm *happily* married to a sociopath who hits me!"

"Then file! You could do it literally right now, and I'd help!"

"I *can't*!" I scream. "What about my father? Or Camille?!"

"*Fuck* Camille!" He roars. "A, she's a conniving, manipulative, emotionally abusive bitch. B, she's got enough money to hire her own security."

"And my father? I guess just fuck him too, and let Massimo come after him while he's in a coma?!" I yell back. "He's my *father*, Alistair!"

"Yes, you seem to have so much respect for a man who sold you to Massimo fucking Carveli for some *smuggling operation*. Real class act, that father of yours. I can see why you care so much."

My face turns to stone as I look at him coldly.

"That's not fair."

"That's reality."

"Don't you *dare* project your own parental issues onto mine!" I seethe.

The hotel suite goes silent.

Fuck.

Instantly, I cringe inside. That was the line, and here I am about a mile past it.

"Shit, Alistair—"

"It's fine," he snaps. He glares at me before turning and striding across the suite. He grabs his clothes from where they got flung earlier by the couch and starts yanking on his pants and his shirt.

"Wait, Alistair, I'm sorry."

"Yeah? Good for you."

I pale when he grabs his keys off the floor and then his jacket off the back of the couch.

"Wait! Where are you—"

"I need some air."

My face falls.

"Hang on, please—"

"I'll be back once I sort through my *family issues,*" he snarls, yanking the hotel door open. He pauses in the doorway without looking back. "Don't wait up."

The door slams, and my heart sinks.

Shit.

30

ALISTAIR

"WHAT DO YOU THINK?" I grunt, nodding to Kratos. "We doing one more?"

He groans, looking as drunk as I feel as he shoves a big hand through his dark hair. "I mean…we could do *one* more."

We've been saying this for the last three hours that we've been sitting in Bar Great Harry, in Brooklyn. Before that—which is the reason every single part of me hurts, especially my face—we were at the fights out in Bushwick.

I glance at Kelly, the bartender who's been serving us way later than she should, and grin.

"Two more?" she chuckles from the far end of the bar, looking up from her book.

"Please and thank you."

I drop my eyes to the book in her hand, which looks like the LSAT textbook to prep you for law school.

"You want to be a lawyer?"

She nods as she pours Kratos and I two more whiskies. "In a perfect world."

"Cool, I'm hiring. I can't work with my existing associate anymore. Personality conflicts."

She grins and shakes her head. "Yeah, you mentioned that."

"Like, ten times, dude," Kratos mutters.

When Kelly goes back to her book, I turn to my friend.

"Hell of a night."

He whistles. "Yeah, you wanna warn me the next time you invite me out for fight night if you're going to be using it for therapy?"

Okay, tonight was a bit much. I can usually manage three fights in a night. If I'm feeling angry or need to work through some shit, I can do five.

Tonight Kratos dragged me away after eight.

He nods at me. "How's the face feeling?"

"Like I slammed it into a bus, thanks."

He nods. "And the rest of you?"

"I'm fine, Kratos."

"I'm not talking about from the fight, if that wasn't obvious." He exhales slowly. "You wanna talk about the trouble in paradise back home?"

"I think I'm all set with barroom therapy, Kratos, but thanks."

"Yeah, you're right. *Eight* fights and then drinking until dawn is definitely a much healthier way to deal."

I scowl. "It's dawn?"

I turn and peer through the windows. Fuck me. He's right.

"Jesus, Kelly, kick us out and go home already."

She snickers from her book. "Don't sweat it. My roommates are party animals. I get *way* better studying done here, believe me."

Kratos raises a brow, looking past me. "You're sure you don't want to talk about it at all?"

"Positive."

"Well, something tells me you're about to, anyway."

I turn as the door to the bar opens. Bleary-eyed, I blink as Taylor fixes me with a "what the fuck is wrong with you" look.

"Thirsty, Taylor?"

She rolls her eyes as she marches over.

"What the fuck are you doing?"

"Having a cocktail."

She glares at me. "It's five-thirty in the morning, Alistair."

"I was working late."

Her gaze lands on my left eye, which is starting to swell. "I can see that," she mutters dryly. "Too busy being a drunk to answer your fucking phone?"

I frown, pulling out my cell. Shit. I've got like twenty missed calls and two dozen texts between her and my brother. There's even a few worried ones from Tempest.

I raise my eyes to Taylor. "How'd you find me?"

She nods to Kratos. "His sister-in-law."

He frowns, sipping his drink. "Which one?"

"Elsa. Hades mentioned this was one of your haunts. I figured, correctly, that my absentee partner would be here with you."

"What can I say," Kratos grunts. "Kelly's the best."

Taylor turns to level a cool eye at our bartender. "*Kelly* is also serving you both almost two hours past the legal serving time in New York," she says pointedly.

"*Hey*," I wag a finger at Taylor. "Be nice. She's going to be our new hire."

"She's reading an LSAT study book."

"As soon as she goes to law school and then passes the bar, she's going to be our new—"

"Outside," Taylor mutters, grabbing my collar. "I need to talk to you."

Outside the bar, I groan as I lean against the wall, shoving my fingers through my hair.

"You look like shit, by the way."

"Good morning to you, too, Taylor." I frown. "Aren't you supposed to still be in Chicago?"

"I came back a little early." Her lips thin. "Roberto Chinellato wants to speak with you in person. Like, now."

I give her a look. "Yeah, that's not happening. Sounds like a Gabriel job."

"He specifically asked for you."

I groan. "Okay, *fine*. I'll grab a cab—"

"He's in gen pop at Fairview now."

I tense. "Wait, *what*?"

There are two kinds of criminal who are generally "fine" in the general population of a large prison: the small guys no one gives two shits about, and the big fish who are so well protected that nobody fucks with them.

Roberto Chinellato is the unlucky type that falls right in the middle. He's not small time, but he's not a kingpin, either. And he's been in this game long enough to have a list of enemies a mile long. Worse, even *I've* heard the rumors of Roberto being a snitch here and there a decade or so ago.

Taylor nods grimly. "He got moved last night. That's why I've been calling you, and why I flew back early."

Son of a bitch.

"Who the fuck authorized that?" I hiss, suddenly far more sober than I should be. "He's a walking corpse in Fairview."

"Why the hell do you think I got on a plane at midnight?" Taylor mutters, tapping away on her phone. "It looks like it was the new assistant DA."

"*Fuck,*" I hiss, just as Kratos joins us outside. "We need to go see Roberto at Fairview, stat."

Kratos makes a face. "I'm definitely not driving anywhere right now."

"No shit. Same."

Taylor sighs. "I'm parked up the street. Let's go."

"You look like shit, counselor."

Roberto Chinellato is old-school, dyed-in-the-wool, mama's gravy and meatballs Brooklyn mafia. He's pushing seventy, but still has the look of a man who's spent his life cracking skulls and taking names. A crucifix tattoo covers one forearm, with the Virgin Mary and Child on the other, alongside the Italian flag.

He grins a toothy smile at me, running his fingers through his thinning silver hair.

"Nice shiner, too," he grunts, nodding at my eye.

I take a sip of shit coffee as Roberto leans his elbows on the table between us. We're at Fairview Prison up in the Hudson Valley, about thirty minutes outside the city. Instead of in an indoor interrogation room or visitors hall, we're outside in a fenced-in side yard at one of the half dozen bolted-down picnic tables.

Why? Because that's what they do with prisoners who're suddenly being transferred into protective isolation.

I raise my good eye to the bloody bandage on Roberto's neck, then down to the clean one wrapped around his hand.

"Pot-kettle-black," I grunt, nodding at his fresh wounds.

Roberto *was* moved to Fairview gen pop without warning, despite that being a shitty idea for a guy with as many enemies as him, and sure enough, somebody made a play for his life within an hour of him being dropped off there.

Luckily, Roberto is tough as nails, and managed to wrench the shiv out of the attacker's hands. His hands are pretty sliced up for his troubles, but he did grab the homemade knife before it could damage his neck too badly.

Roberto chuckles as he rolls his shoulders. "You should see the other guy."

I smile wryly. "Well, protective isolation should put an end to that. I've already submitted a motion to extend that as long as we deem necessary, by the way. How's the neck?"

"Enough small talk." His brow furrows. "I asked you here, Mr. Black, because there are some things you need to know."

"Well, I *am* one of your attorneys, Mr. Chinellato. And you're enjoying client privilege right now, even out here. No cameras, no recordings. You can speak freely."

He pauses, then smiles. "You and your gramps aren't exactly on good terms, I hear."

My jaw tenses. "I'd say that's putting it mildly."

"Well," he winks. "It's about to get worse. You know he and I have done some business together, yeah?"

I nod. It's one of the reasons Charles has been hounding Taylor, Gabriel, and I so much about this goddamn case.

"Well, a few months back, I was involved in a deal with some people in Chicago. I didn't know it, but your grandfather also had some money invested with these assholes. When the deal went tits-up and sideways, well..." Roberto grimaces. "I...may have tried to walk with the merchandise and the cash."

Jesus Christ.

"Guns came out, I got two of this other prick's lieutenants, he got a bunch of my guys. The deal was fucked, and needless to say, Charles and me, we had a bit of a falling out. I don't exactly expect a Christmas card from him anytime soon. Still, your gramps and me, we worked out a deal."

"What *kind* of deal?"

"Well, these other pricks wanted my ass, and Charles and me both knew the feds were itching to come down on me too. So we came up with an agreement where he'd get his grandsons—you and your brother—to get me a reduced sentence, since you're a couple of superhero miracle lawyers."

I frown. "Mr. Chinellato, we're planning on getting you no jail time *at all*. You're going to get those charges dropped entirely."

He smiles thinly. "Yeah? What about until someone makes another play at me in here while we wait to go to trial?"

I shake my head. "You don't need to—" I frown. "Sorry, what exactly was this deal?"

He shrugs. "I paid him and everyone else back what they lost when that other deal went south. And, well, let's just say I know more than a few of the skeletons your gramps has in more than a few of his closets. So I promised to keep my mouth shut about those. In exchange, he said he'd look out for my family on the outside. I lost a bunch of my crew in that bad deal, and there are lots of people out there who want me deader than disco."

What the *fuck*.

I stare at Roberto. "Mr. Chinellato, all due respect, why the *hell* are you telling me all this?"

His face darkens. "Because your gramps is going back on his word," he snaps, jabbing a finger at his bandaged neck. "This was *him*."

I arch a brow. "Mr. Chinellato, again, with all due respect, you have a number of enemies—"

"I know who my enemies are, counselor," he growls quietly. "Why the fuck do you think I spared the little bitch who tried to cut my throat after I turned his own blade on him?" He sneers. "Your gramps is *cheap*, and he hires dumb motherfuckers who'll give up whoever hired them once they're in trouble themselves."

Holy *fuck*. I stare at Roberto, my blurry hangover and fighting pains receding as my brain begins to crank up to high gear.

"You're telling me this man literally told you that Charles Black hired him to fucking kill you?" I mutter coldly, my pulse racing.

"Does the Pope wear a big-ass hat and work Sundays, counselor?"

"You'd testify to this?"

"Last night?" He shakes his head. "No, because I ain't a snitch..." He smirks. "Well, unless Uncle Sam is paying me to be one. Also, I settle my own debts...*plus*, the man was watching over my family. But after this morning?"

I raise a bewildered brow. "What the hell happened this morning?"

Roberto's face turns a deadly shade of red. "Someone tried to take out my mom, my sister, and her kids. I don't believe in coincidences."

Holy shit.

"I haven't heard about this at all," I snarl, yanking out my cell phone.

"That's cause the few guys I've got left stopped it and took my family somewhere safe—somewhere your prick grandfather can't touch 'em. The little bitches they caught trying to ambush my family?" His lips curl dangerously. "They were some of Charles' go-to thugs. My guys recognized them."

Fuck me sideways.

I lean back from the table between us, my brain going a million miles an hour as I try and make sense of the facts and the timeline.

Charles and his buddy Roberto have a falling out. Roberto's got some bad guys after him now, plus the feds are looking to put him away for murder and racketeering. So my enterprising shit-stain of a grandfather cuts him a deal: pay back what he owes, and Charles gets his grandsons—Gabriel and yours truly—to do what we do best and get Roberto off on all charges, or at the least get a reduced sentence. And in return Charles will protect Roberto's family in the interim.

But aside from Charles being an asshole, why the hell would he go back on that deal? And why the hell is he trying to kill the very man he wants us to get out of jail?

Shit.

Abruptly, it clicks.

Charles has never, ever forgiven a debt, or a fuck up, or being crossed. Not once. I mean hell, he stopped sending my siblings and I fucking Christmas presents because of *our dad* defying him. Why the hell would he forgive Roberto for a deal that went bad that cost him, Charles, money?

He wouldn't.

He *wants* us to fail. It's why he's been slowly stacking the board against us, including voting in his own wife, Caroline. Then when we *don't* get Roberto out of prison time, because

Charles has him killed while awaiting trial, our grandfather can sway the board to boot us from our own firm, citing gross incompetence.

Or more likely, to *own us.*

It first came up years ago, when we were setting up the firm that would become Crown and Black. Charles bullied his way in, offering money, connections to city licensing boards, access to clients, and so on. In return, we'd act as his own personal weaponized legal team, that he could use as a bargaining chip with his shady buddies. As in, "Do business with Charles Black, and you get access to his hotshot grandsons and their little friend who all happen to be killer lawyers".

We ended up bargaining him down to just a seat on the board. But again, Charles never forgets *shit*. And now this is his pay: torpedo the Roberto Chinellato case, and thereby own us.

Roberto smiles coldly as the realization spreads across my face.

"You connected those dots yet, counselor?"

"You could say that," I growl. My brows knit. "Mr. Chinellato, can you prove any of this?"

He snorts. "Yeah, I can prove it. I just need to stay *alive* to do it."

I nod. "Protective custody is a start—"

"But not enough. You need to get me *out* of here, counselor," he growls. "I know too much about too many players."

"I can protect you from my grandfather and his people."

Roberto snorts. "So can I," he grunts, pointing to the bandage on his neck. "But that ain't who I'm worried about, Mr. Black."

I frown. "Who else wants you dead?"

His face hardens. "Massimo Carveli."

Fuck.

"Why would Massimo want you dead?"

Roberto smiles coldly. "Because of what I know about him that he *knows* I know."

When I raise my brow, Roberto just purses his lips and shakes his head. "You don't wanna know, counselor."

"On the contrary, I actually *need* to know if you want me to help you, Mr. Chinellato. Again, you're enjoying attorney client privilege here."

He exhales slowly, looking away. "You can get me out of here?"

"I need six hours, at least. But yes."

He nods. "Okay, fuck it." Roberto slowly swivels his gaze back to me. "Two things. The first is that Massimo probably doesn't want anyone looking too closely at that will his pops left, giving Massimo full control of the Carveli family."

My brow cocks. "What do you mean?"

"I mean if it stinks like horseshit, counselor, you should open your eyes and look around for Mr. Ed."

"Are you suggesting that will is fake?" I say grimly.

"I'm not *suggesting* a thing," he mutters back. "I'm just saying I knew Luca, and he fuckin' hated his prick of kid. He wasn't going to leave him a goddamn dime. Yet now, the little shit is king."

My fingers drum rapidly on the table between us, my pulse thudding.

"And the other thing?"

He swallows, looking away.

"Sometimes, counselor, it's best to let things lie."

"Excuse me?"

"Look, the will is the one that matters."

I frown. "Mr. Chinellato, *what else do you know about Massimo that he doesn't want getting out?*"

He taps his foot, his eyes darting around the yard nervously.

"You got a good relationship with that brother of yours, Mr. Black?"

The fuck? My brow furrows as I nod. "I do."

"You got a sister too, yeah? You two get along?"

"We do."

He nods, swallowing again before his gaze swivels back to me and intensifies.

"Mr. Chinellato, I need to know—"

"You ever wonder where you came from, Mr. Black?"

Something icy shivers through me.

"You're referring to the fact that I was adopted as a child. And the answer is no, not really. I know who my family is."

"But I'm talkin' about your *real* family."

My eyes narrow. "Generally speaking, Mr. Chinellato," I growl, "I take great offense to anyone insinuating the people who raised me are in *any* way not my 'real' family."

He rolls his eyes. "You know what the fuck I mean."

"The answer is still no," I grunt. "I don't know, and *I don't care.*"

He smiles quietly. "You might want to start."

I tense. "What the hell is that supposed to mean?"

"It means—"

The coffee cup right next to my hand suddenly explodes. A corner of the plastic picnic table we're sitting at sublimates into plastic mist.

Oh FUCK.

"Roberto!" I roar, lunging across the table. "Get the fuck dow—!"

Blood explodes from his mouth to splatter against my shirt and jacket. His eyes roll back, and just as I grab him to yank him to the ground, he goes limp.

...And blood begins flowing from a quarter-sized hole in his back as the prison alarms start to wail.

31

ELOISE

I SCREAM when he walks through the door, his shirt covered in blood.

"It's not mine," Alistair instantly chokes out.

Before he can stop me, I slam into him, wrapping my arms around his body and holding him tight. Alistair's muscled arms surround me as he buries his face in the crook of my neck.

"*I'm sorry,*" he hisses, hugging me tightly. "Christ, Eloise, I'm so fucking sorry for everything I said—"

"No, *I'm* sorry," I choke, twisting to kiss his face and lips over and over as tears pool in my eyes. "I'm sorry, and can we go straight to the part where we forget that stupid argument ever happened?"

He smiles, cupping my face and kissing me. "I had no right to attack you like that, or your father—"

"It's okay," I choke, a tear sliding down my cheek before I kiss him again. I pull away, my hand flying to my mouth when I truly take in the sight of him. "What…"

"Roberto Chinellato," he growls, unbuttoning his blood-soaked shirt and dropping it on the floor. "He was shot right in front of me in the yard at Fairview."

"Oh my God!" I blurt. "Are you—"

"I'm not hurt," Alistair murmurs. He starts to pull my t-shirt over my head, and I realize it's because I have blood all over me from hugging him.

He drops my bloodied shirt to the floor, and then he's pulling me close, lifting me into his arms, and kissing me as he walks toward the shower.

"I just need you."

I DON'T LOVE the idea of Alistair having dinner with Massimo. So I find myself pacing the suite after he leaves for Keens, chewing at my cuticles—a habit I seem to have picked up in the absence of drinking the last few days.

Since my marriage to Massimo, I've explained away the amount of drinking I do as "necessary". Darkly, like self gallows-humor, I've jokingly referred to it as my "medicine" —something I *need* to get through even a single day living under Massimo's reign of terror.

But Alistair is right: it's too much. It's taking over, and becoming a problem. It's not "medicine", it's a crutch, and I know I have to stop.

It's thinking back to Alistair catching me drinking vodka out of a fucking paper coffee cup that stops me from calling down to room service—though I wouldn't put it past Alistair to have thought that far ahead and warned the concierge desk about letting me order a drink.

Part of me wants to be annoyed by that.

The other part silently thanks him.

I jump, startled, when the house phone rings.

"Ms. White?"

I'm incognito, obviously, so I have a code name.

"Yes?"

"We have a package down here for you that was just delivered by courier. It's addressed to a Ms. LeBlanc, but the courier was most insistent that your suite was the intended recipient."

My brow furrows, but then it clicks.

"Is it from a Rosa Faucher, in Paris?"

"Yes. It was first delivered to a loft building in Soho, who redirected it here via the courier. Shall I send it up, Ms. White?"

Alistair's building. "Please, and thank you."

A few minutes later, a bellhop delivers a documents mailer to my door. I retreat to the living room and to what has become my favorite reading chair in the few days I've been here. I tear open the mailer, and sure enough, it's the papers Rosa said she found while cleaning my dad's office.

Immediately, it becomes apparent they're not *all* meant for me. Yes, the envelope on the top of the stack has a post-it note with my name on it. But the three other documents "attached" to it seem to have been included only accidentally, when the envelope for me managed to get stuck in the same paperclip that's holding the other three pages together.

The first is a valuation of a building in Montpellier, France that it seems my father was at one time interested in purchasing. The second is just the itinerary from some vacation he and Marie took three years ago. But when I flip to the last document, I stiffen.

It's a copy of my father's living will.

I've read bits of it before, of course, after it was made known to me that—surprise—I was being forced to marry Massimo Carveli, sadistic psychopath extraordinaire.

Just the same, I scan through it. Some clauses are to be enacted in the event of his "incapacitation", like a coma. Things like his underbosses taking over various aspects of the business and voting in a new head of the organization from a list of trusted men. Other clauses only become relevant in the event of his actual death, like the stipulation that his wealth and assets be evenly distributed amongst Marie, Camille, and myself.

I scan the parts I've read before, and then, for whatever morbid reason, I flip to the last page.

The page where my fate is sealed to Massimo.

I sigh as my eyes drop to the bottom of the page…and then I frown.

There *is* no "marriage in the interest of the organization" clause.

My brain glitches as I re-read the page again, over and over. Have I missed it somehow? I flip back to the beginning and read the whole thing through again more carefully, but there's nothing.

Not a goddamn thing about me marrying Massimo.

I stare at it a moment longer, theorizing that this must be an earlier draft. But then I skip to the last page again, and glance down at the signatures. It's been signed by my father, and two of his lawyers, on the date of the original signing. Underneath, there are additional signatures from the last time the will was approved and ratified.

What the fuck.

I freeze when I look at the date next to my father's last signature.

...Three days before he fell into his coma.

My pulse races as I keep staring at the will, not quite sure what the hell this means. Quickly, I snatch the envelope with my name stickied to it and rip it open.

It's a photocopy of a letter, but it's not written to me.

It's to Luca Carveli, Massimo's father.

> *Dear Mr. Carveli,*
>
> *In the age of mobile phones and email, I know this may seem outdated. But, like you, I am an old-fashioned man, and I consider important matters deserving of the respect of a hand-written letter.*
>
> *While you and I have not always seen eye-to-eye, and indeed, have at times been enemies, I've always respected you as a man of business. We are both old-school fighters trying to carve a place in this modern world for our children and their children. Yes, we have had*

our differences, and bloodshed between us. But business is business, and you have, at least to me, always conducted yourself with honor.

I want to thank you again for your condolences when my first wife passed. And I hope you know I grieved for you when your son died.

I stiffen, staring at the words.

When your son died.

What? Massimo is, unfortunately, still walking amongst us. He's also an only child.

My eyes dip back to my father's immaculate penmanship.

I cannot imagine a loss like that, and please know I held you in my thoughts and prayers during that trying time.

Now, regarding your proposal. I have given the matter much thought, and I agree there are many benefits both our organizations could reap from such an arrangement. However, I have always cherished the hope that my daughters would be able to choose their own destiny in life and would not be forced into the sort of arrangements that men like you and I were expected to enter into in our youth.

To that end, and with my most sincere apologies, I cannot agree to your proposal that my younger daughter, Eloise, marry your younger son, Massimo.

I hope that you know this letter comes to you with my most sincere respect and admiration.

Best regards,

Andre LeBlanc

The letter, like the will, is dated three days before my father's coma.

What. The. *Fuck*.

32

ALISTAIR

"You're sure?"

"Positive," Taylor says icily. "They're both locked out of anything and everything at the office. I even had their keycards for the lobby deactivated."

Charles is going to raise hell when he realizes we've shut him and Caroline out of Crown and Black. But with these allegations that he's involved in the hit on Roberto?

Yeah, no fucking *way* does he get to stick his nose in our business. Not until we figure out what to do next. Before that, though, I have to get through this fucking dinner with Massimo, and Gabriel has to drop the bomb on Judge Hawkins and get the Chinellato case shut down.

"What about the board members loyal to Charles?"

Taylor sighs. "No. We can duke it out with Charles and Caroline whether or not we have the right to lock them out, but if we start clamping down on everyone on the board who disagrees with us, it'll look bad, and give Charles the ammo he'd need to turn *all* of them against us."

I hate that she's right. But she *is* right.

"I'm having IT monitor any data access from board members, though. We can individually shadow-block them from certain files if it looks like they're snooping for Charles."

"Good idea. Thanks, Taylor."

She exhales. "Any update on Roberto?"

"Other than that, Mrs. Lincoln, how was the show?" I sigh. "He's still knocked out after the surgery, but stable."

I'd like to credit myself for startling Roberto enough when we were sitting at that picnic table that he flinched, thereby causing the yet-unfound sniper to miss. But the more likely reason that he's still alive is that the shooter was garbage.

Which, not for nothing, sort of points at Charles and his tendency of hiring the cheapest guys for jobs you should probably be paying top dollar for.

"Gabriel's submitting his motion to Judge Hawkins to indefinitely delay any proceedings as we speak."

"Good," Taylor sighs. She pauses for a second. "Are *you*--"

"I'm fine."

"Alistair, you were shot at," she says tersely.

"I've got forty-sixty odds that whoever was pulling that trigger couldn't have hit me if I were standing still and glowing in the dark," I mutter. "But in any case, I think we both know I wasn't the target."

She exhales. "And you're seriously still getting dinner with Massimo?"

"Now, Taylor. I wouldn't want to insult the man."

"Yes, *cancelling on steaks*," she says dryly. "I'm sure that's what it is about you and your actions as of late that would insult him."

I roll my eyes and glance up at the front of the venerable Keens Steakhouse in midtown, where I'm meeting with Massimo.

"Does that conclude your super motivating TED Talk, Taylor?"

"For now. Good luck, Alistair."

"Thanks," I grunt into the phone as I step into Keens. "Gotta go."

I end the call and am following the maître d' to Massimo's private dining room when I notice a familiar face at the bar. Carmine Barone arches a brow in recognition as he stands from his bar stool.

"Mr. Black," he growls, extending a hand.

"Mr. Barone," I nod back, shaking it.

He glances at the maître d'. "Would you give us a minute?"

When we're alone, he gestures to the bar. "What are you drinking?"

I hesitate. "I'm actually about to sit down with Massimo…"

Carmine snorts. "So, that would be a *yes* on a drink?"

I chuckle. "Sure. A fast one. I'm buying."

"Is this where you pay me back for the other night?"

I stiffen, glancing at him. "It was just a poker game, Mr. Barone. There was nothing else going on under the surface, despite what you seem to think."

He smirks. "First of all, my friends call me Carmy."

"Are we friends?"

"I did do you a solid the other night. I'd say that makes us friends, don't you?"

When I pointedly don't respond, he sighs and high signs the bartender. The man strolls over and pours us two whiskeys before drifting away again.

"We don't know each other very well, Mr. Black."

"I thought we were on a first name basis now?"

He nods. "Alistair, then. Something you might not know about me is that I consider myself a bit of an expert when it comes to married women."

I look pointedly at the lack of wedding ring on his finger.

"You mean women married to *other men*."

He lifts a brow, shrugging as he sips his drink. "What can I say? The heart wants what the heart wants." He turns to level a hard look at me. "Bu when it comes to *your own* preference in…shall we say, *unavailable* women?"

"Mr. Barone—"

"It's Carmy, and please, I'm not an idiot, Alistair." He looks at me coolly. "Be careful."

"Of?"

"Massimo."

"I thought you were buddies."

He laughs coldly. "*Fuck no*. But let him think that as long as he wants. My point is, Massimo might come off like a buffoon, but he isn't nearly as stupid or reckless as he makes himself out to be." He gives me a significant look. "I really mean that. It's all an act. That fucker is *way* more calculating and devious than he lets anyone think. *Be careful*."

"Mr. Black?"

The maître d' materializes at my elbow.

"Your guest is expecting you."

Carmy arches a brow. "You got balls, counselor, I'll give you that. Dinner with the man whose...*possessions* you're coveting?"

"I'm sure I don't know what you're talking about."

"Well," he nods as he finishes his drink. "Let's hope Massimo doesn't either."

I WON'T LIE, I'm on edge when I step into Massimo's private dining room after Carmy's miserable attempt at a pep talk. But whatever tension I'm holding in my jaw melts away when I realize A, how drunk Massimo already is, and B, how much of a bullshit dinner this is going to be.

There's no weird tension. No suspicion. The man doesn't even *mention* Eloise or the fact that she's been on a business trip with Taylor for almost four days. The "dinner to discuss business" truly is just that: talking business, drinking, and eating fantastic steaks.

It's an odd sensation, sitting across from the man whose wife I've essentially claimed for myself. Even though they're not a real thing, and even though this hardly constitutes an "affair" given that their "relationship" is purely transactional and has never once been physical, there's still this rush of...something...in my veins.

Smugness, maybe. Triumph.

Mostly, I'm just ignoring him, with my thoughts squarely on Eloise.

...And all the ways I'm going to make her scream the second I get back to the hotel after this absurd meal.

My filthy thoughts and Massimo's ramblings about trying to get a casino license for the city of New York—yeah, good luck with that—are interrupted by my phone ringing on the table next to me. Glancing down, I see Gabriel's number.

I grin. My brother *was* submitting a petition to Judge Hawkins tonight to delay all proceedings, given the attempt on Roberto's life. But that's not the only thing Gabriel was delivering to Judge Hawkins. He was also submitting Valerie's sworn deposition concerning her affair with Roberto, which also acts as his airtight alibi.

In all probability, even after she sees Valerie's statement, Judge Hawkins would still go ahead with the trial. But she *could* decide that this is enough evidence to merit tossing the whole case out *tonight*.

"Mr. Carveli, apologies, I have to take this."

He shrugs casually, deep in his whiskey. "Go ahead. I'm going to get that waitress with the ass back in here for another round," he grins.

Yeah, you do that.

I step out of the dining room and slip around the corner before answering.

"So," I grin. "Am I ordering champagne—"

"Valerie Siff is dead."

A cold sensation rips down my spine.

Valerie, as in the spurned wife of the deputy mayor of Montclair.

As in, the cornerstone to our entire defense alibi.

"*What the fuck*?!" I snarl.

"Double tapped to the head, execution-style," Gabriel spits. "We are *fucked,* Alistair."

"*Shit*!" I swear, whirling and stopping myself just before I punch the wall. "Judge Hawkins?"

"Heard the news same as me, about five minutes before I walked into her chambers waving that deposition." He swears. "She's tossing that as inadmissible now, by the way. Seeing as the prosecution can't cross examine Valerie anymore."

"Mother*fucker*!" I hiss. "How the fuck did anyone *find* her?"

For obvious reasons, we've been putting Valerie up somewhere safe until the trial. It's a fairly common practice with witnesses in big cases involving the mafia, and it's hardly the first time we've done it.

Nobody but Taylor, Gabriel, and I knew that Valerie was staying under an assumed name at a spa up by Buffalo, New York.

"That's…" Gabriel exhales slowly. "That's why I'm calling."

I barge ahead. "Okay, we need to make a list. Any associates, interns…whoever had access to that information—"

"We don't need a list, Alistair," he growls. "You *know* who had access to that information. You, me, and Taylor, and we all kept it on absolute lockdown in our offices. No one has access to my office without me present, same goes for Taylor."

My jaw begins to clench.

"Be *very* careful what you say next."

"We're past that, brother," he says quietly. "Who had access to your office without you being there?"

"*Stop talking.*"

"Look past your feelings!" he snaps. "Look past whatever the fuck you're doing with Eloise and read the fucking writing on the wall!"

"We're not having this conversation—"

"The fuck we aren't!" he barks. "Look at the goddamn *facts*, Alistair! Like dad would!"

"*Fuck you,*" I rasp.

"She had access, Alistair."

"She's not—"

"She's screwed you over before."

"Shut the *fuck* up!!!"

"She's *married to Massimo*!"

"What the *fuck* does that have to do with anything!?"

Gabriel sighs heavily. "Hang on, I'm conferencing in Taylor. You need to hear this for yourself."

I hear a click as the third line connects.

"Alistair?" Taylor says quietly.

"*What*?" I snarl, my very skin sizzling with rage.

"I just got a call from Vinny Glaudini."

Vinny's the acting boss of the Pastore Family while Tony Pastore is in prison. He's also one of our clients in Chicago that Taylor flew out to talk with.

"And?" I hiss.

"While I was out there, he was all business. But he called just now as a show of respect to let me know that we've been getting fucked without even realizing it."

"Elaborate," I grit through clenched teeth.

It's not Eloise. There's no fucking way she has anything to do with any of this shit.

"You know how Massimo's been up our asses asking about the Chinellato case? Because they're old buddies, and business associates, and he's so concerned for Roberto?" She laughs coldly. "Yeah, that's all horseshit. Roberto and Massimo had a huge falling out in Chicago a couple of months ago. There was a deal that went bad, and a gunfight ensued. Roberto's guys took out two of Massimo's top lieutenants, and apparently ran off with both the cash and the weapons they were there to make the deal for."

Fuck. Me.

The deal Roberto was telling me about in the prison yard, before he was shot? The one where he tried to rip someone off and got burned for it?

That someone was *Massimo fucking Carveli.*

I don't have time to wonder how fucking stupid Roberto had to be to think he could pull a scam like that on the head of the entire Carveli family.

...I'm too busy focusing on the fact that *Charles* was in on that deal too.

With Massimo.

"They're not buddies, man," Gabriel hisses. "They're enemies, and Massimo's only interested in the case because he wants Roberto fucking *gone*."

"Gabriel," I hiss. "You need to listen to me—"

"Open your fucking eyes!" my brother roars.

"They're fucking open!" I snarl back. "But *listen* to me! Before he got shot, Roberto told me that Massimo and Charles are into some shit *together*. The deal that went bad in Chicago? *Charles* was in on that with Massimo."

"Fucking *hell*," Gabriel grunts. "Can you prove that?"

"Not yet. But when Roberto is talking again, I'll—"

"We need to be focusing on the obvious right now. We all know Charles is a piece of shit, but this is bigger. Alistair, I know you don't want to hear this, but Eloise is the *only* loose end—"

"You have no idea what you're saying!" I hurl back. "Taylor, back me—"

"Alistair," she says quietly. "I mean...come on. She's the only one who could have possibly known where Valerie was staying—"

"*Fuck you both,*" I snap. "You're being insane."

"And you're being an idiot!" Gabriel spits. "She's—"

"I'm *allowed* to find happiness!" I roar back. "I am *allowed* to—"

"With her?!" Gabriel yells. "She's fucking *married,* you idiot! To *Massimo*! I mean how many fucking red flags need to be waved in your idiotic face before—"

I hang up abruptly, seething.

Fuck him.

Fuck Taylor, too.

I *know* Eloise.

I *know* her. I mean, yes, I've been down the mistrust road with her before, and it ate me alive for ten years.

But I'm done with that.

I jam my phone into my pocket and stalk back toward the private dining room. Right outside the door, I freeze when I hear Massimo's voice from inside.

"Eloise worked perfectly," he chuckles.

Holy shit.

Massimo laughs quietly again into the phone.

"It went exactly how I said it would go. See? I *told* you Eloise would be an asset at that law firm."

The floor drops out, and my fucking world crumbles.

I MANAGE to keep my expression neutral as I tell Massimo that a work thing needs my attention at the office. Then I'm staggering out of the private dining room and calling Gabriel back.

"Look," my brother sighs as he answers. "I'm fucking sorry, man. I truly mean that. You *do* deserve happiness, Alistair, and you have to know how much it pains me to—

"Gabriel."

My voice is razor-sharp steel.

"What's going on," Gabriel says quietly.

"You're at the office?"

My blood feels like napalm in my veins. I'm looking with tunnel vision at the wall in front of me as my face turns to a stony mask.

"I am," my brother says.

"Go to my filing cabinet," I rasp. "The keys to it and my office door are on a pink lanyard in Katerina's top drawer. Do it now."

"Gimme a sec."

I wait, listening to Gabriel running. Then there's the sound of my office door swinging open.

"Okay." Gabriel clears his throat. "I'm in. What am I looking—"

"Top drawer."

It's all horribly clicking into place, and suddenly I know why seeing Katerina's keys in my office rang a bell somewhere in my head.

It was the day I walked in on Eloise in my office in her panties, with chai latte spilled on her skirt.

...The same chai latte I found sticky and dried on my carpet and splashed on the side of my file cabinet later.

And when I think past *her* that day, past kissing her, and tasting her, and falling for her *bullshit* all over again, I know where I saw Katerina's keys on the pink lanyard.

They were *in* the lock of that file cabinet.

God in heaven.

It was her.

Eloise was in my private files, seeing where Valerie was being kept, and reporting that back to Massimo, who just had her killed.

But Valerie Siff's fake name and whereabouts aren't the only things I had in that locked file cabinet.

"Okay," Gabriel mutters. "Where in the top—"

"Halfway back. You're looking for the folder labeled Carveli," I growl. "*Luca* Carveli."

I hardly knew Massimo's father. I mean, I know was a piece of shit, just like his son. But for some reason, he chose

Crown and Black for his east coast legal representation, even though he lived in LA.

We met maybe three times, mostly for run-of-the-mill legal issues like signing off on a contract he needed for a construction project, or a residential building he was looking at purchasing.

But there *was* one big thing I did, legally speaking, for Luca Carveli.

His will.

There's the sound of rummaging for a second.

"I have it."

"His will is in there. I need you to read it."

"Give me a sec." Gabriel clears his throat. "Well, no surprises. Everyone knows Luca and Massimo were at odds for years. This is the previous version of his will, where he stipulates that Massimo never becomes the head of the Carveli family, and doesn't get a dime of Luca's money—"

"Look at the last page."

"Hang on..." I can hear my brother's breath catch. "*Holy shit...*"

I know what he's looking at.

The *day before* Luca flew to Paris, where he eventually died either a day or a week later, depending on which rumor you believe, he stopped by Crown and Black since he was in New York anyway. He had me fill out an addendum to his will, signed and dated that day.

The addendum clarified that everything in the original will, specifically the part where Massimo gets nothing, was his most up-to-date wishes. The wording was…emphatic.

"This is dated like a week before he died," Gabriel growls. "Jesus, he doesn't pull any punches. 'My spoiled, idiotic, insufferable weakling of a son, Massimo, will not take my place as leader of the Carveli organization. He also receives one dollar of my fortune and nothing else'. I mean…holy shit."

I grimace. "What the fuck do you think the odds are that they hugged it out and made up sometime between a day or a week after that, right before Luca's 'heart attack'?"

"You're the betting man, Alistair," my brother mutters.

"Yeah, well, I call odds like that slim-to-fucking-*none*," I spit, my pulse thudding in my ears.

"So Massimo forged his dad's will to become king. Fucking hell," Gabriel breathes. "If the other families in The Commission found out—"

"Which is exactly why he had Eloise trying to steal *that* will you're currently holding from my office."

My brother exhales heavily. "I'm calling Taylor. How soon can you be at the office for a war-room sit down?"

"Soon." My eyes narrow. "There's something I have to take care of first."

"Alistair—"

"See you soon."

I hang up abruptly and storm through Keens for the front door, making a detour to the bar first.

Carmy Barone jumps as I grab his shoulder from behind and yank him around.

"Jesus Christ, Alistair," he grunts, glaring. "You scared the fuck out—"

"What would it be worth to The Commission to know that Massimo Carveli is the wrongful head of the Carveli family as a result of forging his father's will?"

Carmine's mouth draws to a line.

"Alistair—"

"I'm fucking serious, Carmy," I snarl.

His eyes narrow. "Do you have proof?"

"Plenty."

The corners of his lips curl dangerously.

"I'd say it'd be worth quite a fucking lot to The Commission to know that," he growls. "*Quite* a fucking lot."

After that, I go directly to the hotel.

To *Eloise*.

Because I have to look her in the eye and know if I'm going crazy, or if I've just fallen for her bullshit all over again.

33

ELOISE

THE NEWS ARTICLES and tidbits of gossip I find online don't help much. There are a few stories here and there about Luca's death—that he was in Paris when he had a heart attack—but even that isn't clear.

Some sources whisper he was with a prostitute when it happened. Others claim it was while sitting on a toilet. One even has him at church, of all places.

Basically, it boils down to whichever source each gossip blog interviewed, and how they wanted to paint Luca.

The thing that jumps out at me is that there seems to be some confusion about *when* he actually died. According to the earliest reports, Massimo officially announced his father's passing three days after Luca's death. This all coincided with his ascension to the Carveli throne.

But there's *another* story with one of Luca's drivers reporting him as missing in Paris almost a full week before Massimo's announced date of death. It's suspicious as hell, but given that Luca Carveli was a notorious *crime boss,* nobody's exactly looking into it too hard.

Either way, there's nothing on this mysterious first-born son of Luca's—Massimo's alleged older brother—who appears to have died young. The boy my father went out of his way to tell Luca he'd grieved for.

I exhale as I sit back in the bed, glancing at my phone nervously.

Obviously, Alistair having dinner with Massimo has me on high alert, even if he's assured me that it's all fine. But I haven't heard from him at all, and it's getting late.

I want him here, with me. I *need* him here, with me. And not just for the sex—for the animalistic way he pounces on me, or the way he fucks me with this intoxicating blend of primal aggression and slow, sensual ecstasy.

I need him because I just *need him*. All of him. His warmth, and his arms. His comfort, and his strength.

I need the way he just seems to fit and makes me feel safe.

The way he feels like home.

I glance at my father's letter sitting on the bed next to me. I don't know why I'm so fixated on it, but I can't stop thinking about my discovery that Massimo had a brother.

Frowning, I go to my laptop again and bring up Google. There's obviously *lots* of information about Massimo—mostly about his playboy lifestyle, and his violent public tendencies. There's even a nauseating puff piece in some gross celebrity gossip blog that focuses on the mafia world concerning *our* wedding, with some blurry paparazzi shots of Massimo grinning at the altar while I look like I'm heading to the guillotine.

But there's also plenty about *Luca's* decadent lifestyle and playboy antics. By all accounts the man was a vile, cruel, abusive asshole, yet seems to have had mistresses and scandalous affairs all over the place.

A washed up movie starlet, a US Senator's wife, the daughter of a Council Minister of Italy... It's like bad reality television, reading about this crap. It's all *total* trash, but somehow I can't drag my eyes away from the litany of Massimo's father's scandals.

There's even some crazy story involving Will Cates, the missing-presumed-dead bass player for the band Velvet Guillotine, stealing one of Luca's girlfriends and taking her on tour, which resulted in Luca literally trying to storm Madison Square Garden with a small army of mob enforcers during a concert.

No wonder his son is an angry asshole with zero impulse control.

Then I find another story about Luca. This one details yet another mistress of his dying in a horrible car crash while allegedly trying to escape from Luca himself, who may or may not have orchestrated the actual crash.

I wince as I scan the pictures in the old news article, which show a horrifically twisted wreck of a car where it landed after being slammed off the West Side Highway and bouncing and rolling *eleven* times.

Obviously, the poor girl was killed. What makes it even more heartbreaking is that there were apparently two other passengers in the car that died—another adult, and…horribly…a child.

I look away, shaking my head. Then, slowly, I turn back. My eyes widen as I scroll back to the top of the article and read the publication date.

The crash was twenty-eight years ago.

Something starts whining in my head—a small noise I can't quite ignore.

You're insane.

Just the same, I go to the Crown and Black website and click on the "About the Partners" tab. My mind flashes to what feels like a hundred years ago, in the dark heat of an elevator during a blackout, when Alistair told me things he'd never told anyone before.

How he came to live with the Black family. How his parents had been killed in a horrendous car crash.

I click on his bio on the website, telling myself over and over how utterly insane this is, and that I'm connecting dots that aren't there. But when I start to read, my face pales.

The bio mentions Knightsblood, and law school, and how he and his brother—sons of the much-loved Vaughn Black, attorney at law—befriended Taylor Crown and founded Crown and Black.

It's a very standard, paint-by-numbers, LinkedIn-style bio.

But at the very end, almost as a footnote, it gratefully mentions his adoption by Vaughn and Marilyn. How he'd been involved in a near-fatal car crash that took the lives of his birth parents before his adoptive ones gave him a new chance at life.

My face goes numb.

A car crash that occurred when he was six, twenty-eight years ago.

On the West Side Highway, in New York.

The little whining noise in my head becomes a full-blown air raid siren.

Holy. Shit.

I grab the letter from my father with shaking hands, re-reading it again.

"I hope you know I grieved for you when your son died."

The letter falls from my hands. In a daze, my head spinning, I slowly close the laptop, slip out of bed, and start to pace the room.

There's no way.

There is *no fucking way* that—

I gasp as my phone rings. My arm jerks out to grab it, my heart pounding as I look for Alistair's name on the screen. But then my brows knit.

It's not Alistair. It's Rosa, my father's caretaker.

The color drains from my face as I answer the call and cautiously bring the phone to my ear.

"*Rosa…*" I choke. "My father—?"

"Ms. LeBlanc!" she gushes excitedly. "It's okay! Your father… He's waking up!"

I almost drop the phone. My hand clamps down on my mouth to stifle the scream rising in my throat.

"*What?!*"

"*Oui!*" She almost screams herself. "I am at the hospital with him now! The doctors are helping him slowly come out of his sleep, and he's waking up!"

I start to sob big, happy tears of utter relief.

"*How?!*" I blurt.

Curiously, Rosa doesn't immediately respond.

"Rosa?"

"Ms. LeBlanc," she says quietly, caution suddenly in her voice. "I… Are you safe?"

My brows furrow. "Yes?"

"I mean *really*, Eloise," she murmurs.

"I'm safe, Rosa." I frown as I wet my lips. "I'm actually not even with Massimo. I'm…hiding."

"*Bien*," she exhales. "I don't mean to frighten you, it's just…"

"What the hell is going on, Rosa?"

"Eloise, you know I'm a registered nurse, *oui*?"

I do. It's required for her in order to be my father's full-time caretaker, given his condition.

"Yes. And?"

"I'm not sure I've ever mentioned that I've been working as a private caretaker while I am back at medical school, studying to be a doctor. Neurologist," she clarifies.

"No, I didn't…" I swallow. "That's wonderful, Rosa—"

"That isn't why I'm calling," she says cautiously. "Eloise, your father had a doctor who would visit once a month and bring the various IV drugs that he needed while he was in his coma. Except that doctor was due a few days ago, and never came. I called, but his mobile number had been disconnected."

I frown.

"Obviously I didn't want your father to go without his meds. One of my professors at school said she could fill the script for me, so long as she knew specifically what the prescriptions were for. I didn't know, so I brought an empty IV bag for her to test."

My frown deepens. "Rosa, what—"

"Eloise, the doctor who stopped coming wasn't giving your father medicine," she hisses urgently. "He was giving him Propofol."

"I've never heard of that. What's—"

"It's a nonbenzodiazepine sedative, Eloise," she says, her voice tinged with fear. "They use it to put *and keep* people in medically induced comas."

It feels like I've been punched in the chest. The air leaves my lungs. My throat closes. I stumble backward until I fall back into a sitting position on the edge of the bed, numb.

What the FUCK.

"I've given the police the name of the doctor who disappeared. I have a picture, too. Can I text it to you, as well? In case you recognize him?"

I'm unable to speak.

"Eloise," she says softly. "I'm so, so sorry. But your father, he's going to be okay! They're going to gently wean him off the Propofol and he'll be up as soon as—"

"Text me the picture," I croak. "Please."

"*Oui*, of course."

My phone dings. I pull it from my ear and tap on the text Rosa's just sent me, and my stomach plummets through the floor.

The missing "doctor" is *Rocco*.

"Rosa?" I hiss, my heart pounding. "Are you safe where you are?"

"I.. *Oui*, yes?" she says cautiously.

"I need you to call the police. Tell them that 'doctor' they're looking for is a member of the Carveli criminal organization."

Rosa's breath catches. "*Mon Dieu…*"

"I'm booking a flight right now," I blurt. "Just, please, *please* be safe, yes? I'll text you when I'm enroute to the airport. And Rosa?"

"*Oui?*"

"*Merci*."

My hands are shaking as I open my laptop again and start frantically looking for the soonest flight to Paris. Suddenly I gasp, startled by the sound of the front door to the suite banging open and Alistair walking in.

I grab the copy of my father's will and the letter and bolt into the living room, desperate to tell him *everything* I've learned.

Part of me is terrified that I'm digging into his past where I shouldn't. Or insane for even going there with this.

But I also know it's going to be okay, because he's him, and I'm me.

And together, we're *us*. The us that might have been ten years ago. The "us" that might despite everything still have a shot, somehow.

My heart races as I walk around the corner and see him, his back to me as he stands over the bar cart in the corner, his shoulders hunched.

"Hey!" I blurt. "I… This is crazy, but I have to tell you—"

The smile fades from my face as he turns and levels the single most sinister, bleak, downright *malevolent* look I've ever seen on his face at me.

"Alistair?"

He keeps staring death at me. I swallow nervously.

"How was dinner—"

Immediately, I'm gasping sharply and tripping away from him in fear as he storms toward me. His lips curl into a vicious snarl, his eyes blue fire as he surges into me. I scream, but it dies in my throat when he grabs it tight and slams me back against the wall.

"*Was it you!?*" he snarls with fury.

"*What*?!" I choke.

"WAS. IT. *YOU*?!" he roars. Fear cuts through my chest like ice, turning me numb.

"I—I don't know what you're talking—"

"I'm talking about *you* stealing private files from *me* to pass to your fucking *husband*!!"

I want to tell him everything. I want to say how Massimo forced me. How he threatened Camille. I want to say I hated doing it every step of the way, and that I could hardly sleep some nights from the guilt.

But none of that comes out. None of that *can* come out, not with the way he's looking at me, and not with the way I feel my face fall.

Instantly, I know my guilt is written clear as day on my face.

"*Jesus*," he says quietly, shaking his head, a sneer on his lips. "Je. *Sus*."

"Alistair!" I blurt as his hand drops from my neck and he steps away from me, unblinking, staring at me in horror and disgust. "Please! Let me—"

"No, Eloise," he hisses thinly. "Just…*no*. I don't trust a single fucking thing that's *ever* come out of your fucking mouth."

It feels like both a slap in the face and punch to the stomach. I gasp for air, my eyes burning as I stare at him.

"*Please—*"

"This…" he growls quietly. "Whatever the *fuck* this was?" His jaw grinds. "It's *done*. I was an idiot to ever trust you."

"Alistair!"

He's turning, striding across the room.

"Alistair!"

"Don't *ever* fucking contact me again," he hisses as he reaches for the doorknob. He stops and glares pure malice at me over his shoulder. "Needless to say, you're fucking fired."

He opens the door. And then, it's like the whole world goes into frame-by-frame slow motion. I hear myself scream as if listening from another room as the gunshot explodes.

As Alistair wrenches sideways in a spray of blood and tumbles backward into the room.

As his white shirt quickly blossoms to red as he drops to the floor.

This isn't happening.

It feels like my body is frozen; like my brain is numb, and reality has stopped making sense. I'm still staring at Alistair lying on the ground when Massimo steps into the room, a gun in his hand, flanked by five of his men.

Oh God.

My heart turns to ice as he smiles dangerously at me.

"What an age we live in," he says with a sardonic grin on his lips. "Chicago, Illinois, right here on Central Park West."

I bolt toward Alistair. Massimo's men grab me and I try to scream but a hand slams over my mouth. I choke on my own breath as Massimo and his goons surround me, my heart jackrabbiting. Massimo's eyes land on the letter and the will on the ground. He stoops to pick them up, his brows arching.

"My, my, my," he muses quietly. His gaze slides from the documents in his hands to me. "I think we have a lot to talk about, don't we...*wife?*"

Two of his men grab a motionless Alistair under the arms. I try to scream again, but a gag wraps tightly around my mouth.

A bag is yanked over my head.

And then all I know is darkness and fear.

34

ALISTAIR

My father used to talk a lot about "perspective". He'd walk in on Gabriel and I fighting over a stupid video game or something, pull us apart, then sit us down and tell us we needed to see things from the other's perspective.

"If you only view the world through your own eyes, you'll miss out on some great views," he'd tell us.

That's what I find myself thinking about when I come to, lying flat on my back on a cold, hard floor.

Perspective.

Granted, my *first* "view" when my eyelids open is looking up at a grimy metal and concrete ceiling with two bare bulbs on wires hanging down, with no windows. So my initial "perspective" is that I've died and gone to Hell, which, for whatever reason, looks just like the set from one of the *Saw* movies.

Then, as I try to focus, a face lurches into my field of vision, staring down with big blue eyes, her long blonde hair hanging down over me.

"*Alistair*!" Eloise chokes. Her eyes fill with tears, and she puts a hand over her mouth as she starts to cry.

"*Hey…*" I croak.

I try to sit up, but I'm abruptly knocked back by excruciating pain exploding through my side. Pure fire claws at my ribs as I glance down.

My shirt is ripped open, stained red. A blood-soaked hoodie is wrapped around my torso, over the pain in my ribs.

"*What the fuck…*"

"Don't move," Eloise says quietly. Her hands take one of mine, squeezing as her eyes pierce into mine. "You've been shot."

Shit.

I glance down at the hoodie again and grimace.

"I… You were bleeding badly," she says softly. "So I took my hoodie—"

"*Thank you*," I murmur, wincing. "How bad?"

Her face is bleak. "I don't know. It looks like the bullet sort of…" She makes a face. "Carved a channel through your side, like a knife slash?"

Okay, not great. But it could be worse. I don't have a hole clear through me, or a bullet lodged in my body. My brow furrows as I replay opening that hotel room door and finding myself face-to-face with Massimo, holding a gun.

I remember the muzzle flashing, and the white-hot knife stabbing into me.

I start to snort, but then groan as I keel over, the pain slicing into me again.

"Whoa, hang on," Eloise hisses, grabbing me and helping me lie back down. She fixes me with a look. "Were you just trying to *laugh*?"

"That..." I grunt, biting back the pain. "That fuckstick shot me from two feet away and almost missed," I chuckle, wheezing again as my torso burns.

I exhale as I lie back down. My eyes slide up to hers, and I slip my hand into hers.

"I'm sorry," I growl quietly.

Eloise starts to cry, shaking her head.

"I *hated* doing it," she chokes. "But...he...he threatened Camille, and with my father in a coma—"

"Eloise."

I grit my teeth, ignoring the pain as I wrench myself to an upright position.

Perspective.

I have it now. I've actually had it ever since this woman walked into my firm and back into my life. And I don't have to "forgive" her for anything she did spying on my firm for Massimo.

Eloise is not the enemy. She never was.

She's the woman I've loved since the day she walked around the corner of the stables back at Knightsblood and asked me why I kept getting into fights. The day I told her if she had a brain, she'd stay away from me.

Thank fuck she didn't.

"I love you."

Her eyes are filling with tears as her lip quivers.

"I—the things I did—"

"You did because you had to. Like we all do," I growl, leaning my forehead against hers.

"Alistair..."

"I love you, Eloise," I say quietly, again.

The tears begin to flow hotly down her cheeks as she wraps her arms around me.

"I love you too."

I hold her like that, letting her cry against me as we hold each other in the dark, dank, coldness of the windowless concrete room. Her sobs begin to hitch harder and louder, getting more frantic as she clings to me, choking and gasping.

Shit, she's having a panic attack.

"Eloise—"

"We're going to die in here!" she screams, clutching at me and shaking. "Oh God, Alistair, he's—"

"Breathe," I hiss, pulling back and holding her face in my hands, maintaining eye contact. "I need you..." I grunt, swallowing back the pain and nausea from the wound in my side. "I need you to breathe, princess."

Her lips twist. Her eyes latch onto mine.

"I used to hate it so much when you called me that."

"I know."

She grins wryly at me. "Dick." She swallows, her hands coming up to grip my wrists as I cup her face. "I… I don't hate it anymore."

A tremor ripples through her, and I can see the color drain from her face again as the reality of our situation creeps in.

"Tell me something no one knows about you."

She chokes out a half-sob, half-smile as her eyes lift to mine again.

"I know what you're trying to do."

"And?"

"*And* it's not going to—"

"*Or* you could just stop being a pain in the ass and go with it."

Her teeth rake over her lower lip as she smiles a watery smile. "You already know everything about me, Alistair."

"Apparently not," I growl quietly, my eyes dragging over our surroundings.

She looks at me sadly. I just smile and lean my forehead on hers again.

"He—Massimo, I mean," she says quietly. "He was going to hurt Camille. And, I know, I know, she's…" Eloise shakes her head slowly.

"Family is family," I grunt quietly. "I get it."

"I'm sorry," she whispers.

"I know." I kiss her forehead. "Now, tell me something anyway. Something no one knows."

"Alistair..."

"I'm sure there's something, Eloise. I don't know everything about you—not yet, at least."

Her throat bobs as her eyes lift to the ceiling. "He might be listening."

I shrug. "Fuck him." I glance up at the darkness of the concrete and metal framed ceiling. "*Fuck you,* Massimo!" I yell before glancing back at Eloise. "Tell me."

Her face reddens before she looks away.

"That night..." she murmurs. "The party at Worthington Tower, and the elevator..." Her face turns pink as she chews on her perfect, plump lip. "I was sad to leave you," she says softly. "I didn't want to, but it felt like I should."

Her mouth twists again as her beautiful baby blues raise to mine.

"And when I was leaving and you were still sleeping—" She stops and rolls her eyes. "Ugh, this is stupid."

"*Tell me,*" I growl, taking her hands in mine, my eyes burning into hers. "Just tell me, Eloise."

She swallows. "I..." she rolls her eyes again. "I whispered *part of you is mine forever* into your ear."

The room is quiet as she takes a slow, measured breath. She's still blushing as she visibly cringes in front of me. "Jesus, I can't believe I just told you—"

"I didn't want you to leave, either," I murmur quietly. "The next morning, when I woke up alone..." I shake my head, my eyes never leaving hers. "I was so fucking mad when you weren't there."

Eloise's lips curl slightly in the corners.

"And when you were asleep in my arms earlier that night, right before I crashed myself, I said something to you, too, you know."

I lean close, my lips almost on hers as her breath catches.

"What did you say?" she whispers.

"You'll always be mine."

My lips press to hers. It's no ordinary kiss. It's a kiss over ten years in the making, picking up where we left off in the daybreak gray of an elevator car. It's every curse I sent her way, every speck of my anger, every black scorch mark of rage being purged from my system.

A cleansing fire.

A rain to wash away the bloodied battlefield between us.

I don't kiss her because I want her.

I kiss her because she's already mine.

Always was.

Always will be.

My hand slips up her face to tangle in her hair, pulling her close and kissing her as my pain and the past melt away around us.

Until the single door across the room wrenches open with an ear-splitting shriek. We both whirl, but I don't make any effort to pull away from Eloise.

Let that fuck see with his own eyes that she's mine.

Massimo comes in, dressed in black. His eyes land on where Eloise's hand and mine are entwined, and smugness surges inside of me at his dark look. But the feeling shatters when two of his men stride into the room behind him, carrying a limp body with a bag over its head.

Wearing a Tom Ford suit I know too well.

"*No—!*"

A barely conscious, badly beaten Gabriel groans as the bag is yanked off his head. Massimo's goons carry him over to Eloise and me, letting him drop to the ground in front of us.

"*You son of a bitch,*" I hiss, choking and feeling pain explode through my torso as I try but fail to lurch to my feet.

Massimo chuckles quietly as one of his men leaves the room, the other remaining, standing right behind his boss.

Massimo shakes his head as he grins, his gaze dragging from Gabriel to me and back again.

"I almost didn't take him," he sighs. "But, where would the fun be in that? Besides," Massimo shrugs. "He walked into Roberto Chinellato's hospital room to check in on that piece of trash just as one of my men was putting an air bubble into his IV drip." He grins widely. "Roberto's dead, by the way. I suppose there goes your case."

I don't honestly give a shit. Especially when I'm writhing in pain, staring at Gabriel lying almost motionless on the ground.

"It's touching to see you care so much about a man who is not even your blood," Massimo murmurs.

Rage bubbles up in my chest.

"Fuck you."

He shrugs. "But he *isn't,* Alistair. As much as you've trained yourself to think differently, this man, and his biological parents, and his dear sisters, are *not* your flesh and blood. They never were, and no amount of good thoughts will change—"

"I don't give a fuck what you think about family, Massimo," I hurl at him. "Considering yours is pure toxicity."

He smiles coldly. *"Isn't it, though..."*

His eyes turn to Eloise, who's gone white.

"I know *you* know, dear wife," he snarls before his lips curl dangerously again. "But does *he*?" He nods his chin at me. "Does your little boyfriend here know the truth?"

Eloise is silent, looking stricken as I squeeze her hand.

"What truth," I growl.

His gaze slides back to me, and his lips curl into a leer.

"It would seem we have a *lot* to catch you up on, *brother.*"

35

ALISTAIR

PERSPECTIVE GOES RIGHT the fuck out the window when life punches you in the throat.

Every cell in my body wants to deny the word he's just hurled at me. To ignore it and strike it from the record, as if he never said it at all. I want to laugh in his face for trying to get into my head so blatantly, and so stupidly.

But it's her expression that gives it away. It's the pain shattered like broken glass across Eloise's face and reflected in her wide eyes that brings me to my figurative knees.

Massimo could bellow it a hundred times and I'd never believe him.

Eloise says nothing, and I know in my heart it's true.

Oh God.

I want to go to Gabriel to see how bad he is. I want to hold Eloise in my arms. I want to spring to my feet, charge Massimo, and rip him apart piece by fucking piece.

I can't do any of that right now. I can't do anything but stare at him.

Icy cold wraps around my heart. A sick feeling washes over me as I drag my gaze from Eloise to Massimo. And when his eyes lock with mine, a dam inside me breaks, sending a tidal wave of nausea and resentment and horror crashing over my entire life.

Every memory. Every moment. Every scraped knee, and every triumph.

I look back at Eloise again, but there's no coming back from this. No erasing it. And when I turn back silently to Massimo again, I know. It's real.

Gradually, I start to notice the horrible likenesses. The way our noses are the same. Our mouths, too. The same sharp glint of blue in our eyes, so different from the hazel gray-green eyes of my siblings.

Slowly, Massimo's grin widens.

"You know it, deep down," he murmurs quietly. "Through the memories you've forgotten or blacked out, through the parts of childhood we erase." He grins. "It's still there, Alistair. Or"…his grin spreads even more…"should I say, *Bruno*."

Something wrenches inside my brain. Something snaps into place and into memory.

…Bruno, baby, it's time for dinner…

…Come hug your mother goodnight, Bruno…

I physically flinch as vague hints of memories maraud through my head and coalesce. Broken, shattered events I've long forgotten or shoved aside laugh cruelly as they claw their way back to the surface.

A mother's kiss.

The screeching whine and sickening crunch of metal on metal. Of tires popping and shredding. Of a little boy's terrified screams as his world shatters, and of the scent of gasoline and blood.

My screams.

"Alistair!"

Eloise catches me as I start to keel over in a numb haze. I cling to her, gritting my teeth as my vision swims.

Massimo laughs coldly.

"The thing is, *dear brother Bruno,*" he growls, "is that I found out early on in life that I enjoyed taking things from you." He lifts a shoulder. "I suppose it started with *your mother.*"

I flinch. I know Massimo's birth story. It's no secret that his…*our*…mother, Allegra, died giving him life. It's even been whispered that *that,* atrocious as it sounds, is what started Luca's disdain for Massimo.

He chuckles. "Yes, I took her from you merely by being born, didn't I? And then, when her sniveling pussy of a brother, Angelo, and one of my father's more soft-hearted whores removed you from our home that night, only to drive off the fucking West Side Highway…"

Eloise holds me even tighter, her breath catching sharply as I stare right through Massimo in a daze.

"Well, so many doors were suddenly open to me, weren't they? I took your position as first-born son. I ascended the throne after our father's death." He grins darkly. "I took the woman you love, too, didn't I?"

"You..." I grimace. "You forged your father's will."

He laughs. "*Our* father, dear brother," he grins. "And obviously. I got a deal when I had the forger do *her* father's, too." He nods his chin toward Eloise. "I had to *take* what was owed me, *Bruno*. You were always his favorite." His eyes narrow. "*Always*," he snarls. "I knew that at fucking *five*. Even after he thought you were dead and gone, he never did look at me the way he used to look at you."

"When did you find out," I hiss, glaring at him.

Massimo smiles. "That you survived the crash? The same time our father did. When you opened your law firm, and your picture was up everywhere as this hotshot young lawyer, *the adopted son of Vaughn Black*," he sneers. "That's when he figured it out. I mean for Christ's sake, our father even went to *you* to have the very will that cheated me out of my inheritance drafted. The fucking *gall*, Bruno!"

Eloise's hand tightens in mine, and she gasps as Massimo reaches into his jacket pocket and pulls out a heavy looking six-shot revolver.

"And today, dear brother," he says icily, "I get to take one more thing from you."

He opens the gun and tips the bullets out of the wheel and into his palm. He looks up and grins as he pockets all but one, which he holds up for me to see.

"Don't worry. You get to choose what it is I take."

He loads the single bullet into the gun with a metallic click.

"You get to pick, Bruno."

My eyes narrow. "Pick *what*."

He smiles. "Who lives: your love…"

I snarl, ignoring the pain and lunging to shield Eloise as he points the gun at her.

Massimo chuckles. "Or…"

I groan again, scrambling over in front of Gabriel as the gun barrel swivels to him.

"Your fake brother."

What the fuck.

Massimo smiles again as he hefts the gun. "One bullet, Bruno. What's it gonna be?"

I'm about to tell him to shove it up his own ass and pull the trigger, when he suddenly flips it around and hands it to me, grip-first. I stare at it, then up at him.

"Go ahead, brother," he murmurs. "Take it."

I snatch the gun from his hand, swallow my pain, and lurch to my feet. I glare pure hatred and darkness as I level the revolver at Massimo's face and draw back the hammer.

"How about option C—"

The dull click of a gun being cocked draws my attention to the single guard standing behind Massimo who's now leveling a Beretta at me. A second click drags my gaze back to Massimo, pointing *another* Beretta at Eloise.

Fuck.

I lower the revolver.

"I'm insulted that you think I'm that fucking stupid, brother," Massimo says quietly. "Now, you can drop the gun, or you can pick one of these two to die. Or," he smiles. "If you're *so* hell bent on an option C, I can pick for you. But, spoiler, I'm going to shoot *both* of them in that case."

My pulse roars. My breath is coming raggedly, and my eyes dart from Massimo, to his guard, to Gabriel, and then to Eloise as blood leaks down my side.

"One bullet, Alistair," Massimo growls thinly. "Tick-fucking-tock—"

"You're a betting man, aren't you, Massimo?"

I don't really know what I'm doing here. I'm putting the pieces together as the words leave my mouth, desperate for a solution, and I figure the longer I talk, the longer my brain can try and find one.

I'm not going to pick. I refuse to watch *either* of them die.

Massimo eyes me curiously. "You know I am."

"Well then," I grunt. "Let's make it interesting."

His eyes narrow on me, darkness swirling behind them. Slowly, his lips curl, and a spark of something I know all too well ignites in his face.

The thrill of a bet. Of wagering, and watching to see where the ball lands, or which horse pulls ahead, or what card the dealer flips next.

Massimo and I share the same genetics? *Fine.* That means that the same poisonous draw to gambling that flows in my blood flows in his.

And like a good lawyer who's spotted a weakness, or a good gambler who's spotted a tell, I'm going to use that any way I can.

Massimo sucks on his teeth. "Exactly how would you suggest making this more interesting?"

"Simple," I grunt. "One bullet, one gun, right?"

He smiles. "You're reaching, brother. It's the lawyer in you—"

"Let's play Russian Roulette."

The windowless room goes silent. Massimo eyes me coldly. Slowly, his eyes crinkle into a grin and he starts to laugh.

"Oh we *are* family, aren't we?" He chuckles darkly as he eyes me. "*Interesting,* Alistair. Very, very interesting."

"Yes or no, Massimo."

"Who are you suggesting plays this game?"

"You and me."

Eloise makes a strangled yelp behind me. Gabriel groans something unintelligible, trying to roll onto his back. I turn just in time to see Eloise rush to him, gingerly pushing his blood-matted hair away from his bruised, beaten face.

My eyes narrow viciously as I turn back to Massimo. "You and me," I hiss. "Are we playing or not?"

He grins. Slowly, his chin nods.

"Okay, counselor."

"*Sir—*"

Massimo stops his guard with a raised hand. He slips his gun back into his pocket and eyes me.

"I think the more the merrier, brother," he murmurs. He nods down to where Eloise is crouched beside Gabriel. "These two play, too."

Fuck.

"No," I growl.

"You're mistaking this for a negotiation, Alistair," Massimo growls. "It *isn't*. I'm intrigued, and I want to play." He reaches out a hand. "Give it to me. Now."

I hand him the revolver as he turns to his guard.

"Leave us. Lock the door, and don't either of you come back in until you hear a gunshot. Capice?"

The man looks at his boss like Massimo has completely lost his mind. But he nods.

"Yes sir, Mr. Carveli."

After the man leaves, Massimo turns to grin at us with a psychotic look in his eyes. "Shall we?" His gaze lands on me. "Please, *sit*, counselor. Right here will do."

With a wave of dizziness, I lower myself to the ground.

"And you, my dear, dear *wife*," Massimo snarls at Eloise. "Right there." He gestures with the revolver. Her eyes meet mine, and I nod quietly before she sinks to the ground, too.

Gabriel, slumped on the ground looking half-dead, she and I now form a half circle. Massimo grins as he sits cross-legged across from me, making it a full one.

"You surprise me, brother—"

"I'm *not* your fucking brother," I spit venomously.

Massimo just smiles. "Apologies. Would you care to go first, *Bruno*?"

"I think the host should go first."

He chuckles. "Well played. But—no." He abruptly spins the wheel of the revolver and then snaps it shut.

"Let's split the difference."

I balk as he suddenly points the gun at Gabriel's head.

"Your fake brother can go first. And since he seems to be snoozing instead of playing, I'll help him out."

"NO!"

I lurch and choke on my breath as the gun snaps a hard metallic sound and dry fires. Eloise screams.

Jesus fucking Christ.

Massimo lets out a wild whooping sound, gleefully looking between me and Eloise like a child who's just watched a birthday clown pull a fucking quarter out of someone's ear.

"*Fuck yeah*!" he shrieks, looking even more manic than usual. "That's a *rush*! Holy shit, how have I never played this before!"

He lets out another whoop before he exhales.

"Okay, ladies next?"

He starts to turn toward Eloise.

"I'll go," I blurt, ripping his attention from her. She snaps her head to me with a haunted, horrified look. "I'm next around the circle anyway."

I want to tell her it's going to be okay. I want to tell her I can save us.

But I can't.

Because even if I manage to use the revolver to kill Massimo, his two guards will come in, guns blazing, and all of us will die.

The only way out is to play Massimo's game.

And fucking *pray* for a miracle.

Massimo cocks a brow before he flips the gun around and hands it to me.

"Well, counselor...*your turn*."

36

ELOISE

When life turns surreal, waking moments become a dream-state. As if nothing you're experiencing is real, because it *can't* be.

I *can't* be in one of Massimo's torture rooms deep in a basement who-knows-where.

Alistair *can't* be slowly bleeding out from the bullet wound in his side, which is frankly a lot worse than I told him.

Gabriel *can't* be lying on the floor across from me looking like he's been beaten to within an inch of his life.

And above all else, we *can't* all be in a circle playing *Russian fucking Roulette* with Massimo.

Yet, here we are.

Reality has left the building.

I watch numbly as Alistair takes the gun from Massimo. When Alistair's fingers close around it, I almost want to scream to Alistair to just *shoot* the psychopath already.

But we all know what happens if he does. Even if Alistair manages to kill the kingpin, Massimo's guards come charging in, and the rest of us die quick deaths here in this hole.

Slowly, Alistair glances at me, his fingers wrapped tight around the stock of the revolver.

"Your turn, counselor," Massimo grins.

He's got that same look in his eye I've seen him get when one of his girls pleads with him to stop, or slow down, and he just starts to go even harder, because inflicting suffering is what excites him.

He's enjoying this game.

Alistair glances at his brother on the ground. Then at me. His jaw grinds before his gaze drags back to Massimo.

"You're right," he says calmly. "It *is* my turn."

My eyes bulge as he raises the gun, points it right at Massimo, and squeezes the trigger. Massimo and I flinch.

Nothing happens. Nothing aside from a sharp, metallic *click* echoing through the room.

I unclench my eyes just before Massimo does. I stare at Alistair, my breath coming quickly.

Massimo grins as Alistair gives him a hard, cold smile.

"*That* is for pointing a gun at me that night at Venom, you psychopathic piece of shit."

Massimo chuckles quietly. "Touché, brother. Touché."

"We're not brothers," Alistair insists coldly.

"Our genetics say otherwise," Massimo shrugs, "but whatever. Potayto, potahto. *Your turn.*"

A chill rakes its nails down my back. "He… He just went!"

"Trying to shoot *me* doesn't fucking count," Massimo snaps tersely. "Your *turn*, Alistair."

My pulse starts racing faster, my chest rising and falling rapidly with every breath as I turn to Alistair.

"You—"

I shudder as he spins the revolver wheel, his eyes locked on Massimo as he snaps it shut. His nostrils flare, and he points the barrel at his own temple.

Oh God...

His eyes shift to mine, holding my gaze steadily as he takes a deep breath.

"For fuck's sake!" Massimo grunts. "Just fucking—"

I choke back a scream as the gun dry fires with a loud *click*. My pulse is pounding so hard, I wonder if I might have a heart attack before I or anyone else dies of a gunshot wound.

Massimo smirks. "Well done, *brother*." He turns to grin at me, his eyes full of malice. "Your turn, wife."

Alistair's mouth is a thin line as he hands me the gun. I shiver when I take it from him, hefting it in my hands.

It's a lot heavier than I thought it would be.

"You've never shot one before, have you?" Massimo asks.

My throat bobs as I shake my head.

"Well, lucky for you, it's easy. Point the business end at something you want to kill, squeeze the trigger, and try not to sneeze. Think you can manage that?"

I swallow again as I nod quickly. My pulse is roaring in my ears as I turn to stare at Alistair with wide, horrified eyes.

"Do it," Massimo snarls.

I raise the gun to my head, my vision dotting from the way I'm hyperventilating. My eyes are locked with Alistair's as I clench my jaw.

"I love you," he whispers.

"I love you, too..."

My eyes close. I take a deep breath and hold it as every muscle in my body tenses.

My finger squeezes.

Click.

"Holy fucking shit," I sputter, sucking in air. I'm shaking as I shove the gun at Massimo, desperate to get the thing away from me.

The Carveli king hoots loudly. "Fuck *me,* this is good!" he blurts gleefully, like he's getting off on this. His eyes dart around the room with a crazed look in them. Then he takes a deep breath, spins the wheel, locks it, and jams the barrel against his temple.

"Carpe fucking diem," he hisses.

Click.

Massimo exhales in a whoosh, his eyes positively dancing.

"*FUCK,*" he yells, grinning like a madman. His eyes snap across to Alistair. "Fuck me sideways, counselor," he pants. "What a fucking *rush*! Fucking hell, I wish I'd played this years ago!"

"We all do," Alistair growls, glaring at Massimo.

The Italian chuckles as he shakes out his arms. Then he spins the wheel again, locks it, and aims it at Gabriel, lying on the ground.

"Given that he's still choosing to *nap* during what could be the most thrilling fucking moment of his life..." Massimo hisses gleefully.

My breath sucks in sharply.

"Say cheese."

Click.

Holy fuck.

Massimo crows in excitement, bouncing up and down as he hands the gun to Alistair.

"Don't stop!" he barks. "Keep going! Fuck me, I could *come* from this shit!"

Alistair glares pure hate at him. Then his eyes swivel to mine as he locks the wheel and puts the gun to his head.

Click.

I flinch, barely biting back a sob as my nerves begin to shatter.

"Your turn," Alistair says quietly, not even blinking as he presses the heavy gun into my hands. "*Almost over,*" he murmurs.

Massimo snorts. "Oh, I second that. I can *feel* it!" He shoots me a venomous look. "Might even be you, wife. *Do it.*"

Every nerve in my body is frayed, laid bare, and about to snap as I press the cold metal to my temple and squeeze my eyes shut.

Click.

A sob wrenches from my chest and I start to cry as Massimo hoots with laughter and plucks the gun from my fingers.

His is another dry fire.

So is the one for Gabriel.

"Holy *fuck*, I am so hard right now!" Massimo blurts. The look in his eyes is completely unhinged as he stares across at Alistair.

"I almost want to stop this, you know."

Hope burns in my chest.

Massimo grins. "I mean, we're just getting to know one another—"

"I already know you *far* more than I ever want to, Massimo," Alistair says coldly.

"I meant as brothers."

Alistair's head shakes side to side. He glances at Gabriel, and my eyes blur with tears as he reaches a bloody hand out to lay it on Gabriel's unmoving chest. His gaze slides back to Massimo.

"We will *never* be brothers."

"Now you're just being rude," Massimo pouts sarcastically. He starts to chuckle again, turning away as his peals of laughter fill the room.

It's then that I realize Alistair is looking right at me. His eyes dart hard to the side. Then again. This time, I follow to where he's looking.

Holy shit.

He's got one hand behind his back.

...And he's holding a bullet. Not just any bullet, either. It's *the* bullet, the one Massimo put in the revolver when we sat down for this death sentence of a game. Suddenly, I'm replaying the moment a few minutes ago when Alistair pointed the gun at Massimo and fired.

How Massimo and I both flinched and turned away, closing our eyes.

It was barely a second. But enough.

I know what I'm looking at. And more importantly, I know what I have to do.

"*Oh! God!*" I cry out, doubling over as my face contorts in mock pain.

Massimo lifts a brow. "What the fuck is wrong with you?"

"I...*merde*," I choke. "When your men took me, one pinned my arm too hard behind my...*ahh*...my back! I've pinched a nerve or something!"

Massimo rolls his eyes and turns to look at Alistair. "Well?" He spits. "Help her."

Alistair shrugs. "She's your wife."

"I'm not the one fucking her!"

Alistair shrugs again. "I'm over her. You're the one in charge, Mass—"

"Fuck this."

I'm half expecting it, but I still cry out when Massimo lurches over to me and backhands me hard across the mouth.

"Shut the *fuck* up!" he barks viciously, sitting back in his spot. "Christ, we're trying to play a fucking *game* here, you cunt."

I wince from the pain in my face. My eyes snap to Alistair, seeing such hate and darkness burning in his eyes as he looks at Massimo that it honestly scares me.

...But both of his hands are back in front of him, empty. And the gun is cocked and ready.

Massimo sighs, shaking his head. Then he grins as he wags a finger at Alistair. "You know, that was intriguing to see. That was ice fucking cold." His lips twist. "Seems you *are* my brother after all, doesn't it?"

"I already told you, we'll never be brothers, you fuck."

Massimo shrugs. "Well, either way, it's your turn."

Alistair nods. He glances at me, his eyes burning and sharp before he turns them on Massimo and raises the gun to his own head.

Massimo's lips pull into a lecherous grin.

"You know, brother," he smiles cruelly. "When I'm watching you bleed out? I might finally consummate this marriage."

Alistair's nostrils flare. His jaw grinds.

Massimo grins wider. "I never did touch her. It felt weird before." He shrugs. "I suppose I never had an inclination to put my dick where my own brother's been before. But when you're dead?" His smile curls. "Well, I think in that case, I could gladly—"

BANG.

I'm still processing the image of Massimo's head snapping back in slow motion, a mist of blood spraying out the back of it as he falls to the floor, when Alistair lurches to his feet.

I hear muffled yells from outside the room, and the heavy metal door being unlocked.

Alistair groans, dropping the revolver and scrambling over to Massimo's body. He yanks the other gun out of Massimo's jacket. Even as the door begins to open, and as Alistair raises the gun, the color fades from his face.

The gun drops from his hand.

His body slumps to the ground.

I don't think, I just *do*. I scramble over, lift the gun in my hands, and aim it at the door as it swings open.

Point the business end at something you want to kill, squeeze the trigger, and try not to sneeze. Think you can manage that?

I spit at Massimo's body. Yeah, I can manage that.

Fire erupts from the barrel of the gun in my hands. The first man through the door screams and slumps to the ground. The second comes charging through, then suddenly clutches his knee and topples to the ground.

"Eloise."

I'm still staring at the two men lying on the ground as Alistair struggles to his feet and gently wraps a hand around the gun I'm holding. I let him take it, my whole body shaking as I watch him turn, grimace, and limp over to them.

"Don't watch."

I flinch and look away, jolting when two shots explode through the room.

I scream when arms grab me from behind. Then I'm choking back my tears as I realize it's him, and I turn to wrap my arms tight around him. I let out a cry of relief as he cups my face and kisses me hard, over and over and over again as I collapse into his arms.

"I love you," I sob.

"I love you too," Alistair murmurs, holding me close.

"And...I..."

Both of us whirl to where Gabriel is slumped on the ground.

"Am still. Fucking. Dying over here," he croaks. *"In case anyone cares?"*

EPILOGUE

ALISTAIR

"Is that all of it, Charles?"

My grandfather purses his lips petulantly.

"Do *not* make me ask again, Charles."

There's an edge in my voice when I want there to be these days that I'm not sure I used to be able to pull off. Being locked in a basement playing Russian Roulette with a psychopath will do that, I guess. I'll be honest, I'm excited to whip out the new hard-edged voice in court and see who I can make shit their pants.

Until then, though, that pant-shitter looks like it's about to be my grandfather.

He pales. "Yes, that's it."

"If I find out—"

"I swear to you, *that's it.*"

"Good."

I glance around the room—at Gabriel, his face still bruised but healing, his arm in a sling. Taylor stands next to him, and then Tempest. Caroline is glowering behind her idiot husband, and of course Eloise is next to me.

This is the last bit of business we need to wrap up in New York before Eloise and I hop on a jet to Paris, where I'll officially be meeting Andre LeBlanc.

I'll also be telling him my intention to marry his daughter. Like, soon.

I proposed. Of *course* I did. She's divorced now—well, annulled *post-mortem*, as it was never consummated. But yes, I'll be marrying Eloise. I was an idiot to let this woman go the first time, and I never will again.

So yes, this is my big "meet the father" moment now that Andre's out of his coma—the one that Massimo put and kept him in, with the help of two dishonorable fuckers in Andre's organization who sold him out.

Luckily, "dishonor" doesn't get you very far with the French Mafia. The French are pretty hardcore about the whole "*Liberté, Egalité, Fratnerité*" thing, and now that he's awake, Andre's people have...*dispatched* the traitors in their midst.

At least, that's what I hear. I'm merely an attorney, after all.

Massimo and the traitors, of course, took Andre out to secure the marriage deal that Luca had first floated and Massimo now wanted too. Not because he had any real interest in Eloise romantically, obviously. But because he wanted Andre's smuggling route, which was apparently far more lucrative than anyone was letting on.

On a more insidious level, his obsession with "taking things from me" was also part of why he married her, I think.

How's that working out for you, fuckwit.

There's a tiny part of me that wonders if I should mourn the loss of a brother. We've looked into it, just to be sure about everything, and Massimo was telling the truth for once.

I *am* Luca Carveli's oldest son. My mother *did* die giving birth to Massimo. And Luca's side-piece of the month, Gia, *did* help my uncle Angelo, who—pay attention, this will be important—was a lawyer, *did* take me away from Luca. Gia, it seems, took pity on me and the life Luca was forcing me into. She'd also, apparently, been a friend of my mother, and so she reached out to my uncle Angelo for help. It would seem their intention was to take a baby Massimo, as well, but were stopped in the attempt by Luca's men.

When the accident which probably wasn't an accident on the West Side Highway took their lives and somehow spared mine, a man who'd worked for years alongside Angelo found me in the hospital.

That man was Vaughn Black. The only real father I've ever known.

The only real father I *choose* to have.

I am not, nor will I ever be, Bruno Carveli.

My name is Alistair Black, and my life is my own.

"You're sure this is it?" I growl at Charles as we stand in the library of his lavish mansion on the Upper East Side, in a half-moon around the fireplace.

"I promise you, Alistair," he hisses quietly, nodding at the folder in my hand. "That is the very last scrap of evidence on earth connecting you, Alistair Black, to—"

"You don't need to say the name out loud."

I draw in a breath and look at the folder—a tether to another world where I'm another man.

But I don't want that world.

When my uncle and Gia were killed, I was also presumed dead. In fact, they called it in the ambulance, and only changed it when the EMT caught the faintest hint of a heartbeat just as they arrived at the hospital.

Apparently, I *have* been a fighter my whole life.

When Vaughn arrived after getting wind of what happened, he, his wife, and a close attorney friend of theirs knew what kind of a life Angelo and Gia had been rescuing me from, and what they had to do to save me from that life.

Money was palmed where it had to be. The EMT who found my pulse "un-found" it, and changed the paperwork when his school loans were miraculously paid off.

So Bruno Carveli died from blunt force trauma to the body and head, at the age of six.

And Alistair Black was brought into a different family, and shown love.

What I'm holding is the very last shred of physical evidence that ties me to the boy I once was, and the crime family whose bloodline I've just ended.

Without another thought, I hand it to Eloise.

"You do it."

She smiles at me, her eyes twinkling. With a flick of her wrist it goes into the fire, and I watch it curl to ash.

"You understand, of course," Gabriel growls, glaring at Charles and Caroline, "that if you ever speak of this—"

"W-we won't!" Caroline stammers, looking pale. "I swear to God!" She turns to me with a panicked look on her face. "I *swear*, we'll never tell a soul!"

"Indeed. I…" Charles clears his throat, eying me. "I'm aware of what you're capable of, Alistair."

I start to chuckle.

"You're worried about what *I* would do to you?"

I grin.

"You're not getting this, Charles. The Carveli family still has a few guys out there. Sure, the other Commission families are hunting them down, but a few will manage to stay hidden. And if you spill any of this, Charles," I growl. "And it gets back to them?" I shrug. "I mean, they'll probably come for me, first…"

Charles looks confused.

Here comes the right hook.

"But I've prepared documents stating unequivocally that it was *you* who killed Luca Carveli. You *were* in Paris when it happened, after all."

Charles' eyes widen. "I was in *Zurich*!"

"Zurich's not even a ninety-minute flight from Paris," Gabriel mutters with a shrug of his good shoulder.

"If *anything* happens to me in the way of retribution from the Carveli family, Charles," I growl, "that information becomes public. And I don't believe the remaining Carveli men, who, by-the-by, liked Luca a *lot* more than they liked his son, will enjoy hearing that on the eleven o'clock news."

Charles swallows hard. "You have my word. This never gets spoken about again."

"Wonderful," I say amiably. "Which brings us to the best part."

I nod to Taylor, who opens a file folder and sets it down on the desk by the window.

"Try as I might, Charles—and trust me, I've tried," I sigh. "I can't stomach sentencing my own grandfather to die in prison."

"Now, *listen,* Alistair—"

"It would *behoove* you, Charles," I mutter, "to shut the *fuck* up right now."

His mouth snaps shut.

"You're out. Done. Finito."

His brow furrows. "With?"

"With everything. All of it," I shrug. "You're done at the firm, for a start. Clean cut *gone*. No board seat, nothing." I level my gaze at him. "And don't you fucking *dare* try and fleece us or poach any staff on the way out. It will not end well for you."

I glance at Gabriel and Taylor to see them smirking at me. I flash them a quick grin and then return my wrathful gaze to Charles.

"You'll get your contractual payout, no more. Caroline, you *have* no contract, since you're only on that board because you gave our grandfather enough blowjobs. So you get *shit*."

I savor the moment the panic hits her face.

"If either of you even walk back into Crown and Black, you'll be arrested on sight for trespassing. Oh, and all the other shit you're into, Charles? The wheeling and dealing where you try and relive the glory days when you actually *were* a king-maker?" I grin. "That's over. You're out of that now, too."

Charles' mouth falls open. But he's got the good sense to not say anything.

"Look on the bright side, Charles," Gabriel says cheerfully. "Now you get more time with your dear wife!"

Which sucks for him because, well, Caroline is *Caroline*. And it sucks for her, because she's probably going to have to let the old guy fuck her more often, if he still can, because he'll be around more often.

I take a deep sigh, letting this knowledge warm my spirit before I tap on the contract laid out in front of us.

"It's all in here. If you choose to go another way, I dig up every single skeleton in your closets, and I swear to fuck, I will put you away for the rest of your life."

I tap the contract again.

"Sign this or die in jail. Your choice, Charles."

He's staring at the contract, fury etched on his face, together with fear.

"I…" He shakes his head. "I could take you down with me," he mutters. "You… I know you shot Massimo."

I chuckle. "Charles, please. The things I know about you, your business dealings, and your clients? Go ahead, take me down with you. I'll get three years. Five, max." I shrug. "You, however, are looking at *twenty*-three years, minimum. And with your record at the DOJ?"

"*Yikes*, Charles," Gabriel sighs dramatically, shaking his head.

I smile at our grandfather. "That's twenty-three years without the possibility of parole." I wince. "Big ouch, Charles. Big, *big* ouch."

He grits his teeth, still staring at the contract.

"*Charles…*" Caroline mumbles next to him.

I hold out a pen and dangle it in his face.

A second later, he snatches it from me, clenches his jaw, and furiously signs the document.

We're done here.

Taylor, Gabriel, and Tempest end up coming with Eloise and me to the airport, where Andre's jet is waiting for us.

I hug my sister fiercely, then Taylor. My brother goes to shake my hand, but I roll my eyes and pull him into a bear hug, even if it makes us both wince.

He's the only brother I've got, after all.

On the jet, I pull Eloise into my lap. My lips find hers as we completely ignore the "fasten seatbelt" sign.

"You got lucky, you know," she murmurs, grinning as she pulls away.

"You mean when I got *you*, right?"

Eloise blushes deeply, biting her lip. "*No,* I meant…you know," she looks down. "Before. Back in…that basement."

I shake my head. "I've told you before. I make my own luck."

"Slipping a bullet out of a gun while the bad guy isn't looking is *luck*, not manifest destiny."

I grin. "Objection."

"Overruled!"

I grab her hand and place it on my bulging crotch. "Tampering with evidence."

Eloise giggles. "Bribing the witness…"

"Agree to disagree?"

"I can agree that I love you," she grins.

"Only if you agree that I love you, too."

"Counselor, we have an accord."

"Good. The defense rests."

"I'm glad," she murmurs, pulling me close to her by my tie. "I don't want to talk anymore."

Neither do I. So I kiss her, and keep kissing her as the plane lifts into the sky, and we fly toward the rest of our lives together.

The Venomous Gods series continues with Gabriel's story in *Poisonous Kiss*.

Haven't gotten enough of Alistair and Eloise?
Get their extra scene here, or type this link into your browser: http://Bookhip.com/VXMNRNW

This isn't an epilogue or continuation to *Devious Vow*. But this extra hot "follow-up" story is guaranteed to keep the steam going.

ALSO BY JAGGER COLE

Venomous Gods:

Toxic Love

Devious Vow

Poisonous Kiss

Corrupted Heart

Dark Hearts:

Deviant Hearts

Vicious Hearts

Sinful Hearts

Twisted Hearts

Stolen Hearts

Reckless Hearts

Kings & Villains:

Dark Kingdom

Burned Cinder (Cinder Duet #1)

Empire of Ash (Cinder Duet #2)

The Hunter King (Hunted Duet # 1)

The Hunted Queen (Hunted Duet #2)

Prince of Hate

Savage Heirs:

Savage Heir

Dark Prince

Brutal King

Forbidden Crown

Broken God

Defiant Queen

Bratva's Claim:

Paying The Bratva's Debt

The Bratva's Stolen Bride

Hunted By The Bratva Beast

His Captive Bratva Princess

Owned By The Bratva King

The Bratva's Locked Up Love

The Scaliami Crime Family:

The Hitman's Obsession

The Boss's Temptation

The Bodyguard's Weakness

Power:

Tyrant

Outlaw

Warlord

Standalones:

Broken Lines

Bosshole

Grumpaholic

Stalker of Mine

ABOUT THE AUTHOR

Jagger Cole

A reader first and foremost, Jagger Cole cut his romance writing teeth penning various steamy fan-fiction stories years ago. After deciding to hang up his writing boots, Jagger worked in advertising pretending to be Don Draper. It worked enough to convince a woman way out of his league to marry him, though, which is a total win.

Now, Dad to two little princesses and King to a Queen, Jagger is thrilled to be back at the keyboard.

When not writing or reading romance books, he can be found woodworking, enjoying good whiskey, and grilling outside - rain or shine.

You can find all of his books at
www.jaggercolewrites.com

Made in the USA
Monee, IL
20 November 2024

70675937R00243